About the Author

Lexie Winston has been an astronaut, rock star, princess and time traveller. In her dreams. But none of the dreams have lived up to what becoming an author has been like. She gets to live in a world of pure imagination, and her heroines get to do the things she's always wished she could.

When not writing books, Lexie is a mother of two gorgeous teenagers and the wife to a patient and understanding man. They live in Western Australia and are lorded over by a black toy poodle. She loves camping, reading and if her iPad was stolen, her world would explode. (It has the kindle app on it.)

And you can find all my links at

www.lexiewinston.com

ICE ME OUT

LEXIE WINSTON

Also by Lexie Winston

Neighpalm Industries Collective 4-6

Seductive Sins Collection

(Reverse Harem Series)

Glorious Gluttony

Gangs, Guns, and Glory

Galaxy Circus

(Sci-Fi Reverse Harem Series)

Apprentice

Stagehand

Whisperer

Mama - Galaxy Circus Novella

Performer

Ringmaster

A Night Most Wicked - Galaxy Circus Novella

Broken Promises

(Dark Poly Romance Series)

Secrets Kept

Lies Untold

Trust Broken

Love Found

M.I.T.H.O.S

(Contemporary RH)

Spies Like Me

Standalones

Ice me out

(Contemporary Sports Secret Baby Romance)

For all the English teachers over the years, but especially you Jan. See I didn't always talk in class, sometimes I paid attention.

First published by Neighpalm Publishing in 2023

Ice Me Out

Mobi format: 978-0-6455262-6-4
Print: 978-0-6455262-7-1

Cover design by Dazed Designs
Editing by Elemental Editing

 Created with Vellum

CHAPTER 1

Miriam

"Jorja, honey, you have exactly thirty seconds to get your cute butt down here so I can do your hair, or you are going to school with a bird's nest on your head," I call up the stairs to my wayward daughter.

"Coming, Mama," my daughter's high-pitched voice calls back, so I head to the kitchen with my fingers crossed, hoping she doesn't get distracted by something on the way.

Pouring coffee into a travel mug, I add sugar and milk before taking a sip of the sweet, rich brew, causing my tastebuds to sing. Hopefully my tired and travel weary body will start to function more normally.

I lean against the counter and survey my kitchen. The cupboard and counters are shabby, and the wooden floorboards need to be stripped and resealed, not to mention the stove needs to be replaced, but I can't help but marvel that it's mine. My kitchen! My house. It was left to me by my eccentric great-aunt—the same woman who took me in when my own family sent me packing. I loved her like a mother, and she had certainly been better to me than my own flesh and blood.

They felt shamed by their seventeen-year-old daughter's accidental pregnancy, too Catholic for an abortion and too social climbing for a pregnant teen. I was sent to live with Aunt Jocelyn in London so I wouldn't embarrass them. They didn't even give me a chance to tell the father of his impending father-hood, and they haven't talked to me since except to say I was not welcome back in my family home. In fact, I was cut off from everyone. My grandparents and friends all seemed to forget I exist.

When the will was read after Aunt Jocelyn's untimely car accident, I was shocked to discover that while she bequeathed most of her vast fortune to her immediate family, she left me her house in my own hometown and a large sum of money in which to renovate it and take care of ourselves. I was like the granddaughter she never had, and she was thrilled to call me that. Her only son hadn't cared. In fact, he'd been happy for me, but he warned me it had been empty longer than I had been alive, so not to expect too much.

After living in London for the last six years, I bid them farewell with many tears and hugs and returned to the States with my five-year-old daughter in tow, both excited and nervous for the next stage of my journey.

We only arrived a few days ago, and while the house was partly furnished and livable, it really was in desperate need of some work, but that would all have to wait. Now that Jorja was in school full time, I was going to college. I finished high school in the UK, while Jocelyn watched Jorja for me. When I decided to come home, I applied to college in my hometown and was accepted.

Today is both of our first days, and I can't say I'm not excited.

The sound of little feet on the staircase has me cringing as I wait for her to slip in her rush, the rickety staircase another priority on the long to-do list, but she apparently manages to navigate them with ease. She comes in carrying her *Paw Patrol* backpack and throws it up on the counter before climbing onto the stool sitting next to it.

She's small for her age. I had a difficult pregnancy and was bedridden for the last three months, and she arrived at only thirty weeks. Each and every day was a struggle, seeing her in the NICU fighting for her life, but she must have a lot of her father in her, because she didn't give up. Eventually, I was able to bring her home. She was a sickly baby, always catching everything that was going around. Some days I just wanted to cry, and that was with the support of Aunt Jocelyn. Thankfully she got better, and apart from slow growth, everything else about her is perfect.

"Mama, can you give me two braids today?" Jorja holds out her brush and a couple of pretty hair bands to go on the ends. She recently lost both of her front teeth and lisps all her words at the moment, but I try my hardest not to smile because it upsets her.

"Of course, princess." I take the bows and brush and untangle her long, unruly black curls, which she does not get from me. I have white blonde, dead straight hair and brown eyes, but Jorja is the spitting image of her father with her bright, Caribbean blue eyes. I always feel a pang of longing when I look into them, wondering if he still lives in town and succeeded in his dreams, or if he ever thought about me after I was shipped away.

My parents confiscated my phone and had

someone scrub my social media accounts so I practically didn't exist, and I didn't know any other way to contact him. I begged them just after I arrived to tell him where I was, but they told me he had moved on, that he was dating someone and that he hadn't asked to see me at all. I tried to contact his sister, who I thought had been my best friend, but I got no response, so I gave up. I had a new life growing inside me, and by then, I was so sick that I didn't have the energy to worry about anything else except getting her to full term.

"Mama? Are you going to do it or not? I don't want to be late for my first day." She shakes me out of my memories, and I smile at her.

"Sorry, baby. Let's tame the wild beast, and then we need to get moving." I start to gently brush her knots, and I make a note to grab some detangling spray when I go to the store. Thankfully, Jocelyn left me enough money so I could afford to live and go to college without needing to get a job, so I don't need to worry about money for groceries or bills, and there is a car in the garage.

Seamus, Jocelyn's son and my mom's cousin, sent a mechanic out to make sure it was running. Imagine my surprise when we opened the shed on the back of the house and discovered a mint condition Chevy Impala sitting under a dust cloth. It needed a service and some new tires after sitting for so long, but when he got it started, the thing purred like a beast, and the guy promptly offered me a decent sum of money for the thing. I turned him down of course. Being a huge *Supernatural* fan, I was excited to drive the same car as Dean.

I quickly work Jorja's unruly curls into some semblance of neat braids. Hair is not my forte. If she wanted a ponytail, then I was her girl, but I had spent many nights watching YouTube videos to keep my little girl happy. I'm not great, but I try, and that has to count for something, right?

"Okay, done. What do you want for lunch?" I ask her, and she spins around on her stool.

"Mama, they give us lunch at school," she says, her eyes wide with excitement.

I screw up my nose. "Oh, baby, that's not necessarily a good thing," I protest, but she shakes her head.

"No, Mama. I want to eat at school, please." She tries to flutter her eyelashes in a way she saw on TV, but she just looks constipated. Again, I hide my smile.

"Okay, you can today, but if you don't like it, we can make it tomorrow. Deal?"

"Deal." She looks pleased as she holds her hand out for us to shake on it. We do, and then I lift her down from the high seat and pass Jorja her backpack.

"Okay, munchkin, let's rock and roll. I need to drop you off at school then hurry to my first class." I pick up my phone from the counter and check the time. Yup, we need to get moving. I grab my keys and my backpack, which has my books and laptop, and follow her out the door that leads to the attached carport. She opens the back door and climbs in, and I strap her into her child seat before jumping in myself.

"Okay, baby, don't fail us now." I pat the car's steering wheel and cross my fingers, turning the key over in the ignition. Thankfully the engine roars to life, and Jorja cheers as I breathe out a sigh of relief. Although it runs like a dream, she has been temperamental when starting, and I haven't had time to get the mechanic to look at it, but today we are good to go.

Shifting it into gear, I slowly back out of the drive. Despite having learned to drive here in the US, I got used to driving in the UK, so I'm cautious of driving on the opposite side of both the car and road, but I manage to get us onto the street and to Jorja's school without horns beeping at us or being flipped off, so I call that a win.

I pull the car into a spot and then help Jorja out

of the car. All around us, moms are parking with their BMWs and Mercedes. My Impala looks a little out of place, but I don't care. Seamus paved the way for Jorja to come to this private school and is paying for it. He and his husband adore us both, and they said that if they can't look after us in person, then they will from afar.

I thought Jorja might be nervous for her first day at a new school, but she practically drags me up the path and through the door. We had a tour a couple of days ago, so we know exactly where to go, and she beelines to her class despite all the other children milling about. My daughter most definitely has single-minded determination, and not much stops her.

When we get to the classroom, her teacher, an older matronly woman named Mrs. Brady, greets us with a warm smile. "Good morning, Jorja and Miriam. How are you today?"

"I'm great, thanks, Mrs. Brady," Jorja replies, looking around the classroom with excited eyes.

Behind Mrs. Brady's voluminous skirts, I see a little dark-haired girl peek around. Mrs. Brady sees where I'm looking and steps to the side. A little girl, slightly taller than Jorja, with dark hair and a tearstained face, is standing there.

Mrs. Brady takes her by the hand. "Jorja, this is Lola."

"Hi, I'm Jorja." My vivacious five-year-old skips over and gives the girl a hug before she can get out a word. "We're going to be best friends," she declares.

"Oh, honey, go easy there," I say, trying to temper the rabid beast, but Lola's eyes widen with interest.

"But, Mama, Lola and I have to be best friends. She likes *Paw Patrol* too." She points at the girl's backpack, which matches hers. I am almost certain ninety-nine percent of the class is going to be into *Paw Patrol*, but before I can point that out, Lola giggles.

"You talk funny."

Mrs. Brady frowns and is about to say something, but my confident daughter just shrugs.

"That's because I'm from London. That's all the way across the ocean. We came in a big plane to get here, and Uncle Seamus paid for us to have the good seats so we didn't have to slum it with the oi polloi." Jorja mangles the last bit, but Mrs. Brady snorts with smothered laughter, and Lola doesn't care either way. Her lips round in a big O.

"You know what? I have a map. Why don't we get you two settled, and then I can show you both on the map where London is and where Storm View is?" Mrs. Brady takes one in each hand and leads them away.

All around the room, parents kiss their children goodbye, but all I get is a quick wave over the shoulder. "Bye, Mom," Jorja calls before they disappear into the crowd.

Well, fuck. I guess it's my turn to go and make friends. With a small lump in my throat, I hurry back to the Impala and make my way across town to the university campus. I won't deny that a few tears trickle down my cheeks as I take a moment to be sad in the car before I get moving. Jorja is starting a year after she's supposed to. Being sick so often meant I couldn't start her schooling when she was supposed to, and this will be the first time we've been apart for a whole day since she's been born. I guess it's long overdue, but it's extremely hard when it's been her and me against the world for what feels like forever.

Apart from Aunt Jocelyn, Seamus, and his husband, Darcy, I didn't really have friends in London. I devoted all my time to Jorja, and this next step is fucking nerve-racking, but I suck it up and turn the key. Hell, at seventeen, I was kicked out of my house and moved across the world, and just before my eighteenth birthday, I gave birth, so college is going to be a breeze.

The campus is on the opposite side of town, and I have to drive through my old neighborhood to get to it. Thankfully I don't have to drive past my parents' house, because I'm not ready to face any of that yet. I have no doubt that I'm not going to be able to avoid them forever, but for as long as possible works for me.

My father's family is wealthy, and my parents and my dad's parents live in mansions next door to each other. I used to be very close with my grandparents, but I guess they must have been just as ashamed of me as my parents were, because not once did they reach out to me.

Aunt Jocelyn was my mom's aunt and the black sheep of that side of the family. She had been disinherited by her father for being a little too wild. Aunt Jocelyn married three times—once to a woman— and had outlived them all. People would whisper about the fact that she was now a very wealthy woman due to being widowed three times, and maybe she had something to do with it, but each of her loves died from a tragic accident or natural causes. After the third time, she swore off marriage and had many lovers. She said life was too short to be tied down and live within society's confines. At sixty-five, she was still going strong when she was taken from us.

When I grow up, I want to be just like Aunt Joce-lyn, not worrying about how people look at me. I just want to love and be loved and screw society and its ass-backward rules. It's my life goal to be as happy as she was.

I drive through town in a daze, and before I know it, I'm pulling into the student parking lot on campus. After hopping out and locking the door, I hurry across campus to my first class.

I took a virtual tour online because I hadn't had a chance to come in person, so the building I need isn't too hard to find. I pass plenty of other students gathering around or hurrying between buildings—thankfully no one I recognize from when I attended high school six years ago. Most of them wouldn't be freshmen like I am, although my first class of the day is mixed, so I cross my fingers, hoping I won't run into anyone I know.

My marketing class is half full, and I quickly take a seat at the back of the classroom. I'm so nervous. I haven't studied since I graduated high school when Jorja was two. I worked in Seamus and Darcy's flower shop while raising Jorja. I loved it and decided I wanted to do something similar. The two men offered to finance a store here in town for me, but I decided that I needed to take some business classes before I accepted their blind trust in me. I wouldn't want to let them down by not being able to manage the business side as well as the creative one. They agreed, but Seamus said he would keep an eye out for a suitable building for us.

All the classes I'm taking are business based. I have marketing, accounting, and business law this semester.

I'm so distracted with taking out my laptop and notebook that I don't notice anyone approaching my corner of the classroom until they slip into a seat in the row in front of me. He has his hoodie pulled up and slumps down in his chair like he doesn't want to be noticed, so I leave him be. As nice as it would be to make some adult friends, I'm not going to force myself on someone who looks like they want to avoid contact. Every time someone walks into the classroom, I see him stiffen until they take a seat elsewhere. His body relaxes minutely until the next person gazes around the classroom for a seat. It's an interesting few minutes until a teacher finally walks in, closing the door behind them.

The woman looks to be in her early fifties. She's dressed in smart work attire, and her heels click on the parquet flooring as she smiles at the class.

"Good morning, I'm Sarah Carlyle." There are a few gasps amongst the crowd, but I have no idea why. "Your original lecturer was in an unfortunate accident over the summer, and the dean has asked me to fill in for him as a favor. For those of you who don't know me, I am the CEO of the Carlyle Agency. We are one of the biggest marketing firms in the US, and this semester, we will be covering everything, including how to brand your business, social media marketing, and consumer behavior. This was a last-minute thing, so while I read through the curriculum, I want you to talk to the person closest to you about famous brands and which ones have marketing that resonates with you. Make some notes on why, what attracts you to their brand, and why you think it appeals to you. I'll give you half an hour, and then we're going to discuss them."

The class is silent for a moment.

"Well, get to it." She gestures for us to get moving.

The only person close to me is hoodie boy, so I lean forward and tap his shoulder. "Hi, can we work together?"

CHAPTER 2

Bentley

The slightly accented voice has me sighing before turning to look at the woman. I noticed her when I first sat down, but I really hadn't paid any attention. I wasn't looking to draw unwanted attention to myself, and her section of the room had the least amount of people in it. Knowing that if I don't answer her, I 'm going to come off as rude, I slowly turn to face her. Normally I wouldn't care about being rude to a social climbing sorority girl, but her slight English accent has made me curious.

I expect to see some kind of recognition in her eyes, so I'm surprised when she smiles blankly at me like she doesn't know who I am. Maybe my mother is right and I have become too arrogant and self-important, assuming everyone on campus knows who I am.

Looking down at her outstretched hand, I take it as I give her a closer once-over. She has white blonde hair with light eyebrows, so I'm assuming it's not from a bottle. Her warm caramel eyes sparkle with amusement as she allows me to look my fill, a slight blush tinging her cheeks. Her thick black lashes, which have to be tinted, flutter slightly, but she holds her ground and uses the time to look me over. I can't tell how tall she is, but she has some curves on her with an ample chest hidden behind a graphic T-shirt. A pair of jeans, which aren't so tight that she needs oil to get into them, and a pair of sneakers top off her look. She's beautiful and so unlike the rest of the coeds here. She has the kind of natural beauty that smacks you in the gut and makes you look twice, but it seems like she doesn't even realize it.

Her cheeks pink at my continued perusal. "Hi, I'm Miriam. Would you like to work with me?" she asks again, bringing me back to the situation at hand.

I shake her hand, unsure if she's working an angle or if she really doesn't know who I am. "Bentley. Sure, why not," I reply, pushing back my hoodie.

If she's working me to get a good grade, then she's going to find that she's not going to get anywhere with me.

"Oh hey, great, thanks." She picks up her stuff and climbs forward over the seats to take the one next to me. I watch in amusement, even more intrigued by the girl. "This is my first class, and I really want to do well."

My stomach drops, and I frown. So she is using me for my connections.

"I was really looking forward to having Professor Smith. He is supposed to be fantastic, so I'm a little bit disappointed we have this woman. I don't know anything about her. Do you?" she says as she puts her bag on the spare seat next to her and picks up her pen to take notes.

I let the breath I was holding go and relax minutely. "You could say that," I tell her, but before she can ask anything, I distract her. "Tell me about some of your favorite brands."

Her eyes flash with excitement, and she becomes completely animated as she talks. I'm so captivated by her enthusiasm and complete lack of guile that I lose track of what she's saying. There are no airs or graces or any mention of my mother's brands, so I know she's not trying to impress me at all.

"What did you say this brand sold?" I interrupt

her, trying to get back on track. Her smile drops when she realizes I haven't really been paying attention. "I'm sorry, it's not one I'm familiar with."

She shakes her head with understanding. "No, of course you wouldn't be. They are a UK based company. They sell kids' wear." She pulls her laptop between us and googles the brand—Jellybabeez Clothing. A bright, colorful page with on point branding pops up. I can see how it would be appealing to both children and parents alike. Their logo is cute and colorful, and their catalog is filled with happy, smiling children and parents, and their price range looks to be affordable.

"Oh yeah, they certainly did their market research and are nailing their demographic." I'm impressed and make a note to tell my mother about the company. She's always looking for new and exciting challenges. "What about it attracts you? I mean, apart from your interest in marketing, you aren't the demographic they are aiming for," I point out, and the brightness dulls in her eyes as she forces a smile.

"Oh yeah, but their ads appeared on TV at prime time, and their theme song is catchy, so it sticks in your mind," she tells me.

"Ah, yes, catchy tunes are most certainly an effective marketing strategy."

"What about you?" she asks politely, and I rattle off a number of exclusive brands, explaining about market demographic and other boring facts that have been hammered into me over the years.

I trail off when I see her frown. "What's wrong?" I ask, and she shakes her head.

"I don't mean to be rude, but I thought the point of the exercise was to talk about brands that we are attracted to." Her voice lowers, and she looks around the room like she's unsure of herself.

"It is," I tell her, and she wrinkles her nose up in an adorable way. It's all I can do to stop myself from reaching out to smooth her skin.

"Well, everything you just talked about are big, expensive brands aimed at the wealthy. None of them are fun or average. It kind of feels like you just learned a whole heap and are rattling them off because they are important. What appeals to *you*?" she asks, and I'm speechless. If I wasn't already sure she didn't know who I am, this would have sealed it. Anyone who knew my family would know that every one of the brands I mentioned is in my daily life.

"I love the branding for Beaver Booze Whiskey and Gnomies Candy, and I love the marketing for the Storm View Titans hockey team," I blurt out, and she loses the confused expression and regains her smile.

"I'm familiar with the hockey team from when I lived here in my teens, but I don't know either of the other two. Will you show me?" She nods at her computer, and I pull up the whiskey page and the catchy slogan. "Strong enough to break a beaver dam."

She snorts at the suggestive phrase and the sleazy, winking beaver. "Oh, that is good. I'll have to grab a bottle and see how it tastes and if it lives up to its reputation," she mutters that last little bit, and I'm not sure if I was supposed to hear it or not, so I don't say anything. I don't want to embarrass her. We're only just getting to know one another.

I pull up the candy next, which are gummies shaped like garden gnomes with interesting flavors.

"I don't remember them from my teens. They must be new in the last six years." There's a hint of sadness in her tone, and I make a note to grab a pack for her before our next class.

"Okay, show me the hockey team. The college has a team too, right? I used to love going to games when I lived here before. My grandparents always had season passes..." Her words trail off, and she looks sad for a moment before a shadow looms over the top of us and we look up to find our lecturer smiling at us. There's genuine amusement in her eyes. She points to the candy on the computer screen.

"Are you trying to bring people over to the dark side?" she asks, and I roll my eyes, but Miriam looks confused.

"Bentley is always trying to convert people into eating those horrible things," she explains to Miriam, who still looks confused.

"You only say they are horrible because they refuse to sell out to you," I tease, and my mother grins unrepentantly.

"You bet your ass. They would be ten times bigger if they let me control their marketing campaign. I'm glad to see you're actually doing some work, Bentley. Goodness knows you could teach the class yourself. You picked the right partner, Miss..." Mom waits for an introduction, and I roll my eyes again at the interfering wench.

"Miriam Kennedy." She quickly holds her hand out to shake my mom's.

"Any relation to Violet and Calvin Kennedy?" Mom inquires politely, but I can see a glint of curiosity in her eyes.

Miriam pulls away from my mom and fiddles with her pen before replying, "Yes."

There's an awkward silence for a moment before my mother changes the subject.

"Well, it was nice to meet you. Okay, class, let's talk about some of those brands," she says loudly before walking back down to the lecture podium, leaving us on our own.

"How do you know that woman? What was her name again? Sarah Carlyle? You couldn't have said something when I asked?" Miriam hisses.

"Bentley Carlyle III at your service," I say jokingly, tipping my imaginary hat to her, but she just glares at me.

"She made it sound like I picked you because you're her son. I can assure you that is not the case." She packs up her things and moves back to the seat behind me. "I don't need yours or anyone's help to pass this class. I'll show you both."

I turn in my seat so I can look at her. I want to argue with her, but there's a stubborn set to her jaw, and she won't even look at me as Mom asks the first person to share with the class. Sighing, I turn back around, pulling my hood back over my head. Mom catches my movement out of the corner of her eye and looks up at us, raising an eyebrow. I shake my head, and she goes back to paying attention to the student who's talking.

She's going to grill me about that next time I see her, no doubt about it.

By the end of the lesson, we've heard from a lot of students in the class about brands and broken down a few of the key elements of why they appealed to them, but as the bell rings and everyone starts to pack up, my mother makes an announcement.

"Alright, you will have a semester assignment, which I need you to grab the outline for as you leave." She points to a pile of papers on the table. "You'll be working in pairs, and it will be the person you just discussed brands with." There's a rumble around the classroom, and my mother holds up her hands. "Nope, I don't want to hear it. In the big, wide world, we don't always get to choose whom we work with, and we damn sure don't always like the people, so this will be a chance to get used to that. Please don't come crying to me. Sort out your problems between the two of you, but let me tell you this, I want to see that both parties are contributing to the assignment, or you will both fail." On that ominous note, my mother gathers up her things and sweeps out of the classroom, already in work mode.

Standing up, I turn to look at the girl behind me. Her mouth has dropped open in shock, and she has a pure, stubborn expression on her face.

"No way, this can't be happening. I'm screwed," she mutters, and it's all I can do to stop myself from chuckling. She jumps to her feet and pokes my chest. "Listen here, buddy. This might be an easy A for you, but I need this class, so you better think twice about slacking off just because your mother is our lecturer." She keeps poking, and this time I do chuckle. I can't believe the words coming out of her mouth. Anyone else would think they hit the jackpot and that we wouldn't have to do any work for the same reason.

I grab her finger, stopping her from poking the same spot once more. "Oh, don't worry. I assure you my mother will be harder on us than any other group in the class, so you better be ready to bring your A game," I tell her before dropping her finger and sweeping my own stuff off my desk.

I take one last look at her, finding that wrinkle is back on her nose, so I have to stuff my free hand into my pocket and walk away before I actually reach out to smooth it. My hoodie falls off my head, and when people realize it's me walking through the classroom, I get inundated with students asking if I want to swap partners, asking where Noah is, if Kashton is ready for the season's first game, and if we are throwing a party after it. They try to get me to talk about whether his contract has been renewed by the

Titans, but I know not to comment on anything like that. Speculation is still rife, and until there's an official announcement, I'm not going to be blamed for letting anything slip.

I grimace at all the attention and look back once more to find her watching me quizzically. Damn it. I actually enjoyed her not knowing who I was. I hope she doesn't google me or my mother's names, but the likelihood of that not happening is slim.

Sighing, I turn back around and shuffle my way through the crowd, answering some questions and ignoring others. That was my only class for the day, so I made plans to meet the other guys at the rink.

I head across campus to where I parked my car, unable to shake the sound of Miriam's laughter when I showed her Beaver Booze.

CHAPTER 3

Miriam

It took all I had not to gasp when Bentley lowered his hoodie, revealing drop-dead gorgeous green eyes, platinum blond hair, and cheekbones that could cut ice. The man is extremely attractive, so it's no wonder he had his hoodie up, but then when I found out he'd been playing me all along, it infuriated me. I bet he thought I knew who he and his mom were. He had that kind of arrogance —arrogance that is super familiar to me. After all, I grew up with some semblance of wealth with parents who had the same kind of attitude. Joke's on him, though, because I didn't know him from Adam. Sure, my parents probably know his family, but they'll have made damn sure to make my name mud to anyone who counts... although Sarah did look at me with curiosity, not malice.

My stomach sinks in disappointment as I watch him walk away, suddenly surrounded by people now that his hood exposes him to everyone else. I know boys like him. Shit, Jorja's father was exactly like him—popular and someone people gravitated toward. I couldn't believe it when he decided to pay special attention to me. He said all the right things, but I guess they were all lies. Once he got what he wanted, I became a distant memory, especially once I was no longer in his life.

Finding out that I'm going to have to work with him for the rest of the semester was like a kick in the gut. What a way to start my first semester of college. I can't afford to flunk out because he's some frat boy who doesn't take college seriously and is cruising through on his good looks, charm, and family name. I just have to pray that he brings enough to the partnership that I can pass this course.

The rest of my day passes quickly. My other two classes are interesting, but I don't speak to anyone else, and with a sigh of relief, I jump in my car and head toward the school to pick up Jorja.

She is happy and chats nonstop, telling me about her day right up until I pull the car into our driveway. Seeing my neighbor collecting the mail, I wind the window down and stop the car.

"Hi, Mrs. Wilson," I call out to her.

She looks up and smiles, waving to us. Mr. and Mrs. Wilson are a delightful older couple who live in a beautiful Victorian mansion next door. They tell me it's been in their family for years. It's what mine would look like if it hadn't been abandoned for close to thirty years.

"Ah, Miriam, how many times do I have to tell you to call me Mae? Hello, pretty girl, how was your first day of school?" She comes over and leans down, waving an elegant hand to Jorja who bounces up and down in the seat.

"Hello, Mae! I have a friend, her name is Lola, and we're going to be best friends forever," my hurricane tells her in a flurry of words.

"Well, that's lovely, dear. Why don't you go and put your bag inside and then come and have a snack? I baked some snickerdoodles this afternoon and told Fred he wasn't allowed to have one until you came home."

My little girl's eyes widen with excitement, and she waves her hands in the air. "Come on, Mom. Hurry up! I can't let Fred eat all my biscuits." She uses the British word for cookies, which has Mae smiling.

"Alright, hold your horses. Are you sure? She can be a handful," I warn my neighbor, but she snorts.

"Please, we have five grandsons. I'm sure she is no more of a handful than they were. Each and every one of them was constantly up to mischief."

"Well, okay, thanks. I'll walk her over in a few," I tell her.

She steps away from the car and waves goodbye. "I've made a pot of tea too," she calls, and I know she's got me.

Tea is something I have been missing from London. Sure, I can grab some bags, but it's not the same as the tea ritual Aunt Jocelyn and I had every afternoon at three thirty. When Mae discovered this, she was thrilled. She also loves to serve tea in the afternoon, but her husband is a "heathen" and will only drink coffee. Since I met them a couple of days ago, she's been inviting me for a pot of tea every afternoon, and it's hard to say no. Both Mae and Frederick have taken us under their wing, which has been somewhat of a blessing. I had been feeling lonely and isolated, much the same as I had when I first left town six years ago. Having them next door gives me a sense of comfort that had been missing since I left London, and I couldn't appreciate them more.

I pull the car forward into the carport, and Jorja

scrambles out of her car seat, throwing open the car door and racing up to the side entrance of the house. "Come on, Mom. Apart from Mae, there's nothing Fred likes more than snickerdoodles, and he sneaks them when she's not looking. None will be left by the time I get there."

Hauling my backpack over my shoulder, I follow my hurricane at a more sedate pace. "I'm sure he won't eat them all. He would probably get in trouble with Mae if he did that."

Jorja snorts indelicately and bounces up and down on the spot. I put the key in the lock and wiggle it, shoving my shoulder against the old wooden door. It's warped and gets stuck, but it finally swings open. Jorja doesn't wait, she just pushes past me, tossing her backpack on the kitchen counter and tearing off to her room to change out of her school uniform.

"Hold it, missy," I call after her, and she practically skids to a stop. "Your school bag does not live on the kitchen counter. Take it with you, please." I point to the item, and she huffs but turns around to get it, rolling her eyes in my direction. I smother the smile that wants to break free—my girl is so sassy—but she does as I ask and continues on her way. I hang my own backpack on a hook next to the door and pull out my phone. There's a message from

Seamus wishing us both an amazing first day of school. He must have gotten the time difference mixed up again. I shoot him a message saying it went well and that I'll call him tomorrow morning. They are seven hours ahead of us, so I'm sure they are probably already in bed and asleep.

I pull open the old fridge and peer inside. It makes creaking and clanging sounds, and I know it's going to need to be replaced, but I haven't had time yet. Maybe Mae can suggest some places to go shopping, and Jorja and I can go on the weekend. It's looking pretty empty except for some milk and a few pieces of fruit and cheese. Wrinkling my nose, I decide that takeout is on the menu for dinner. I haven't learned how to cook. Both my parents and Jocelyn had chefs that prepared our meals, and I have never had the need. It is on my list, but so far, my one attempt resulted in us needing to open all the windows to air out the house. Apparently you need to pay attention, otherwise things burn if the gas is too high under the pot.

The sound of a herd of horses above me makes me lift my head and close the fridge. I'm not sure why I was standing there staring at nothing anyway. It wasn't going to magically fill with food.

Jorja safely navigates the stairs again.

"How does it sound like there are ten of you

running along the hallway when there is only one tiny little girl?" I ask her, crossing my arms and leaning against the kitchen bench as she tears into the kitchen.

She's breathing heavily, and I can see she made an attempt to pat down all the flyaway hair that worked free from her braids during the day. She's also wearing a pretty pink dress that Seamus and Darcy gave her, which is all pink tulle ruffles. She uses any excuse to wear it, and afternoon tea with the Wilsons is apparently another suitable occasion.

"I don't know?" She stares at me with wide-eyed innocence.

"Were you running?" I ask, and she shrugs, unwilling to admit to it. "I've told you to be careful. This house is old, and there are things that need to be repaired. I don't want to see you get hurt," I scold her lightheartedly.

I know it must be difficult. She hasn't had a lot of friends over the years and has learned to entertain herself. This big house is a veritable treasure trove of places to explore, and the floorboards make such delightful noises when you walk across them. She's taken to learning where they creak and jumping over them. If she were a teenager, I'd suspect she was learning to sneak out, but I have a few more years before I have to worry about that.

She hurries forward and grabs my hand, pulling me with her. I only resist long enough to grab my phone and tuck it into my pocket before I allow her to drag me out the back sliding door and across the overgrown garden to a secret door in the fence between our houses. The Wilsons used to be great friends with Jocelyn and put in a fence to facilitate traveling between each other's houses with ease. Fred had shown Jorja the secret door on the day we met just after we moved in. It opens up to a small hedge maze in their backyard, and there is a special poem to say so you know you are going the right way. Of course he shared that with her too, and while she still needs help with left and right, she memorized the path perfectly.

A strong breeze kicks up just as we leave the maze and walk across a perfectly mowed expanse of lawn, blowing leaves across the pristine surface. Their gardener must have been here today, because the smell of freshly cut grass is strong, as well as the familiar smell of an electrical storm. I look up and find dark clouds rolling across the sky despite the fairly warm temperature.

Frederick and Mae are watching us from the glass conservatory that overlooks their backyard. I see Fred wave enthusiastically, and Jorja tears her hand out of mine and scampers across the rest of the distance. I can't stop the smile of contentment that crosses my lips, because despite not having friends my own age and family nearby, I'm happy. These people have welcomed us like we're family, and I can't be more grateful.

Jorja leaves the sliding door open for me, and I pull it closed behind me as I enter the cooled room.

"Phew, it's starting to turn dark. It looks like we may be in for a summer storm. That will be a nice change to all this warm weather," Mae says, peering outside.

I grimace. "Well, let's hope that my roof doesn't leak. I've found some disturbing water stains on some of the floors. I haven't had a chance to get anyone in to look at it yet." I sigh as Mae passes me a cup and saucer, taking a small sip of my perfectly brewed tea before sighing again. "I haven't had time to do much. I think I'm going to need new appliances too. Maybe you could point me in the right direction."

"Of course we can," Fred booms, a snickerdoodle in his hand and a smattering of crumbs across his belly. Jorja is also munching on a snickerdoodle, her own cup of tea in front of her. Aunt Jocelyn believed it was important to start appreciating tea at a young age. "Our grandsons work in construction. I'll give them a call and ask if one of them could pop by and take a look at the whole house for you. They can work out what needs to be done to make it safe, and then we can go from there." I start to argue, but he won't hear it. He just holds up a hand and tuts at me. "Let us do this for you. It's one less thing on your plate, and either Mae or I can be here to let them in while you two pretty ladies are at school." He winks at Jorja who giggles and reaches for another cookie, passing one to him first before grabbing one for herself. He beams with delight as Mae glares at him. "I can't disappoint the girlie, now can I?" he argues, taking a big bite. Mae rolls her eyes and shakes her head.

"Thank you, that would be wonderful," I tell him, and he wears a smug smile. I know when I'm outclassed.

"Now tell us about your day, Jorja. You said you made a friend?" Mae distracts them both, allowing me to enjoy my tea in peace and quiet.

Their big, fluffy ginger cat saunters across the room and leaps up onto the chair next to me, settling herself in my lap and purring loudly. I stroke an absent hand over her fur as I hear Jorja tell them about her new friend Lola.

"And did you know someone asked if we were sisters? We both have blue eyes and black hair," Jorja gushes, and I think back to the little tearstained girl

I'd met this morning. She was taller than Jorja by about a head, but she did have bright blue eyes and dark hair. Unlike Jorja's unruly mop, hers looked like a sleek waterfall of black silk. Obviously her parents gave her good genes or they are more organized in the morning if they have time to straighten their daughter's hair before school.

"That's just lovely. You'll have to have her over for a playdate so we can meet her." Mae smiles at my daughter's enthusiasm. Jorja's eyes widen and her mouth pops open as she turns to look at me.

"Can I do that, Mama? Can Lola come for a play-date?" She sounds hopeful, and I see her cross her fingers on one hand, and my heart aches. Poor baby has never had any real friends before. How could I ever deny her this?

"Of course, my sweet. I'll see if I can talk to her mom about it. We also need to find some after-school activities to sign you up for. What would you like to do?" I ask, and she bites her lip as she thinks about it before a big grin spreads across her lips.

"I want to do ice hockey."

I stifle the groan that tries to escape. Of course she picks that. There's barely anything to her, and she wants to play one of the biggest contact sports. I blame Darcy and Seamus. They had her on skates as soon as she could walk, skating on the pond in the backyard when it froze over for winter. They had a little stick custom made for her, and they put up a net for her to shoot goals into. Damn men, why couldn't they have been stereotypical gays who took her to ballet or encouraged her to do ice dancing?

"Oh, honey, we've talked about this," I start, but she gets a stubborn set to her lips and a frown forms as she crosses her arms and glares at me.

"Ice hockey? My grandsons play ice hockey. We are huge ice hockey fans. We have season tickets to the Titans, the Typhons and Frozen Fury! Maybe you could come with us to watch it one day," Frederick adds unhelpfully as Mae and I both glare at him. He takes the hint and shoves another snickerdoodle into his mouth, but it's too late, the damage is done. Jorja is bouncing in her seat again.

"They do wear lots of padding," Mae says quietly, patting me on the knee. "She will be okay. They will put her in a level appropriate to her skating skills."

"That's what I'm afraid of. She's a demon on ice," I tell them, and their eyes almost bug out of their heads. "Don't be fooled by her tiny stature. She skates almost better than she runs. Is the junior league still cutthroat here?"

I remember what it was like when I lived here

previously. I'm no slouch on the ice myself, and I played all through high school in the local league.

"Yes, hockey is still considered God's work." Frederick chuckles, and I sigh heavily again, but I will do anything for my girl, so I guess I need to make inquiries about tryouts.

CHAPTER 4

Miriam

We ended up staying for dinner with the Wilsons, and it's dark and considerably windier and cooler when we eventually leave. Jorja carries the flashlight that Fred gave her, but instead of going back through the maze, we leave via the front door, and it's only a short walk down their driveway and up ours. Jorja's beam is drooping by the time we reach the front door, and she can barely keep her eyes open. I guess the first day of school was more tiring than she realized. I kind of know how she feels, but I'm going to pour myself an adult beverage and find some TV show to zone out to before I hit the hay.

"Alright, chickadee. Teeth, pj's, and bed. You can

have a shower in the morning," I tell her, and she groans.

"Do I have to clean my teeth?" she argues, and I shrug.

"I don't know. Do you want smelly breath and rotten teeth when you're older?" I counter, and she shakes her head vehemently. "Well, there you go." She grumbles under her breath but hands me the flashlight and trudges up the stairs. "Oh, and Jorja." She stops and looks back at me. "Do a good job. One swipe of the brush is not enough," I tell her, and she heaves another sigh before continuing up the creaky stairs.

A crack of thunder breaks the silence, and she jumps and squeals before giggling nervously.

"It's okay, it's just the storm. I'll be up there shortly to tuck you in." I see the sky light up out the front door, thunder following the lightning. It looks like it's going to be a big one.

"Can I sleep with you, Mama?" she calls out quietly.

"Of course, but you still need to do everything before you hop into my bed, okay?"

She nods and continues up the stairs, hitting every possible light switch on her way.

I close and lock the front door, tossing the keys onto a little side table before making my way to the kitchen, also turning on every possible light. The house is old, and it creaks creepily, so I'm not risking anything. I've seen that horror movie. Maybe I need to think about getting a dog, or at least an alarm system. I make sure all the windows and doors are closed and locked before making my way to the fridge. There isn't a lot in there, but I did manage to grab some duty-free vodka when we flew in from London, and I always make sure we have some orange juice in the fridge because Jorja loves it. After pouring vodka and orange juice into a glass with a few cubes of ice, I make my way upstairs, switching off all the lights I turned on apart from one lamp in the living room. I make sure to grab my backpack too. I can use my laptop to watch some TV while Jorja goes to sleep, and it probably wouldn't hurt to look at my marketing assignment.

When I get to my bedroom, Jorja is already in bed with Paddington Bear under one arm. Seamus and Darcy gave it to her before we left England, and she's barely let it out of her sight except to go to school. I'm almost certain she didn't clean her teeth as well as I'd like, but I'm going to overlook that for the moment.

"Mama," Jorja starts hesitantly as I place my laptop and glass on the bedside table before stripping, putting on my own pj's, and climbing into bed.

"Yes, baby?" I fluff my pillow and put it up against the headboard before sitting against it.

"In class today, we introduced ourselves and shared a little bit about our family." My heart lurches, because I'm almost certain I know where this line of questioning is going, but I reach for my glass and pretend I'm not suddenly as tense as a bowstring.

"Mm-hmm, and what did you tell them?"

"I told them about you, Uncle Seamus, and Uncle Darcy and how sad I am that Aunt Jocelyn isn't with us anymore."

"Mm-hmm." I reach out and grab her hand as she bites her lip in a manner I'm super familiar with.

"But Billy Cole, who's a big fat bum head—"

"Jorja Kennedy, we don't talk about people like that," I scold, and she gets this stubborn gleam in her eyes.

"Uncle Seamus says I don't have to like people who are mean to me."

"Well, no, but what did Billy Cole say that was so mean?" I ask, and she shrugs.

"He asked why I didn't have a daddy and said that we must have done something wrong for him to leave us. Did I, Mama? Did I do something wrong?"

Big fat tears well in my daughter's eyes, and I

want to strangle Billy Cole and his parents who have obviously put wicked ideas in his head.

"Oh no, baby. You did nothing wrong, I promise." I wrap my arm around her shoulders and haul her up against me, hugging her hard and pressing a kiss to her head. "Your daddy didn't leave us, and I'm sure if he knew about you, he would love you so much. But things happened in Mommy's life that made it so she and Daddy couldn't be together, and I had to do what was best for both of us to keep us safe" It's really hard. I can't tell Jorja that her dad dropped us like a hot potato the minute we were in his rearview mirror. They may meet one day, and despite my animosity toward him, I think she deserves a chance to make her own judgment.

I thought about going to their family home and confronting both him and his sister, my former best friend, but then I thought better of it. Too much time has passed, and I think there is too much between us now to even consider rekindling any kind of friendship. Maybe one day when she's older. I have a feeling this is probably only just the start of all these questions now. Children are inherently curious, and I'm sure this is only the beginning of inquiries from her peers, though I'm certain the nuclear family is probably an exception to the rule these days, but maybe not at an expensive private school like Storm View Prep.

I can see Jorja mulling over what I said. It's nothing she hasn't heard before. She started asking when she saw a family spending time in the park. She even called Seamus Daddy once. Darcy just about pissed his pants laughing at that before I quickly set her straight, but mostly it doesn't seem to bother her. Maybe I need to find her a child therapist to talk to. I'll keep an eye on her, and once we've settled into a routine, maybe I'll find one for her.

I also need to check out the youth hockey league tryouts. I sigh loudly as I feel Jorja relax and fall asleep, no longer able to keep her eyes open. Being a mother never seems to let up. It's always one constant worry after another, which was fine when Jocelyn, Seamus, and Darcy were always around, but now I have no support system. It's Jorja and I versus the world, and it's daunting as fuck.

I settle Jorja on her own side and put my computer on my lap. Taking a sip of my drink, I pull up the syllabus for my marketing class, reading over the outline for our major assignment that is worth eighty percent of our grade.

An irritated shiver goes up my spine when I think about how animated Bentley Carlyle III was when he told me about the candy and whiskey businesses, a stark contrast to the bored way he talked about all those fancy labels. The sparkle in his green eyes and the dimple that popped up when he smiled entranced me, but then I realized he was just another entitled dude bro who doesn't even need to pass the class because Mommy is the lecturer.

I huff as I read through the directive. We need to create our own company and brand it to appeal to our target audience. My head bangs back against the wall as I contemplate how Bentley and I are ever going to come to an agreement on the kind of company we would like to create. If I was working on my own, I'd use my own florist business that I want to run when I finish school. It would be a good head start, but I'm almost certain Bentley is going to turn up his nose at that idea.

Thunder rolls across the sky, shaking the house, followed by another flash of lightning as the gentle sound of rain starts to pitter-patter on the roof. I cross my fingers, hoping the roof doesn't actually start leaking in the middle of the night. It's the last thing we need. Deciding to call it a night, I drain my drink before closing my laptop and placing it next to the bed. I quickly brush my teeth and use the bathroom before climbing back in next to my little girl. She's snoring this quiet, little girl snore that makes me smile as I reach up and flip the light switch handily located above the bed. Tomorrow is a new day, and I don't plan on letting Bentley snow me with his pretty boy looks.

An almighty crashing sound has me screaming and flinging myself over the top of Jorja. Debris flies around us, and Jorja sobs, scared from being woken by me throwing myself over her. I feel wind and rain soaking through my pajama top, something that is most certainly not supposed to be inside the house. When I peel my eyes open, finally getting the courage to look, it's dark, but I can clearly make out the night sky during the next flash of lightning and the great big branch that is now half inside my house. My stomach sinks at the thought of how much damage it's done, but I'm also incredibly grateful that it missed the bed completely.

I grope around, trying to find my phone on the bedside table, switching on the flashlight to get a better look, and sure enough, it stabbed a big hole in the roof, but everything seems to be relatively sound.

"Mama, what's happening?" Jorja sobs, and I gather her up in my arms and crawl out the other side of the bed with her. The branch is blocking me from getting into my closet or bathroom, so I'm stuck in cotton underwear and a tank top.

"Okay, baby. The big tree next to the house decided it didn't need one of its branches and threw it into the roof."

"Like the whomping willow?" she asks, and I smile at her apt Harry Potter reference.

"Yup, you bet. Come on. I'm not sure what we're going to do, but we can't sleep in here tonight."

I don't want to tell her I'm afraid to sleep in her room either. That tree has limbs hanging over her room too.

"How about we sleep on the floor in the living room?" I suggest.

"Like a sleepover?" she exclaims, and I nod.

"Yup, just like that. I don't know about you, but I could use a glass of warm milk to settle my nerves before I go back to bed. What do you think?"

"Yes!" She claps her hands and tucks Paddington tighter to her chest, and we leave the now damp, and getting damper, room. Shit, that's not going to be good for the floor. I hope I won't have to get that replaced as well. I try to turn on the light for the landing, but it doesn't respond. Shit, the power must be out or that tree did more damage than I thought.

"Alright, chickadee, we need to be careful since the lights aren't working. Grab my hand and I'll use my phone to light the way. We can grab Fred's flashlight from the side table next to the door." She takes my hand, and we carefully make our way out the door and down the stairs in the dark. We just make it to the side table next to the front door when someone bangs on it. I freeze, deciding whether or not I want to be *that* girl.

"Miriam, it's Fred, are you okay? Shit, Mae, call Noah. We may need his help."

I hurry to the door when I hear my neighbors, not wanting them to disturb anyone else. "Hi, Fred, Mae, we're okay." I turn the latch and pull open the door. My neighbors are standing there, both wearing yellow raincoats and looking adorable. I smile despite what just happened.

"Thank goodness. We heard the tree go through your house. We were worried you were hurt." Mae grabs Jorja and hugs her, forgetting she's dripping with water, but Jorja just giggles.

"We're fine. It destroyed the roof over my bedroom, but we're unharmed," I assure them. "Our power is out though."

"Yes, it took down the line that leads from the

street to your house as well. Come on, we have plenty of spare bedrooms. You two can stay in one tonight. I'll get someone over here to at least stop some of the rain from coming in." Fred has his phone in his hand, and he pushes past and heads up the stairs, using the flashlight in his other hand to light up the way. I just gape, looking from him to Mae who just rolls her eyes.

"Come on, let's get you some dry clothes. I only have grandsons, but my daughter-in-law has a few shirts and things she leaves just in case. You can have something of hers to wear."

"But..." I look back in the direction Fred went.

Mae just tuts and waves a hand. "He'll take care of it and make sure the damage isn't going to spread."

I guess I must be a little shocked, because I let her lead us out of the house. I carry Jorja over to her place, which is blazing with light, a stark contrast to my sad, dark, dilapidated heap.

She ushers us inside, and before I know it, we're both in borrowed shirts and up in a cozy spare bedroom that has photos of five boys in various stages of their lives. I don't look too closely, but the one thing that stands out is that they all look incredibly happy. I feel a pang of longing. Even before I'd been kicked out, we didn't have that. There were no family holidays or events that I can remember being excited to attend. The only time I felt that way was when I went and stayed with my grandparents, but I'm not sure any of that was ever real, nor did anyone think to take any photos to document that time in my life. I've made sure to do the exact opposite with Jorja. I've kind of gone overboard, but she won't ever think she wasn't loved.

"Should I go back and help Fred? I kind of feel bad leaving him to deal with that mess," I ask, turning my attention away from all the happy family photos.

Mae tuts and shakes her head. "Pfft. Fred used to own a construction company. He knows what he's doing, and I'm sure he already has a couple of the boys on the way to help him."

"But it's midnight!" I yelp.

"Yeah, but they are good boys. They'll grumble, and I'm sure they will all come over here for some hot chocolate and snickerdoodles. Why don't you settle Jorja in for the night and come on out?" I look down at my bare legs and the T-shirt barely covering my panties. I'm not wearing a bra, and I'm not sure meeting new people at midnight while looking like this will go over well.

Mae chuckles like she knows what I'm thinking. "I'm almost certain you would make the trip worth their while if they came over and saw you in that, but why don't I find you a robe?" She hurries out of the room as Jorja climbs up onto the bed. It's a huge, wrought iron thing with elegant iron work and a big plush mattress.

"Look at this bed, Mama! It looks so fancy." Jorja bounces up and down on her knees and grins with excitement.

"Okay, settle down." I pull the sheets back, and she climbs over, Paddington tucked under one arm.

She snuggles under the blankets with a little frown on her face. "Is our house okay, Mama?"

I lean in and press a kiss to her forehead, pushing back a stray curl. "Yes, of course it is, or it will be. We'll be able to see how bad the damage is tomorrow and go from there, but you and I are uninjured, so we're fine. Sleep now. You've got school again tomorrow, and you can tell your new friends all about your nighttime adventures."

"Okay, Mom. Lola will be so surprised." She rolls over and closes her eyes, and she's out within minutes. I press another kiss to her head, wondering how I got so lucky. She's always been such an even-tempered little girl and so resilient. I'm so glad we seem to be over all our illness hurdles.

I leave the door open a crack so I can hear her if she calls out and wander downstairs in search of

Mae. I hear her and Fred talking in the kitchen, so I push through the door, only to immediately stop when I notice three young men sitting at the counter, drinking from mugs—three young men whom I recognize from the pictures on the wall in our temporary bedroom.

"Shit." The word slips from my mouth before I can stop it, drawing everyone's attention to me. Ranging in age from a teenager to about my age, all three of them have the same sparkling chocolate brown eyes. The youngest and oldest both have a head of chestnut-colored curls. The middle one might too, but his is cropped close, so it's hard to tell. The youngest grins and gets a good eyeful of everything as he slowly peruses my body, but the other two's eyes narrow suspiciously, which I guess I can't really blame them.

Mae hurries over, holding out a robe as I take in the three men before me. "Sorry, Miriam, I got side-tracked. Let's get you covered up."

I take the robe, my cheeks heating with embarrassment at their continued perusal. I can't even meet their eyes. I wasn't good with the opposite sex previous to being banished to the UK and giving birth to Jorja, and the lack of interaction since hasn't helped. It was different with Bentley because that was a school thing, but socially, I'm a little bit of a mess. My ex-bestie, Kira, always took the lead.

"Come on, grab a seat, and I'll pour you a hot chocolate and help you warm up. Noah, move over and make some room for Miriam." Mae smacks the larger man on his broad shoulder, and he quickly does as she asks, making room for me to grab the stool between two of them.

CHAPTER 5

Noah

When my phone rang, I begrudgingly got out of bed and hurried over to my grandparents' place. My brother Ethan pulls up at the same time I do. He still lives at home with Mom and Dad and my other brother Dylan, who is in the passenger seat, his curls sticking out at all angles. He perks up when he sees me and waves. He's perpetually cheerful, kind of like a Labrador.

They both grunt a greeting when they get out. I grab the requested tarps from the back of my truck before handing Dylan a powerful flashlight as Ethan gets the ladder. We're about to head to our grandparents' home, which is surprisingly lit up, unlike what I assumed, when a shout draws my attention.

Grandpa is waving from the porch of the house next door to theirs, so we change direction and walk up the drive to the pitch-black house. The rain has let up slightly, and now there's only a light drizzle, but the wind is still blowing from the summer storm, and I shiver as the drizzle dampens my shirt and the wind blows straight through it. My bed had been so nice and warm, and I was having such nice dreams.

"Hey, Gramps, what are we doing here?" I ask as Dylan shines his flashlight around the front of the house.

"I thought this place was unoccupied," Ethan, my middle brother, remarks, scratching his head.

"It was, but Jocelyn's great niece inherited it when she passed and has recently moved in. The big sycamore tree in the backyard lost a branch in the storm and went through the master bedroom roof and took out the power. I want to secure the hole to minimize the damage for the poor girl." My grandpa looks really upset, and I can tell that he likes his new neighbor.

"It's okay, Gramps, we've got this. Why don't you show us the damage, and the boys and I will see what we can do?" I suggest.

My grandpa is responsible for teaching us everything we know. He passed the business to Dad, who will pass it to us once he's ready to retire, but he's not there yet. In the meantime, I work, go to college, and take business classes so that when it's my time to take over the family business, I won't fuck it up. Ethan works full time for dad. He's happiest working with his hands and being the day-to-day face of Wilson Construction with Dad. Dylan is still in high school and is hoping to play hockey at college, just like my roommate Kashton, so that's his focus now.

Grandpa leads the way up the steps, and Ethan shines the light around and whistles. "This place needs a lot of work," he mutters as the stairs creak under our feet.

Grandpa grunts. "Yes, it's been empty nearly thirty years at least. I was going to suggest to Miriam that she get you out to do a quote for everything when she mentioned needing a contractor, but I got distracted. Once we're done here, I'll take you over and introduce you to her. It will be nice for her to know someone more her age."

More her age? How old is this new neighbor of theirs? I assumed she'd be in her thirties or forties, but I guess I was wrong.

Gramps shows us to the master bedroom, and Dylan whistles as he catches sight of the damage a few feet from the large bed in the room. "Wow, the owner was really lucky that it didn't land a few feet closer," he says as Ethan puts the ladder down and studies the damage.

"Dylan, run back to the truck and grab a hammer and some nails. We'll nail these tarps in place so it will keep the weather out tonight and come back tomorrow with the cherry picker and a chainsaw to remove the branch. Then we can see what it's going to take to fix it."

"Can you have a look at the tree and see if there are any more potential problem branches? I wouldn't want anyone getting hurt." Gramps wrings his hands, and Ethan assures him he will take care of it.

Dylan disappears and returns quickly with the requested gear, and the three of us make short work of getting the tarps up.

"If the rain is heavy, I'm not sure how effective this will be, but I guess it's better than nothing," I muse out loud.

"After I've done that tomorrow, I can have a look around and see what else needs to be done, and work up a quote for the owner," Ethan offers, always in business mode.

"I have a morning class, but I can help you once it's finished," I tell him, and he nods.

"Yeah, that would be great, thanks. I have a job I can't put off in the morning anyway, so how about we meet here at one? Will the owner be home? In fact, where is she now?" Ethan's brow creases, and I realize he's right. Where is she?

"She's at home with Grammy. She's going to stay the night with us. The poor thing was shaken," Gramps explains as we pack up our gear and head back downstairs. "Come over and have hot chocolate and snickerdoodles before you go, and you can ask her if she's going to be home."

"Yes! Grammy has been baking." Dylan fist-bumps the air and hurries out without waiting.

"I swear that boy thinks with his stomach." Ethan chuckles, shaking his head.

"Like you don't." I elbow him as he picks up the ladder, and I gather the rest of the stuff Dylan conveniently left behind.

Gramps chuckles. "Your poor mom swears the three of you made their grocery bill skyrocket the minute you all had your growth spurts."

"I'm sure it did, but I blame her cooking. She's an amazing cook," I argue, and he smiles.

"Yes, she is, your dad chose well, and hopefully you three will be as smart as him."

Ethan chuckles. "Noah doesn't need a wife who can cook, he has Bentley."

The two of them chuckle as I roll my eyes, but he's not wrong. My roommate Bentley is an amazing cook. He learned everything from their chef at home, then continued his education overseas. The kitchen in our house is his domain, and heaven help us if we mess it up. It's his way of contributing to the household. He says that both Kashton and I are too busy to cook, and we'd eat takeout all the time if it wasn't for him, and he's right. He prides himself in preparing delicious, healthy meals for us so that Kashton stays in top physical shape. Dylan asked for a few of his recipes for Mom to make so he can eat as healthy as his idol. It's weird the way that my brother worships my best friend. To me, he's just a dude who leaves wet towels on our bathroom floor and forgets to wash his stubble out of the sink after he shaves. To Dylan, he is a hockey god.

"I don't see either of you assholes complaining when he regularly feeds you too," I comment as we exit the run-down house and put our gear in the back of my truck. The rain seems to have blown through for now, but the wind is still pretty strong.

"Hell no. I know when I'm getting a good thing. It's why I'm happy to offer to clean the dishes every time I'm there and do any repairs he or his family needs done for cost. He scratches my back, and I scratch his."

Our families have been friends for years, though Kash and Kira went to a different school than

Bentley and me. Every year we would head to the lake for summer holidays together. The Carlyles have their cabin, which is really a three-story log mansion with enough space for us to well and truly spread out. The five of us boys, Kira, and Bentley's younger sister, Ginny, would spend the summer swimming and fishing and using the jet skis and genuinely getting up to mischief.

Our grandparents' house is brightly lit, a stark contrast to the forlorn house we just left behind. "You need to get the owner to call the power company so they can come out and get their power working again," I remind Gramps, who nods.

"Yes, I'll do it first thing in the morning. It's supposed to get hot again, and I want her to be able to use her fans."

"No AC?" I ask, and he shakes his head.

"No, the house hasn't been lived in since the late eighties, and AC wasn't installed in it. There's a lovely pool area in the backyard, but it's overgrown, and the pool is empty. Miriam wants that to be one of the first things fixed so she can use it while the weather is still warm."

We make our way into the kitchen where Dylan has already made himself comfortable at the kitchen island. A steaming mug of hot chocolate sits in front of him along with a plate piled high with snicker-doodles.

"Boys!" My grandma pushes away from the counter she was leaning on and holds out her arms to give us a hug, but she has something draped over her arm, so it makes it a little awkward. Ethan and I still manage to give her a side hug and a kiss on the cheek. "Thank you so much for coming out so late. We really appreciate it, and I'm sure Miriam does too. Grab a seat, and I'll pour you some cocoa. You know you can all just crash here instead of returning home," she suggests, but I shake my head as I take a seat.

"I have class in the morning, and Dylan has school," I remind her, and he grumbles, glaring at me, even though I know he wouldn't skip it. He won't do anything to jeopardize his spot on the hockey team.

"And I have a job over at the Kennedys' place. Violet is redoing their guesthouse and wants the bathroom retiled. Dad asked me to go over and give her a quote." Grammy's eyes light up at this.

"Is she really? I can't wait to see what she does with it. Why they need such a big place when it's just the two of them, I have no idea." She and Grandpa exchange a glance that I can't interpret, but Ethan snorts.

"At least I'm dealing with them and not their son, Eric. He's a raging asshole. There is a stick firmly lodged up his ass, and he thinks he is so much better than everyone else. I told Dad that I won't do any work he requests, and I make him go instead," Ethan grumbles before taking a large sip of his hot chocolate.

"Yes, how he became that way, I have no idea. Violet and Calvin aren't anything like that," Grammy says. "Both he and Leticia are trying people."

Before any of us can say anything else, the door to the kitchen swings open. Grammy's eyes widen as a gorgeous, curvy, blonde-haired siren steps into the room wearing nothing but a T-shirt I recognize as one of my mom's that she leaves here, but shit, it never looks like that on her. I just about swallow my tongue as I take in her long, shapely legs and curvy body tantalizingly hidden beneath the baggy shirt.

She stops suddenly, and I hear her mutter, "Shit." The word is slightly accented, and I see her cheeks pinken under our scrutiny. Dylan is smiling like a damn fool as he looks at the pretty girl, but Ethan's eyes narrow in suspicion. This is their new neighbor? She was not what I was expecting at all.

Grammy hurries over, holding out a robe. "Sorry, Miriam, I got sidetracked. Let's get you covered up.

Come on, grab a seat, and I'll pour you a hot chocolate and help you warm up. Noah, move over and make some room for Miriam." Grammy smacks my shoulder and gestures for me to move over so she can squeeze another seat between Dylan and me.

I do as she asks, and the girl reluctantly moves onto the chair, biting her lower lip. She smells like vanilla and strawberries, and a sudden urge to bite her lip rolls through me. I grab hold of the counter to steady myself. Damn it, I haven't had such a visceral reaction to a woman like this before. Women are easy for me. They practically throw themselves at me. I'm friends with Kashton Young and Bentley Carlyle, and I'm one of the heirs to Wilson Construction, a multimillion-dollar company. I'm considered quite the catch, and when I first started college, I took advantage of that, but I quickly grew tired of meaningless flings. I want something like what my grandparents and parents have—love with a solid amount of friendship and respect.

"Boys, this is Miriam Kennedy. She's been living in London for a few years. She is Jocelyn Smart's great niece, and she is our new neighbor."

Did she say Kennedy? As in Violet and Calvin Kennedy? No, she's too young to be their child. They are the same age as Gramps and Grammy. My eyes widen, and Ethan and I exchange a loaded glance. Holy shit, the rumors of a long-lost daughter are true. For years, people have whispered about it at fancy parties. Apparently, Eric and Leticia used to have a daughter, and she disappeared. They said she got mixed up with the wrong crowd and ran away with a drug dealer or a motorcycle gang or something. It was always different every time I heard the gossip, so I stopped believing any of it, and here she is, right in front of me, and not what I thought she would look like at all.

"These are my grandsons Noah, Ethan, and Dylan." Grammy points to each of us, and Dylan waves and smiles. I nod and grunt, unsure if I'll embarrass myself if I say anything now.

Ethan, of course, is unshakeable, and he holds out a hand. "Nice to meet you, Miriam."

She shakes his hand, and a small smile appears on her lips, which just makes her even prettier. "Thank you so much for coming to help in the middle of the night. I wasn't sure what we were going to do until Fred and Mae came to our rescue," she says quietly in that slightly accented voice.

I smother the groan that wants to escape. This girl is certainly pressing all my buttons, and I know nothing about her. She sounds so posh, and I can just imagine her moaning my name as I do wicked things to her body.

"Sure thing. Any friend of Gramps and Grammy is a friend of ours. We've secured some tarps over the hole, but that's about as much as we can do tonight. Noah and I will come back tomorrow after lunch with the cherry picker and a chainsaw and remove the branch. We can check the other branches while we're up there, and then we can assess what needs to be done to fix the hole."

Miriam heaves a sigh of relief next to me. "Thank you. I really didn't know what to do. Owning a house is a completely new concept for me. I'm not even sure how livable it is, but it's our only option for now. The staircase feels like it's one wrong move away from killing me." The words tumble out like she can't stop them.

"Hey, it's okay." I reach out and touch her hand, and goosebumps appear on her arm. We both look at them before our eyes meet, and I swear I hear angels singing a chorus. "Ethan is amazing at what he does. He will go through the house with you if you want and assess everything, and make sure nothing is going to fall down around your head. He'll also give you a quote for anything he feels needs to be repaired. If you want a recommendation,

I can give you a few numbers to call for people who we've done work for in the past."

"That would be wonderful. You have no idea how much I've been worrying about this. I don't need any of those numbers. If Fred recommends you, then that's good enough for me." Out of the corner of my eye, I see Gramps' chest puff out with pride, and I smile.

"And they won't do anything sketchy either. I taught them better than that," Gramps says, and she smiles at him.

"Of course you did. I wouldn't expect anything less."

He beams, and I can tell he and Grammy are completely smitten with this girl. They always wanted a granddaughter, but they were stuck with me, my brothers, and our two cousins.

As much as I don't want to leave, since I would love to get to know her a little better, it's late, or should I say very early, and we all need to be up in a few hours.

"Will you be home after lunch, around one?" Ethan asks, and she nods.

"Yes, that's fine, I need to go somewhere around three, but you can leave the keys with Mae and Fred if you get done before I return."

I'm dying to ask where she needs to go. I want to interrogate her and find out every possible thing I can about her, but if I come on too strong, I'm going to seem like a psycho.

"Okay, well, we need to get going then. It was nice to meet you, and we'll see you tomorrow." I stand up and push my stool back.

Ethan and Dylan quickly follow suit, Dylan grabbing another cookie before we leave. He's been quiet the whole time, but I think he's probably still half asleep. He trains hard and crashes equally as hard. I was surprised to see he came with Ethan, but he does like to feel like he's contributing to the family, even in a small way.

"It was nice to meet you, and again, thank you all," she calls as we trail out of the house, kissing Grammy on the cheek and waving goodbye to Gramps.

"Dude, what the fuck was with you two?" Dylan asks, leaning against Ethan's truck. "What was that look when you heard her name?"

"Explain it to him on the way home," I tell Ethan, who nods, and he and my little brother leave.

I get into my own truck, my mind stuck on the beautiful and intriguing Miriam Kennedy. I'm dying to know her story now, but I'm pretty sure patience and kindness is going to be necessary to find out the truth. There was something a little fragile and wary in her eyes—a look I didn't like at all—but I will do everything I can to get her tale. There's nothing I like more than a juicy mystery, and she's one all wrapped up in a delicious package.

CHAPTER 6

Miriam

I head up to bed not long after Fred and Mae's grandsons leave. I'm feeling a little off-kilter at my reaction to the oldest, Noah. He had this calm, gentle presence despite his rather large frame, and my body reacted when he put his hand on my arm. Goosebumps broke out, and I gritted my teeth at the shiver of desire that wanted to make itself known. I mean, I know it's been years since I've felt the touch of the opposite sex, but am I really that fucking needy?

Tall and rugged, all three of them looked fit and athletic. I remember Fred saying they all played hockey, and I don't doubt they didn't dominate on the ice. Construction work must keep them in shape, but it was the look of interest in Noah's gaze that shook me to my core. Ethan kept everything all businesslike, and I think Dylan was half asleep, but there was something in Noah's eyes that told me he might like what he saw, and I can't tell you how much that actually means to me to know that I am desirable to someone. He also knows absolutely nothing about me or my situation, so there is no pity or false looks of understanding, but I'm sure once he finds out that I am a mother, that interest will quickly dry up. It happened time and time again back in the UK. We'd be out for the day, and the minute someone realized Jorja was mine and not Darcy and Seamus's, they would quickly find someone else to flirt with.

It was my biggest concern when I returned to Storm View. Rumors, gossip, and innuendo always dominated conversation, whether it was at school or in social situations, and the thought that I became fodder for those gossip mongers makes me sick. I only hope my mother and father buried it as deeply as I think they did and I can start over fresh. I considered changing my surname to Smart—Jocelyn would have been ecstatic—but I couldn't bring myself to do it. I kept Kennedy in the blind hope that, one day, maybe either Kira or her brother would come in search of me. It was probably stupid of me, but there's still a small part of me that continues to hope that they didn't believe whatever lies my parents fed them and they are waiting for me to resurface. I haven't been able to force myself to stalk them on social media in the time since I have been gone, not wanting to add another level of hurt from seeing them both move on.

I toss and turn a little in the strange bed, but I eventually fall asleep, only to be woken a short time later by the alarm on my phone. Jorja doesn't even flinch, sleeping the sleep of the dead like she normally does. It's still early, so I leave her and get up. I'll go back to our place and get changed and bring her some clothes. She'll be fine here with Fred and Mae if she does wake while I'm gone, which I'm almost certain she won't. I get out of bed and throw on the robe Mae gave me last night. Pulling the door almost closed behind me, I head out. I'm going to make a mad dash down their driveway and back up mine and pray that no one is out early, walking their dogs, but voices in the kitchen stop me. I poke my head through the door and wave at the older couple.

"Hey, I'm just running back to get changed and grab my and Jorja's bags and something for her to wear. Can you listen out for her?"

"Good morning, Miriam. Of course we can. I'll

have some coffee waiting for you, and the muffins will just be coming out of the oven when you return," Mae tells me as Fred waves.

"That would be wonderful, thank you."

"Miriam, don't panic when you see the state of your bedroom. The boys will get it fixed up for you, I promise," Fred assures me. "Things always look worse the next day. Oh, and before I went to bed, I called the power company. They already fixed the power because that live wire was dangerous and risked setting things on fire."

My stomach rolls at the idea my house could have burned down. "Thank you so much, I hadn't even thought of that."

"It's no problem. I didn't want you to worry. You just look after yourself and your pretty girl, and my boys will get your house fixed up for you in no time." I hurry over and smack a kiss on his cheek, super grateful to both of these people. Their kindness is something I hadn't been expecting when I returned to my hometown, but I'm not going to turn it down.

"You two are the best. I don't know what Jorja and I would do without you."

"Go on, get away with you," he grumbles, and Mae giggles at his reaction. "It's just plain, common decency. Anyone would do it."

"No, Fred, no they wouldn't," I reply, and he and

Mae exchange a glance. I'm pretty sure they know my family story. Jocelyn spoke to them on a regular basis, so they weren't surprised to see me when I turned up a week ago. I think Seamus probably told them when he called to tell them of Jocelyn's passing, but neither of them have pried, which I'm thankful for.

"I won't be too long. I'll drive my car back so we can leave straight from here. I have another morning class, but I will be back in time for Ethan and Noah."

I'm in luck when I hurry over to my house. It's still too early for anyone to be out and about, and the storm has blown through, so the sky is blue, and it feels like the sun is gearing up to make it a hot day.

This neighborhood is mostly people Mae and Fred's age. I am by far the youngest here. My parents and grandparents live a couple of streets over from here in a suburb a step up from this one. Don't get me wrong, this is still a beautiful neighborhood, but it's not on the same level as that one. My grandparents are old money, but when I lived at home, they firmly believed my father had to learn to make his own way in the world and not live on family money. He's in investments, but I didn't actually pay that much attention. He and my mother were so busy trying to impress people they didn't have time for me. The only reason we lived in such a wealthy neighborhood was because my grandparents let them build a house on their estate. It all belongs to them and not my parents. Personally, I would want my own things and not to rely on others, but not my mom and dad. They can say they live in the Kensington area of Storm View, and that's all that matters.

I roll my eyes at how my thoughts have turned back to my parents. Thinking about them always makes me equal parts angry and sad, so I brush thoughts of them away.

I put my key in the lock and push the front door open. Daylight drifts through various windows, making it easy for me to make my way through the house. I still flick on one of the light switches, though, and sure enough, the power is on, which means I can have a hot shower if I can get into the bathroom. The branch was sitting right over the top of both the closet and the bathroom, but I didn't get close enough to see if it did any damage to either of those rooms.

Hurrying upstairs, I go to Jorja's room first and grab her a clean uniform, shoes, and socks for school. I stuff them in a bag she has in her closet before making my way to my own room.

I hesitate at the closed door, dreading seeing the damage from the night before, but I take a deep breath and push it open. The sight that greets me has my heart sinking. It looks so much worse now that I can actually see the damage. Despite the tarps that have been nailed around to keep some of the rain out, I see that there's a fair amount of rain damage to the floors and, well, there's a huge hole in the roof. Luckily it missed both the bathroom and the closet, and I should be able to duck under to get to both of them. Sighing heavily, I put Jorja's bag down on my bed and strip off the borrowed robe and shirt and my underwear before crossing to the bathroom. I turn the water on hot and step under, feeling my body relax for the first time in days.

Moving halfway around the world is stressful, and being a single mother makes it extra stressful. Add both of us needing to start school, and I haven't had a moment to breathe in weeks. Showers are the only time I get to fully destress, so who cares if I stand here a little longer than is acceptable? Especially because I know Jorja is safe and sound asleep and not poking around this big house, which could tumble down around our ears at any moment.

I think about last night's adventure, and despite the major inconvenience of having a tree branch through our roof, I feel like it was serendipitous. I wanted to get a contractor in anyway, and now I feel quite confident that the Wilsons are going to be reliable and honest. There's just something about Fred and Mae that makes me feel like they raised their children the right way, teaching them right from wrong and that being fair and kind is a better way to keep clients than being ruthless and cutthroat.

I make quick work of washing my body and hair, aware Jorja could wake up at Fred and Mae's at any moment. The morning was already feeling fairly steamy, so I find a pair of denim shorts and a shirt before shoving my feet into socks and my Converse. I throw my wet hair up into a ponytail and swipe some mascara across my blonde lashes, calling it good. After picking up Jorja's toothbrush and a hairbrush, I ease back under the branch. I remember to grab my laptop from my nightstand, grateful the branch wasn't any closer than it was—Jorja and I could have been seriously hurt. Lastly, I grab her packed bag from the bed and hurry downstairs, shoving my laptop into my own bag before collecting Jorja's. She's going to have school lunch again. Luckily she said it was really good yesterday. I guess private school lunches are on a whole other level compared to public school. Mae assured me that Storm View Prep's lunches were good. Her two sons and three of her grandsons all went there. I went to Storm View Public because my grandfather believed public education was good enough for him, so it was good enough for his son and grandchild. My parents argued vehemently, but Grandfather put his foot down, and they caved. I wasn't upset. I met Kira on my first day, and we had been tight ever since.

Grabbing my car keys from the side table, I hurry out the door and into the carport. I pull open the driver's side door and throw everything into the passenger's seat before sliding into the Impala. I turn the key, and the car roars to life, and I breathe a sigh of relief. I make the short trip between the two houses, parking in their driveway before grabbing the bag with Jorja's clothes, then I knock on the front door.

"Miriam, dear, you don't have to knock. If it's open, just come on in," Mae tells me as she pulls the door open.

"Sorry I took so long," I apologize, and she waves her hand.

"Pfft, don't think anything of it. Jorja woke up about ten minutes ago, and she and Fred are having breakfast. Why don't you go and join them?"

I follow Mae back to the kitchen, and I hear Jorja giggling and Fred chuckling before we've even made it halfway.

"She really is such a delightful little girl. Fred and I are completely smitten with her," Mae tells me as she pushes the door to the kitchen open, and I find the two of them eating waffles with maple syrup and strawberries. Jorja waves at me, and I smother a groan. I feel sorry for her teacher with her starting the morning with that much sugar, but I'm sure she will run it off in no time.

"Hi, Mama, hi. Fred said that his grandsons are going to fix our house. Can they fix the pool too? I want to go swimming!" The words rush out, and she bounces up and down on her seat, knocking into her fork and almost sending it to the floor.

"Hey, easy," I caution, putting the bag on the ground and grabbing a seat at the island next to her. Mae puts a steaming hot mug of tea in front of me as well as a plate of fruit. I see the strawberries, peaches, cherries, apricots, and raspberries. Behind Mae and Fred's maze is a small orchard, and all the fruit are from their trees and garden. "This looks lovely, thank you, Mae." I smile warmly at the woman, and she pats my hand before turning to my daughter.

"Maybe after school, Jorja would like to walk with me in the orchard and pick some of the ripe fruit?" Mae asks her, and she bounces up and down on her seat again.

"Oh yes, that would be awesome. Can I, Mama?"

All three of them turn to look at me with hopeful eyes, and I just chuckle.

"I can't win with you three. That's fine, now hurry up and eat your breakfast. We still have to get dressed, clean your teeth, and brush your hair, and we don't have a lot of time." We make quick work of our breakfast as Mae pulls a steaming tray of muffins out of the oven before placing them on the stove top to cool.

I finish my fruit and my perfectly brewed tea just as Jorja finishes her waffles and wipes her mouth on her napkin.

"Okay, grab your bag and get dressed, and don't forget to clean your teeth. I'll do your hair when you're finished."

She jumps down from the high seat and quickly hurries off to do as I instructed, and I blink in shock.

"What was in those waffles?" I ask, turning to face the elderly couple. "She didn't protest." I know I sound shocked, but we usually go through some kind of song and dance about getting ready in the morning. Now that I think about it, though, she didn't give me one yesterday. "Going to school really is exciting for her. I wonder how long that will last."

They both chuckle. "Hmm, I think the boys were probably about ten when they started to grumble about school," Fred says, smiling fondly as he thinks back.

"And then they hit puberty, and God help us, it almost took a bulldozer to get them out of bed. The grandsons were the same," Mae adds.

The three of us are having a quiet conversation about my house when Jorja returns in a flurry of activity. She has managed to dress herself, but the buttons on her top are done up wrong, and her skirt is twisted around backward. She's carrying one of her shoes, and her hair desperately needs to be brushed.

"Wow, that was a great effort," I praise her, hopping off my chair to help her button the shirt properly and tug her skirt around the right way. I lift her up and smack a kiss on her cheek, causing her to giggle, before sitting her in my vacated chair. I take the remaining shoe and place it on her foot before doing up the laces. I take the brush from her and try to tame her mane of curls into some semblance of neatness, but without the detangling spray, it's somewhat of a chore. Eventually, I get it up into a ponytail, then wet my hands and comb them through the back, trying to dampen the frizz, which works slightly.

"That will have to do," I announce, placing the brush on the table.

"Gorgeous," Fred declares, and Jorja giggles. She really does love them as much as they love her.

"Okay, I hate to eat and run, but we have classes," I tell them, grabbing my plate and coffee mug and setting them in the dishwasher for Mae. She gets up and grabs a ziplock bag, shoving one of the fresh muffins into it before handing it to me.

"In case you get hungry in class. I'll send the rest of these home with the boys this afternoon. They all like to eat them for snacks." I'm not surprised, because they look delicious.

"Thanks so much for last night. I'm not sure what I would have done without you both," I say, giving them both a kiss on the cheek before picking up the hairbrush. "We will see you this afternoon."

"Miriam, you two are welcome to stay as long as you need to until the roof in your bedroom is fixed, which I'm sure the boys will make a priority, so don't you worry about anything, okay?" Mae reassures me, and I feel a rush of relief.

I was worried about that, actually, but I shouldn't have been. I guess I've been let down by the people who are supposed to love me so often that I forget that not everyone is like that.

We all say our goodbyes, and I hustle Jorja out of the house and into her car seat before setting off toward school. I left the school backpacks in the car, so we have everything we need.

I get Jorja settled at school, and again, she doesn't look backward once she finds her friend Lola. She gives me an absent kiss on the cheek before they both run off together, but I don't feel so sad about it today. I'm just pleased she has a friend and is happy to be here.

CHAPTER 7

Miriam

My morning class flies by, and before I know it, I'm headed back to my house to wait for the Wilson boys to remove the branch from my bedroom. The day has turned humid and hot, and my back is sticking to the leather seats of the car. It has no AC, so I have the window down, but that's not even helping.

Pulling my car into the carport, I take a small breath. My class this morning was boring, and I sat away from the majority of the students. I am never going to make friends this way, but when I hear their mindless chatter about parties and who's hooking up with who, all I feel is bored. My life is so much more complicated than theirs. I have nothing in common with any of them.

Gathering up my bag, I head inside my house, which is also a hot box. I hang up the bag and toss my keys in the bowl, then I go around and open up a few windows. I am so not used to this heat after living in the UK for so many years. I make myself a cup of tea and take it outside onto the back patio. There is a huge, climbing wisteria plant that covers the whole thing, creating shade and bringing a beautiful scent to the backyard. It's completely over-grown and definitely needs some work. I'll pop by the hardware store and grab some pruning shears and gloves and tackle it this weekend.

The offending tree is at the far end of the patio, its huge branch shading a good portion of that side of the yard. Hopefully the rest of the branches are in better shape than the one that plunged through our roof, but Fred assured me the boys would check it out.

I take a seat on an old bench that's on the patio and add new outdoor furniture to the never-ending list in my head. I have to check out the shed and see what's in there. Apart from getting the car out, I haven't had time to poke around yet. My eyes drift to the empty pool. It's an old-fashioned tiled one, but it has a layer of sludgy grime after last night's rain, so I can't see if there is a pattern in the tile or what kind of condition it's in. Maybe Ethan or Noah can suggest a pool restoration service, because Jorja is dying to swim. I'd try to tackle the job myself, but I don't know the first thing about pools.

I finish up my tea to the sound of birds singing and insects buzzing, but the heat is oppressive, so I quickly head inside and decide a cool shower is exactly what I need. I check the time, and it's only half twelve. Ethan said they'd be around by one, so I have time to cool off. I run upstairs to my room and strip off my clothes, ducking under the branch once more before turning the shower on decidedly cooler than I had it this morning. I wash away the stickiness the heat caused and turn off the taps, wrapping a towel around me before heading out to find some clean clothes to wear. I'm just ducking under the branch when I hear footsteps. I freeze like a stereotypical horror movie girl as they get closer, unsure what to do except grip my towel tighter.

I heave out a sigh of relief as sexy Noah Wilson enters my bedroom, completely distracted by the phone in his hand so he doesn't even notice the half naked girl in the room. I clear my throat, and he startles, looking up. His eyes widen like a deer caught in the headlights, and he spins around, giving me his back.

"Holy shit. I am so sorry. I knocked and called out, but when no one answered, I tried the door, and it was open. I just figured maybe you were next door with our grandparents, and I let myself in. I am so sorry." The words flow out of his mouth in an embarrassed rush.

"It's okay. As you can see, I was in the shower, so I didn't hear you at the door. If you give me a moment, I'll get changed and out of your hair," I tell him, a little disappointed he didn't try to get a better look.

"Yeah, sure, take your time. My class finished early, so I thought I'd get started. I just wanted to see what it looked like in the daylight before I brought tools up, but I'll go grab them out of my truck so you can get dressed. Again, I'm sorry." He hurries away, and I snort out loud. I wouldn't have thought a half naked chick would be that scary to a young, red-blooded male, but he took off like a bat out of hell. Maybe he's gay, or he has a girlfriend and is one of the good ones and not interested in checking anyone else out. Lucky girl.

I find a pair of shorts and a top. It's what I've been living in since we arrived. Acclimating is not easy, and I've found the heat stifling.

By the time Noah returns, I'm decent again, but he knocks on the doorjamb anyway. "Come on in," I call out, and he eases through the doorway with his ladder. He sets it up close to the branch and steps back to get a good look. I'm not sure if he's too embarrassed to look at me again or if he's just keen to get started on the job. I hope it's the latter. I step up next to him and look up at the damage, wincing at how it destroyed the gorgeous, corniced ceiling.

"Well, it's certainly made a mess of the ceiling, but it looks like it might have missed the structural beams. Once we remove the branch, we'll be able to tell what kind of damage it did to the roof," he says, sounding all businesslike.

"Will you be able to fix it?" I ask turning away from the damage to look at him. I find him already looking at me, and I conjure up a shy smile.

"We'll be able to fix it. Victorian roofs are a specialty of ours since there are so many in this area. We may not be able to match the exact color of the slate you have since it's over forty years old, but we can get it close enough so no one will notice after a bit of weathering. As for the ceilings, we have a man who works for us who is a master at cornicing. He should be able to match up the design without any problems," he reassures me. "Ethan should be here soon, and we'll get started."

"Would you like something to drink while you wait?" I ask him, and he looks at his watch.

"Yeah, that would be great. I hadn't realized how early it was. Again, I'm sorry," he apologizes, and I wave it off.

"Don't worry about it. You said classes. Are you going to college?" I ask him as I lead the way out of the damaged room and back down the stairs. The stairs creak and groan with his weight as we descend them, and I hide my wince.

"Ah, yeah, I'm doing a business degree. I almost have all my credits. I just have one or two classes to finish, and I graduate at the end of the semester."

My ears perk up at hearing he's doing business as well. "Really? I'm doing business too," I say, but as I turn around, I find he's stopped and is banging on a couple of the stairs.

He looks up when I clear my throat. "Oh, sorry. They were loud, so I wanted to check the integrity. I wouldn't want you falling through one of them."

My heart skips at the thought of Jorja falling through a step, and I am thankful for his thoughtfulness. "What's the verdict?" I ask casually despite feeling anything but.

He looks up at me and grins, which has my heart skipping for an entirely different reason. "Despite sounding like something out of a horror movie, they are actually fairly solid." His eyes drift to the balustrade, and he shuffles over and grabs the railing and gives it a solid shake. I watch in horror as the whole thing sways precariously. "This, on the other hand, needs work." He moves down a step and looks at the base of the next post. "It looks like the wood shrank over the years and is not as solidly fitted as it was years ago. We could put wedges in to stabilize it, but I would highly recommend replacing the whole thing."

I think about Jorja hanging onto it as she jauntily skips down the steps. I'm relieved she's not going to fall through them, but horrified that she could quite easily go over the edge if they decide to give way. "Let's replace it," I tell him quickly, and he nods, pulling out his phone and swiping his finger across it.

"I'll start a list of things and share it with Ethan, because I am sure he's going to want to go through the house with you."

He follows me the rest of the way to the kitchen. "Is soda okay?" I ask, pulling open the fridge and peering at the limited contents. "Or I have juice or wine."

He chuckles. "A little too early for me for wine. Soda would be great. You said you're doing business. What classes do you have?"

I tell him about the four classes that I have this

semester, and his eyes light up when I mention having marketing with Sarah Carlyle.

"Oh, hey, Sarah is great. She really knows what she's talking about. You're lucky to have someone with so much firsthand experience teaching you. I would have killed to have her as my lecturer when I did that class." He talks about her in an almost familiar way, but before I can ask about it, there's a knock on the door, and I go to let Ethan in.

"Hey, come on in. Do you want a drink?" I ask him as I lead him back to the kitchen. He and Noah fist-bump as Ethan takes a seat at my island.

"Soda would be great, thanks. It sure is hot outside. Damn storm just made everything worse," he grumbles. "I had my AC on high in the car, but it all goes to shit as soon as you step outside."

"You are preaching to the choir," I reply, grabbing another soda out of the fridge and sliding it over to him. "Try moving from cloudy old England to this heat. This house has no AC, and the pool is nothing but a mud puddle." I wave a hand in the direction of the backyard.

Ethan takes a long drink of his soda before wiping his mouth with the back of his hand. "Okay, how about Noah and I deal with the branch currently sticking out of your ceiling? I had a good look around the tree outside, and the branch has broken clean off. I think we should be able to cut it up bit by bit and drag it through. Then we can assess what kind of repairs we need to make to the roof and ceiling. After that, we'll head outside and take a look at that pool for you. You can't spend the rest of the summer sweltering, and the AC is not so easily fixed."

"If you can fix my pool, I will kiss your feet," I gush, and he laughs while Noah rolls his eyes.

"I don't think you need to go quite that far," he grumbles good-naturedly.

"Well fine, how about I have both of you and Dylan around for a BBQ and a swim? I haven't ever grilled before, but how hard can it be?"

The boys' eyes widen, and Ethan gasps dramatically. "You've never grilled?"

"My roommate would have a heart attack. He's an expert griller. If you allow me to bring him too, then we can put him to work."

"It's a deal. I'm sure I can manage to make some good sides. Mae must have half a dozen recipes for me to steal."

They both grin. "You bet she does, but I bet she'll just invite herself and Gramps and make them all for you."

I throw up my hands in defeat. "I'll provide the beer."

Ethan holds out his fist, and I bump it before they both drain their drinks and stand up.

"Can I help with anything?" I ask them.

"Nope. I'm just going to grab the chainsaw and wheelbarrow, and we'll get started. I think we'll just toss the pieces of wood out of the window if there isn't anything under it."

I follow them both back out to the foyer. "Oh, hey, there's this thing if it will be easier for you." I go over to the dumbwaiter I found when I explored the house one night after Jorja went to bed. She hasn't found it yet, thankfully, or I'm almost certain she would have climbed in it by now.

Ethan pops his head in and looks up, giving the mechanism a tug. "Seems pretty solid, but I'm not sure if I would want to risk it before giving the mechanism a service." He presses the button on the wall to the side of it, and we watch as the rope or chain or whatever it is starts moving, but there is a grinding sound, and it comes to a stop.

"Ah, I guess you were right."

"So back to plan A, I guess," Noah says, his arm brushing against mine as we all step away from the broken mechanism.

"Well, let me know if you need a hand. I have somewhere to be at three, but I'll be around until then. I want to start cleaning out all the rooms. All of them are furnished, but most of it isn't to my taste. I want to call a charitable company to come and get anything I don't want."

"Oh hey, my mom volunteers for a program that helps women get back on their feet when they've gotten out of a broken relationship. I'm sure she would take anything you'd like to get rid of." Noah fishes around in his back pocket, pulling out a wallet. He takes out a business card and passes to me, looking a little sheepish. "She makes us carry them for this exact reason. When people do renovations, they tend to want new furniture too."

I take the card, and he runs a hand through his chestnut curls. I think it's adorable that he helps his mom out. They are obviously a close-knit family.

"Awesome! I'll give her a call once I've sorted things into piles."

He and I continue to stare at one another until Ethan clears his throat.

"Right then, shall we get going?" He slaps Noah on the back and nods to me as they both start out the door. My eyes drift to Noah's pert ass, and it's as lovely watching him go as it is watching him come. There's something building between us, and maybe I will work up the guts to ask him out. I've never had to do that before, and I have no idea how to. Maybe Reddit will have some advice.

I hurry off to find my laptop, dragging it into the formal parlor which is where I'm going to start. I sit down on the uncomfortable Queen Anne chaise and do a Google search. I will get an answer before I start cleaning out the room. It faces the back of the house, and I think I would like to tear down a wall, put in glass doors, and turn it into a small conservatory like Mae's with lots of plants and light. I'll have to ask Noah and Ethan their opinion, but first, I need to know how to ask a man on a date.

CHAPTER 8

Miriam

The sound of the chainsaw jolts me out of the Google rabbit hole I found myself traveling down, and I slam the lid shut on my laptop.

Get it together, Miriam, it's just asking someone out, not rocket science, and you need to ask Mae and Fred if they would watch Jorja for you before you can do anything, I scold myself.

I sigh and look around the room. There's a chintzy cabinet with a lovely tea set that I am definitely going to keep, but I think I'll get a more modern cabinet to hold it. I'm also going to donate this chaise I'm sitting on, which is not comfortable in the least. I look over at the small table and two uncomfortable chairs on either side of it. Yup, they need to go too.

When I sit here and look out at the world, I want to be comfortable. I imagine replacing the old-fashioned furniture with plush armchairs that I will really sink into. Wallpaper and carpet also need to be added to the list. I slide off the chaise and crawl along the floor until I get to the edge of the room, where I pull back on the seam, searching to see if there are wooden floors under this garish monstrosity that someone called carpet. Sure enough, I see roughened wood peeking out. I'll ask the guys if it's possible to sand and polish it. I like the idea of wood floors with maybe one or two plush rugs. My eyes drift to the fireplace. They are placed throughout the house, and while I love the idea of a wood fire, the practicality of it, especially for a single woman, is pretty low. Maybe I'll just keep one or two—the one in here and the one in the library— and convert the rest into gas fireplaces.

In the chintzy cabinet, there is a whole heap of knickknacks. I guess I should probably ask Seamus if he wants to keep any of these things. I dig my phone out of my pocket and look at the time difference. It's about eight thirty in the UK, but Seamus and Darcy are night owls, so they should still be awake. I press the button to dial him, and within seconds, he's answering.

"Mimi, darling, we were just talking about you!" Seamus's posh accent comes down the line, and he must have me on speaker phone, because I hear Darcy in the background.

"Hello, gorgeous girl. We miss you both so much."

A rush of warmth flows through me at hearing their voices. They really are wonderful, and I miss them both dreadfully. "Hey, guys, we miss you both so much too," I reply.

"We were just wondering how your first day of classes went. Seamus wanted to call last night, but I made him wait. I thought you'd both be exhausted after your first day," Darcy tells me, and I can practically hear Seamus roll his eyes through the phone. I smother a smile as they bicker for a moment.

"You were right. We had dinner with Mae and Fred and went to sleep quite early, but we had an interesting night." I go on to tell them about the tree branch and subsequently meeting the Wilson brothers.

They both gasp in shock when I mentioned the branch, and I hear Darcy mutter something about how they never should have let us come out here alone, but by the time I get to the Wilson brothers, they are over their agitation.

"Hmm, if they are anywhere near as handsome as their father was, then you have some lovely eye candy to keep you occupied at least," Seamus says, and I can practically hear his cheeky grin.

"Well, I haven't met their father, but I can confirm that they are a treat for the eyes," I hedge, but even through the phone, they can pick up on my hint of interest.

"Oh, and pray tell, which one has caught your eye? Or is it all three?" They titter with amusement, Jocelyn's penchant for multiple lovers making them both open-minded and encouraging of polyamory, even though they are in a committed, monogamous relationship.

"Ah, no, one is still a teenager, but I can't deny that I'm attracted to the oldest."

"Well, Mimi, you're not getting any younger, and it would make both of us less worried if there was someone in your life you could depend on."

"I have Fred and Mae next door. They've been wonderful," I argue, and Seamus sighs.

"Yes, well, that's all well and good, but neither of them are making you feel all tingly on the inside, are they?"

"Well, no, but before either of you give me the

third degree, I already considered asking Noah out for a drink, and I'm having them all over for a pool party once I get it cleaned out and filled up again, so I am making an effort."

They cheer dramatically and gush, but I quickly change the subject, knowing I could be stuck here for an hour with the two of them giving me dating advice. "Let's discuss all the things in this house."

We talk for the next half hour about the few things they'd like me to put aside for them. There are a couple of paintings they would like and some of the antiques, but everything else is mine to do with as I please.

"Mimi, honey, I'm sure Mother would want you to have any jewelry in the safe," Seamus tells me.

"Safe?" I ask, looking around the room for a safe. I'm not sure why, it could be anywhere.

"Yes, in the library behind the painting of the poker playing dogs." I get up and head in that direction, leaving the parlor behind. The library is a few doors down, and when I push it open, the musty smell of leather and books hits me, and I grin. Although I'm not a big fan of classic literature and will probably donate a lot of these books, I am a huge fan of reading and plan on refilling the shelves with all my favorite romance authors.

I cross the room and step behind the big, presidential desk and look up at the garish painting. I wonder if it's one of the originals or a knockoff. Knowing Aunt Jocelyn, it's probably one of the originals.

"If you feel behind the bottom right corner, there will be a latch," Seamus explains, and I do as he suggests, feeling around before hearing a click as the painting swings slightly forward. Reaching up, I pull it back and reveal a safe behind it. It's an old-fashioned digital safe.

"The code is..." He rattles off some numbers, and I input them. The screen lights up green, and the safe opens with a loud beeping sound. I pull the heavy door open and peer inside and gasp. There are stacks of money and a large jewelry box.

"Holy crap, that is a lot of cash," I mutter, and Seamus chuckles.

"Dad was quite the lucky gambler, but he had a thing against banks. He would stack all his winnings in the safe, saying he was saving them for a rainy day. I guess this is that day. Use the money to fix up the house. They both would have wanted that." When Jocelyn's first husband and Seamus's father passed, they packed up and moved to the UK. Jocelyn said she couldn't stand living in the house surrounded by so many bittersweet memories. "She would want you to make new, happy memories."

We talk for a little longer before I hang up. I'm not quite ready to look inside the jewelry box. I'm feeling a little sad now, and seeing Jocelyn's pretties won't make it better. Instead, I close the safe, leaving everything untouched, and reposition the painting. I know the money is there now if I ever need quick cash.

"Miriam?" I hear someone call and quickly go in search of them. I find both Ethan and Noah in the foyer at the bottom of the stairs. Ethan is examining the balustrade, while Noah leans against the wall with his phone in his hand.

"Hey, is everything okay?" I stutter, almost swallowing my tongue. Noah has removed his shirt, and all his beautiful, golden skin is on display. He has a tattoo on his left bicep, but I would have to get closer to see what it is, and I don't want to give away that I'm completely ogling him.

He looks up from his phone. "Hey, there you are. We finished cutting up the branch. Do you want to come upstairs, and we'll explain what needs to be done to fix the damage?"

"Ah, yeah, sure." I'm slightly flushed, and I fan my face. "Is it hot in here?" I ask no one in particular, and Noah smirks at me, his brown eyes twinkling.

Before he can answer, Ethan steps back from the staircase. "You're right, Noah. The wood has shrunk, making it all very wobbly. I would suggest we fix this as well as the roof as soon as possible. I would hate for you to hurt yourself if it gave way. We have a master carpenter working for us. I'll take some photos and measurements before I leave today and get him started on it right away."

"Seriously?" I ask, and he just smiles and nods.

"Yes, Miriam. Gramps said to make you a priority, so that's what we are going to do. That man never asks anything from us, so it's the least we can do after everything he's given us."

"Call me Mimi. All my friends do," I tell them. Only my parents actually called me Miriam, and now Fred and Mae, I guess, but they say it in a loving way, not with the cold, annoyed tone my parents frequently adopted.

"Come on." Noah grabs my hand, and we start heading up the staircase.

His palm is rough with calluses, and if I ever needed proof that he works with his hands, this is definitely it. I watch the muscles play across his back as we climb the staircase, Ethan leading the way. I wait for Noah to drop my hand, but it doesn't happen, so I leave it there. Who am I to argue? And it's nice to be touched, even if it's platonically.

When we get to my room, bright sunlight shines

through the previously filled hole, and the chopped up branch is stacked against one wall.

"We couldn't throw the pieces out of the window because there wasn't an area where we wouldn't hit another roof. We'll carry it all downstairs in a bit," Ethan explains, gesturing to the pile of wood.

"Can I use it for firewood?" I ask before he can continue, and he shrugs.

"I don't see why not. It would have to dry out more, since it's still a bit green, but we can stack it in your shed and cut it into smaller sizes for the fireplace if you want."

"That would be great. I'm thinking I'd like to keep one or two downstairs, and maybe even this one." I wave to the one opposite my bed. Thankfully the branch missed the chimney. "The rest I'll convert to gas."

"That's smart. I'm pretty sure that dumbwaiter was mostly used for firewood for the upstairs rooms. Once we get it fixed, you can use it for that again," Noah adds, still holding my hand.

Ethan looks at our clasped hands and raises his eyebrow at his brother, so I tug mine free, feeling my cheeks heat with embarrassment. Noah winks at me again, and butterflies take flight in my stomach.

"As for the roof, the branch did some damage to

a couple of cross beams, but they are an easy enough fix, and I have a contact who works in demolition who may have access to the same shingles. We should be able to have the roof and ceiling fixed by the end of next week, but for now, we'll put a couple of sheets of plasterboard up so that no critters get in the house and you can sleep without worry," Ethan finishes, and I heave out a sigh of relief. As much as I appreciate Mae and Fred's offer to stay with them until it's fixed, I don't like to feel like a burden. I've already felt like that enough to last me a lifetime.

"You guys are amazing," I gush, beaming at them. "You have no idea what a relief that is."

"As for the floor, I would recommend tearing up the carpet. It's damp, so you don't want it to sit there and rot the wood underneath. I can have someone out here to do that tomorrow if you want," Ethan offers, and I bite my lip with worry.

"I have classes all day tomorrow," I tell him, and Noah huffs.

"Just give Gramps your keys. He'll be happy to come over and supervise, or as I call it, get in everyone's hair."

"Yeah, okay, that will work." My phone beeps in my pocket, reminding me that I have to pick up Jorja.

"I've got to run. If you finish before I get back,

can you lock up behind you?" I ask them, and Ethan nods and waves his goodbyes before turning his attention to loading the branches in the wheelbarrow. It must have taken both of them to get it up here, and it will take both of them to get it back downstairs.

"Um, Mimi..." Noah follows me out of my bedroom. I stop and wait as he runs his hand nervously through his hair. "I was wondering if you'd like to get a bite to eat this weekend and maybe see a movie or an ice hockey game?"

Internally, I'm a teenage girl squealing with excitement, but I try to control my outward reactions so I'm not quite so lame. "Ah, yeah, I'd like that," I reply, smiling, and he loses the nervous frown and grins, his eyes sparkling again.

"Great. Can I get your number so I can call you?" He pulls his phone out of the back pocket of his jeans, and I try not to swallow my tongue at all the delightful muscles that ripple with the movement. I rattle off my digits, and he puts them into his phone. Mine beeps, and he looks up. "And now you have mine too. Feel free to call or text me if you just want to chat."

He winks and turns back to my bedroom, leaving me kind of breathless. I shake off my daze and hurry into Jorja's room, grabbing some clothes she can pick fruit in. I don't want her to get fruit juice stains all over her uniform. Pulling the door closed behind me, I head downstairs. I don't want to leave my little girl waiting, and I'm sure she will be impatient to come home so she can pick fruit with Mae.

As I get into the car and back out, I contemplate telling Noah about Jorja. Do I let him know that the woman he asked on a date is a single mother? Is that first date information? If I don't tell him, I guess that could be considered misleading. Not everyone is interested in dating a mom, I know that firsthand, but on the other hand, the date could be bad anyway. Maybe I should just wait and see. Ugh, or I guess I could ask Mae for advice. I wish I had a girl-friend I could call.

I drive in the direction of Jorja's school and put the decision out of my head for now. For all I know, both of them will still be there when we get home, and it will be a moot point. I won't hide my child, but if the subject doesn't come up, I'm okay with that. I don't know how Jorja feels about me dating, and I'm not sure I'm ready to talk to her about it either. God, what a mess.

CHAPTER 9

Miriam

I'm a little early when I arrive at Jorja's school, and instead of sitting in my sweltering car, I grab a seat under a shady tree just inside the gates. It's a nice, grassy area and considerably cooler than my car. I'm just scrolling through my phone when a shadow falls over me.

"Hi, you must be Jorja's mom. You're the only person I don't recognize. Lola had lovely things to say about your daughter."

The voice is one I haven't heard in six years, but as I look up, the sun blinds me so I can't be sure whether I heard right or not.

"Holy shit," I hear the woman mutter before she says, "Well, look what the cat dragged back into town. What cesspool did you crawl your skanky ass out of?" The tone is acrid and bitter, and I know that feeling quite well. I'm just not sure why she's aiming it at me.

Standing before me is none other than my former best friend, Kira Young. What are the odds? And did she say Lola was her daughter? She would be a year younger than Jorja. When I left, Kira was hot and heavy with Liam, her boyfriend of two years. He went to the Storm View Private school but played hockey with her brother.

I scramble to my feet, unwilling to have Kira stand over me, and get my first look at her. She looks like the rest of the moms here at the school—designer outfit, perfectly coiffed hair and nails, and that same, disapproving sneer I've seen aimed my way. She's nothing like the Kira I left behind who didn't care about designer clothes or being seen despite her family's wealth. The Youngs were one of the most down to earth families I knew, very much unlike mine. I loved hanging out at their place, and I was always made to feel incredibly welcome by both of her parents.

"Kira, look at you. I never thought I'd see the day when you became a carbon copy of my mother," I sneer back, unable to hide the hurt in my voice, much to my dismay. I see her gear up to bite back, but before she can answer, the bell rings, and a swarm of children descends on us. A lump forms in my stomach, because I know the minute she sees Jorja, she's going to know who her father is. I try to push past her so I can intercept Jorja, but she grabs hold of my arm, digging her perfectly manicured nails into my skin.

"Well? What do you have to say for yourself? You just picked up and left without a word. You disappeared off the face of the Earth with no explanation, and then your parents told us you'd taken off with a motorcycle gang and you were addicted to drugs. You sure had us fooled. Did my brother mean anything to you? He was fucking heartbroken." The polished façade drops, and I see a glimpse of the real Kira Young.

"And you believed them?" I snap, unwilling to cave under the pressure. "After everything you knew about me and my relationship with my parents, you decided to trust the words out of their mouths?" I shake my head in disappointment. "Obviously I didn't mean as much to you as you did to me. You moved on a few weeks after I left and found yourself a new group of friends. They made sure to let me know."

Her eyes widen at the venom in my voice, but

before either of us can say another word, two little girls push between us.

"Mama, hi!" Jorja wraps her arms around my waist, giving me a hug, and Kira has to release my arm to turn her attention to her own child.

"Hey, baby. Did you have a good day? Are you ready to pick fruit with Mae?" I ask, but Jorja's not paying any attention to me, she's staring at Kira.

"Is that Lola's mama? Can you ask her if we can have a sleepover?"

Fucking hell! I would do anything for my daughter, but I'm not sure her having a sleepover at Lola's place is a good idea. I think maybe that ship has sailed, though, because Kira is staring at Jorja like she's seen a ghost. Jorja really is the spitting image of her brother.

"Holy shit," she says, and both girls' mouths drop open, and Lola's eyes widen.

"Oh, Mommy, you said a naughty word. Daddy is going to make you put a dollar in the swear jar."

Kira isn't paying any attention to her daughter. Her gaze flits back and forth between me and my daughter before it finally settles on me. A stubborn gleam comes into her eye, one I am very familiar with, and she sets her hands on her hips. "Lucy, you got some 'splainin to do," she drawls, and just like that, I'm taken back to the summer when I was seventeen, hanging out with Kira at her place, giggling with my best friend and stealing kisses with her brother when no one was looking.

Jorja and Lola watch us with undivided attention, and it's not something I want to talk about with little ears listening in. "Look, I have to get Jorja home. Our neighbor is taking her fruit picking."

"Are you staying at your parents' place?" she demands, not accepting my casual brush-off one little bit.

I try to hide the flinch, but she sees it, and a knowing look shines in her eyes. "Ah, no. I have a place a couple of blocks over from theirs."

Before I can steer Jorja away, she grabs my phone out of my pocket and sends herself a message. "I will text you for the address, and after I get this one asleep, I will bring over a bottle of wine. It seems like we have a lot of catching up to do," she tells me, handing the phone back, and I know she isn't going to take no for an answer.

Heaving out a sigh, I nod my agreement before herding Jorja away with the promise that we can arrange a sleepover another time, but before I leave, I turn back to Kira. "Please don't tell him. I want him to hear it from me."

She crosses her arms, and her chin sets stubbornly. "Fine, but you better not take too long, or I will tell him. He deserves to know."

I snort. "Does he? Seems to me he was perfectly happy and didn't even notice I was gone."

She gapes at me like a goldfish, but I don't wait to hear what she has to say. That's a conversation for later, and with less of an audience.

I drop Jorja off with Mae, and she changes out of her uniform before the two of them disappear down the back of the property, hand in hand. I leave my car in their driveway, since the two of us are going to stay there again tonight, and Fred walks back to my house with me.

"I want to see what the boys have done," he explains, and I smother my grin at his nosiness. Mae told me he gets bored and likes to keep a finger in the pie at Wilson Construction. I guess my house is his new pet project.

"They were finishing up when I left to get Jorja. Noah said he was going to take a look at the pool for me. I promised them a pool party if they could get it finished as soon as possible."

Fred chuckles. "I'm sure an invite from a pretty girl was pretty enticing."

I leave him to run upstairs to look at the roof and ceiling now that the branch is gone and make my way out the back. It's only then that I recognize the sound of the lawn mower and stop on my patio, watching the delicious sight of Noah Wilson mowing the jungle that is my backyard. The smell of freshly cut grass tickles my nose as the sun beats down on us, his muscles glistening with a light sheen of sweat. I'm mesmerized. He is one well-formed man.

"Hey, you don't have to do that," I call out to him, and he looks up and waves, but I'm not sure he heard me because he keeps going.

The area around the pool starts to emerge. It's a nice, flat, grassy expanse that I can put some sun loungers on. I'm pretty sure there is a fire pit down there somewhere, as well as a smaller sunken area, but I haven't had a good look, too afraid to walk through that tall grass without boots on. I sit down on the steps of my patio and wait for him to finish. About ten minutes later, he finally turns off the lawn mower, and at the same time, Fred and Ethan come outside.

"You didn't have to do that," I call out to him again as he grabs the shirt from his back pocket and wipes the sweat from his face. He just grins at me.

"I can't fix the pool if I can't actually get to it," he jokes as Fred and Ethan stop behind me.

"Let him. It's good for him," Fred remarks, and Noah and Ethan chuckle at their grandpa's words.

"We've been hearing that our entire lives. Hard work is good for the soul," Ethan adds, and Fred beams.

"And I'm right. Look at the two of you. Successful men with good hearts. I know what I'm talking about." He winks at me. "I'm heading back home. You're in good hands here, and it's too hot for me. I'm going to put on the game and sit in the AC. I'll see you boys later." With that, Fred disappears.

"We have to get going too, Mimi, but we put a temporary patch over the roof, so don't let my grandparents browbeat you into staying with them if you don't want to. We know how easily they can railroad you."

"Thanks, Ethan. Let me grab you a spare key so you can come and go as you need to, even though I might not be here." I leave them talking on the patio and run inside. I grab Noah a cold bottle of water from the fridge and the spare set of keys from the bowl in the foyer for Ethan before returning.

They are both over by the pool, peering in from

the side Noah mowed flat. I join them, passing Ethan the keys and Noah the water. He smiles gratefully and cracks the top before downing half of it. If I watch a little too closely as a drop of water slides down his chest, well, I'm only human and slightly touch starved at that.

"One of the boys will be back tomorrow to drain all of that water from the bottom, and then we can assess the state of the tiles and go from there. You'll probably need a new filtration system, something more modern, so I'll work up some invoices for you," Ethan says with a funny grin on his face as he looks between Noah and me.

"The hot tub and the fire pit will need to be cleared out as well," Noah adds, "but I'll use the string trimmer to clear that out and go from there."

"Hot tub?" I peer at the overgrown mess, and he points out a smaller tub on the other side of the pool, surrounded by thick shrubbery.

"Yeah, there's a small rocky outcrop that surrounds it to keep out any breeze, and the fire pit is next to it."

"I do like a hot tub. I can't wait to get that going and sit in it with a glass of wine in the evenings." We stare at one another, and I wonder if he's imagining sitting in the hot tub with me.

"Alright then, I'm off. I'll see you both later,"

Ethan says, but Noah and I don't stop looking at one another. Ethan's chuckle fades as he disappears into the house, and I wave an absent hand in his direction.

"If the tiles in the pool are okay, we should be able to have it full by the weekend, but it probably wouldn't be a bad idea to put in new grout to avoid any possible leaks. It looks like it's holding water, but it might be slowly draining through," Noah says, finally taking another drink of water and breaking our intense stare.

I look away, flustered by my reaction to him. "It was empty when we arrived. Seamus couldn't remember if his mom emptied it or if it just evaporated or leaked out over time," I explain, and he raises an eyebrow.

"Seamus?"

"Yeah, Great-aunt Jocelyn's son, so I guess my cousin. He and his husband Darcy are still in the UK, but give it time, I'm pretty sure both of them will be out to visit soon. They like to meddle in my life as much as possible, and they can't do it across the ocean, so it won't surprise me if they move out here." That thought makes me feel warm and cozy. I would love to have them close by.

"It must be hard having family so far away. Do you have any here in town?" I know he's curious, and my family name is recognizable, but this line of questioning instantly makes me wary, and I shut down.

"Yes, but I don't have anything to do with them." I turn on my heel and head back up to the house.

"Mimi! Hey, Mimi," he calls behind me, but I don't wait. His hand grasps my arm, stopping me. "Hey, I'm sorry. I didn't know it was a sensitive topic."

I snort and turn around to face him, raising my eyebrows. "Really, Noah? Because despite not having lived here for years, I remember what Storm View was like, and it was always rife with gossip. I'm sure you've heard the Kennedy family gossip at the country club, or did my parents manage to hush it up completely?"

He has the grace to look sheepish and releases my arm. "Look, I might have heard some rumors about the missing Kennedy daughter, but I wasn't sure if that was you or not."

"Well, I can tell you that whatever you heard is as far from the truth as you could possibly get. Now, if you'll excuse me, I have homework. You can let yourself out."

I leave him on the patio and make my way inside. The last thing I want to do right now is homework, but I also don't want to stand there and feel the weight of his pity. Not everyone has a wonderful family like Fred and Mae Wilson, and I hope he appreciates what he has.

His question left me feeling vulnerable and out of sorts, though, and I know I was probably a bit harsh, but it's a sensitive topic for me. Maybe one day, I'll be able to talk about it without it affecting me so dramatically, but that is not today. Seeing Kira earlier didn't help either. My emotions are all over the place, and poor Noah was an easy target. I'll apologize to him when I see him next.

I hear a car door slam out front and head to the room that overlooks the front yard. I peer out the gauzy window coverings and find Noah staring at the house with a deep frown on his face. I give him a tentative wave, and the frown eases slightly before he waves back, starts his truck, and drives away. Yeah, I really owe him an apology. Maybe Mae can tell me what his favorite baked good is, and I can do that as a way to apologize. I mean, it didn't feel like he was fishing for gossip, just curious, and I shouldn't have blown up at him like I did.

I drop the curtain, and instead of doing homework, I pack overnight bags for Jorja and me. One more night at Fred and Mae's isn't going to hurt, and it's nice to feel loved.

CHAPTER 10

Kashton

"Hello?" I call out as I push through the garage entrance and into the kitchen. I throw my keys and the contracts on the island. I was expecting to find Bentley in the kitchen, since it's almost dinnertime, but he's not here. Frowning, I make my way through our house, looking for my roommates. I have some amazing news, and I can't wait to share it with them. "Hello?" I call out again.

"I'm in here," Bentley replies from the living room.

I find my roommate stretched out on the sectional with *Inside Hockey* magazine in his hand.

He waves it around before dropping it on his

chest when I walk in. "Hey, did you know that Rigby Engman and River Cooper from the Ann Arbor Ice Caps are in a polyamorous relationship with a woman and another man?"

"Huh?" I ask in confusion, my own news forgotten for the moment.

He sits up. "The article says that the three men are in a relationship with this one woman named Nova. They are raising a child, and they say it's a relief for the two of them because it means someone is around when they have to be away for so many weeks of the year with team commitments."

I roll this information around in my mind. I think I remember some breaking news about this, but as long as no one is hurting anyone, I don't care what a player does in their private life. "Well, I mean, in theory it sounds like a solid idea, but I'm not sure if I could do it in practice. I guess it would depend on the woman."

Bentley's eyes are unfocused, but before I can ask him what he's thinking about, our other room-mate appears. Noah has a towel wrapped around his waist, and water droplets glisten on the rest of his exposed skin. He rubs a second towel through his hair.

"There you are. Did practice run late?" he asks, throwing himself down on the single chair.

"Have you been at work?" I ask, and he nods.

"Yeah, doing a job for Gramps. His neighbor lost a tree in the storm last night. Where were you? And what's for dinner?" He looks at Bentley, who is still lost in his own thoughts.

"Pizza," he mutters, and we gape at him.

"Dude! What's wrong with you? You've been weird since I walked in here," I remark.

Bentley is usually a bundle of energy. He has ADHD but has learned to manage it well, but normally he's a flurry of movement and activity. It's why he learned to cook in the first place. It kept his hands and his mind busy and out of trouble.

He flops back on the couch again, puts the magazine over his face, and mutters something.

"What? I didn't catch that," I ask, and he sighs and pulls the magazine off to look at us.

"Chef John had a go at my foie gras foam. He said it was lumpy. The fat fuck sits at the back of the kitchen and doesn't lift a finger while I do every-thing, and yet he takes all the credit for it. Let's see if he can keep his Michelin star without me."

"You quit?" Noah asks, dropping the spare towel in his lap and leaning forward.

"Yes, I'm done cooking fancy-ass food that won't fill you up. Mom always said that if I finished college, and I only have that last credit that I need, then she will lend me the money I need to open my own place."

Bentley has talked about wanting his own place for a long time now, and although he could probably teach the marketing class, I know he wants to prove to his mom that she taught him well.

"So you're finally going to do it. It's about time. You know I would lend you the money," I tell him. "Especially since the Titans just offered me another three-year contract." I drop my own good news into the conversation, unable to hold it back anymore.

"Dude, that's awesome! Congratulations. Is that where you were?"

Bentley and Noah jump to their feet, and we all bro hug, Noah clasping his towel as it starts to slip as we all sit back down.

"Yeah, upper management asked to speak to me after practice, and Louella Eastern was there. She's such a down-to-earth woman. You'd never know she's one of the richest people in the state. She was wearing jeans and boots and was gushing about how Liam and I are one of the best combinations she's had the pleasure of having in a first line."

My best friend Liam and I both went to college on hockey scholarships, and we both signed with the Storm View Titans in our fourth year. I've been playing with them for the last two, and my contract had been coming up for renegotiation. To say that I'm stoked with what they offered me would be an understatement. It's also a massive relief that I can stay in my hometown, close to my family and friends, especially my two roommates. We've been friends for years. The only reason Liam doesn't live with us as well is because he wifed up my sister when she became pregnant just after she graduated. I thought they were crazy, but I was slightly jaded back then. Now, I'm super envious of their relationship and want something like that for myself.

I'd gone crazy in my first couple years at college with all the puck bunnies that literally threw themselves into my lap, but that quickly got old. Now, I'm looking for the one, but I'm afraid I already had that and let her get away. They say lightning never strikes twice in the same place.

"Dude, that calls for a celebration. I'll get dressed and grab us some beers to have with our pizza." Noah jumps up and hurries out of the room.

It's not long after that when the doorbell rings and Bentley gets up to pay for the pizzas. I stay where I am, since I know both of them will return here. We usually sit at the table and eat as a family —Bentley insists—but he seems like he has something on his mind.

He returns with two boxes and some napkins

and plates. Noah is behind him, dressed in sweats and a T-shirt, with three bottles of beer in his hand. He passes them around as Bentley dishes up slices of pizza and hands them to us.

"So what are you going to do?" Noah asks Bentley around a mouthful of pizza. "You have your business plan already, so don't you think it's time you went ahead with it?"

Bentley chews and swallows before answering. "Yeah, I went to Mom and Dad's before I came home and spoke to them. Because I only have the one class to finish, Mom said she will transfer the start-up capital into an account for me. I'm going to use the final assignment to work out a marketing strategy. I have an appointment with a realtor to look at some locations tomorrow after class. I just hope my class-mate, whom I have to do the assignment with, is okay with that." A funny look crosses his face.

"What is it?" I press, and he shrugs.

"You know, she didn't know who I was. She didn't know who Mom was either."

Noah and I chuckle.

"Oh, so she didn't fall for the old Bentley Carlyle III schtick?" I ask, and Noah and I clink our bottles together, mocking him.

He scowls. "No, but it was kind of refreshing,

and then she was pissed when she did find out. She accused me of coasting on nepotism and said I expected an easy A because my mom is the lecturer."

This has Noah and me laughing even harder. "Holy shit, if only she knew your mom is going to be the hardest on you. I hope she's willing to bring her A game." I take a sip of my beer.

His frown turns quizzical. "Yeah, I really think she is. She's new. I've never seen her before. She's gorgeous, all long blonde hair and curves for days. You should have seen everyone staring at her when she wasn't looking. The girls looked mad, and the guys looked interested, and she just seemed oblivious. She's going to get eaten alive if she's not careful. Storm View U can be vicious."

Bentley seems to have taken a shine to the girl. Well, I hope she's nice, because we've had girls try to come between us before or use one of them as a stepping stone to get to me. All three of us have become incredibly jaded when it comes to women, and this is the first one he's shown actual interest in longer than it takes to get his cock sucked.

"Going to take her under your wing and look after her?" I ask, and he shrugs, trying to brush it off.

"Hmm, not sure she even likes me." He sounds sad about that but changes the subject, quickly turning to asking me how practice is and if we're ready for our first game this weekend.

"What about you? Do you have any more classes this week?" I ask Noah a short time later as I down the last of my beer. I'm starting to feel tired. practice was intense, and the high of renewing my contract is wearing off. I want to call my family and tell them the good news before I go to bed.

"One more on Friday. I only have three this semester. I am so ready to be done with college."

"Ugh, me too," Bentley grumbles, closing his eyes and leaning his head back on the sectional. "If I get asked if we're going to party hard this year one more time, I'm going to scream. I don't even know half the people who approach me to talk about you or ask if we're going to throw a party after the game."

"No parties this year. If we want to celebrate, we can go to Lou's Place, but I'm done having strangers tramp through my house, especially after finding that naked freshman on my bed at the end of last year. That was a fucking lawsuit waiting to happen, and I won't risk my career to keep other people happy." I lay down the law, and my boys don't even think to argue because they are just as over that shit as I am.

"Oh, hey, Bentley, I might have told our client

today that you'd grill for us if she threw a pool party once it's restored."

"You talked your grandparents' neighbor into having a pool party?" I ask him, feeling confused. "Why would you want to do that with old people?"

"Well, she's not old. She's gorgeous and friendly and smart, and I really like her." Noah sighs, and it's my and Bentley's turn to gape at him.

Noah has been off women since his ex-fiancée cheated on him with one of the football players. I couldn't stand the girl, she kept hitting on me when he wasn't around, but he wouldn't listen. It took him walking in on her in her dorm room to get a clue. She wasn't the smartest person. Ginny, Bentley's sister, is in her sorority, and she wasn't going to stand for that. She invited him over and, well, the rest is history, but it left him anti-women for a long time.

"Jesus, what's in the water? Maybe I shouldn't drink it. Both of you in the same week," I tease, but inside, I'm worried.

We've been the three musketeers for so long that I'm not sure I can take playing second fiddle to a woman in their lives. It was different with Liam. He and Kira were attached at the hip for as long as I can remember, and nothing changed. Sure, he didn't come out and party with us as much, but that was his choice, not because she demanded it. He wanted to stay home with her and my niece, Lola, and I respect that. He still comes out occasionally for a drink after the game, and we have them over here for dinner, or we go to their place at least once a week, but who knows if these girls they are interested in will be as relaxed as my sister.

"Don't be like that, man. We know you had your heart broken, but life's too short to be a lonely, jaded old man at twenty-four. Your time will come, and then we will be the ones teasing you."

I think back to the summer when my heart broke in two. The girl I was madly in love with disappeared, and all her parents could tell me was that she was cheating on me and had fallen in with a bad crowd and was doing drugs. Initially, I was so angry, I couldn't see straight, but when I thought about it, I realized there was no way they were telling the truth because she spent all her time with me. We would sneak around because her parents were assholes and it was exciting, but then she started avoiding me, giving me excuses as to why she couldn't meet up, and then a week later, she was gone.

I looked for her for a while, but it was like she disappeared off the face of the earth. I even approached her grandparents, and they were just as shocked and hurt as I was. They didn't believe it either and hired a PI to search for her, but he wasn't ever able to turn anything up. Eventually, we had to believe her parents. For a long time, every time I saw a blonde with long hair, I looked twice to see if she was my girl. Even now, I sometimes get caught looking twice at the crowd at our games, especially the ones interstate, in the hopes that maybe I'll see her amongst the teeming people. God, I miss her even now. If I ever see her again, I will shake her and demand answers, but my biggest fear is that she became just another Jane Doe and is buried in an unmarked grave with needle tracks littering her arms.

"You know, those Ann Arbor players might be onto something," Bentley muses, nodding at the hockey magazine on the table.

"Huh?" Noah wasn't here for that conversation, so Bentley explains what he's talking about, and Noah's eyebrows jump in surprise.

"So they are all in a relationship with the same woman?" he asks, and Bentley nods.

"Yeah, you know, it makes sense. Instead of dating women who always try to come between us, maybe we should find one who can love us all."

"I don't know, man. That sounds like a possible nuclear implosion for our friendship."

"These guys say communication is key, and it's

not like we're strangers. We've been friends for years. Instead of seeing each other as competition, we should work as a team to keep one woman very, very happy." He's grinning with enthusiasm by the end of his sentence, but Noah is frowning.

"But I really like this girl," he says, and Bentley's face falls, and he slumps back down.

"Yeah, and I really like the one in my class."

"Well, I guess it's a moot point for now," I say, getting up. A wave of irrational jealousy washes over me at the thought of my friends in relationships. "I need to call my parents."

Noah misses nothing, damn observant asshole. "Are you okay, man?" Noah asks, looking at me closely, and I force a smile.

"Yeah, I'm good. Pre-season is kicking my ass. I just need an early night. Thanks for dinner," I reply, gathering up the plates and sliding the leftover pizza into one box. Their "goodnights" echo behind me as I take it all into the kitchen. I put the trash in the bin and place the leftovers in the fridge before grabbing a glass of water and heading upstairs.

I showered after practice, so I only need to brush my teeth. I do that and strip, leaving on just my boxer briefs before climbing into bed with my phone. I select my parents' number, and it rings twice before my mom picks up.

"Hello?" The sound of her voice makes me smile.

"Hey, Ma," I say, and I can practically hear her smiling.

"Kash, baby. How are you? We were just talking about you. Dad was just saying how much he's looking forward to the opening game on Saturday. He even bought Lola and him new jerseys."

I can't help but smile at my mom's words. My family is so supportive of my career, and Mom and Dad were nothing but supportive when Kira got pregnant and decided to keep the baby. They adore Liam like he's their own and welcomed him into the family with open arms, unlike his own family which, apart from his grandpa, disowned him. People can be such assholes. Kira, Liam, and Lola lived with Mom and Dad for a few years while he went to college, but as soon as he signed with the Titans, he bought them a house. Kira is happy being a stay-at-home mom for now, but she has taken a few night classes. Now that Lola is at school, she's trying to figure out what she wants to do with her life.

I tell them my good news, and they both gush about it, Mom having put Dad on speaker phone. When I get off, I'm out of my funk. My family never fails to make me smile. I should call my sister and tell her, but I'm sure she and Liam are celebrating his own contract renewal, so I'll talk to her tomorrow.

I make myself comfortable, but as I drift off to sleep, the image of the one who got away slips into my mind once more, and I wonder if she's still alive and what she's doing with herself.

CHAPTER 11

Miriam

I consider avoiding Kira by just not being home when she comes over. We're supposed to stay at Fred and Mae's tonight anyway, but that's just cowardly, and the sooner I can get this talk over with, the better.

I make our excuses to Fred and Mae and prepare to take my daughter home. She's sticky and has red lips from eating her fair share of the picked fruit.

"I tried to stop her, explaining she might get a sore tummy if she eats too much, but she wasn't particularly interested in listening," Mae apologizes as she walks us to the door.

I look at my daughter with disappointment. "It makes me sad to hear that you weren't willing to listen to Mae. If you aren't going to listen, then I won't be as willing to allow you to do fun things like that," I tell her, and her bottom lip drops into a pout before she sticks her thumb into her mouth.

"I'm sorry, but they were just so yummy," she replies quietly, realizing she's in trouble.

"I'm sure they were, but when an adult makes a suggestion or tells you something, you really should listen to them, okay? Most of the time, they know what's best for you." I try to soften the blow, but she really does need to learn to listen to others. She's really headstrong and thinks she knows better than everyone else.

"Thank you for having her," I tell the older woman who smiles, her eyes crinkling in the corners.

"Any time, dear. She is a delight. And good luck with your friend. I can't deny the rumors flying around when you first left, but another scandal happened not long after, and your family drama was overtaken by something more interesting. Just tell her the truth. Anyone who knows your parents will believe they are capable of doing what they did, and Jorja is proof. She was your best friend. I'm sure she still loves you, but she's hurt from what happened, just like you were hurt by what your parents told you she did. What do you think the odds are that they lied to you just as they lied to everyone here?"

"Oh, I wouldn't put it past them at all. That's why I've been able to let go of my hurt over the years, but at the time, I was pregnant, alone, and incredibly sick. Back then, I hated everyone here. I hated that they could be sucked in so easily by my parents' lies and that they didn't try harder to find me, and then I was too worried about trying to keep Jorja that it all slipped to the wayside anyway. We have lots to talk about, but hopefully we can reestablish some kind of relationship, especially for Jorja's sake."

"You know, if Mary and Simon Young had known you were pregnant, they would have fought tooth and nail to get at you. Your friend Kira became pregnant just after graduation, and they were so supportive of her and Liam. I don't doubt they wouldn't have done the same for you as well," Mae says quietly, but Jorja's eyelids are drooping, and I don't think she's paying any attention anyway. I hand her my phone, and she takes a seat on the stoop, distracted by whatever game is on my phone.

"I loved Kira and Kash's parents. They were amazing. But my parents basically put me on house arrest the minute the maid showed my mom my pregnancy test. They took away my phone, my laptop, and every possible communication device. They locked me in my room while they made arrangements for me to go to London. Then they paid someone to escort me to the airport and supervise me until they could put me on the plane. They made sure I had no money and no way of communicating or asking anyone for help."

Mae's eyes narrow in anger, and her fists clench. "When you're ready, we need to tell your grandparents what they did. I will also ensure that their reputations are destroyed. They won't be able to show their faces at the country club again."

A rush of warmth washes over me. "I'm not sure my grandparents care. They had the means and opportunity to find me over the years, but they never did," I tell her, trying to hide my hurt.

Her anger disappears, replaced with soft sympathy. She reaches out and puts her hand on my arm, giving it a squeeze. "No, honey, they did. They hired a private detective to look for you, but they were going off the lies your parents told them. I don't think it occurred to them that they should look for you overseas. They have someone who travels to all the states and searches the homeless population and drug addicted, flashing your photo. The same person calls around to various state coroners' offices to make sure someone of your description has not wound up in the morgue. They have never given up hope."

Tears well in my eyes, and a lump settles in my throat at Mae's words. "Really?" I choke out. "Aunt Jocelyn encouraged me to reach out to them, but I was stubborn, especially in the beginning. Mom and Dad told me that my grandparents were so ashamed of me and wholeheartedly supported them in sending me away."

"Oh no, honey, and I wouldn't want to be your mom or dad once they find out." The anger is back now. "Would you like me to arrange for them to come over for some afternoon tea? That way Fred and I can be there as a buffer. You probably don't remember us, but we've been friends with them for years."

I bite my lip and think about the offer. What if they are ashamed when they find out about Jorja? They never gave me those kinds of vibes before. Grandma used to volunteer a lot, helping at women's shelters and always donating to causes that helped get single mothers back on their feet, but what if that is only her public face? My parents are very much like that—one face for the public and then one just for me.

"Um, can I think about it? I know I'm not going to be able to avoid them forever, and gossip is eventually going to catch up, and someone will tell them I'm back in town."

"Sure, just let me know what you decide. It's better to control that kind of news than to let them find out from some other source."

Jorja and I say our goodbyes and make our way back to our place. I'm able to keep Jorja awake long enough to feed her a grilled cheese and make her have a quick shower to wash off all the fruit juice and brush her teeth. I don't even make it through half a story before she's snoring those adorable little girl snores. I give her a kiss on the forehead and flick on the nightlight before turning off the main one, then I leave the door open in case she wakes up and head back downstairs.

I'm just checking the contents of the fridge when the doorbell rings. Fuck, I really should have grabbed something on the way home from school. There's a dribble of orange juice left in the bottle, a quarter of a bottle of wine, and a few random sodas. It's not particularly impressive, and from the looks of Kira, she seems to be living the fancy life.

Sighing, I close the fridge and make my way to the front door, dragging my feet. I'm not looking forward to this conversation at all, but it's one we definitely need to have, even if it's just to clear the air. I mean, I'd love to get back to where we used to be, but I'm just not sure that's possible with all the lies that have been told. Both of us have been hurt, and it wasn't through either of our actions, but it would be nice to have a friend again, someone my own age who actually knows what it's like raising a child. Who would have thought that both Kira and I would be young moms?

I pull open the door to find my former bestie, and boy, does she look different from this afternoon. Gone are the designer clothes and heels, and in their place are a pair of cutoff shorts, a T-shirt, and a pair of sparkling flip-flops. Her perfect makeup and hairdo have vanished, and she is makeup free with her long, black hair tied up in a messy bun. She's holding two bottles of wine in one hand, and a box of pizza in the other.

"Ah, hi. Thanks for coming," I say, and she rolls her eyes and pushes past me.

"Shit, Mimi, like you had a choice. Now, I bought a bottle for each of us. Liam dropped me off, and I will uber home later. We have six years to catch up on, and I want to hear everything."

I follow her in a daze as she pokes around until she finds a room that makes her happy. "This house is amazing. It has great bones, but wow does it need an update." She wrinkles her nose in much the same way I had when I had first seen it. "Don't worry, my mom still does interior design. She's in demand, but I'm sure she will make room for you." She drops the pizza on the coffee table before placing the wine bottles down more gently. Putting her hands on her hips, she looks around. "Well, where will I find glasses?"

It's my turn to roll my eyes. Kira was always the steamroller in our relationship, and I guess it's going to continue how it's always been.

"In the kitchen." I point in the direction and follow her as she heads that way.

She pushes through the door and gazes around the room, a look of horror crossing her face. "Who the fuck thought baby poo brown was a good color for all those cupboards?"

A snort of laughter escapes as I remember thinking something similar when I first saw the room. I can't control it, and I start to giggle, and it must be contagious because she joins me. Before I know it, we're both doubled over in laughter, but when she straightens up, I stop laughing instantly. Tears stream down her face, and she looks torn.

"Mimi, can you ever forgive me for believing your parents? For not looking harder for you when you disappeared without a trace? What kind of friend was I to believe them?" I start to say something, but she holds up her hand. "I should have guessed that the images they showed me were fabricated. I should have demanded in person proof and pushed them to give me the details of your whereabouts so I could have confronted you directly. I'm a horrible person."

I don't say anything, because if I do, I'll probably start crying too. I'm sure it's inevitable, but I'd like to delay it for as long as possible. I just grab two wine glasses out of the cupboard, two plates from another, and some paper towels from the roll on the counter before turning back to her.

"Come on, let's pour a drink and compare stories." I lead her back to the living room, and we're quiet while we both have a slice of pizza. I had a grilled cheese earlier with Jorja, but who can say no to a slice of steaming hot pepperoni? The wine she brought is sweet and exactly the same one we used to steal from my mom's wine fridge when they left us home alone. It brings back so many memories of us sharing a bottle and giggling over boys. It was always Liam for her, and I never admitted that I had a huge crush on her brother.

The four of us were in the same junior hockey league, and I'd been on track to play hockey at college. Storm View Frozen Fury is the women's college team, and it was my dream to play for them. I'd been in love with Kashton for years, but it wasn't until that last summer that we had gotten together. He had just graduated, and we were out celebrating their scholarship offers when things just happened. We kept it from Liam and Kira because we wanted to just see how things went. I was afraid if we didn't work out that it would affect my friendship with his sister, but it was like we'd been together forever. We just seemed to meld seamlessly into a couple. It wasn't just the physical attraction, which was off the charts, but we also had everything in common, and before I knew it, I was head over heels in love with him. We fucked like rabbits, unable to keep our hands off one another, but we'd been careful, always using condoms, and I was on birth control, because neither of us were willing to jeopardize our future goals.

When I asked my doctor in London how I had gotten pregnant, we worked out that it was a broken condom, which hadn't bothered us when it happened because I was on birth control, but a course of antibiotics had made my birth control ineffective, so it was a recipe for conception. I contemplated an abortion for a hot minute, but in the end, I chose to have my baby. I decided that fate had interfered. Both of us had been so careful, yet I still ended up pregnant, and this baby was going to be loved, even if it was only by one of its parents.

I thought about begging my parents to give me Kash's contact information, but they probably would have used the information against him and his family.. I'd even searched for him online, but when I pulled up his Facebook page, I discovered he was in high demand with women at his new college. There were photos of him with a different girl on his arm in every shot. It didn't take me long to figure out that I hadn't meant anything to him. I was just a warm hole to keep him occupied before he went off to college. I felt cheap and heartbroken, so I closed the laptop and never searched again.

"So I can't help but notice how much Jorja looks like my brother," Kira comments quietly, jolting me out of my memories. "I didn't even know you two were together until after you disappeared. I mean, I suspected, but I thought you would have told me." She sounds hurt, and I feel bad.

"We were going to tell you, but we kind of wanted to see if we worked first. I insisted because I didn't want to have to make you choose between me or your brother if we didn't work."

She scoffs and rolls her eyes. "Like I would have chosen. If you hadn't worked, it wouldn't have been from something you did. You don't think I knew you had a crush on him? Your eyes followed him whenever you thought he wasn't watching." I blush, and she chuckles. "But don't think it wasn't recipro-cated. He was infatuated with you, and I couldn't understand why he didn't make a move. Having my brother and my bestie together was like a dream come true."

I go on to tell her about that summer, including sneaking around and how I found myself pregnant, and that before I could even tell Kash, our house-keeper had found my pregnancy test when she cleaned my bathroom and told my parents.

"That bitch. I can't believe she did that!"

"Oh, I can. I'm pretty sure she was sleeping with one of them. I'm not even sure which one. It could have been both." I giggle as Kira's eyes become round with surprise before she wrinkles her nose.

"Dude, gross."

"Yeah, and when I got home that afternoon, they cornered me, demanding to know who the father was. I refused to tell them, because knowing my parents, they would have blackmailed him or your parents or something. I mean, he was off to college on that scholarship, and there was no way I was ruining that for him. They would have insisted we get married."

"What?" She looks confused. "Why?"

"They pretend to be Catholic, remember? The church is a great way for Father to find investors.

Shit, I think he manages most of their local church funds. Having a pregnant teenager out of wedlock would have had them shunned, not to mention if I had an abortion and that gossip had gotten out. No, they were firmly in panic mode and decided hiding me on the other side of the world was the best idea. Before I knew it, I was shipped off to Aunt Jocelyn."

She tears up when I tell her how my pregnancy was and moves over to put her arm around me. She then tells me about the vicious lies my parents told both Kira and Kash when they turned up looking for me. They lied, saying I had developed a drug addiction and that I shacked up with some dude from an MC gang and ran away with him. They told them they were looking for me, but the next week, when Kash and Kira confronted them, they had photos proving that I really was where they said.

"Kash lost his shit, and that was when I put two and two together, but when faced with proof, neither of us could deny it any longer, and we let you go."

We cry together, mourning the years we missed and that our girls could have grown up together.

I suddenly realize something. "Holy shit. Jorja is going to be thrilled when she realizes that she and Lola are actually related," I say, wiping tears from my face with one of the paper towels, passing her one as well. She uses it, but I can tell by the look on her face that the question I've been dreading is coming.

"When are you going to tell Kash?" she asks me, and I shrug. "Look, can I ask you to wait until after this weekend? His first game of the season is on Saturday, and I think if you told him, his focus would be off."

"The college has a game this week? I thought that wasn't for another week or two." My brow creases in a frown. I'm sure I saw a poster at school advertising the first game of the season, and it wasn't for another two weeks.

Kira chuckles. "It doesn't, but Kash doesn't play for the college team. You've been gone six years, Mimi. He plays for the Storm View Titans. Both he and Liam do."

My heart skips a beat, and a grin crosses my face as I realize that his dreams and hard work paid off. "He went pro? Gosh, you must be so proud of him."

"We really are. But how about I organize for him to come to dinner on Monday night? You and Jorja can be there, and Liam and I can be a buffer."

"What if he doesn't forgive me? I won't ever deny him access to Jorja, but it would be easier if her parents didn't hate each other."

She winces, and my stomach sinks. "You know

Kash. He has big emotions. He loves hard, and I'm certain he was in love with you, but he also has one of the biggest hearts I know. Once he has all the facts, I don't doubt that your parents will be in the firing line, and he will make them pay for taking away the chance to support you through your pregnancy and Jorja's first five years." Kira's voice is hard, and I know that she will support him all the way.

"And your parents?"

"Oh my god, Mimi, they are going to be over the moon. When Liam and I weren't as careful as we should have been, and I ended up pregnant with Lola, they supported us in every way. Liam's parents kicked him out, and he came to live with us. Only his grandpa supported us, but he lived with Liam's parents, and he couldn't change their response." She grins wickedly. "They sure regretted that when Liam was signed by the Titans. Then Grandpa passed last year and left his vast fortune to Liam. They are constantly trying to kiss our asses, but he won't have anything to do with them."

"I'm so happy for you, Kira. The two of you were couple's goals, even in high school."

Kira sighs dreamily. "Yeah, we're great. Come on, let's have another glass of wine. We have six years to catch up on."

CHAPTER 12

Miriam

I'm dragging ass the next morning and regretting the two whole bottles of wine we managed to polish off during the hours we talked for. Kira didn't leave until after one in the morning, and I almost crawled my way up the stairs to my bed. I haven't had that much to drink in years. I was still coherent enough, though, not to lean on the precarious balustrade and tumble to my premature death.

I stumble into the kitchen the next morning after my alarm makes me jump out of bed entirely too early. Groaning at the bright sun shining through the kitchen windows, I throw my arm up against the offending sight. I turn on my coffee machine and wait for it to warm up, but the voices in the backyard instantly make my hangover slip away, because one of those voices is high-pitched and belongs to none other than my wayward daughter. I can only pray that it's Mae or Fred as I hurry toward the backdoor, but Ethan did say he would be sending someone over to start draining the pool this morning.

I step outside, the bright sunlight burning my fragile retinas, and I heave a sigh of relief when I find my daughter turning cartwheels on the freshly mowed grass, chatting happily with Noah, but then the relief turns to dread as I realize that although I don't have to worry about him harming her, he now knows my secret.

He's smiling gently and answering her barrage of questions as he watches her finish her cartwheels and wobble on the spot. He leaps forward to steady her, and she smiles up at him.

"Wow, thanks, Noah, I was so dizzy. See how good I am? Lola and I have been practicing. Lola is my bestest friend in the world." She continues chattering and starts to prance, pointing her toes and throwing her arms around. "We're going to play hockey together. Lola says she loves skating too, just like me, but none of that girlie crap where they wear pretty dresses and do twirls, no, we're going to kick ass and score goals."

"Jorja Kennedy, where on earth did you hear that kind of language?" I demand, putting my hands on my hips.

She stops prancing and grimaces as she looks up at me. "Well, that's what Lola said her daddy said, and that she wasn't to tell her mama, but because we're best friends, she shared it with me. Besides, Uncle Darcy said I kicked ass all the time."

I shake my head, trying to control the laughter that wants to bubble up, and I can see Noah is struggling too. Trust Liam to teach Lola that kind of thing. "Well, how about you get your cute butt inside, have some breakfast, and get ready for school, and maybe we keep the words crap and ass from your vocabulary for now? Those are adult words, and you know it."

She hangs her head slightly at the scolding, but recovers quickly. "Okay, but Noah looks like he could use a coffee. Don't you think, Mama?" she says, grabbing her new friend by the hand and dragging him toward the patio. To his credit, he lets her, dropping the hose he held.

"Is that okay?" he asks as hurricane Jorja drags him up the steps and drops his hand, leaving the two of us alone as she races inside with a cheeky grin on her face.

"Yeah, sure, come on in. It's not easy to cope with the little miss first thing in the morning without some caffeine. I have no idea where she gets it from, but the moment those eyes open, she's on the go and doesn't stop until they close at night."

He smiles, and I try to judge how he's reacting to the news that I have a daughter, but he seems to be taking it in stride, so I turn and lead him inside the house. The coffee machine has thankfully finished its warm-up cycle and is ready to dispense blessed caffeine relief. Noah takes a seat at the island next to Jorja, who already has a box of cereal and milk out and is trying to pour it on her own. The milk is a little too heavy for her to manage without spilling, but before I can jump to help her, Noah reaches over and assists her. Instead of taking over, he steadies it, and they pour it together. She grins at him, her gap-toothed smile wide with the achievement.

"Thanks, Noah," she says as she takes the first mouthful. "Mama, did you know that Noah is Fred and Mae's grandson?" she asks with a mouthful of cereal. I raise one eyebrow, and she winces. "Sorry."

"I know I taught you better than to talk with your mouth full. I'll let it slide because I know you're excited to meet Noah, but don't do it again," I caution her, and she jams her mouth shut and chews the rest of her food carefully, nodding her head. "I did know that. He and his brother Ethan were here yesterday, patching the roof in my bedroom."

"The tree fell through it. It was really scary, but I didn't cry," she tells him now that her mouth is cereal free.

He nods solemnly. "You were very brave. That must have been very scary."

"It was, but we got to sleep at Fred and Mae's. I love Fred and Mae. I wish I had grandparents like them. I miss Aunt Jocelyn and Uncle Seamus and Uncle Darcy." The last few words are said quieter, and I go around and give my girl a hug.

"Oh, baby, I know you do. I miss them all too. I'm sure Aunt Jocelyn is watching us from heaven, and she wouldn't want you to be sad, and Seamus and Darcy will come visit soon, I'm certain."

She hugs me back before returning to her food, her sadness brief and fleeting as she takes another mouthful of cereal, allowing me to ask Noah how he takes his coffee.

"Creamer and sugar please. The sweeter the better, just like me." He winks at Jorja, and she giggles as I roll my eyes.

"Getting used to American coffee again has been

a challenge," I tell him as I grab both things from a nearby cupboard and slide them over to him. "They drink it very differently in the UK, and I adjusted to that, although we mostly drank tea. Today is definitely a two-cup morning."

He grins. "I wasn't going to mention that you looked a little rough this morning. I didn't think it was a polite start to a conversation, but now that you mention it..." He trails off, and I pretend glare at him.

"It's not nice to point out a lady's hangover, but yes, you are correct. I caught up with an old friend from my past last night. Lots of wine was had, along with tears and laughter. It was great."

"Oh, a male friend?" he asks casually as he finishes doctoring his coffee and taking a sip.

"Nope. Mama doesn't have a boyfriend. It was Lola's mama. She and my mama were friends before I was born," Jorja shares loudly, and I roll my eyes. My daughter is an oversharer, but before I can say anything, she hurries on. "What about you, Noah? Do you have a girlfriend? Mae was saying she wished her grandsons would find nice girls and settle down."

Holy fuck, my daughter is nosy. "Jorja," I scold as I turn around to finish my coffee, but I can't say I'm not interested in the answer, so I'm not too harsh with her.

"No, I don't have a girlfriend, Jorja, but I was kind of hoping that maybe I could take your mom out on a date. What do you think about that?"

I whirl around and stare at him, my mouth wide in shock, but Jorja looks pleased as punch. I can't believe the balls on this guy.

"Oh yes, my mama would love to go on a date with you!" she shouts, clapping her hands.

He's grinning, and she's cheering, and I narrow my eyes and mock glare at him.

"Noah Wilson, that was very sneaky. I thought you were a good boy, but now I see I will have to keep my eye on you."

The sparkling joy in his eyes turns heated, and I feel a shiver of desire run down my spine. "I wouldn't want it any other way," he says as I hear a knock on the front door. His grin drops, and he frowns.

"Expecting someone?" he asks, and I'm just as confused as I shake my head.

"No, I don't think so, but it might be Fred or Mae."

He gets up and goes to the front door to let whoever it is in, and I sit on one of the spare chairs, but it's not Fred and Mae. I hear another high-pitched child's voice, and I remember something from last night when Kira offered to take Jorja to school.

"Who is that, Mama?" Jorja asks and tries to climb down, but I hold up a hand, stopping her.

"Hurry up and finish your breakfast so you can get dressed. Lola and her mama are taking you to school today," I tell her, and she cheers and starts shoveling her cereal into her mouth, swallowing without even chewing. "Slow down, you'll make yourself sick, and then you won't be going anywhere."

She slows to a much more reasonable pace as the other three return to the kitchen.

Kira looks around. "Nope, not any better in the daylight." She goes over and grabs a mug, sticking it under the machine before turning around and putting her hands on her hips. She's dressed like a private school mom again, but the light in her eyes is the same Kira I always knew, and I brace myself for the words about to come out of her mouth. "So imagine my surprise when this hunk of delicious-ness opened the door to my best friend's house so early in the morning." She points at Noah, who's returned to his seat.

"How come Uncle Noah is at your house?" Lola

asks, climbing up and looking at Jorja's cereal with interest.

"He's your uncle?" Jorja asks, looking at him with renewed interest. "So if my mama marries him, you and I will be cousins?"

"Oh my god." I slap a hand over my mouth and just stare at the floor with embarrassment. Kira and Noah chuckle, but Lola squeals.

"Yes, oh yes! Uncle Noah, you have to marry Jorja's mom so we can be cousins for real." They hold each other's hand and flutter their eyelashes at him, and I watch him melt. Kira and I exchange a loaded glance. Little do they know, they don't need Noah.

"Well, how about we start with a date?" he tells them, and they cheer.

"Alright, run upstairs, brush your teeth, and get dressed. Remember what I said about the rails on the steps. Make sure you run your hand along the wall until we can get it fixed. Show Lola what to do." I take the empty bowl away and hurry my child along.

"Come on, Lola, come and see my room, and I'll show you where the big branch came through our roof." Jorja and Lola join hands and hurry out of the kitchen. Kira bites her lip, and I can tell she considers following them.

"Don't worry, Jorja won't let her go near the balustrade. They will be fine," I promise her, and she takes Lola's abandoned seat.

"So how do you two know each other?" Noah asks before I can ask the same thing.

"Mimi was my best friend growing up."

"How is it that we never met if that's the case?" Noah inquires, scratching his head and looking confused.

"We went to Storm View Public, remember? And you guys never invited me anywhere when you did things together. I was the annoying little sister, and then I met Liam, and we were friends with different crowds," she grumbles, and he has the grace to look embarrassed before his eyes clear.

"Yeah, I remember. Kash would split his time between hanging with us and hanging with Liam and another group. That all changed once we all hit college."

"And by then, Mimi was gone," Kira points out, and I flush with embarrassment at the reminder of all the rumors, but Noah's eyes shine brightly with knowledge.

"The rumors said you hooked up with some motorcycle gang and ran away with them. I take it that wasn't true?" he asks, and I sigh.

"It's so far from the truth, it's ridiculous."

His gaze turns shrewd, and his eyes lift like he's trying to see through the ceiling to the rooms upstairs. "I can't help but notice how much Jorja and Lola look alike. It's kind of uncanny." My heart starts to race as Noah puts all the pieces of the puzzle together. "The summer before college, which I guess would be six years ago, Kash was absent a lot. Turns out he'd fallen in love and was spending all his time with a secret girl. He claimed it was because he wanted to be sure before he introduced her to everyone. We didn't see him often, but when we did, he was the happiest I've ever seen him until he wasn't. One day, it all just stopped, and he became evil Kash, or that's what we called him. His drinking and partying were out of control. We knew something must have happened, but he wouldn't ever talk about it. That was you? You were his secret girl?"

There's a lump in my throat now, and I can't answer aloud, so I nod.

"Before you get upset with her, everything we know was wrong," Kira jumps in, defending me like the friend she has always been, but Noah doesn't look mad, he just looks sad—sad for me, sad for Kash, and especially for Jorja.

"Jorja is his?" he asks, and I can hear the disappointment in his voice.

I nod again. "Yes, and he doesn't know because my parents made sure that no one did," I explain, and he nods slowly as all the information rolls around in his brain.

"Are you going to tell him?"

"Yes, Monday after the game. Kira said she'd have us over for dinner, but she didn't want me telling him before the opening game of the season."

He nods slowly. "Yeah, that's probably a good idea. His head wouldn't be in the game."

We're silent for a moment before Kira stands up. "I'm just going to see what's taking the girls so long."

I nod at her, grateful she's giving us a moment. I told her about my attraction to him last night when the wine hit me, and surprisingly, she told me to go for it. "*Life is too short not to grab hold of everything you want, Mimi.*"

He's quiet, and I don't interrupt his thought process. He deserves to make his own decision.

"I don't know what's going to happen between you and Kash, but I still want that date," he announces suddenly, and a small amount of hope kindles within me.

"Really? Even not knowing the whole story?" I ask, worrying my lip with my teeth.

"Well, it will be a hell of a first date, won't it?" He shrugs, and a smile spreads across his lips. "You deserve to tell your side of the story, but I'm not going to judge you, Miriam. We have all had to make difficult decisions."

I shake my head. "I can assure you, all of the decision-making was taken out of my hands, but it is what it is, and I can't change the past."

"So let's just try to make the most of the future. Is it okay if I pick you up at six on Saturday? I thought we could have dinner and then watch the opening game."

I freeze at the thought of the game. I love hockey with a passion, but I worry that I might see Kash before I'm ready. He must see my reaction, because he starts shaking his head.

"Don't worry, Kash won't know you're there, but it's a tradition for us to go to the first game of the season and support him."

Kira returns with two small girls in tow. "We can have Jorja sleep over if she wants, and we'll go to the game too. We all sit together, even Mom and Dad." The girls jump up and down and shout their joy at having a sleepover.

"But what about—" I break off and nod in my wayward daughter's direction. She and Lola are chatting and not even paying attention.

"If they don't see you, they won't put two and two together. They'll just see a friend of Lola's from school. You'll have to sit somewhere else for this game," she tells Noah, who quickly agrees.

"That's fine. Kash probably won't even notice."

"And if Mom and Dad ask where you are, I'll just tell them you're on a date. Are your parents going?" she asks him, and he nods.

"Of course. We all have season tickets. Gramps and Grammy too, as well as the Carlyles."

"You know Bentley?" I ask, unable to hide the surprise in my voice, and Noah's eyebrows jump in surprise.

"You know Bentley?" he counters.

"Yeah, he's in my marketing class. We're going to do a project together."

Noah groans and thumps his head down on the table. "Of course you are. I should have put two and two together. Blonde and curves for days with an accent."

"Is there a problem?"

Kira has an amused look on her face, and she waves a finger at Noah. "Noah and Bentley are my brother's roommates. This just got very interesting.

This is going to be so much fun." She rubs her hands together and shoos the girls out of the house with a breezy wave. Jorja gives me a kiss and follows along, leaving Noah and me alone.

I can't look at him, so I get up and make myself a second cup of coffee, but I hear his chair scrape on the floor, and all of a sudden, his arms cage me in place, my front to the coffee machine and his breath on my ear.

"Don't think that just because you have history with one of my roommates and the other is intrigued that I'm going to bow out so easily. I like you, and I like a challenge, and who knows, the possibilities are endless." His words are quiet, and my nipples pebble as his hard body presses against mine.

"Me being a single mother doesn't bother you?" I ask quietly, and he scoffs, spinning me around to face him. When I look up, the desire I feel is echoed in his gaze.

"Not even a little bit. I love kids and hope to have a dozen of my own one day." My eyebrows jump, and he shrugs. "Okay, maybe not a dozen, but it doesn't scare me at all. She's adorable, and I look forward to getting to know both of you."

"Okay, then six on Saturday sounds good."

He grins and leans in, brushing a brief kiss

across my lips. "Good, it's a date. Now, I have a pool to clean."

Before I can do anything but touch the place he kissed with my fingers, he disappears out the back door, leaving me breathless and giddy and hoping that Saturday comes quickly.

CHAPTER 13

Miriam

I have my marketing class again today. I have it twice a week, and all my others are only once. I'm dreading it because I really don't know what to say to Bentley, especially since I now know he's roommates with both Kash and Noah. I wonder if Noah has talked to him about me. Also, we didn't end our last interaction on the best of terms, but I don't have time for playboy assholes who coast by on their family name. Was I even right in accusing him of that?

I, of all people, should know better than to judge someone by their name. Shit, my parents are the perfect example of what you see is not necessarily the truth. On the outside, they seem like they would be good and kind, donating to worthwhile charities and attending church regularly, but that couldn't be any further from the truth. Neither of them has been faithful to each other for years, probably since I was born. I once caught my mom fucking the pool boy, which is such a fucking cliché. I'm pretty sure Dad has been having an affair with his PA, or at least he was before I was kicked out. They both drink and indulge in illegal drugs, and if my dad's investments are clean, I would be surprised. I think he launders money for a local drug dealer too. When they used to fight, they weren't particularly discreet, and I heard all sorts of things they probably didn't want me to know.

As I get dressed, I decide I'm going to go in with an open mind and give him a chance. He was so animated when he finally cut the bullshit snobbery and told me about the things that appealed to him. I could see the side of himself he hides behind his carefully crafted rich boy façade.

Noah is outside, and he has a pump running, draining the sludge out of the pool. He ran the wastewater hose through the fence and into his grandparents' orchard, telling me the trees will appreciate the extra water. I just cross my fingers, hoping there are no chemicals or anything that might kill any of their beautiful fruit trees. He assured me, however, that it's been so long since there was anything in there that it should be fine, but I did make him go over and ask Fred just to be sure.

"Noah, I'm off. I have a class, and then I have an appointment with a realtor to look at a few buildings."

He comes over to the patio and looks up at me, shading his face with his hand. "Realtor?"

I roll my eyes and nod. "Yes, apparently Seamus made an appointment for me without asking. He wants me to check out some storefront locations."

"Storefront locations?"

I can't help but giggle at his confused expression. Of course he has no idea what I'm talking about. "Seamus and Darcy own a chain of florist shops in London. I worked for them part time while I was there. I loved it, and I was good at it, so they offered to support me in opening my own here. It's why I'm taking all the business classes. I'm good with the creative side, but I want the business knowledge too, so I won't let them down."

His confusion clears, and he nods. "That makes sense. It's why Bentley is doing them too, so he can open his own restaurant."

Now it's my turn to be confused, and I wrinkle my nose. "Bentley cooks?"

"Oh yeah, he is so freaking good."

"Huh..." He just gave me another side of the playboy that I never would have even guessed existed. "Alright, if I don't see you before, I'll see you Saturday, right?" I ask, and he grins and nods.

"You bet, but I'm sure we'll talk before then."

I wave goodbye and hurry out to my car, driving across town to the college campus. It was nice not having to worry about Jorja this morning but kind of weird too.

When I make it to class, Bentley is already sitting in the seat next to the one I had last time. His hood is up, but he hasn't managed to slip in incognito this time. There's a girl standing next to him, and she is very obviously flirting up a storm. She flips her hair and giggles as she runs a hand down the front of his hoodie. I try to get by her, but she's blocking my way.

"Come on, Bentley, your mom's the lecturer! I'm sure if you ask, she'll let you change partners. Seriously, a freshman is just going to drag you down."

Well, okay then. Thanks, bitch. If that's what he wants, though, I won't stop him. I clear my throat, and Bentley startles—he hadn't noticed me—but the girl doesn't flinch. Oh yeah, she already knew I was here.

"You wouldn't mind if Bentley changed partners, would you? I mean, you're only a freshman, so you can't give him what he needs." She looks me up and down, and I can tell she's not impressed with what she sees.

Today, I'm wearing a cute skater skirt and a tank top with a pair of sparkly flip-flops. If I dressed knowing that I'd be seeing him, well, I'll never admit it. I can tell by the way Bentley's eyes heat when he looks at me that I look good, but this girl is wearing designer jeans that look like they were airbrushed on and a top that is cut so low it's almost indecent. She looks like she should be clubbing, not going to a college marketing class. Her hair is perfectly straightened, and her makeup is on point. She is completely put together, and not a hot mess single mother.

"Bentley is free to do what he wants," I say, shrugging. "But that's my seat there, and I'd really like to sit in it." I point to the one next to him. "So if you could move, that would be great."

She glares at me, but before she can say anything, Sarah's voice sounds out through the lecture room.

"If everyone could take a seat, I'd like to get started."

The girl doesn't move. Instead, she crosses her arms and stares at me. Rolling my eyes, I shrug and settle into a seat across the aisle. She grins and takes a seat next to Bentley. When I look up, Sarah is watching us with interest.

She shuffles some papers around. "Sitting with the person you're doing your final assignment with would be beneficial, because you can use what we discuss when you work on your project."

The girl who basically took my spot waves her hand in the air. "Bentley and I would like to work together if that's okay. I'm sure we have much more in common and will have similar ideas, especially since my daddy works with you. I'm sure we think the same."

"Your daddy works *for* me, Rebecca," Sarah says dryly, "and I already said there will be no partner changes. Why don't you move back to the spot you were in on Monday and be quick about it so I can start the class?"

Rebecca's mouth drops open in surprise, and her cheeks pinken slightly. I'm not sure if it's from embarrassment or anger. "But," she starts, and Sarah lifts her head and glares at her, so she quickly shuts her mouth, gathers her notebook and back-pack, and moves down a few aisles, taking a seat next to another pretty girl who is basically a carbon copy.

"Alright, now that that's settled, let's talk about

demographics. When you're trying to work out a marketing campaign, knowing your demographic is imperative. Can anyone tell me why?" Hands rise into the air, and I feel a piece of paper hit me on the shoulder. I turn to find Bentley looking at me, his hood pushed back now, letting me see his green eyes sparkling with mischief.

"What?" I mouth, and he nods at the chair next to him.

I glare and shake my head, trying to pay attention to the person answering the question, but no sooner than I face the front, another piece of paper hits my shoulder. Damn it. The annoying asshole isn't going to let it go.

I gather my crap and move into the seat next to him. He wears a satisfied smirk, but he doesn't say anything, allowing me to listen to the lecture. We spend the next hour talking about how important it is to know your target audience, both of us taking notes along the way.

After a PowerPoint presentation, Sarah turns the projector off and turns to face us. "Okay, so I'm going to give you the remainder of the class to talk to your project partner. You need to come to a consensus on the business you will be presenting and start looking at what your target demographic is, because until that is established, you won't be able to come up with an effective marketing strategy. Also, make sure you are working on this out of class, so exchange numbers, emails, whatever, but I don't want to get to the end of the semester and hear any excuses as to why you couldn't present your marketing strategy, and that's what you will be doing. You will present a marketing campaign to a prospective client—me. It will be in class, and let me tell you, if I am not excited by what you present, you will find yourself with a passing grade only. I will want to see that you have taken everything we have discussed here in class into account, so if you can't make it, make sure your partner is here or you are getting the lecture notes from the class dashboard. Don't assume you can half-ass this assignment. In week four, we will be watching presentations from my own staff to prospective clients. Pay special attention to them, because every single one of them has been successful in landing the client. Alright, get to it."

The lecture hall descends into noisy chaos as everyone starts to talk with their partner about their project.

"Hi, look, I think maybe we might have gotten off on the wrong foot on Monday," Bentley says, looking at me earnestly and passing over a small bag of candy. When I look down, I find the Gnomies he was telling me all about last class, and I feel my heart flutter at the notion that he was thoughtful enough to remember to bring me some. "My mom is not going to let me get away with a subpar presentation. In fact, she will be harder on you and me than anyone in class."

I sigh and angle my body to face him. "I'm sorry for my reaction. It was uncalled for, and I shouldn't have jumped to conclusions. I know what it's like to be judged, and that wasn't fair of me," I say, offering up my own apology. "Thank you for these. I can't wait to see if they are as awesome as you said." There's a moment of awkward silence before a smile creeps across his face.

"No, you were mostly right. I can be a spoiled little rich boy. It's what people expect to see, and I'm pretty good at giving people what they want."

"But that's not all there is?" I probe, and he shrugs playfully.

"Well, you're going to have to find that out yourself."

I roll my eyes, but I can't stop the small smile from forming on my lips. "Shall we talk about this project? I have an idea for a business."

"Oh? I do too," he says, and I remember what Noah said. I chew on my lip.

"How is this going to work if we both want to do different things?"

He shrugs. "I'm sure most groups will have the same issue. I think Mom made it this way to see if we can cooperate. How about you tell me your idea, and then I'll tell you mine. I mean, we can even draw up two campaigns and then present the one that is the most solid."

Bentley's proposal is solid and surprisingly reasonable. I thought he'd be stubborn and insist on doing his idea, but he seems open to hearing what I have to say.

"Yeah, okay, that sounds good. You tell me about yours first," I insist, hesitant to tell him about mine. What if he hates it? What if he thinks it's stupid?

He looks surprised but slowly nods his head. "Oh, I thought you could go first, but yeah, okay. Um, so up until recently, I was working as a chef in a restaurant in town. I've parted ways with that establishment, but the goal was always to eventually open my own."

"You're a chef?" I'm unable to hide my surprise.

He chuckles, not looking the least bit upset. "Yeah, I spent a year at the Cordon Bleu

in France. Our chef growing up was always putting me to work to keep me out of trouble. I have ADHD, so keeping my mind and hands busy was always a smart idea, otherwise I just got into shit. Anyway, I fell in love with it. I love being able to feed my family and know they are getting healthy but tasty meals."

Wow, I never would have guessed it just from looking at this man, but they say not to judge a book by its cover.

"Anyway, as much as there is a place for fancy fine dining, I think there is a need for family friendly restaurants with good food at a reasonable price. Most families have two working parents these days, and who wants to cook a substantial and healthy meal for their family when they spent all day working? I know neither of my parents did, but we were in the position where they didn't have to. People are grabbing take-away on their way home, and most probably don't even sit together to eat it. Everyone is on their devices, and people don't talk and interact anymore. You see it even at fancy restaurants. I want to create a place where you get good, home-cooked meals, no artsy-fartsy crap, and have fun as a family while doing it. My idea is to have each table be board game themed with a box to lock all phones and devices inside for the duration of the meal. You only get them back once you pay. I also want to have an old-fashioned arcade with whack-a-mole, basketball hoops, and shooting games —all those fun things you can do as a family when you go to the fair. My idea is you pay to use them, but the tickets you win can go toward paying for your meals or drinks. There will be fun cocktails and mocktails that smoke or light up, and a menu with good, wholesome family food, like mac and cheese, brisket and slaw, and surf and turf. Homespun cooking in a fun environment. Basically, it will be a place where all your worries can disappear for even a short period of time, and when you leave, your sides will hurt from laughing and having a good time and your belly will be full—" He breaks off suddenly, and I see him blush. "Sorry, I'm kind of passionate about it."

"Don't be embarrassed. I think it's amazing. I'd love to go to a restaurant like that. I know what it's like to be passionate about something that someone else might find boring—not that your idea is boring, it's awesome! I would so eat there."

"Well, tell me about your passion. I want to hear what excites you." He winks, and I roll my eyes.

"My idea isn't nearly as fun as yours, but I want to open a flower shop. I used to work in one part time back in the UK, and my cousin is going to back me to open one here in Storm View. I want it to be the kind of place where you can get your high-end bridal and special occasion flowers, but also the kind of place where you could drop in and grab a plant or a bouquet of flowers to give to your mom when you go to visit."

"Sounds nice," he says diplomatically, and I snort.

"I know it's not very innovative, but the other service I want to add is what makes it kind of unique. Unfortunately, flowers don't last. That special bridal bouquet, your prom corsage, or even the flowers from your loved one's funeral end up withering and dying. I want to offer a service where you bring them in, and we preserve them in resin. Whether that be a paperweight, or something else like a cutting board or coasters, they will be as perfectly preserved as the day you first got them, while also serving as a keepsake to remind you of a special or momentous occasion. Darcy and I were trying out a few different options before I left England." I pull out my phone and pull up the video of the wood and resin platter we made, imbedding some irises in the resin. It turned out beautifully, and I actually have it in a box, waiting to be unpacked at home.

He takes the phone and watches the video I put together of us making it. "Wow, that turned out really nice. My mom loves irises. She would love something like that. What a clever idea. I'm pretty sure there is no one doing anything like that in Storm View."

"There isn't. I did a bit of research online. None of the florists in this area offer it. Most of the florists in Storm View only do high-end bridal and special event flowers. There aren't many that cater to the general population. I mean, sure, there are internet places where you can order a bouquet to be sent to someone, but people often like to see the flowers they are sending. They want to know what they choose actually looks like, not just hope they are similar to the photo on a website. And instead of the usual chocolates and teddies that most of the florists encourage you to add to bouquets, I want to source a local supplier of body products, soaps, and candles—things that people can actually use instead of items that are just going to end up in landfills. Instead of adding a teddy bear to a bouquet for a new mother, how about adding stretch mark or nipple rash cream? For a graduation bouquet, how about a relaxing bath bomb or bubble bath? It shows you're making more of an effort while thinking about the person."

"Huh, I never thought of it that way, but it makes sense. I can tell you've put a lot of thought into this."

"Yeah, I guess I'm kind of passionate about it. I

actually miss getting my hands dirty so to speak. I miss the smell of the flowers and the hustle and bustle of the flower markets. We'd go at least once a week as a family. Darcy and Seamus would haggle with the vendors, and the rest of us would just enjoy being surrounded by the beauty of it all. I miss the chill of the cold storage and the humidity of the hothouse for the orchids and other tropical plants we kept stocked."

"Wow, so we have two amazing choices. I say we build marketing campaigns for both and then decide which is the strongest to present during class. We will both benefit in the long run, even if it will be extra work and mean we'll have to spend a lot of time together." He says this with a straight face, but his eyes are sparkling. There's the cheeky playboy.

I guess it will be no hardship spending extra time with him, especially if he's going to work hard, which I have a feeling he will. He's just as passionate and enthusiastic about his business venture as I am. I have an idea.

"Hey, I have an appointment with a realtor this afternoon. They are going to show me some shopfronts. Do you want to tag along? You might find something that is suitable for you too," I offer, feeling guilty that I misjudged him.

"I don't have any plans after class, that sounds fun. I'm sure what I need and what you need are vastly different, but it still doesn't hurt to see what's around. Oh, and the other thing we should do is scope out our competition and check out their marketing strategies, see what's working and what isn't," his eyes twinkle with what I'm learning is mischief

"Oh yes, that's a good point. Here, let's swap numbers so we can text each other if we have ideas. Shall we get together later this week to start hashing things out?" I think about what I have for the rest of the week. "I have a class Friday morning, but that's it."

"What about Friday night? We can scope out one of the competitors and turn it into a working dinner." As much as I would like to do that, I'm going out with Noah on Saturday night, so I don't feel like I could leave Jorja on Friday night as well.

"Ugh, sorry, I can't do Friday night. What about for lunch?"

"Hot date?" he asks, his eyebrow rising.

"Yeah, something like that." I'm not ready to explain myself to him, nor should I have to.

"Lunch is good. I'll make us a reservation at one of the places I think will be my biggest competition. It won't hurt to start there."

"Sounds great," I tell him as the bell rings.

"Alright, I hope you made some headway in your assignment. Next week, we'll taking a deeper look at what I will require from you for your assignment.. Have a great weekend," Sarah calls as everyone gathers their stuff.

"Want to grab a coffee and talk some more?" Bentley asks, and I look at my watch.

"Yeah, that sounds good. I have an hour before my appointment."

"Bentley?" We look up and see his mother waving at him, and he groans under his breath.

"Raincheck on coffee and the realtor?"

"Absolutely. Text me the details for lunch on Friday. I'll meet you there."

He nods and moves in the direction of his mother, and I leave. I have time to grab some groceries before Jorja finishes for the day. Today, I'm going to make a bigger effort to cook a meal, even if it's nothing fancy. We have to stop eating takeaway.

CHAPTER 14

Bentley

My mom watches Miriam over my shoulder as I approach her, but she quickly smiles at me. "Hey, how are you? If you really don't want to work with your partner and want to swap to Rebecca, I could probably facilitate it," she offers with a grimace. "But if she's anything like her father, she's lazy and coasts off other people's work. I wanted to fire him years ago, but you know what your father is like. He's such a damn softie, and they went to college together. I think the man's a moron myself but—" She breaks off and raises a perfectly plucked eyebrow.

"God, no!" I shout, shuddering before looking around, hoping no one heard that. Thankfully the class has emptied out, and Mom and I are the only ones left. "I made the mistake of making out with her at a party last year when I was drunk, and now she thinks she and I will be the next power couple like you and Dad. Why do you think I was hiding in the back on the first day of class? I slunk in behind some tall dude, and thankfully she was distracted. No, I don't want to work with Rebecca. She's clingy and needy, and she used to come around the house all the time. It took Ginny telling her to fuck off to get her to stay away."

My mom giggles. "Your sister is so protective of her boys. Could you imagine if Kira had been in college too? None of you would have seen any action with the way they would have gate kept you."

I shrug. "That might not have been a bad thing. Ginny has always been great at getting rid of hangers-on. Noah and Kash think she's amazing."

"Hmm, I wonder what she'll think of the Kennedy girl." And now we finally get to the subject I know she's been dying to explore. "You do know the rumors about her, don't you? Her grandparents are good friends with Nana, Pop, Fred, and Mae. When your dad was young, he, Eric Kennedy, and Mason Wilson were friends, but during college, he fell in with a crowd that they didn't like and they kind of drifted apart. Thank goodness, though, because from the rumors I hear, Eric and his wife are horrible people. I can't understand why, because Calvin and Violet are wonderful, kind, caring, and loving. They were devastated when Miriam became addicted to drugs and ran off with a biker gang. It was like she disappeared off the face of the earth. They had a private detective looking for her for years. He still does a round of the morgues in major cities once a year to make sure she didn't become a Jane Doe." A shrewd look fills her eyes as she stares in the direction Miriam went. "I have to admit, she looks really good for a drug addicted whore."

My mind is fucking blown. "Are you serious?" My eyes follow the same path as my mom's as we look in the direction she disappeared.

"Oh yes, Eric and Leticia milked sympathy for months, but then she was never spoken of again."

I grit my teeth. "I wonder how many drug dealing motorcycle gangs have exchange programs with their British counterparts."

"What?" My mom sounds confused.

"Miriam just moved to Storm View from London where she's been living for years. She said she worked in her cousin's flower shop over there."

My mom gasps. "Well, that certainly thickens the plot, doesn't it? I wonder if I should pay Calvin and Violet a visit. I'm sure they would be interested to hear their granddaughter has returned to town. I wonder if her parents know."

My hand snaps out to my mom's arm like she's going to go do it right now. She looks down in surprise. "Sorry, but don't you think if Miriam wanted them to know, she would have already been to visit? You would have heard the gossip. I'm thinking there's a reason, especially if she was close to her grandparents."

"Yes, they practically raised her, what with Eric and Leticia traveling or socializing. Unlike us, they didn't care for their children, and they only had the one, I guess, to carry on the family name. I also know they wanted a boy and that having a girl was a disappointment."

"Man, people suck. Have I told you recently what amazing parents you and Dad are, and that I am so grateful for all of your support? I know Ginny feels the same way."

Mom blushes but gives me a hug. "We do our best. Now, did you convince your partner to work on your restaurant? Maybe you could have her over to the house, and Dad and I could help you brainstorm." She leans her butt against the desk.

I chuckle and pull my backpack up on my shoulder. "I'm pretty sure it would be considered cheating if the lecturer helps with the assignment."

She wrinkles her nose. "I guess you're right, but there's nothing stopping Dad from helping you, and he is half of the dynamic duo that is Carlyle Marketing."

"Slow down, Mom. We're meeting on Friday afternoon to scope out the competition."

My mom grins. "Oh yes, you are so sneaky, scoring a date with a pretty girl under the guise of working on your assignment. Where are you taking her?"

"Actually, I'm going to take her to Lou's Place. I'm pretty sure they will be my biggest competition, and every time I've been there, it was in a social capacity, so now I want to study it in a business capacity."

She nods. "That's a good idea. They are a popular place, but I'm not sure they will be your competition. They target the college, sports, and young adult market, so it's not family friendly. While your idea will still appeal to that market, it's aimed at families. Actually, you know what would be smart? If you had split mealtimes. An earlier seating aimed at families, and then a later one with a more casual bar menu aimed at the college and young adult crowd. They will spend more money on drinks and games with their expendable income."

"Yeah, I'd already thought about something

similar. I'm also going to have kids under the age of ten eat free with a paying adult to make it enticing to families. I might even do afternoon sessions for parties. I wasn't planning on opening for lunch, but maybe on the weekend and during summer."

"Bentley, I am so proud of you. Seriously, Dad and I think you're going to be amazing. Maybe even later down the track, if it goes well, we can look at franchising it."

I almost burst with pride at my mom's words, but I wrinkle my nose at the franchise suggestion. "I'm not sure I could turn over control of my baby to someone else."

She laughs and gathers up her things, and we leave the lecture hall. I look around, hoping Miriam is still in sight, but to my disappointment, she's gone. Giving my mom a kiss, I say farewell and make my way home. I'm going to spend the afternoon googling recipes. I have a good idea what I want to put on my menu, but I still need a few more options. I wonder what kind of food Miriam likes. I remember a weekend trip to London from Paris with a couple of my classmates and sampling some of the local food and feeling underwhelmed. Hopefully she didn't acclimate to their food, and she's a little more adventurous, or maybe I'm just going to have to teach her the wonders of flavor. I'm totally up to the challenge.

I'm busy making the sauce for the stir-fry for dinner tonight when Noah returns home from whatever job he's been working on today. He's red in the face, and there's a line of sweat down his back, plastering his shirt to his skin. He grabs a beer out of the fridge and takes a seat at my counter, taking a piece of carrot out of the pile of chopped veggies.

"God, it's hot out there," he complains, taking a big sip of his beer before munching on his stolen carrot.

"Dinner won't be long. Why don't you take a shower so your stench isn't putting us off our food?" I say, and he flips me off, but then a curious look fills his eyes.

"How was class? Did it go well with your project partner?"

I dip my finger in the sauce and taste it before adding a sprinkle of sugar. "Yeah, it went well. We're going out for lunch on Friday to work on our project.

I called it scoping out my competition, but I just wanted to spend more time with her and not in a school setting," I tell him as I look up. He's smiling like he knows something.

"Oh, and where are you going to take her?" he asks innocently.

"Lou's Place. It's not too intimate where it will scare her off, but the food is great there. It's the only place I worry about giving me hard competition."

"Yeah, you're not wrong, but it's not really suitable for families, so I still think there's room for both of you. Well, I hope it goes well. It just so happens I have a date too. You'll have to find your own way to the game on Saturday," he tells me, smiling like the cat who got the canary.

"You're bringing her to the game. That's a bold move, man, subjecting her to all the families on the first date."

He grimaces and shakes his head. "Fuck no, she and I will be sitting elsewhere. I won't have everyone bombarding her with questions. I'm going to grab a quick shower, but I'll be back in a moment." He grabs another piece of carrot before slipping out of the room.

I roll my eyes and put my wok on the stove, turning up the heat. The garage door opens again, and this time, it's Kash. Unlike Noah, he took the time to shower after practice, so his hair is still slightly damp, and he has his workout bag over his shoulder. He groans as he drops it on the ground before taking a seat.

"Hard session?" I ask, and he lays his head against the countertop.

"Fuck, man, the coach is going to kill us. He's determined to go to the playoffs this year, and we haven't even played our first game."

"Is the team looking solid?" I ask him. Sometimes, I go down and watch him train, but the week leading up to the first game has closed sessions only, so I haven't been able to see what everyone looks like.

"The team is on fire. I really think this is going to be our year. I feel it in my bones." He sounds determined, and if anyone can achieve something through sheer determination, it's him.

"Well, you can rest on Sunday."

"Yeah, I think I might soak in the tub for a little bit after dinner." Liam says. "Youth tryouts are on Sunday, and Lola is trying out. I want to go down and support her."

I can't help but grin. "Lola's trying out for hockey? Wow, I can't believe it. It only feels like she was born yesterday. I am so there. Uncle Bent will be cheering from the sidelines."

I cook dinner—chicken and veggie stir-fry with a black bean sauce—while Kash has a micro nap. I know if I send him to the couch or up to his room, he'll be out and won't eat. With his practice schedule, he can't afford to skip meals. I've prepped some jars full of fruit and protein powder, so all he has to do is blend them in the morning, as well as some high protein mini quiches for him to eat after he works out. The team usually eats lunch together, their chefs preparing them meals, but he likes to come home to eat dinner with us, so I make sure everything is lean and healthy and full of vitamins and minerals when he's in training to keep his body in tip-top shape. Liam teases me, saying that I'm like Kash and Noah's wife, but I love to cook, and I get satisfaction knowing they are eating well.

"You know, I was thinking about this." Noah walks back in freshly showered, holding the hockey magazine I was reading the other day.

"Thinking about what?" I ask as I plate the food.

He drops the magazine next to Kash's head, startling him awake before placing three place settings at our small kitchen table. We have a bigger one in the dining room, but when it's just the three of us, we tend to eat in here. "You know, those players from Ann Arbor might be onto something."

"The ones who are into polyamory?" Kash asks,

rubbing at his eyes and picking up the magazine, looking at it with bleary eyes.

"Yeah, I mean, how many times have girls tried to come between us or use us to get one of the others?" Noah takes down three glasses and fills them with water before placing them on the table as well.

"All the time," Kash grumbles, feeling guilty that many of the girls Noah and I were with were only sleeping with us so they could make a play for the pro hockey player. Luckily, neither of us were looking for Mrs. Right and only Ms. Right-Now, so it took the sting away.

"Or tried to make us choose them over each other, like Missy did. She used the excuse that I always put you two ahead of her, which is why she cheated on me," Noah points out, and Kash rolls his eyes as we all sit down.

"That's a load of bullshit," I explode. "She constantly came on to me and Kash. Shit, she walked into my bathroom while I was in the shower butt naked one morning after you'd gone to work. She offered to wash my dick with her mouth. I told her to fuck off, and that was when she started whispering in your ear about me coming onto her."

"She was clueless. Like I would believe her over

my childhood friend. That's when she got mad and slept with that other dude."

"Seriously, you dodged a bullet there," Kash tells him before shoveling food into his mouth and groaning at the taste. I smirk, proud of my cooking, but Noah smiles sadly.

"Yeah, I did, but at the beginning, I thought we had something. Look, all I'm saying is what if we found someone to love all three of us? Bentley and I could keep her safe and well-loved while you're at away games, and there will always be one of us around if Bentley has to work a late shift at the restaurant or I have to put in overtime with the company."

I kind of like the idea. I think about Miriam and how I would feel if she showed an interest in my boys. I don't think it would be something that I would be mad about, but who knows if she'd even be interested in that kind of arrangement?

"I don't know, man. We've never been interested in dating the same woman before." Kash shakes his head, reaching for his glass of water and taking a long drink.

"Yeah, but that's because none of us have really thought about settling down, but I kind of want what Liam has. I want a family and someone to come home to at night, but I also don't want to give up my friendship with you either. It means too much to me." Noah stares down at the table like he can't quite meet our eyes with that confession, so I decide to throw him a bone.

"I really like the girl I'm doing my project with," I tell him, and he looks up and smirks before he quickly hides it.

"Yeah, and I really like the girl I'm going out to dinner with on Saturday. Look, all I'm saying is keep an open mind, you never know what might happen."

He drops the subject as we fall silent and eat the meal I prepared. We talk about a few things, but mostly we're all lost in our heads. Maybe he's onto something, but I'm wondering if it's too late. I'm not sure that kind of relationship would work with two women.

After we've eaten and the boys thank me, Kash heads out to the hot tub to soak away his aches and pains while Noah and I clean up. Normally I wouldn't let Kash get away with it, but it's opening week, so he gets a free pass this week, but that's all.

"Listen, I have to call Ethan and talk to him about the job we're doing for my grandparents' neighbor," Noah tells me, hanging up the dish towel once he finishes drying the wok.

"Yeah, okay. I'm going to head to the supermarket. I feel like ice cream, and we're out," I tell him, grabbing my keys off the hook next to the door and shoving my wallet in my back pocket.

"Can you grab me a tub of mint chocolate chip?" he asks, and I chuckle. He's been eating that since we were ten, and very rarely does he deviate.

"Yeah, of course. I'll catch you later, and say hi to Ethan for me. He hasn't been over for dinner in a while. Make sure everything is okay, yeah?"

Noah nods, and I wave as I walk out the door and get in my car. It's a black Aston Martin that my parents gave me for my twenty-first birthday with the license plate Bentley 3. It's over the top, but I love it, and I love to drive around town in the evening, listening to music and letting all my worries float away. Most of those worries used to be hating on my former head chef. I feel so much lighter now that I quit, though, I've had a few calls from the owner of the restaurant. I'm not ready to return to them yet, maybe tomorrow. Today, I'm going to find a pint of raspberry ripple and a good movie and enjoy not having to cook for people who aren't appreciative of the food I put on their plates.

CHAPTER 15

Miriam

"Mama, I don't feel so good."

I turn away from where I'm doing the dishes at the kitchen sink to find Jorja standing in the doorway. I put her to bed half an hour ago, and I'm surprised to find her awake again so soon.

"Aww, baby, what's wrong?" I dry off my hands on a nearby dish towel and hurry over to her.

She looks flushed and glassy-eyed, and when I put my hand on her forehead, she's damp and feverish. Shit! I don't have any Tylenol to give her to help bring down her fever. I bend down and pick her up. My heart races as I pray that this is just a normal, run-of-the-mill childhood thing and not anything to do with how sickly she was before. I mean, she just started school, and it's full of germs, so I'm sure she just picked something up from there. I'll monitor her for a few hours before I start to panic. Her immune system was so crappy from being born prematurely, so the smallest thing worries me.

"Okay, honey, hang on. Let's get you into the car, and we'll run to the grocery store and get something to make you feel better, okay?" I grab my keys and phone and hurry out the door, Jorja's sweaty little body wrapped around me.

"My head hurts, and so does my tummy," she whines as I strap her into her car seat.

"Oh, baby, I know. You must feel terrible. How about we get you some ice cream for later when you feel better?"

"Okay, Mama, I might like that," she says, trying to smile, but then she groans and curls in on herself.

I drive just over the speed limit to a nearby supermarket. Not wanting to leave her in the car, I unstrap her and carry her inside. Her head flops against my shoulder, and she's heavy in my arms because she's not holding any of her weight. I look around with panic. I'm not really familiar with the layout yet, and have no clue where to find the medicine. I find a teenage boy stocking shelves and hurry over to ask him. He tells me which aisle, and I hurry over and grab a bottle of liquid Tylenol. Remembering the promised ice cream, I detour to the freezer aisle. I'm just checking out the selection with Jorja still wrapped around me like a koala, her eyes shut and her breathing shallow, when I hear a voice.

"Miriam?" I turn around and find Bentley looking between me and Jorja curiously.

Before I can respond, Jorja mutters, "Mama, I don't feel so good," and proceeds to puke down my front.

"Holy shit," Bentley mutters as I look down at my vomit splattered body.

"I'm sorry, Mama," Jorja sobs.

"Oh, baby, no, it's okay. Are you feeling a little better now?" I ask, pushing her hair back from her face, but her eyes are closed. What the hell am I going to do now?

Before I can even think, Bentley holds up both hands. "Hang on. I'll go find something to clean you both up. Just wait here. I'll also tell one of the workers to clean the floor. Just wait, okay? I promise I'll help. Everything is going to be okay." He sounds kind of flustered, and I can't help but find that cute. A smile twitches on my lips, but my daughter moans, and he whirls around and takes off.

Either he's freaked out and never returning, and I'm going to need a new project partner, or he's actually going to try and help. I guess all I can do is wait.

The smell of vomit has me gagging, especially because I'm wearing a good amount of it, but within what feels like hours, although I'm sure was only a few minutes, Bentley returns, followed by an employee pushing a mop bucket. In Bentley's hand is a roll of paper towels, baby wipes, a bottle of Gatorade, and what looks like a change of clothes.

"Okay, here we go," he says breathlessly. "So what we're going to do is clean the little lady first, because she managed to miss most of herself, and then you're going to pass her to me and you can clean yourself. I grabbed you some clean clothes, and we'll put yours in a bag. Susan here is going to show you where you can get changed, okay?"

I just stare at him in shock as Susan starts mopping up the splatter on the floor.

"Miriam, are you okay?" he asks, and I just nod my head slowly, still speechless at how helpful he's being. He turns his attention to Jorja, whose eyes are slightly open as she looks at him.

"You're pretty. Who are you?" she mutters, and he smirks. She's not wrong, he's blonde with dimples and sparkling eyes, he's smoking hot. The fact he's kind and funny makes him even hotter.

"This is my friend Bentley from school. This is my daughter, Jorja," I say, introducing them.

"You're pretty too. Now how about you help me make Mama pretty again." He puts his supplies on a nearby shelf and grabs the roll of paper towels, pulling some off. He holds her arm and wipes it before doing the same thing with the baby wipe. He looks her up and down, seeming satisfied that her arm was the only place she didn't miss on her body before holding his hands out to her. She happily lets go of me and reaches out to him.

"Okay, baby, how about you hang with me for a moment while Mama goes and gets changed? You did a good job of getting puke all over her. That was great aim."

"I have excellent aim," Jorja mutters proudly, resting her head against his shoulder and closing her eyes, inhaling deeply. "You smell good."

Bentley chuckles and shoos me away. "Go get changed. I promise we'll be right here when you get back. Here, take my keys. I won't be able to go anywhere." He holds out his key fob, but I shake my head. My gut tells me I can trust him, and Jorja didn't even hesitate. In the past, she's been wary of adults, having had stranger danger drilled into her since she could walk.

"Thank you so much. You have no idea how

much I appreciate this," I tell him as Susan gestures for me to follow her.

She shows me the employee bathroom, and I quickly strip off my vomit-soaked shirt. Using the baby wipes, I clean off any residue and pull on the plain blue shirt he found me. My shorts are just as gross, so I use the baby wipes to clean my legs, because they didn't get missed either. I replace my denim cutoffs with a pair of men's, drawstring sports shorts and tie them tight so they don't slip down. My flip-flops are also victims, but they are easy enough to wash in the sink and dry with paper towels. Throwing all the trash in the bin, I put my own clothes in a plastic bag Susan supplied. I still smell bad, but I'm not sure if that's me or just the smell stuck in my nostrils. At least I can get us home without messing up my car.

I head back out, passing Susan on the way. "Thank you so much, and I am so sorry."

"Ah, hun, don't you worry. It happens all the time, but your hubby was certainly a lot more helpful than a lot of the other dads I've seen." She walks away, pushing her bucket. I guess she's going to empty it somewhere.

My hubby? I guess Bentley could be mistaken for that, and he was certainly attentive enough. A small rush of warmth flows through my body as I think about it. Having someone to help with the good and the bad would be amazing. One day, I would like that, and hopefully they will be as kind and understanding as he is.

I stop daydreaming and rush back to the freezer section to find Jorja perched on a freezer and Bentley holding the drink for her. "Just a small sip, because we don't want it all to come back up again, but it should help you feel better."

She takes the bottle of bright blue liquid from him and takes a sip, screwing up her nose at the unfamiliar flavor. "That's not very nice."

Bentley chuckles. "I guess to some it's not, but arctic blast just so happens to be my favorite Gatorade flavor."

"Jorja, honey, how are you feeling?" I hurry over, dropping my clothes bag on the floor. "Thank you so much." I put my hand on Bentley's arm. "You have no idea how much I appreciate this." I turn to my daughter, putting my hand on her head. She still feels warm. "How are you feeling, baby?"

"I'm still so hot, Mama. Maybe I should have ice cream to cool me down?" Her eyes slide to the side, looking into the freezers.

"Ha, what a sneak." Bentley is impressed by her cheekiness.

"I don't think that's such a great idea, but we'll

take a pint home with us," I tell her, and her bottom lip drops and starts quivering. Bentley buckles under the emotional torment.

"No, no." He holds up his hands. "Please, pretty girl, don't cry. I'll grab you a pint to take home. What do you want? Are you a chocolate girl or do you like the ones with the things mixed in? I'm partial to raspberry ripple and my room mate like mint choc."

"I like the one with the gummies," she points to the one that has a whole heap of candy mixed in. Bentley looks at me like he's asking if it's okay, and I nod. He opens the door and reaches in, grabbing a pint of mint chocolate chip, one of raspberry ripple, and the one Jorja pointed out. Jorja yawns, and I can't help but copy her. "Okay, how about I grab some other things that might help make you feel a little better and then I drive you two home?"

Before I can argue, he grabs a nearby basket and throws the ice cream in. He takes the Tylenol from where I placed it and adds it to the other items, as well as the leftover towel and wipes, Gatorade, and the tags from my clothes. "Alright. You two go and hop in your car, and I'll pay for all of this and meet you out there."

I start to argue, but he just shakes his head. "Go, Miriam. I've got this," he insists, so I accept his help.

I pick up my girl and carry her out to my car, which is parked just outside the front door. There is a black Aston Martin a couple of spots down with the license plate Bentley 3 on it, and I can't help but chuckle, shaking my head. Of course the playboy has vanity plates and an expensive car.

It's not long after that before Bentley comes out carrying two shopping bags. I'm leaning against the front of my car when he stops and whistles. "Wow, I noticed that when I came inside. That is a sweet classic car." His eyes roam over my vehicle.

I push off the hood and hold my hands out for the bags. "I can't thank you enough. How much do I owe you?"

His eyes narrow. "Nothing, now let's put this in the trunk and get you two home." He holds out his hands for the keys, and I slowly hand them over.

"But what about your car?" I nod in the direction of his.

"Don't worry about it. I'll come back and get it later," he assures me, and I just decide to let it go. It's been so amazing having help that I don't want to argue.

I climb in the passenger seat and look back at Jorja. She's fast asleep, but I can see she's still sweaty.

Bentley climbs in the driver's seat, and thankfully the car starts right away. "Whoa, that sounds mean." He chuckles as he puts it in reverse and backs out of the parking spot. I give him directions to our place, and it's not long before we're pulling into our driveway, but when I look over, Bentley is frowning and looking next door.

"You live next door to Mae and Fred?" he asks as he pulls the car into the car port.

"Yeah, they've been amazing," I tell him, pretty sure I know what the next question is going to be. I worry my lip with my teeth as I brace myself.

"So that means you're the neighbor Noah has been helping out. The branch went through your roof," he surmises, not sounding angry. If anything, he sounds curious and hopeful.

"Ah, yeah. I'm sorry I never said anything. Noah mentioned you guys were roommates, but I guess I never thought to bring it up."

He sits there for a moment, and I can practically see him turning it all over in his mind, but instead of being mad like I thought he would be, a smile spreads across his lips, and he nods. "Yeah, okay, this is good. Right, let's get the pretty princess inside, shall we?" He gets out of the car, leaving me sitting there, reeling.

Well, okay then, I guess it's not a big deal. Good to know. By the time I get moving, he's already unstrapped a sleeping Jorja from her seat and lifted her out of the car. He has her wrapped in his arms as he passes me the keys. "Show me the way," he says when I just stare at him in surprise again.

Coming to my senses, I put the key in the lock and open the door wide for the two of them. "Just up here. Be careful of the balustrade, it's wobbly. Ethan is getting someone to fix it this week," I tell him as I show him the way to Jorja's room. I push her door open, and he follows me in and lays her down on the bed.

"Why don't you get her settled, and I'll bring the things in from the car?" Before I can say anything, he's gone again, so I strip off her sweaty clothes and give her a sponge bath with a cold cloth before dressing her in some clean pajamas. By the time I'm done with that, he's back with the Tylenol and a glass of water.

"Here." He passes it to me and then hurries out again.

Gaping at the empty doorway, I just shake my head and pour the required dose. I shake my daughter slightly, and she cracks her eyes open. "Here, baby, take this. It should make you feel better," I tell her, leaning her up so she can swallow the medicine easier.

She doesn't argue, just takes the medicine with

her eyes half closed. I think she's asleep again before I lay her back down again. As I brush tendrils of curls back from her face, I notice she's not quite as hot as she was before. Hopefully that was all the vomit we are going to see, but just in case, I need to grab something to put next to her bed. I might also slip a towel under her just in case. It will save me from having to change sheets every time she vomits.

Out in the hallway, I grab a towel out of the linen closet, as well as a bucket, which I place next to her bed before maneuvering her so I can spread the towel out underneath her and the pillow. Happy with my preparations, I leave her to sleep. I'll come back and check on her shortly, but I want to see what happened to Bentley. Did he leave? Or is he still here?

As I make my way downstairs, the smell of onions cooking hits my nose. Is he cooking? When I get to the kitchen, I stop and stare. Bentley has something frying on the stove, and he's cutting up celery and carrots like a madman. He looks up as I enter and smiles.

"Hi. How is she?" he asks as he scrapes his carrot and celery pieces into the pot on the stove.

"Out like a light. I gave her some Tylenol and cleaned her up. Hopefully that was the extent of the vomit, but I doubt it."

He wrinkles his nose. "No, it usually isn't. I haven't had the stomach flu in years, but I remember when both Ginny and I had it as kids. Poor Mom and Dad were run ragged for a few days. Our housekeeper did so many loads of laundry so we didn't run out of sheets."

"What are you doing?" I ask as he pulls a cooked chicken out of the grocery bags.

"I'm making Jorja some chicken noodle soup for when she's feeling better. I know she probably can't have it right away, but it freezes well, and I remember enjoying it after having been sick. I grabbed some crackers and a couple more bottles of electrolytes as well for when she wakes up."

Holy crap, and just like that, my heart wants to leap out of my chest and throw itself at this gorgeous man who is pulling apart a chicken in front of me. "I don't have time to make the stock from scratch, but this works just as well." He nods to the carton of chicken stock on the counter.

Without even thinking about it, I step around to the side that he's on and turn him to face me. Putting my hands on his cheeks, I pull him toward me and kiss him hard. When I move away, he's blinking and looking slightly dazed before his eyes heat. He pushes me out of the way and moves to the kitchen sink, turning on the water.

Shit, did I do that wrong? Is he leaving? It's been so long since I've had any male interaction that maybe I read the signs wrong. I'm about to apologize when he finishes washing his hands and turns off the faucet, drying his hands on his shirt.

He takes two big steps toward me and wraps his arms around me, pulling me against his chest. "Couldn't do that with chicken on my hands," he explains before leaning in and kissing me.

He starts cautiously, almost hesitantly, like he's asking permission to continue, but the minute his tongue darts out to lick my lip, I groan and sink into him, giving him the green light to kiss the hell out of me, and he does. Hesitation turns to full command as his tongue explores my mouth, tangling with mine and leaving me breathless, aching for more, when he pulls away.

He moves back reluctantly. "As much as I'd like to continue this, I'm going to burn Jorja's soup if I let you distract me anymore."

"Ah, okay." I step back, feeling flushed and turned on as well as slightly awkward. What happens now? "Ah I might just go check on Jorja," I tell him.

He opens his mouth to say something, but I don't wait to hear it. I hurry out of the room like my pants are on fire.

I get up to her room and find her sleeping soundly, and when I place my hand against her head, she seems a little cooler. I hurry to my own room, closing the door behind me. I sag against it, my fingers coming up to feel my lips. They are swollen and sensitive, and I feel so incredibly guilty. What am I doing, kissing one man when I have a date with another on Saturday night? How can I feel equally attracted to both of them? That's not how it works. It's been bad enough knowing the gossip that circulated in this town about me previously, so what would people say if I was seen dating two different men? Fuck, I'm in so much trouble, because I like both of them equally. Knowing I'm going to have to choose is heartbreaking. Maybe I should just say no to both. The fact that they are friends makes it worse. There is no way I want to come between them, and then there's also the fact that they are Kash's roommates. As much as I wanted to be free and easy like Aunt Jocelyn, the reality is so much more intimidating, it's a fucking disaster waiting to happen. No, I'll go back downstairs and pretend that kiss never happened.

I take a deep breath and blow it out, trying to calm my racing pulse. When I think I finally have myself under control, I leave my room and head back down. Before I can make it to the kitchen, though, there is a knock on my door.

CHAPTER 16

Miriam

When I open the door, my mouth drops open when I find Noah standing there with a frown on his face. He steps forward, grabbing me with both hands. "Are you okay? Is Jorja okay? What's going on?"

"Huh?" I'm so confused right now. Why is he here?

"B called and said you needed help, so I came right over."

Well, fuck my life. This is just perfect. The man I have a date with turned up at my house just after his best friend kissed the hell out of me. I feel myself blush. "B? You mean Bentley called you? He's in the kitchen making soup," I tell Noah who wraps his arm around my shoulders and sweeps me along with him.

"Why is he making soup? Is someone sick? He didn't tell me anything except that I needed to come over. Bastard wouldn't answer his phone when I tried to call him back." He pushes the kitchen door open, and Bentley looks up and smiles.

"Awesome, you're here."

"What the hell, man?" Noah demands, helping me onto a seat before sitting himself. "You can't leave me hanging. I thought something was really wrong. You left to get ice cream and never returned. Kash went to bed, and I waited to make sure you were okay, and then you gave me a call like that. I was freaked out."

"You didn't tell him?" Bentley looks at me, and I just stammer.

"He didn't give me a chance to. Jorja has the stomach flu. We ran into Bentley at the grocery store. I needed Tylenol, and Jorja puked all down my front. He helped us, and now he's making her soup," I say, pointing unnecessarily to the pot.

Noah heaves out a sigh but doesn't lose the worried look. "Is she okay? Do we need to call a doctor to come look at her?"

Ugh, these men. Their concern for my daughter

is heart wrenching. They have no idea what they are both doing to me.

Bentley is watching us closely as I shake my head. "No, I think she'll be fine. She seems to be getting better already."

Noah sighs heavily. "Good, that's good."

"I left my car at the grocery store because I drove them home in Miriam's car."

"You got to drive the Impala? How was it?" Noah sounds excited, and I just roll my eyes.

"It was awesome, but when I realized Miriam was the neighbor you had been helping, I thought you could give me a lift back to mine." Bentley is glaring at Noah, and Noah runs a hand through his hair, shrugging sheepishly.

"I put two and two together this morning. I haven't had a chance to say anything because Kash was there this afternoon," he explains, and my stomach sinks. Shit ,we haven't gotten to Kash yet.

"Kash?" Bentley asks, and Noah looks at me, raising an eyebrow.

I just shake my head, and he groans.

"Shit, sorry, Mimi, I thought he would have realized like I did."

"You only realized because Kira and Lola were here this morning. It was seeing the two of them together that triggered it," I point out.

"Yeah, fuck, sorry," he says again.

"What am I missing? What do Kira and Lola have to do with all of this?" Bentley puts down the spoon he was using to stir his soup and adjusts the stove. He sounds a little annoyed now.

"Come sit down if you've finished your soup. There's something you should know," I say then decide to put on my adult pants. "Actually, there are things you should both know."

Noah raises his eyebrows as Bentley takes a seat but stays quiet.

"Fuck, I don't even know where to start," I tell them, so Noah does.

"Remember the summer before college when Kash was avoiding us? He'd met someone and was sneaking around, wanting to see if it all worked out before he introduced us."

Bentley nods. "Yeah, I remember, but it must not have, because he suddenly turned into a complete ass and nailed anything that walked."

I flinch, not liking the truth but unable to avoid it either. I sigh and spend the next half hour explaining exactly what happened. A range of emotions flows over both their faces during the story—anger, sympathy, outrage, and finally, comprehension.

"Jorja is Kash's? Fuck, how could your parents do

that to both of you?" Bentley asks, repeating the same thing Noah said this morning.

"Yeah, she is, and yes, I am going to tell him, but after the opening game. I don't want to mess him up in the head before that."

He's quiet as he absorbs everything I've told him, and Noah reaches out and gives my hand a squeeze. Bentley's eyes latch onto the action, and his head whips up and he glares at Noah. "This is why you were asking about that magazine article at dinner earlier, right?"

Now it's my turn to be confused, but before I can question him, Noah starts talking. "Yes. Miriam mentioned she was your partner, and I put two and two together and realized that you and I happened to be talking about the same person."

"And that person is also Kash's baby mama, the same woman he was head over heels for?" Bentley asks as an understanding expression appears on his face, even though I'm still clueless. He starts nodding enthusiastically. "Yeah, man, I'm totally in. It's a brilliant plan."

Noah grins.

"What the hell is going on?" I ask, throwing my hands up in the air in frustration. "I have no idea what you two are talking about."

Bentley looks at me with mischief sparkling in

his eyes. "How about you tell my friend Noah here just how much you enjoyed kissing me? I mean, it's only fair that we're all open and honest considering you're going out to dinner with him on Saturday."

My mouth drops open, and I narrow my eyes at him before hissing, "It wasn't up to you to tell him that." I jump off my seat, but before I can storm out of the room, Noah grabs my arm, pulling me to a stop.

"Hey, hey, it's okay. Bentley was just messing around. Sometimes he doesn't think before he opens his mouth. Ignore him." He gathers my hands in his and pulls me into his body. I can't look him in the eye, but he drops a hand and places a finger under my chin. "No, it wasn't his place to tell me that, but I don't mind."

"You don't mind that he kissed me?" I can't help sounding outraged.

Noah laughs and shakes his head. "If it had been anyone but him, then yeah, I'd be pissed. When Bentley told me he was interested in his project partner, and then I discovered it was the same girl I was interested in, and not only that, but she had a daughter with my other best friend, I thought that was it. There was no way I was going to let a girl come between us. I was going to bow out and let him have you." I don't know whether to feel outraged at his statement or impressed. "But then I remembered something I'd been told about. Bentley recently read an article about two pro hockey players who have a very different personal life than the norm. They share a woman between them and one other man." He pauses and shakes his head. "I'm not sure sharing is the right word, but the four of them are in a relationship together. I don't know what the dynamics are, and personally, I don't care who sleeps with whom, but it made me think. What's to stop us from giving that a go? Both of us like you." He gestures back and forth between him and Bentley. "And why can't we explore that? To be honest, we've had so many women who have tried to pit us against one another that the three of us have given up. None of us have dated seriously in years," he tells me, pushing a lock of hair back from my face as I feel a body approach me from behind.

Bentley's hands settle on my waist, and he leans in, his body pushing me into Noah. "I'm sorry, I didn't mean to upset you. It's just when I finally realized what Noah was suggesting, I got excited. I like you a lot, and if we were in a relationship like that, then it would mean none of us would have to choose between a partner and a best friend. It's like having your cake and eating it too."

"You're talking about me being in a relationship

with both of you?" I ask, trying to make sure I got this right. I'm not unfamiliar with polyamory. Aunt Jocelyn had a number of paramours, as she called them, and they all knew about each other. She wasn't sneaking around, and they all seemed happy with the arrangement, but I just want to make sure all the cards are on the table before we go any further. Maybe her free and easy ideals won't be as hard as I first thought.

"Yes, and Kash if he's on board, because I have no doubt that once he knows your story, nothing will stop him from rekindling whatever you had beforehand. He loved you so hard, and had I not met you, that wouldn't be a problem, but I have, and now I'm not stepping back," Bentley continues, his words caressing my ear and making me shiver.

I snort with doubt. "You could have fooled me. Within weeks of me leaving, his page was full of puck bunnies."

"He was in pain and used puck bunnies and alcohol to numb it. It didn't work for long," Noah explains, and I can see the truth in his eyes.

"Okay, so you two, me, and Kash in a four-way relationship? Do you all fuck?" I ask and almost chuckle when horror enters Noah's eyes and Bentley's hands tighten on my waist. Both of them explode.

"No way!" Bentley cries out.

"I love my boys, but not like that." Noah looks down at me, and I can't hold my giggles in any longer, so laughter bursts out. "Oh, see, that wasn't funny," he scolds me, but his eyes sparkle.

Bentley squeezes my waist. "That was naughty. We might not fuck each other, but we are very happy to work together to bring our girl pleasure."

The atmosphere gets tense again. "You've shared before?"

Noah nods. "Occasionally in the past we've had threesomes, but never with the three of us with one girl."

"And would you be seeing other girls as well as me?" I want to clarify this. Although I like the idea of having the three of them to myself—if Kash is even interested, like they think he will be—I don't like the thought that I will have to share with others.

"No, this will be a closed polyamorous relationship. The four of us only, no other women or men."

"And Jorja? Because she is my priority. I will always put her first."

"And we wouldn't want it any other way. Look, think about it. It's a huge thing. There will be scrutiny and gossip, and you've had enough of that to last a lifetime. If you decide to go ahead, we'll do this at your pace." Bentley presses a kiss to the back of my neck and steps away, returning to stir his soup on the stove.

Ugh, my stomach rolls at being gossip fodder for high society in Storm View again, but this time, I can control the narrative. This time, I'm an adult and my parents can't send me away and sell a false narrative. This time, I'm taking charge.

"You can tell me your answer on Saturday on our date." Noah tells me, leaning in and pressing a kiss against my cheek. "I really hope you take a chance."

"Okay, let me finish this soup, and then we'll get out of your hair. You have a lot to think about, and as much as I want to give you an idea of how good it could be in a relationship with both of us" —my heart thuds with excitement at the thought of these two men giving me all their attention— "Jorja may wake up at any time and need her mama, and that's more important than making you feel good."

Seriously, these guys are certainly making all the right moves to win their case. The conversation turns to lighter topics, and we talk about school and hockey and Jorja.

"Hey, how did it go with the realtor this afternoon?" Noah asks, and I groan.

"Ugh, it was a disaster. She didn't show me anything suitable. I don't think she listened to Seamus's requirements at all. Not one of them had a cool room, and when I asked, she looked at me like I was an idiot. She took one look at me and made assumptions, despite having spoken to Seamus. All she could talk about was that she was giving up precious time to show me property, and I shouldn't waste her time if I wasn't serious."

"I didn't want to say anything before, but my dad is in real estate. It keeps him out of mom's hair now that he's handed the business over to Ethan and I. Do you want me to ask him if he has any suitable property?" Noah suggests, and Bentley nods enthusiastically.

"Good idea. Mason is going to show me some places next week, maybe we could do it together."

"Yeah, actually, that would be great. Give him my number, and I'll wait for him to call me."

About an hour later, after we polish off both the guys tubs of ice cream, he pulls all the chicken pieces out of the broth and blends it with an immersion blender before putting it back in. Next, he pours in some tiny pasta pieces before declaring Jorja's soup finished.

"Okay, give her the crackers and the Gatorade when she wakes up if she's hungry. If she manages to keep that down, try the soup," he instructs me as they take their leave.

I won't laugh at him telling me how to look after

my own child, because he's so damn freaking adorable and his concern is so sweet. "Okay, and thank you both. What would normally be a very stressful situation hasn't been so bad because you were here to help," I tell him. "And then you both kept my mind off of it for a while. Jorja's health wasn't great as a baby and, well, it's easy to let my thoughts run away if I'm left to worry."

"Good night, Mimi, sleep well," Noah says, pressing a kiss to my cheek and heading down the steps.

"Mimi, huh? I like it. Sweet dreams, beautiful." Bentley winks and kisses the other cheek before hurrying after Noah, whistling happily. I wave and wait until Noah's truck is down the drive before closing the door.

Holy crap. Although I managed not to lose my shit when they were here, my mind has done nothing but think about being in a relationship with them ever since they mentioned it. Despite the possible backlash, I promised myself I was going to live my life to its fullest, just like Aunt Jocelyn, and I think she's up there somewhere screaming at me to go for it. It would be just like her to be the guardian angel that's orchestrating all of this from above.

I already know what my answer is going to be. How could I not want to see what might develop between the three of us? The only thing that's holding me back is Kash. How is he going to react to seeing me again, let alone finding out about Jorja and the fact that he's missed the first five years of her life? Regrets are kind of useless, but I wish I'd taken Jocelyn's advice and reached out years ago. But who knows, maybe I was never meant to be for just him. Maybe I'm exactly where I need to be now.

.

CHAPTER 17

Miriam

Jorja doesn't vomit again, but she's still not a hundred percent when she wakes up the next day. We spend the day snuggling on the couch and watching movies.

Kira calls just after school pickup when she realizes that Jorja hadn't been at school. "Is everything okay? Lola said Jorja wasn't at school."

"Just the stomach flu, but I'll keep her home tomorrow anyway," I explain.

"They don't have school on Fridays anyway, so it's not a big deal," Kira replies, and this information makes me pause.

"They don't? Crap, I have a morning class on Friday. I was going to ask Mae to watch her for me tomorrow morning since she's sick, but I can't do that every week. I'll need to find a daycare. Can you recommend any?" I'm not hopeful, because Kira has always been a stay-at-home mom.

"Don't be silly, she can come to my place, and I happen to know that my brother has a rest day on Friday because he usually plays that night or on Saturday, so once you tell him about Jorja, he will drop any plans to have her on Friday."

I'm quiet for a moment as I suddenly realize the precarious situation I'm in. I almost want to book a ticket and return to London and hide out. Have I made the biggest mistake of my life by returning to my hometown and putting us on Kash's radar?

"What's wrong? That was some loaded silence," Kira asks, and I can hear the worry in her tone.

I groan. "Fuck, is he going to sue me for full custody? I have some money, but I can't afford to fight him in court."

"Oh, honey, no. At least I don't think so. He'll be angry, but it won't be aimed at you. It will be aimed squarely at your parents, but I'd like to know why you didn't return sooner."

I bite my lip and hesitate. Do I tell her the truth? It's past time that I did, and I haven't told anyone this, not even Jocelyn or Seamus.

"My parents told me that if I returned to town,

they would take Jorja away from me and I would never see her again, and I don't mean they would sue me for custody. They are not exactly the most aboveboard people, and I wouldn't have put it past them to have her kidnapped. It's harder now that she's older, but it's why I've been reluctant to announce my return. If I can live a quiet life and never run into either of them, I'll be happy."

"What the fuck?" Kira explodes and rants for a few minutes about how despicable my parents are, but then she falls silent, and I can practically hear her thinking. "Okay, this is how it's going to work. As soon as Kash knows, he will have to hold a press conference announcing your and Jorja's return to his life. That will put you in the media spotlight. It's not a great place to be, but it will make things harder for your parents. Did you put Kash's name on Jorja's birth certificate?"

"Yeah, I did. I was never going to deny them a relationship. I'm just worried he will hate me and try to cut me out of her life."

"Good, that's even better. I swear Kash will never do that to you. Even if he is mad, he'll come to his senses. If not, Mom and Dad would kick his ass, and so would Liam and I. Your circumstances were out of your control. Anyways, I will pick Jorja up tomorrow, and you can pick her up after class."

"I kind of have a lunch date with Bentley," I mutter, but of course she doesn't miss this.

"Really?" She sounds surprised.

"Yeah, we are going to work on our marketing project together."

"And you have a dinner date with Noah on Saturday?" I thought she'd be mad, but she just sounds curious.

I sigh and tell her about what they suggested last night.

"Oh my god, girl, you are living the fucking dream. Three gorgeous men wanting to share you. Damn, I wonder if Liam has a few friends he can tap on the team."

I laugh at her ridiculousness, pleased she's not being judgy. "I'm not sure, to be honest. I haven't made a decision, and Kash might not be interested."

"It's actually the perfect solution. For seven months of the year, he is away as much as he's home. Having Noah and Bentley around assures that you and Jorja will always be looked after. Bentley wants to open a restaurant, and that's going to make him incredibly busy with very long hours, at least until he's established, so having Noah around will do the same thing. It really is the perfect solution, but how do you feel? Is that something you might be interested in?"

I'm quiet while I think about my answer. "You know Aunt Jocelyn lived a polyamorous lifestyle. None of them lived together, and they were each happy with their own lives, but she regularly went on dates with them or they would come for sleepovers. It seemed to work. I can't deny my attraction to both Bentley and Noah, but how do I know that it's real and not just the product of no male attention since I became pregnant? Bentley and Noah are the only men to show any interest in me since Kash. It's lovely to feel desirable again, but how do I know what I feel for them is real and not just my hormones jumping for joy?"

"Hmm, I guess going on dates will tell you that. If you enjoy spending time with them and doing non-bedroom related things, I guess that's a good start," she suggests, and I groan.

"Don't even mention bedroom things. Pregnancy does things to your body. I mean, being young helped, and most things went back to normal after, but my boobs and ass are bigger, and I have stretch marks despite Jorja not being very big. Plus, Kash is the only person I've ever slept with. I have nothing to offer these guys."

Kira whoops. "Girl, you are preaching to the choir. Lola was a normal pregnancy, but Liam loved me being pregnant. He's been trying to knock me up ever since, but I've been able to hold him off until now. I'm not sure how much longer I'm going to hold out. If he had his way, I'd be barefoot and pregnant permanently. As for those guys, they are not looking for someone who knows their way around a bedroom. Shit, there are a thousand girls on campus or puck bunnies if that's what they want. They want more, and you are the full package—kind, caring, and gorgeous—and the best part is you couldn't care less who they are. Shit, Bentley and Noah are heirs to huge fortunes, and Kash is a multi-million-dollar hockey player, but none of that matters to you, and that's big to them."

"Seriously?" I choke out, and she chuckles.

"Yes, bitch. You are about to become very unpopular on campus if you lock down two of the most eligible guys, not to mention my brother. I need to introduce you to Ginny. She'll have your back."

"Ginny? Is that Bentley's sister?"

"Yeah, she lives in one of the sorority houses and won't allow anyone to give you shit. She's very protective of her brother and his friends. She's been handling thirsty bitches for the last three years."

"Ugh, I don't know what to do." I sag on my sofa, holding my phone against my ear. Jorja is completely occupied by *Paw Patrol*, so she's not paying any attention to my conversation.

"Don't overthink it, just go with your gut and deal with issues as they pop up. Don't create them." Kira's advice is sound. "Listen, how about we meet after your lunch? Youth tryouts are on Sunday, and Lola said that Jorja can skate and wants to play."

"My daughter is a demon on ice, but I'm worried she's too small to play," I explain, and Kira chuckles.

"So is Lola. Liam bought her a pair of skates before she could even walk, and he and Kash took her as often as they could."

"My cousin Seamus was the same," I tell her, and she scoffs.

"Please, bitch, I remember exactly how well you could play hockey too. Don't think I know you're not responsible for your daughter's skills."

"Well, I couldn't very well let him teach her wrong. He loves hockey, but he's terrible at it," I argue, and we dissolve into giggles. "If she skates as well as Lola, you have nothing to worry about. They do the groups by age, and most of the kids at that level aren't great. They will be fine. We're going to buy Lola new gear tomorrow afternoon. Does Jorja need some?"

"Yeah, she left her stuff in the UK. There was no point in bringing it with our limited space, so I figured by the time she wanted it, she would need new gear anyway."

"Okay, text me when you're done, and I'll give you directions to the store. Maybe Bentley can bring you. He needs to spend time with Jorja to be sure that's what he wants."

"Ugh, Jorja thinks he's the best thing ever."

"What? Why?"

I tell her about how he helped us. "He bought her the ice cream with the gummies in it and arctic blast Gatorade which looks really cool but taste terrible. Plus he made her soup, she doesn't need to have tasted it to know it's better than mine," I repeat my daughters words to my friend and she giggles

"Dude, it sounds like he is all in. Most guys would have bolted. Shit, Liam still freaks out when Lola gets the stomach flu. He just starts gagging too and is useless. Mimi, I'm so sorry. I can't imagine how hard it must have been for you all alone."

"I wasn't alone. I had Jocelyn, Seamus, and Darcy, and the three of them embraced me from the moment I stepped off the plane. I think they were trying to make up for my parents' abysmal behavior, but I can't deny that I missed you and Kash like crazy. Then, though, I was too sick to worry about anything but keeping myself and Jorja alive. It really was a struggle some days. I was constantly sick, I couldn't keep anything down for the first four months, and although that eventually stopped, I was confined to bed, and the most movement I was allowed was to walk from my bed to the toilet. I had to sit on a chair to shower with one of the guys on standby in case I fell. To say that the three of us had some awkward moments would be an understatement."

I can practically hear the steam bursting out of her ears. "Oh, I can't wait until Kash and my parents know about what they did to you. They are not going to know what hit them. They will be destroyed socially."

We say our goodbyes, and Jorja drags her attention away from the TV. "Mama, I'm hungry."

She's been nibbling on crackers all day and sipping the Gatorade Bentley bought her, and all of it has stayed down.

"Would you like some of the soup Bentley made you?" I ask, and she sits up.

"And the bread?" she asks hopefully.

Mae ran over a loaf of bread she baked after she'd spoken to Noah earlier in the day and found out about Jorja being unwell.

"Sure, if you're that hungry."

"I'm starving." She pats her stomach and widens her eyes.

"Alright, stay there, and I'll bring you some."

I find a tray in the kitchen and load up Jorja's dinner, getting myself a bowl too. "This is the best soup ever," she declares with wide eyes. "He's a better cook than you, Mama." I chuckle and thank my child for her brutal honesty. "You know, I think he'd make a really good husband. I mean, he can cook, and he's pretty, and he smells good, and he's really nice," Jorja says, listing off Bentley's attributes between mouthfuls of soup.

"You saw him for all of an hour," I point out to her, and she shrugs, looking up from her bowl.

"He dealt with vomit for you, Mom, and he didn't gag once like Seamus or Darcy. He's a keeper." God, some days my daughter sounds like a wise old woman.

"That wins him brownie points?" I ask, and she nods.

"And he bought me ice cream. Oh, and I think Noah would make a great husband too. He's handy and can fix things. If you married both of them, you wouldn't have to do anything."

I just stare at her in surprise. "What do you mean?" I ask, unsure if she actually knows what she's saying.

"Well, Aunt Jocelyn had James, Charles, and

Susan who all came to visit and loved her. Why can't you have the same?"

Holy crap. I guess she never hid anything from Jorja. Aunt Jocelyn wasn't ashamed so she didn't hide her relationships, but I hadn't thought Jorja really knew that they were more than friends.

"Lola only has one mummy and daddy, but one of the other girls in my class has two daddies and a mommy. Why can't I have that too?"

Ah, I get what she's saying. The two daddies in the class are actually a gay couple who co-parent with the mother of their child. It's all kinds of awesome.

"Well, I guess there's nothing saying that you can't have that." I'm not going to shoot down her thoughts. She deserves to have them, and if I am considering a multi-person relationship, then her opinion means the most to me.

"So, you like Noah and Bentley?"

"Yeah, they are great. Did you know Noah skates, and he plays in a social league? What's a social league?" She cocks her head to one side and raises her eyebrows.

"They play for fun," I explain, and she grins.

"Well, maybe we can go skating together one day. Do you think Bentley can skate? We could ask him too."

"Speaking of skating, Kira said youth tryouts are on Sunday. Are you sure that's what you want to do? We can try something else if not. There are dance classes or horse riding lessons." I don't want her to be so tunnel visioned.

"Oh, Lola says she rides horses, and that would be fun, but I definitely want to play. Did you bring my skates and stick?"

"No, sorry, honey. I had to leave them back at Jocelyn's house."

She sags and looks down at her now empty bowl. "Oh, okay." Ugh, the disappointment in her tone breaks my heart.

"But you were getting too big for them anyway, so tomorrow after your playdate with Lola, we're all going to go buy new ones."

"I'm going to Lola's, not school?" She loses the dejected frown and looks excited again.

"Yeah, I have a morning class, and then I'm having lunch with Bentley. I'll meet you at the skate shop after."

"You're going on a date?" she asks excitedly.

"No, we're working on our assignment."

"Oh, so no kissing?" She sounds disappointed, and I can't help but snort with amusement.

"What do you know about kissing?"

"Darcy and Seamus kissed all the time. That's what you do when you love someone."

"No, no kissing," I tell her, but I secretly hope that maybe there will be a kiss goodbye. "Now how about we do these dishes, and then you can have a small bowl of the ice cream Bentley bought for you last night. We can take a photo of you eating it and send it to him to say thanks."

She scrambles off the sofa and picks up her bowl to take it into the kitchen. She's too short to do dishes without a step stool, so she grabs it out of its place and steps up on it. "I'll wash and you dry," she instructs, turning on the taps.

There's not a lot to do, and we get them done quickly. I could use the dishwasher, but I want Jorja to learn some responsibility, and dishes are a good start. She takes her ice cream back into the living room for a little bit more TV before bed. I'm happy to see her back to normal and that it wasn't anything major, but now that I don't have to worry about her, my mind fixates on my other drama.

Not the house, since that will get fixed bit by bit. Today there were people here working outside, regrouting the pool. I asked Ethan to leave the inside alone for today, and I'd let him know how Jorja was tomorrow. I'll shoot him a text to say he can come in tomorrow. No, what my mind is fixating on are the two delicious men who proposed such an outrageous idea. Do I like them both enough to put myself through the hard-core scrutiny of the locals, not to mention if Kash decides he wants in with the even harder scrutiny of the hockey media? Although I'm not all that worried for myself, since I have a fairly thick skin after what my parents did, my worry is for Jorja. Is that something that I want for her? I mean, I know she suggested something similar, but she's unaware of the backlash that will come along with something like this. Or maybe she knows, since she's already received questions from peers about her lack of a father. I guess it's something I need to talk to her about, but not today. I'll see how my dates with the two guys go. I may decide it's not something I'm interested in, and I wouldn't want to get her hopes up.

CHAPTER 18

Miriam

My accounting class is dry and boring, and I find my thoughts drifting to my upcoming date. Bentley called me last night to see how Jorja was, and I told him she thought his soup was the best she'd ever eaten. I could practically hear him puff up with pride through the phone, and I had to smother my giggle. He told me he'd pick me up from my place so we'd only need to have one car.

My class finally breaks up, and I'm walking across campus toward my car when someone steps in front of me, blocking my progress. When I look up from my phone, I find the girl from yesterday and her sidekick. She's looking me up and down with a sneer on her face.

"Bentley may be interested now, but you're just a pretty new face. You have nothing to offer him. He needs someone who understands his family business, someone who can help him take over when his parents retire."

What's this girl talking about? Bentley has no plans to take over his parents' business. He told me that his sister is going to be the ballbuster marketing exec. Before I can answer, a shadow appears behind me, and Rebecca flinches, taking a step back.

"The shit that continues to spew out of your mouth is really astounding. What's worse is that you honestly believe it, and so do your minions." The girl who steps up next to me is tall and statuesque, with a luscious mane of auburn hair. She's wearing a pretty summer dress with a pair of flip-flops similar to mine.

Rebecca swallows and looks around like she wants to make a quick escape. "Ah, Ginny, hi. How are you? I was just telling her that Bentley needs someone who is more appropriate for his station in life. He can slum it for now, but it's never going to last." Rebecca isn't giving up her agenda no matter how nervous Bentley's sister makes her, and I guess that requires balls.

Ginny scoffs. "No, my brother needs someone

who isn't going to take his shit and let him believe his own self-importance. He also needs someone who actually pays attention to him. You are so far off from him wanting to take over from Mom and Dad, you could be in outer space. Give it up, Rebecca. He's not interested. And leave Miriam alone." Ginny tucks her hand under my elbow and leads me away, leaving the girls behind us as Rebecca hurls abuse at the pretty coed.

"Ignore her, she's never been particularly intelligent. In preschool, she used to eat the sand in the sandbox. I hope you don't mind me stepping in. She's been the bane of my existence for years, and I love putting her in her place. My brother's momentary lapse of judgment has been a thorn in his ass ever since he made out with her at a party last year when he was drunk. Thank fuck I was there to stop him from making a monumental mistake. I overheard her talking about poking holes in a condom. I got her kicked out of our sorority for that crime." Ginny's voice is bright and bubbly, and she seems happy to control the conversation.

"Seriously? That's entrapment!" I exclaim, and she shrugs her pretty shoulders.

"Yup, but the law doesn't care too much about that. It would have at least secured her some interest in the Carlyle fortune. Now, enough about her. Kira called and told me all about my brother's mind-blowing plan. You could have knocked me over with a feather. There is no way I would have thought those three would ever be interested in an arrangement like that, but it really is perfect for them now that I think about it."

"Two of them," I correct her, and she stops and turns to me, arching a perfect eyebrow.

"Really? Because my little gossipy friend informed me that you are the former love of Kash's life, and you disappeared due to circumstances out of your control. And not only that, you're his baby mama. Am I right?"

"Well, yeah. Bloody Kira, can't keep her mouth shut."

"Pfft." Ginny waves her hand and starts walking again. "If it were anyone else, she wouldn't have said anything, but we're family, and I think that you are exactly what our guys need. I'm sick of chasing off puck bunnies and gold diggers, and I know they are sick of it too. I am fully on team Mimi. I hear you're off to lunch with my brother. Now don't let his ego steamroll you. It's a façade he uses to protect himself. Most people here don't know he's a chef, they thought he spent a year abroad getting laid." She tips her head to the side and shrugs. "I mean, I'm sure he did his fair share of that, but he worked hard to get where he is today. At his core, he's a care-giver. He wants and loves to care for his loved ones. People tease him, saying he's Noah and Kash's wife, but it makes him happy, so that's all that matters. Let him love you and your daughter, and he will be the happiest man alive. Allow him to spoil you, because we can afford it and it makes him happy. Just make sure you're sure about this before you go too much further. Bentley loves hard and fast, and you will break his heart if you change your mind further down the track. And no matter what happens, Kash will always be in your and Jorja's life, and as an extension, so will Noah and B. They are a team. Where one goes, others follow, so be sure."

I feel her warning deep within my soul and know what she said is true. I'm already half in love with him after everything he did for us the other night, but I will take her warning to heart.

She stops walking, and I look around. We're at the student parking lot. Parked next to my Impala is a beautiful blue Aston Martin with the vanity plate Ginny 1.

"Well, have fun, and we'll have to have a girls' night soon, just you, me, and Kira so I can get to know you. Kira used to tell me about you all the time, and I've been dying to meet you for years. I'm so glad what happened was out of your control and you never set out to hurt any of them. Otherwise, I'd have to hate you." With that warning, she slides into her car and puts on reflective sunglasses. She starts it up with a roar and backs out, leaving without another backward glance.

"Whoa." I breathe out a sigh at the disappearance of stormfront Ginny. Jesus, she and Kira are like two peas in a pod. It's no wonder they are good friends. I heard Kira mention her before, but because they went to different schools, they didn't see each other as much as she and I did. I was kind of jealous when she spent time with her, but maybe now I can get to know her too. I'm just glad she hasn't decided to set her hate on me. That would have been a scary experience. She was so intense, I'm assuming her hate would be too.

My house is full of contractors when I arrive home. There are people working in my room to fix the ceiling and on the roof to patch that hole as well as a team working on the stairs. I find Ethan and Noah in my kitchen, discussing the swimming pool.

"Hey, Mimi. The pool has been resealed. We'll give it a couple of days to dry out, and then we can fill it with water. There will be people here tomorrow to change out the old filtration system," Ethan explains. "When you get a chance, Noah will run through the operation of the new system with you, or we can recommend a pool maintenance company who can come and do it all for you if you want."

"Yes, that one!" I jump on the suggestion, and they both laugh.

"I'll ask Mom who we use." Ethan makes a note on his phone before wandering off to speak to his workers on the stairs.

"Is B picking you up soon?" Noah asks.

I hang my backpack up and grab a glass before turning on the tap, filling it with water. I take a long drink before answering. "Yeah, are you sure you're okay with this?" I ask, looking at him carefully for any signs of problems, but he just smiles.

"I am. I'd crash it, but he deserves alone time with you, and if I did, he would crash our date tomorrow, and I'm selfish, and I want my alone time with you too. I'm sure he'll link up with us at the game anyway."

"Is Kash going to be pissed at the two of you

once he realizes you know who I am? Who Jorja is to him?"

Noah winces. "Probably for a small moment, but he will forgive us."

"I don't want you three fighting over me. I don't want to come between you."

He sidles up to me, grabs my waist, and pulls me close. "And that's what's so amazing. You want our happiness, you're not just thinking about your own. It's fine, Mimi. Everything will work out, I promise. I think you're strong and have survived so much already. The small bumps in our road will be nothing compared to that. You just have to trust us."

He leans in and presses a gentle kiss to my lips, and I melt into him, enjoying the feeling of his arms around me. I love being held. There is nothing better than being surrounded by someone you are attracted to. I used to love feeling Kash lying on top of me, our hearts pounding and our chests heaving after we fucked like monkeys. I would hate it when he rolled off me. There is something to be said for strong, muscular men. They make me feel safe. Although I'm a little nervous, I can't wait to find out if I feel the same way about Noah and Bentley.

Does that make me a slut? Aunt Jocelyn would spank me if she heard me thinking like that. I glance around the room to make sure that her specter isn't lurking before giggling at my behavior. No, I'm not going to think that way. I'm embracing my sexuality and enjoying everything life has to offer, which hopefully includes lots and lots of orgasms.

A knock on the door has me reluctantly pulling away from his embrace, and I think he knows. He tucks me under his arm, and we answer it together. Bentley is there, and he grins when he sees us together.

"Tag, I'm it," he says, punching Noah on the arm before twirling me out from underneath it. "Work hard, Noah, and I'll make your favorite dessert this weekend," Bentley calls without looking back as he walks us to his car.

I glance back to make sure Noah is okay, and he's chuckling, rubbing the spot Bentley punched. He waves at me when I catch his eye before closing the door. Okay, he looked alright, no jealousy at all. Phew.

"You're a little flushed. Were you enjoying my friend's company?" Bentley asks as he opens the passenger door with a flourish.

"Is this how it's going to be? Are you going to want to hear what I'm doing with the others? Is this jealousy or something else?" I demand, not allowing his playful charade to blindside me.

I need to make sure he's okay, because Ginny

was right. Bentley leads with his heart and will need constant reassurance. I push him back against his car and step closer.

"Are you going to want to hear all the details of what I do with each of them? If I get down on my knees and suck Noah's cock, are you going to want me to do the same? Because for the sake of my knees, I could probably suck both of you off at the same time," I'm slightly annoyed, I hope he can hear it.

Bentley's eyes narrow and shine with desire. "No jealousy, I promise. I'm sorry if you thought that. I just don't want you to think you have to hide your relationship with him from me. I want us to be open and honest with one another, and to be honest, the thought of my friend taking care of your needs turns me on. I would fucking love to see you down on your knees, sucking our cocks, and it's definitely on my bucket list, but it's right up there with having you on your back with Noah's head between your legs, giving your sweet pussy love, while I lavish your gorgeous tits with attention."

His voice is all rumbly and low, and the visual he gives me flat out does it for me. "Oh, I like the sound of that." I grab his shirt, press up on my tiptoes, and kiss the hell out of him. It takes him a moment to catch up, but when he does, he doesn't let me down.

The kiss is all tongue and lips and teeth, and when we pull away, both of us are breathless and flushed.

"There, now that that's out of the way, where are you taking me for lunch?" I ask, stepping back and climbing into the passenger seat, trying to calm my rapid breathing.

Bentley isn't much better, and it takes him a moment to get his bearings again. "You are such a minx." He closes the door and hurries around to the driver's side and slides in before pushing a button. The car roars to life, and he shifts it into gear before easing it out onto the road. "You can't just kiss the hell out of me and think I won't get you back, but I'll let it slide for now, just know that payback will be coming."

We're both grinning like loons, and I can't remember the last time I had this much fun. Actually, that's a lie. My summer of sin with Kash was just like this—fun, easy, and full of laughs and love.

CHAPTER 19

Miriam

Bentley takes me to a local sports bar called Lou's Place. He tells me it's the place to hang out after hockey games. The owner, Louella Eastern, actually owns the Storm View Titans and loves having their fans there. "They serve amazing food, and the drinks are reasonably priced, and for those who want more than just a sports bar, there is a dance club in the basement that opens after ten in the evening."

The bar is located close to the hockey stadium, and when he holds the door open for me, I'm hit with the familiar smell of old beer and bodies, but the bar itself is pristine. The smell just tends to get into the walls.

There's still a decent crowd for lunch, but I guess it's Friday. It just seems to be college students and young people in their twenties. A few shout out and wave to Bentley, and while he waves back, he doesn't stop to talk.

He finds us an empty booth, and we slide in. I look around, taking in all the TVs, but it also has Western decor with lots of wood paneling and country themed adornments. Bentley takes out his notebook and starts scribbling things down.

"What are you writing?" I ask, but before he can answer, a waitress sidles up to our booth with a couple of menus in hand, a raised eyebrow, and a sassy hand on her hip. "Now, Bentley Carlyle III, you wouldn't happen to be partaking in corporate espionage, now would you?" Her lavender-colored eyes sparkle with joy. They really are a gorgeous color, and she accented them with black eyeliner and smoky eye shadow.

"Peaches!" Bentley stands up and hugs the girl, who I can now see is probably a teenager. I would put her age at maybe seventeen or so, but it's so hard to tell. She's gorgeous, with long black hair piled into a messy bun on her head with a pencil shoved through it. She's wearing cutoff shorts and a tight T-shirt with Lou's Place embroidered on it. She's fit and athletic with long, shapely legs and a banging body, but she's not looking at him predatorily, so I don't feel the urge to gouge out her eyeballs.

"You caught me. Of course I had to check out the most successful bar in the city if I want to be anywhere near as popular." He tries to butter her up, but she just rolls her eyes and turns to me.

"Be careful of this one, he's sneaky." She hands me a menu as he sits back down.

"This is my friend Miriam. She just moved here from London, and of course I had to take her to eat in your fine establishment. Mimi, this is Priscilla Eastern, her grandma, Louella Eastern, owns this place and the Storm View Titans. She's a living legend in this city."

"Call me Peaches, I hate that name," she tells me and leans against the booth. "How did you get this one to take you on a date? I haven't seen him with anyone for a long time."

Bentley flushes, and I chuckle. "Well, technically this is a school project," I reply, and she throws her hands up in the air.

"Ha, so I was right. Corporate espionage at its finest. You wait until I tell Grams. She was just telling me last night that she heard you told that pig Bellamy to kiss your ass. About time if you ask me. You've been carrying that restaurant for the last year. I wonder how long it will be until it goes under. She said we had to watch out because you would give us a run for our money when you finally committed." She's not angry, and everything is said with affection.

"Peaches came on summer vacations with us growing up. Her grams is friends with our grandparents, and they would often join us on family vacations. She was just a little too small to keep up with us, but she's friends with Dylan Wilson."

Peaches' smile drops, and her eyes cloud. "Ah, yeah, I was, but I ran into some trouble a few months ago and swapped from Storm View Prep to Storm View Public. I haven't seen him for a while."

"What? How come I didn't hear about that?"

She shrugs and tries to smile. "I asked Grams to make sure it didn't get around. I don't mind if you ask Dylan about it, but I don't want to talk about it again."

I reach out and give her hand a squeeze. "That's fine. I understand very well about not wanting things to get around town, although my parents made sure my gossip was spread far and wide to cover their own asses, even though it was all lies."

"You don't get along with your parents?" she asks, sounding curious.

"Fuck no." I shake my head vehemently.

"Yeah, I don't either. Actually, I don't even know

who my dad is, and my mom is a narcissistic bitch," she says quietly, looking down at her hands.

"Hey, if you ever want anyone to talk to, you can give me a call. We can compare family drama. It will be fun."

"Yeah, I'd like that." She smiles warmly before standing up. "I'll give you a few moments to look over the menu, and then I'll take your orders, okay?" She leaves, and I look over the menu, but Bentley is deceptively quiet.

"Are you worried about her?" I ask him, and he nods.

"Yeah, her mom really is a vapid bitch. Lou's basically raised her since she was a baby. I wonder what went down. I'll have to ask my sister, she'll know."

"Speaking of Ginny, I met her today," I begin, and then I tell him what happened.

"Ginny rescued you from Rebecca?" Bentley asks as we both look over the menu.

"Rescued and then basically proceeded in a roundabout way to threaten me. I mean, she was subtle, but the theme was definitely hurt you and die. Actually, hurt any of the three of you and feel her wrath."

Bentley chuckles awkwardly. "Yeah, we're a fairly close-knit extended family. We are basically in each other's pockets all the time, but now that she mentioned it, Peaches hasn't been around for a few months. Lou explained it by saying she's a teenager with her own friends, but maybe it was more." He chews on his lip, and I see worry in his eyes. "I feel like maybe we don't include her as much as we should because she's younger. Dylan too, but he's so busy with hockey now that he's been missing from some of the most recent family things as well."

"Oh, believe me, I think it's awesome, and don't worry too much. Teenagers are feeling their way into adulthood. It's tricky and scary, and sometimes you just have to let them feel their own way. I'm sure if what you say is true, Louella is watching her granddaughter like a hawk. She'll be okay."

"Maybe I should tell Ginny and Kira anyway. They'll make sure she's okay." He pulls out his phone, but I put my hand over it.

"Leave it be for now. I'm sure she knows she can speak to them if she wants to. I promise I'll drop back in another time when you're not with me and see if she wants to talk. Whatever it is, she obviously doesn't want her surrogate big brothers to know."

"Yeah, okay, but I won't let this go. I want you to tell me everything you find out. If heads need to be crushed, me and the guys will take care of it." He's so serious, and he cracks his knuckles to make sure I get the point.

I can't help but laugh. "You're so freaking adorable," I say.

"Yeah, if you like dorks." Peaches has returned to take our order, and Bentley flips her off.

"Takes one to know one," he replies childishly. They banter back and forth, but eventually, we place our order after I hurry to read the menu.

"I'll be back with your drinks in a moment." She gathers the menus and leaves again.

Bentley reaches across the table and grabs my hand. "Tell me about living in London." We spend two hours just talking and comparing London stories, and he tells me about his time in Paris, and we get to know each other a little better. The food is amazing, and while we do talk a little bit about our project, I think we've both accepted that this is a date, not school work.

"Although this has been fun, we really do need to do some work on our project," I tell him after Peaches takes away our dirty dishes.

"Yeah, how about we get together next week at the library or your place and do some serious work?"

"Not yours?" I ask, not thinking straight, and he grimaces.

"I'm not sure where you and Kash are going to

be next week. If he's actively hating you, then having you at our place won't work."

My stomach rolls, and I have to work hard not to bring my food up. I know I have to tell him, but I'm really terrified. Bentley must see that.

"Hey, that's worst-case scenario, and I'm sure it won't be like that."

"From your mouth to God's ears," I mutter, repeating one of Jocelyn's favorite sayings. My message alert sounds, and I look down. It's a message from Kira with the address of the skate shop. "Ugh, this has been so much fun, but I need to be a responsible parent now." Bentley waves to Peaches for the bill. "Can you drop me off at Cold Comfort? That's a cool name."

"What are you shopping for there?" he asks, his forehead wrinkling in confusion.

Before I can answer, Peaches comes over and gives him a kiss on the cheek. "It's on the house for you. Give my love to the gang when you see them next. It was nice meeting you, Miriam." She smiles sweetly, and we thank her before taking our leave.

On the way back to the car, I answer him. "Jorja is trying out for the youth hockey league on Sunday with Lola. Kira is going to help us buy some gear. I had to leave her skates back in London."

"Jorja wants to play hockey? It's a rough sport,

and you have to be a good skater to join a team. Lola's been on skates since she could walk." Bentley is so cute, and his worry for Jorja is endearing.

"Oh, I think she'll do okay. She knows how to skate," I hedge, not wanting to admit what a demon she is on skates.

He chews his lip and opens his car with the key fob. "But she's so little and delicate."

I snort, but I guess he did see at her most vulnerable. He hasn't had the pleasure of meeting hurricane Jorja yet.

I reach over and pat him on the shoulder. "Trust me, she will be fine. Do you want to come shopping? Do you know anything about hockey gear?" I ask him. I know Noah used to play, but I'm not sure about Bentley.

"Yeah, I'd love to." He beams at me. "And yes, I played for years. I was offered a scholarship like Liam and Kash, but I declined it because I knew I wanted to go to Paris. Hockey is fun, but I just didn't have the killer drive like they do. I bet she looks so adorable in all that gear, like the Stay-Puft Marshmallow Man."

I grimace. He better not tease her, because she takes hockey seriously. She's likely to clobber him with her stick.

Before I know it, it's Saturday evening and time for my date with Noah. Shopping for gear was fun, and the girls are fully kitted out for tomorrow.

Jorja is so excited to be attending the hockey game with Lola and Kira. "Mama, Lola's daddy plays for the team we're going to see. Can you believe it? He's amazing," Jorja gushes as I finish getting ready for my date. She's sitting on my bed. My room smells like the paint the builders used on the ceiling, which looks as good as new. Ethan really pushed them to get it finished quickly, which I appreciate. "We have seats right next to the ice. It's going to be so much fun."

"I did know that, and he is pretty awesome. Make sure you use your manners, okay? If you need me, I'll be there, but I'll be sitting somewhere different with Noah," I remind her as I finish applying a swipe of mascara to my lashes. Placing the wand back in the tube, I take stock of my appearance. I'm wearing a pair of black skinny jeans, my heeled boots, and a pretty top. I'll probably be hot at wherever we're going for dinner, but I know how cold the ice rink will be, so I dressed for that.

When I head back into the bedroom, Jorja cocks her head and nods her approval.

"You look really pretty, Mama. You should wear these." She has my jewelry box in her lap, and she's obviously been pawing through it. In her hand are a pair of earrings that make me freeze.

I haven't seen them in years. They were one of the only things I managed to grab before my parents shipped me off to London. Kash bought them for me a few weeks into our relationship. We'd snuck off and spent the day in a neighboring town, which had an artisans' fair. They are a little pair of silver infinity symbols with pink gemmed hearts in the middle of them. He saw me looking at them and snuck back and bought them when I was distracted. They were the first thing in years that someone had given me other than birthday presents I adored them. I didn't wear anything else that summer.

"They are just as pretty as you are. When am I going to be old enough to get my ears pierced? I want to wear pretty earrings too."

I crouch down and take them from her little hand. "It hurts to have your ears pierced," I warn her as I take out my gold hoops and replace them with the infinity symbols. Standing up, I go into my closet, my emotions all over the place, and grab a big, cable-knit sweater with a cowled neck in a shade of pink that matches the gems in my earrings. I also grab the beanie I picked up yesterday. I've always gotten cold whenever I've been a spectator. It's completely different from playing where you sweat like crazy.

"Okay, are you ready to rock and roll? Noah is going to be here soon, and we're going to drop you off at Lola's place."

"Are you going to kiss Noah?" she asks me as she jumps off the bed and follows me out of the room.

She already has an overnight bag packed, and it's sitting at the front door, but she has her scarf and beanie on. I warned her she will be hot, but she doesn't care. She's also wearing a Storm View Titans hockey jersey. Bentley bought it for her, and it has number fourteen on it. He whispered to me that it was Kash's number and asked if it was alright. I couldn't really say no. If he wasn't already a big hit with my pocket dynamo, this basically sealed the deal.

He gave us a lift home, happily swapping her car seat from Kira's car to his. The two of them giggled all the way home, talking about Harry Potter. Apparently, it's their favorite movie. I've only allowed Jorja to watch up to number three because I'm not sure she's ready for the death in four, much to her disgust, but she tried to convince me that she could watch it with Bentley and he could hold her hand if she got scared. You should have seen him puff up with pride at the thought of comforting her. I'm pretty sure they are both going to wear me down. When she heard that he has a sister named Ginny, she instantly demanded to meet her. Apparently that's going to happen tonight, because she will be at the game too.

"Maybe. How do you feel about that?" I ask her as we grab her bag, and I tuck my phone into my pocket. I don't need anything else, since that has everything I need.

She's quiet for a moment as I grab her jacket off the coat rack as I hear a car pull up outside.

I wait, though, because I want to hear her answer.

"Well, it's only fair because I saw Bentley kiss you goodbye yesterday," she announces, reaching for her jacket, and my eyebrows jump.

"You did?" I ask her, and she giggles.

"I looked out the front window when you walked him back out to his car. He put his hand on your bottom." Her eyes are wide when she says this.

"Oh my lord. Jorja Kennedy, you are in so much trouble. What have I told you about being a snoop?"

"But, Mama, how am I supposed to find things out if I don't snoop?" she asks innocently, batting her eyelashes.

"Some things are not for children." There's a knock on the door, and Jorja flings it open.

"Hi, Noah, hi. If you kiss Mama today, you need to put your hand on her bottom and give it a squeeze." She mimes squeezing something with her hands. "That's how Bentley did it."

Fuck my life. My chin drops to my chest, and I feel a wave of embarrassment wash over me, but Noah just bursts out laughing.

"Is that right? Well, I'll make sure to remember that," he promises her, and she nods.

"Good. Come on, let's go." She drags him outside by the hand before either of us can greet one another. I just follow behind with her overnight bag, wondering if there is a crack in my sidewalk big enough to swallow me up.

CHAPTER 20

Noah

I can't stop chuckling as I drive the ten minutes from Miriam's to the Worthingtons' place. Jorja is a spitfire. She talks a million miles an hour, telling me all about the swimming pool is now filled up with water and that they can swim soon.

"I can't wait to go for a swim. Mama said I can have a unicorn floatie, and we're going to get something for Lola too for when she comes to visit so she doesn't miss out. But mine will be the biggest, as big as a house," she declares, holding her arms wide to show me exactly how big.

"How is it going to fit in the pool?" I ask, looking back at her in the mirror with wide eyes, and she giggles.

"Well, maybe not that big, but it will be big and pretty, and if you're good and kiss Mama, then you can float on it with me."

Miriam tenses next to me, and I reach over and give her hand a squeeze.

"Nothing like having your daughter pimp you out," she mutters out of the side of her mouth, and I grin. I love spending time with them both. I'm already head over heels for Jorja, and I'm heading that way with her mother despite not having spent a significant amount of time with her.

"So I have to kiss your mama to be allowed to swim in your pool?" I ask, and she nods sagely.

"Yes, and maybe you and Bentley can have a sleepover with her too, like Lola's mom and dad do. They are always so happy in the morning, and they haven't had coffee yet. They are always smooching and cuddling on the couch. Lola says it's gross, but I like it."

"How do you know this?" I ask, and she just looks at me like I'm stupid.

"Lola told me."

"Of course she did, but if they are anything like what they were when we were teenagers, she's not wrong. Kash and I were always being subjected to gross PDA." Miriam leans her head back on the headrest and closes her eyes behind her sunglasses, smiling like she's remembering. "We were always doing things as a foursome. It's how He Who Shall Not Be Named and I ended up together."

"Voldemort?" Jorja squeaks, and when I look back at her again, she looks horrified.

Miriam chuckles. "Well, I thought he was for a while, but no, not Voldemort."

Before Jorja can ask any more questions, I pull into Kira and Liam's driveway. "Oh look, here we are," Mimi calls, sounding relieved, and Jorja is instantly distracted.

We hustle her inside, and within ten minutes, we're on our way again with Kira's reassurance that Jorja will be fine.

Miriam is biting her lip with worry and keeps glancing back as I drive away. "Hey, Jorja will be okay. Kira's a good mom, I promise." I reach over and grab her hand again, giving it a squeeze.

"Oh, I'm not worried about that. I trust her with my daughter's life. I'm worried about what her parents are going to say. She told me they won't even notice, but I'm worried they will."

"I don't think they will. I only put two and two together because I saw all of you together. They are only going to see Lola's classmate. Bentley and Ginny know the truth and will run interference. I promise, no one is revealing anything until you are ready."

She breathes out a heavy sigh. "Yeah, I'm dreading Monday, but I can't wait until everyone knows. It will be a heavy burden off my shoulders."

"And your parents and grandparents?" I ask, broaching a subject we haven't really talked about, and I know she would like to avoid it, but it's one we need to have.

She's quiet for a moment, and I concentrate on getting us where we are going. I considered heading to Lou's Place, but it will be full of hockey fans pregaming or settling in to watch the game. It will be loud and noisy, and to be honest, I want to be selfish, even if it's for a short while.

I know a relationship like we are trying to attempt will be all about communication and sharing, but we all deserve alone time with her, and I'm going to make the most of mine, just like Bentley did yesterday.

"Ugh. My parents don't deserve to hear it from me, not to mention they threatened to have her taken away. I think I want to make sure everything is solid with Kash first, and if he doesn't want to step up to the plate, then Kira assured me Mary and Simon would help me make sure they can't get her. If I at least have most of my ducks in a row, I'll feel more confident dealing with my parents. Despite everything, they still have the ability to reduce me to a cowering, insecure twelve-year-old every time I'm around them." She sounds so sad, and my soul aches for young Miriam. Some people don't deserve to have children. I'm going to make sure she never feels like that again. "As for my grandparents." She shrugs helplessly, "I'm not sure yet."

"Okay, once we talk to Kash, no matter how he reacts, we will sit down and form a plan. I don't want to hide our relationship from my family, and Bentley won't either. Despite it being unconventional, I'm certain our families will support us. With the weight of the Youngs, Carlyles, and Wilsons behind you, your parents won't stand a chance."

"Okay, yeah, that sounds really good." She looks at me, and I can see the worry in her eyes.

"But for now, I don't want to talk about that. I want to talk about other things. I want to get to the heart of Miriam Kennedy. What makes you tick? Are you ready to get down and dirty with me?" I lighten my tone as I pull into the restaurant parking lot.

The worry clears from her face, and she grins. "You bet I am."

I climb out and hurry around, opening her door for her before she can. I put my hand on her back and escort her to the restaurant. It's the one Bentley used to work at. I'm unsure about what the food will be like now that he's not here, but I'm hoping it's still good.

A hostess shows us to our table as I warn, "Bentley used to work here, but the chef was taking advantage of him, so he quit recently. I'm hoping the food is still okay."

She shrugs. "I would have been happy with a hotdog at the game. I'm just looking forward to spending time with you."

It's my turn to sigh with relief. Thank goodness she's not high maintenance and needy like my last girlfriend. She wouldn't have stood for a hotdog at the game. I instantly feel myself relax. I knew she wasn't like that, but it's a relief to have that reassurance.

The staff members are efficient and professional, and the waitress leaves us with our menus, promising to return to get our order soon. We look at the options, and I start peppering her with questions.

"So what does Miriam like to do when she's not moving, renovating a house, and being a mother and a college student?"

She looks startled for a moment before chuckling. "Sleep?" she replies, but then she shakes her head. "Ah, to be honest, I haven't done more than be a worried mother for the last six years, but I do like to read, and I love going to the movies, but none of that serious stuff. Life is serious enough. I want to go to movies that allow me to escape reality. Superheroes, dinosaurs, robots, explosions, and magic. If the movie doesn't have that then I'm not interested."

I smile and nod, encouraging her.

"I mean, I love to skate, but I never wanted to do something professional. It was a way for me to go to college. My parents informed me they weren't going to pay for me to go."

I gape at her in shock. I thought the Kennedy family was rich. I'm almost certain her grandparents are. She must see my face.

"Oh, I could have asked my grandparents. They had no idea that my parents weren't going to, but it was a big fuck you to my parents not to need them. I mean, it didn't matter in the end. I am almost certain they had plans to marry me off to some old dude for business reasons, but getting pregnant fucked with all of that anyway."

"You're joking." I can't believe what I'm hearing, but I can tell by the look in her eyes that she's not.

"No, I'm pretty sure there is something fundamentally wrong with my parents, but I have no idea why. My grandparents are lovely, wonderful, and kind, or they were, and Mae said they never believed my parents' lies."

"They still are. I have a lot of respect for them, and Ethan loves your grandma's 'personal projects.'"

She raises her eyebrows quizzically.

"She regularly has things done to her house, but it's always something unusual. She just had their guesthouse bathroom redone, and she had it done like a Roman spa, with mosaics and a huge Roman bathtub. She's quirky and fun."

Miriam giggles. "I remember her teasing Grandpa about doing things like that. He would just grunt and pretend to be annoyed, but I know he loved indulging her quirks. I remember when that movie *Fifty Shades of Grey* came out, she threatened to build her own secret sex room. My parents were mortified because she announced it at the dinner table with about thirty of Storm View's wealthiest and most influential people in attendance. Grandpa blushed but didn't complain. It was awesome."

I choke on a laugh and shake my head. "I know Ethan built her a secret room last year, but he thought she just wanted it for a reading room. Oh, I can't wait to tell him what it was."

Miriam shrugs, her eyes bright with amusement. "I mean, it might just be a reading room, but

I'd love to see Ethan's face when you tell him. If Grandma had her way, her whole house would be full of tunnels and secret rooms. I asked why they didn't sell and build again, but she assured me she was happy right where she was. Looking back now, I think maybe she didn't want to go too far from my parents so they could keep an eye on them. Hindsight is an interesting thing, and I see so much clearer now. My parents are not good people, and I think my grandparents knew." The giggles are gone now, and I want to kick myself. I hate seeing her sad.

Just then, the waitress comes back and takes our order. When she leaves, I steer the conversation away from her parents. "Okay, so we have reading, blockbuster movies, and skating. What else makes Miriam Kennedy tick?"

She smiles gently. "Every summer, Seamus, Darcy, Jocelyn, Jorja, and I would go on vacation. London was always so busy during those months, and Jocelyn hated it, so we would do things. We've been to Spain, Italy, France, Scotland, Iceland, and the Greek islands, which were all amazing, but my very favorite time was when we used to hire a house in either Brighton or Cornwall and spend the days splashing on the beach and exploring the towns or 'camping.'" Her fingers lift with the word *camping*, putting them in quotations, and she giggles. "I told them about the couple of times I went camping with the Youngs and how happy I was with them, and they wanted to recreate that for me. But none of them were campers, so we hired a cabin on the lake, and we'd canoe and fish and grill without the bugs and sleeping bags. They tried so hard to make me smile, and I will never be able to repay them. Jorja loves it too, even though she was too small to remember a lot of the trips."

"Hey, that's cool, we all love outdoor summer activities. The Carlyles have a house on the lake. We used to spend a lot of summers there."

"Yeah, I remember. Kira and Kash would go away for two weeks every summer, and I would dread it. The Youngs invited me to come, but my parents would never let me. I spent those two weeks moping and getting sore thumbs from texting Kira."

"Yeah, Kira never went anywhere without her phone in her hand. She said it was like having you close by. I can't believe none of us ever met before."

She opens her mouth to answer but frowns as I feel a hand on my shoulder. Looking up, I groan quietly to myself. Missy, my ex-girlfriend, is standing there, dressed in a skimpy little black dress with thick makeup and a shiny diamond pendant around her neck.

"Noah, how lovely to see you. I was just telling

Jason that we hadn't seen you in a while, and here you are." She nods in the direction of her own table. Sitting there is the asshole she cheated on me with. He's captain of the basketball team, and rumor has it, scouts from a couple of the pro ball teams have their eye on him. He nods his head. He knows what he did, but neither of them feel any remorse, and you can't really expect that with narcissistic people.

"Go away, Missy, I'm not interested," I tell her, and she puckers her mouth with disappointment.

"Don't be like that, Noah. We used to be so close." She's talking to me, but her eyes haven't left Miriam. "Who's your friend?"

"None of your business, and we were close until Ginny caught you fucking Jason while you were supposed to be my girlfriend. Now we are anything but close. Hurry back to your meal ticket before he loses interest." I nod to her table, and she whirls around to find her boyfriend flirting with their server. Her eyes narrow, and she stomps off again without another word.

"God, what a bitch," I mutter. "I'm sorry you had to see that. I've made some errors in judgment in the past."

She reaches over and grabs my hand. "Don't worry about it. She didn't bother me in the least. I'm just sad to see you upset. Now how about I hear all about what makes Noah Wilson tick?" She throws my own line of questioning back in my face, distracting me from Missy.

The rest of the meal is fun, and we connect on a level that just amazes me. It's like we've been friends for years. Eventually, we have to leave if we're going to make it to the game on time, so I pay the bill and we depart. Missy waves to me as we pass her table, but I ignore it.

As we drive toward the hockey arena, I feel Mimi get more and more tense. "Hey, it's okay. I got us seats up in the back, and he won't even know you're there. I promise. He will be too focused on the game."

Out of the corner of my eye, I see her relax a little and nod. "Okay, yeah, sorry. I was getting inside my head. Of course he won't see us, and he won't have any clue who Jorja is. Thanks, Noah. I don't know what I'd do without you and Bentley."

I grin, feeling pretty pleased with myself. I love knowing this woman trusts me, but also that I can help comfort and reassure her.

CHAPTER 21

Kashton

The locker room vibe is edgy and loud as everyone gears up for the first game of the season. I take a moment to sit and breathe, sticking my earbuds in my ear and turning the volume up on my "getting in the zone" playlist. This one is full of calming instrumentals that help me get my mind where it needs to be. I push out all the other worries and stressors in my life and just concentrate on the soothing sounds of rain on a roof or waves crashing against the shore. My body relaxes as I breathe in and out, closing my eyes to block out all the frenetic activity of my teammates. They know to leave me be for a good half an hour. They avoid talking to me or jostling me as they get ready. They respect that this is my way of getting ready to kick ass on the ice and support anything that helps me play better.

I can feel my best friend somewhere by my side, going through his own pregame routine. He likes to watch videos of my sister and his daughter to center himself. I tease him, but I secretly want that. I thought I had it once, someone I wanted to spend my life with. Sure, we were young, but I knew we were it. It would have been hard work but completely worth it to have her permanently in my life. I thought we were both on the same page, and then it all fell apart.

I was so angry—angry that I'd been deceived and tricked into believing I meant as much to her as she did to me. I lashed out in the worst possible way, drinking and partying and fucking random puck bunnies, trying to destroy every dishonest memory I had of her until my sister and Liam staged an intervention.

They dragged me out of the party I was at, some frat thing that some of the hockey guys had gone to. I was balls deep in a chick, and Kira just burst into the room, hauling the girl off me and throwing her to the floor. "This has gone on long enough. Put your dick away and get dressed, you're done."

She left the room, and I remember rolling over and vomiting—not from the alcohol I consumed, but from the look of disgust and disappointment on my sister's face. Liam helped me clean up, and the two of them drove me to a diner, gave me black coffee and some greasy food, and had a come to Jesus moment with me.

"What happened to you? You're fucking everything up. You're going to lose your scholarship if you keep going this way," Liam scolded, and Kira just looked at me with sad eyes.

"You know why. I told you all about it when she disappeared. I fucking loved her. She was it for me," I snarled at him and took a sip of the coffee, shuddering at its bitter flavor.

"Okay, I know you're angry, but have you really stopped to think about this? I was pissed too, but then I thought about everything I know about Mimi and her parents. At first, I was suspicious, since I barely saw her over summer, but dude, according to you, that's because you were shacked up together. You didn't even go to the lake this year with the others. And if she wasn't with you, she was with me. When, exactly, could she have been hooking up with drug dealers and a greasy motorcycle gang? If she wasn't with you, then she was with me. I never saw any evidence of drug use apart from an occasional joint with us at a party." Kira's words were soft, but they packed a punch. "Her parents haven't given two fucks about her since she was born. She either spent all her time with us or staying with her grandparents. I

didn't ever see her parents come to a school event. It was always Grandma and Grandpa Kennedy. When she had a birthday party, it was always at Grandma's place. Grandpa Kennedy taught her to drive. She wasn't allowed to have a job, because her parents didn't want her to be independent. She was always having to ask them for money. They didn't always give it to her either, and she hated asking her grandma and grandpa for anything. Look, I went over there today, demanding to know where she was. Mr. Kennedy threatened to call the cops on me, so I went to see Grandma and Grandpa. They don't believe it either. They've hired a private detective to find her."

My stomach rolled, and I threw myself out of my seat, racing to the bathroom before losing the remaining contents of my stomach. I retched until my stomach was empty, and then I retched a little more. Finally, I flushed the toilet and moved to the sink to wash up. I stared at myself in the mirror and grimaced. In the harsh yellow light, I looked sallow, and my eyes were bloodshot. I was not in peak condition, and it showed in hockey games. I'd become sloppy, and even the coach noticed, moving me to the second line. I splashed some cold water on my face and pushed my hair back from my forehead. It'd grown long and unruly, and I wasn't looking after it like I should.

What if Kira was right? Miriam just disappeared

after we had spent almost every day together for weeks. She was my everything, and I thought I was hers. She was worried about me going off to college, and that with her still in high school, I would forget about her, but I swore I wouldn't. She was my heart and soul. I'd crushed on her for years but was too afraid that she just saw me as a brother figure, but at my graduation party, we all drank a little too much, and she stumbled and I caught her, and before I knew it, we were kissing, and that quickly led to the best sex of my life. We couldn't keep our hands off each other. When I woke the next morning, I was worried she would think it was a mistake, but she just snuggled into my side, and when I told her that I'd loved her for a long time, she said she felt the same way. We became inseparable but decided to keep it a secret for a little while. We wanted to enjoy ourselves before we told anyone, and Mimi wanted to make sure that what I felt was real, because she didn't want to hurt Kira if we didn't work out. Was I too quick to believe her parents? When I thought about it now, all I wanted to do was rant and cry and scream because I believed Kira was right. There was no way she would just disappear without a word to anyone. Not my Mimi. Sure, her parents were assholes, but she had others who loved her. Something wasn't right, and I had been an idiot. Fuck, I didn't deserve her. At the first sign of trouble, I completely fucked up. I felt dirty and sick, and I couldn't even look at myself in the mirror anymore.

I returned to the table with my head hanging, everything in me dying to confront her parents. Kira and Liam could see the comprehension in my eyes.

"Hey, don't beat yourself up. We believed it too for a while." Liam tried to console me, and I shook my head.

"Yeah, but you didn't fuck your way through a good portion of the sororities and a whole heap of puck bunnies and flush your hockey career down the toilet," I argued, slumping on my side of the booth. "She's never going to forgive me."

"If I know my friend, she will. Once she realizes her parents told us lies, she will place any anger and blame solely on the two people responsible—them." Kira was adamant.

"But I didn't have faith in her," I cried out, and Kira got up and came over to my side of the booth, wrapping her arms around me and pressing her forehead against mine.

"Neither of us did in the face of that proof, but it must have been doctored. Grandpa Kennedy is chasing down leads."

After that, all I did was play hockey, eat, and sleep. When I signed with the Storm View Titans, I bought my house, and Bentley and Noah moved in. Sure, we had a few parties, but I never drink until

I'm drunk anymore. My career is worth more than that, and I avoid women as much as possible. Some people have suggested that maybe I'm gay and in a relationship with one of the boys, but it couldn't be further from the truth. I found my true love and lost her. No one will ever measure up to her, and if I'm with someone else, the specter of Mimi will never be fair to them.

That was almost six years ago, though, and Mimi seems to have disappeared without a trace.. There is a passport in her name, but there is no record of her ever leaving the country, so the PI didn't think it was worth searching for her overseas. I guess it's probably time I moved on, but I haven't wanted to. There's still a small part of me that hopes that she will reappear one day. Every time I would go around to the Kennedys' to ask them if they had heard from her, they threatened to call the police until I signed with the Storm View Titans. Now they are happy to associate with me. Eric is always asking me if he can manage my money, but I wouldn't trust him as far as I could throw him. He's a slimy weasel, and Leticia isn't much better. She approached me in quiet corners and blatantly tried to seduce me. They are two disgusting individuals, and how Mimi turned out as kind and loving as she did is beyond me.

I take a deep breath and pull out my earbuds. My centering routine is not working today. Maybe it's thoughts of Mimi and her parents, or maybe it's something else, but I have a feeling something is about to change. I switch my Bluetooth over to the speaker in my locker and swap my playlist to my "pump me up" playlist. I turn it up loud, and the locker room cheers as AC/DC's "Thunderstruck" starts playing.

"Yes, Kash is ready to kick some ass!" Vladimir crows, his Russian accent thick. "It is time to break some bones." He and his co-defenseman, Theo, chest bump, already in their pads.

"You okay, man?" Liam asks quietly, looking over as he laces his skates. "You've been quiet."

"Yeah, I'm okay. Noah isn't going to sit with the family tonight. He has a date and didn't want to subject her to all that entails."

Liam chuckles. "I don't blame him. They are a lot to take all at once."

"But it's kind of messing with game traditions. I know it's stupid, but it makes me feel restless."

Liam snorts. "You don't have to explain anything to me. I've been carrying around one of Kira's thongs since I signed with the Titans. It was in my pocket the night I got offered my contract, and I consider it my lucky charm."

I wrinkle my nose and pretend to gag. "Dude, TMI. I know sports players are ridiculously superstitious, but that's stupid." I pull on my pads, not wanting to know anything gross about my best friend and my sister.

Liam rolls his eyes. "Not as bad as that." He nods at our goalie, who is participating in his traditional, pregame voodoo ritual. Ezekiel "Witch Doctor" Jones is of Cajun descent, and a direct descendant of Marie Leveau. His mocha-colored skin shines in the harsh lights of the locker room. He has something smoking in the little altar he has set up in his locker. He swears it's what makes him such a good goalie, and thankfully our coaching team leaves him be. It's not harming anyone, and we're all used to the smell now. At least he's not slaughtering a chicken, which he has tried before. Coach shut that shit down immediately.

"Alright, assholes, stop fucking around. I want you out on the ice and warming up in ten minutes," the coach shouts. "Play hard, do what you do best, and we will come out winners. I'm excited to see this team go all the way to the playoffs this year. This is our fucking year." He ends his short but sweet motivational speech to cheers of the team.

Everyone puts their hands in and yells, "Titans," before the locker room starts to empty out. The coaching and support staff and most of the team head out onto the ice.

The only people left are the starting lineup. Our center and team captain Joe is a mountain of a man who is coming to the end of his career, but is still fucking dynamite on the ice. Me and Liam are the forwards, with Vlad and Theo as our defensemen, and Zeke rounds us out as goalie. I look up from tying my laces. I'll redo them once I've been on the ice a bit.

"You guys good?" Joe asks, arching an eyebrow. "Heads in the game?"

I stand up and grab my jersey, pulling it over my head—number fourteen. It was the date of Mimi's birthday. Pulling it down over my pads, I strap on my neck guard and pull on my helmet before shoving my gloves on my hands.

"Never better," I tell him as I pull my helmet over my head. "Lead on, Captain." The five of us bow our heads to him, and he rolls his eyes.

"Right. Skate hard and fast, and let's smash those pucks home. May your hands and feet be fast." He smacks Zeke on the helmet and leads us out of the locker room.

I pick up my stick, and Liam and I knock them together in a ritual we haven't missed once since we've played together on the Titans.

The arena is loud, and the atmosphere is electric as I skate out onto the ice to warm up with the rest of my team. Liam and I have a ritual. We do a lap and find Lola in the crowd. She puts her hand up to the glass for a high five, and we give her one, but when we get there, there's another little girl standing next to her, jumping up and down, cheering. She watches Liam give Lola a high five with wide-mouthed awe before sticking her hand up to the glass and looking at me with hope. I put my hand up to hers and give her a glass high five, and she screams and jumps with excitement.

I'm not sure who she is, but she's a gorgeous child, and there's something familiar about her. I'll have to ask Kira. Maybe she's been at their place when I've been there. As I skate away, I see her and Lola jump up and down together, holding hands, and when her back is to me, I see she's wearing a jersey with the number fourteen and the name "Young" on the back. I skate to a halt, and ice flicks up. I frown as I try to work out how I know her, but then Bentley sits down next to her, and she smiles and climbs into his lap, talking a million miles an hour. I watch Ginny join them, and she climbs from Bentley's lap to hers, her little hands reaching for Ginny's auburn hair. I watch as the three of them laugh about something.

"Hey, man, what's wrong?" Liam skates up to me, nudging my shoulder.

"Who is that with Bentley and Ginny? She looks like she's friends with Lola."

"That's Jorja, Lola's best friend from school. She and her mother just moved here from London. Jorja and Lola have become fast friends," Liam tells me. "I haven't met her yet, but she's coming for dinner on Monday when you and your parents do."

"Why is she wearing my jersey, and how does she know Bentley?"

"Her mother was on a date with him yesterday, and they met Kira and the girls to go shopping. Lola needed new gear for the tryouts tomorrow. Lola said Bentley bought her the shirt when Kira bought her one with my number." He shrugs and skates away, and I know that I should too, but there's something eating at the edge of my mind.

I shake my head and know I need to get my head in the game. I have another tradition that I need to observe before I turn my full attention to annihilating the other team. I do a full lap of the rink, my eyes searching the crowd for blondes. Here and there, my eyes catch on one, and my heart jumps only to slow again when I realize it's not Mim. I mean, I know she's not going to be at a home game, and I look harder at the away games, but since that day, I haven't given up hope of seeing her one day. I catch sight of a long, straight blonde ponytail and a curvy ass and do a double take. I can't see the girl, since her back is to me, but she's with Noah. This must be his date. The two of them are making their way to the top of the stands in the nosebleed section. I hope things go well for him so they can sit with the family next time. Heaving out a sigh, I finish my lap and let the distraction and disappointment flow away. It's time to turn my attention to winning.

CHAPTER 22

Miriam

The arena is cold but packed with people, so the cold doesn't last very long. Noah and I have seats in the back, far away from all the action of the ring, and I'm grateful. People shout and cheer for the Storm View Titans, who have just taken to the ice and are warming up.

Noah's hand is on my back in a comforting gesture as we walk up the stairs to our seat. My heart races as we sit down, and I scan the ice for Kashton. I just about swallowed my tongue yesterday when Bentley bought Jorja a jersey that had "Young" on it and his number. Fourteen is my birthdate. Is that a coincidence, or does it mean something more? Is it possible he won't be as mad as I thought he would be? Shit, that's all going to change the minute he finds out about Jorja.

Despite everyone's reassurance, I'm almost certain he's never going to forgive me. I just hope he doesn't try to take her from me.

"Over there." I follow the line of Noah's finger and feel lightheaded as I finally catch sight of the love of my life for the first time in six years. I can't see him properly, because of the glare of his visor, but I know in my heart it's him. His skating style is as familiar as my own. He looks like he's bulked up considerably since high school, but the pads make it hard to tell anything else.

It's not long before the puck is dropped and the Titans skate rings around their competition. The first period is dominated by the Titans with many shots at the net, but the goalie for the other team has magic moves, and despite their many attempts, he blocks everything, so the score is zero-zero at the end of the first period. The Titans' goalie is just as impressive, although he didn't have to defend as often.

My heart is racing, and my stomach is rolling with adrenaline. "Wow," I murmur, speaking to Noah for the first time since the game started. We've both cheered and shouted advice, but neither of us have said a word to each other. I laugh sheepishly. "Sorry I've been so unsociable. It's been a while since I went to a game. I forgot how much I love it."

A grin spreads across his face, and he shakes his head. "No, trust me, it's not a problem. I would have felt rude ignoring you if you tried to talk to me during the game." The relief is instant as he grabs my hand. "You know, it's nice not having to force anything. We can just be. Thank you. Now how about I buy you some popcorn or something?" He pulls me out of my seat, and we battle the crowd on our way to the concession stand. We pass a bathroom on the way, and I duck in quickly before continuing. When I return, Noah has his back to me and he's talking to someone.

"Noah, hi, we're not sitting with the family today because Lou invited us to sit in her box with her for the opening game." Mae's voice is familiar, but the next one has me freezing on the spot.

"Oh, Noah, is Ethan here? I want to thank him again for the amazing job he did on my Roman bath." My grandma's voice hasn't changed a bit in the years I've been gone. I'd still be able to pick her out of a crowd. I'm frozen, trying to decide whether to duck back into the bathrooms or run when someone jostles Noah and he stumbles, exposing me to the view of both ladies.

"Oh!" Mae gasps and puts her hand up to her mouth before turning to look at her friend with shock in her eyes.

My grandma sees me. "Miriam?" It's like she can't quite believe her eyes, and I guess I'm six years older than I was when she last saw me.

"Hi, Grandma," I say, and she pales considerably and sways. Noah leaps forward just in time to catch my grandma as she literally swoons.

"Violet!" Mae exclaims just as I hear another voice behind me.

"Hi, Mama! Hi, Noah! Did you see the game? It was so good!" Jorja appears next to me, and it's my turn to pale as I take in who she's with. Lola and Kira are with her, but so is Mary Young, Kash's mother.

"Miriam?" She looks like she's seen a ghost, but then her eyes narrow, and she looks from me to Jorja, and I can see the wheels turning in her head as she puts everything together. Her hands go to her hips, and she looks at Kira. "What the fuck is going on?"

"Oh my god, I'm so sorry," Kira tells me as Mae pats my grandma's face, trying to get her to come around. She does, but she just stares at me with wide eyes, muttering to herself.

I'm torn between taking care of my grandma and trying to explain things to an irate Mary. Before I can offer up any words, though, Noah comes to my rescue.

"Hey, pumpkin, what are you doing?" He distracts everyone by talking to Jorja who has been looking between all the adults with confusion.

"We're getting popcorn and sodas, but we have to hurry because the game will start again soon." Jorja is bouncing up and down on the spot, oblivious to the nail-biting tension.

"Well, that sounds like fun. Why doesn't Kira take you and Lola to do that, and then the rest of us will head back up to Lou's box so Miriam can explain what is going on?" Mae suggests as Jorja gives her a hug. My grandma and Mary both look at Mae warily, and Mae blushes slightly but stands her ground.

My grandma pushes off Noah, her hand going to his cheek and giving it a pat. "Thanks. I've never done that in my life. Not sure what happened. Maybe we don't tell Cal, because he'll never let me live it down." She straightens up and brushes off her Titans jersey before smoothing down her slacks and patting her hair to make sure it's all in place. "Yes, well, Mae's idea is good. It looks like we have a lot to discuss," she says, her eyes drifting between me and Jorja. I can't help but feel guilty when I see hurt in her gaze, but then I remind myself that none of this is my fault.

"I would say that is a very fuc—damn good idea," Mary says. She is pissed. I feel the urge to cower in the face of her rage, but Kira just reaches out and gives her mom a squeeze on the arm.

"You need to be patient and kind, Mom. Believe me, I know how you feel, and your rage is deserved, but it needs to be aimed at the right people. Come on, girls, maybe we should have a hot dog too."

Jorja and Lola cheer, and they hurry off to the concession stand with Kira as the rest of us follow Mae and Grandma back to their box. The tension between us is off the charts, and Noah reaches for my hand and gives it a squeeze, but when he tries to drop it again, I hold on for dear life. I need to borrow his strength right now, because all I want to do is turn around, snatch up my daughter, and hightail it out of here.

We use the private elevator to get back up to the owner's box, the noise of the crowd completely disappearing as the doors close behind us. The tension is so thick you could cut it with a knife.

"Kash is playing like a demon. He looks good out there," Noah remarks casually to Mary who nods.

"He and Liam are going to be hard to beat this year," she replies without taking her eyes off me. "Hopefully nothing will derail him." I can feel the weight of both her and my grandma's gazes on my face, but I can't bring myself to lift my head and meet their eyes.

The doors open, and we step out directly into the owner's box. The rest of the occupants look up as we walk in, and I see a variety of reactions. Fred smiles when he sees me, but then he blanches when he realizes who else is with me, and he looks at the man next to him with panic. The man next to him turns as white as my grandma did but quickly goes red and jumps out of his seat.

"Miriam, thank fuck you're alive." My grandpa hurries toward me and gathers me up in a hug so tight I can't breathe.

"Oh shit," Peaches swears, and I hear a Southern voice admonish her. "But Grams, this is the girl I was telling you about the other day. The one who was with Bentley."

"Ah, well then, yes. I guess I was right with my guess as to who she is, but it seems to me that maybe a few people weren't aware of her return."

My grandpa's hug is so familiar and comforting,

and just smelling him brings back so many memories that I burst into tears. I sob like I haven't sobbed since I first arrived in London. My entire body shakes, and he whispers words of reassurance and pats me on the back just like he did when I was small. I feel my grandma put her hand on my back too.

I hear people murmuring around us, but the three of us are lost in a small bubble of grief. I finally get control of myself and pull away from my grandfather, though he is reluctant to let me go. He holds me at arm's length and looks closely at me, then his eyes narrow suspiciously.

"You don't look like you've been ravaged by drugs or living the hard life," he growls, and I shake my head.

"She has a little girl," my grandma says quietly, and Grandpa's body stiffens, and his eyebrows jump.

"A baby?" he asks.

"No, she looks to be about six, and I want to know if my son is the father." Mary's voice breaks through our bubble, and I sigh, knowing I'm going to have to explain everything to all these people. I can't wait until Monday, and Kash will be the last person I'll ever have to explain myself to.

Stepping away, I turn to face the angry woman,

but before I can say anything, Peaches' grandma stands up. "Maybe we should leave."

Peaches groans with disappointment, which makes me laugh.

I wave my hand. "No, please stay. I don't want to kick you out of your own box during the first game of the season. Stay and listen or ignore us and watch the game, it doesn't bother me. I'd rather you hear the real version rather than believe the lies my parents spread or the gossip that will eventually come."

"Thank you, dear. I'm Louella Eastern, by the way. You probably don't remember me, but I've been friends with your grandparents for years."

"I do, Ms. Eastern. I remember seeing you at their parties. You were always very kind. I think I came out to your ranch and had a few riding lessons when I was young. It's lovely to see you again."

She beams. "Yes, you did. You were obsessed right up until you discovered hockey, and then you never returned."

"Our Mimi was fierce on the ice, remember? She was working toward a scholarship to Storm View U before she disappeared," Grandpa boasts, and Louella nods.

"Yes, I remember. I'm on the selection commit-tee. I remember hearing talks about her. I was disappointed that her application wasn't there when it was her final year."

A rush of anger flows through me, and I grit my teeth. It's yet another thing to blame on my parents, but I wouldn't go back and change things if it meant I wouldn't have Jorja anymore.

"Shall we all take a seat and Miriam can tell us her story?" Mae is standing with Noah's arm around her, resting her head on his shoulder.

"Good thinking, love." Fred jumps to his feet and brings a couple more seats over so that they are all in a circle. Everyone takes one, leaving me standing with their eyes on me.

"I don't know where to start," I tell them, and Noah gives me a reassuring smile.

"Just start at the beginning," he says, and Mary waves a finger between us.

"Is this a thing?" she demands, and Noah raises an eyebrow at her.

"Mary, you know I love you like family, but you don't get to speak to us like this. I know you are angry, and you have every right to be, but that anger needs to be directed in the right place. Let Miriam tell her story, and we can get to what this is at the end."

A rush of gratitude for Noah rolls over me, and I lean in and give him a kiss on the cheek. "Thank you," I tell him, and Mae and Fred beam at him encouragingly.

Mary's face crumples, and tears well in her eyes. "I'm sorry I'm being such a bitch, but it's all been a shock. We've spent a good portion of the evening with a little girl who is freaking adorable by the way, and now I'm finding out she's my grandchild—a grandchild who I haven't been able to see for the first six years of her life. I want to know why. Did you have a fight? Did you not like us? I thought of you as another daughter. What did we do wrong that you would deny us her?" My heart aches for the woman who was more of a mother to me than my biological one.

I step over and pull her up, hugging her hard. "No, Mary, none of that, I promise. If I had known that you would want to be in our lives and I wasn't worried for my daughter's life, I would have told you, but I was also fooled by lies and manipulated so that I would not seek you out." She hugs me back hard before I sigh and let her go. "Sit down and let me tell you what happened."

It takes a good hour for me to tell my tale with people constantly stopping me to ask questions. Their outrage, especially my grandparents', is a balm to my bruised heart and soul. They all seem to believe me, which is a relief, but I'm kicking myself for not trying to contact them prior to all of this.

The game is basically over by the time I finish telling them what my life has been like since I moved back to Storm View, including the fact that I'm trying a polyamorous relationship with Noah and Bentley. I might as well get it all out on the table so nobody can accuse me of hiding anything.

CHAPTER 23

Miriam

Everyone is silent as they digest all the information I gave them, except Peaches. She's watching me with something that looks like respect. "Wow, both Noah and Bentley. Now that takes some balls, but good for you. I've never considered a relationship like that before, but why the fuck not? Love triangles and monogamy are so last year." I think she's trying to lighten the atmosphere, but none of the adults are paying attention except for maybe her own grandma.

"Ha, I can see you plotting now," her grandmother jokes, but Peaches' eyes cloud, and she shakes her head again.

"Nah, I'm considering lesbianism. Men suck, but then again, so do women. Maybe I'll become a nun."

Her grandmother looks at her with sympathy, but Peaches pretends not to see it. There is definitely a story there, but mine takes precedence today, so I put it to the back of my mind and make a note to reach out in a few weeks.

"I am going to kill them!" My grandpa is sitting upright in his chair, his spine ramrod straight as he practically vibrates with anger.

"Where did we go so wrong?" my grandma sobs, but he shakes his head and reaches out to pat her knee.

"Don't, sweetheart. We did everything right. I'm afraid that maybe nature outweighed nurture in this case."

His comment confuses me, but Mae and Lou exchange a knowing glance.

"What do you mean by that?" I ask, completely confused.

"It's not a secret, but I guess it was so long ago that people forget. Eric isn't our biological child. We adopted him when he was ten. We tried to have children for so many years, but it wasn't meant to be, and I hated seeing Violet so sad every time we failed, so we decided to adopt. We considered a baby, but there were just so many children who needed homes that we decided to go for an older one who might be as lucky as a baby," Grandpa announces to my shock. I had never heard anything about this when I was younger.

"We had a few appointments with the adoption agency and met a few children. Eric was so sweet and loving, and we had a few visits, and then he came and stayed with us a few times. We fell in love with him, so we made it official, but it turns out that Eric had already worked out how to game the system at such a young age."

My grandma sighs. "Not long after he came to live with us, he started to change. He became withdrawn and moody unless he wanted something, and then he was as sweet as pie. It was like he had a dual personality." She wrings her hands in her lap. "We took him to see a psychologist. We thought that maybe he needed to talk about his previous trauma. We know the family he grew up in were all crooks and involved in unsavory practices, and he'd seen things that no child should see. His mother died of a drug overdose, and his father was not suitable for raising a child, according to CPS..." She trails off and swallows hard as my grandpa takes over again, shuffling his chair closer to hers and putting his arm around her shoulders.

"They diagnosed him as a sociopath. He has no

empathy and disregards societal rights and wrongs. We were heartbroken, but what do you do? You don't return a kid because he's not what you hoped, so we did our best, but by the time he was sixteen, we had no control over him. All we could do was regulate his access to funds, but he's smart. He got himself part-time jobs, but he wanted to go to college. We told him we would pay for it as long as he stayed out of trouble. He started exploring where he came from and developed some unsavory friends. We agreed that if he turned his back on them, we'd pay for his degree, and he did for a while, but by his third year, he just developed another group of unsavory friends, but these were all college educated."

"We had such high hopes when he married Leticia and they had Miriam. We thought maybe he was turning his life around. His financial advising business was taking off, and we allowed them to build on our land, wanting to be close to Miriam, but what we hadn't realized was that Leticia was just as narcissistic as he was. I'm not sure if she's a sociopath, but she certainly has no love for either of us or Miriam. I think she loves the money and life-style being married to Eric provides her. We tried to suggest that maybe they and Miriam would be happier if we raised her, but by then, they had joined the local church. Again, I think it's all false, but perception is very important to both of them, and they couldn't be perceived as neglectful." Violet sounds disgusted, and I feel such a wave of empathy for my grandparents. They have so much love to give and no one to give it to.

"We concluded there was nothing else we could do but let them live their lives and do our best to make sure Miriam was safe. They'd never done anything to physically hurt her, even though I'm sure there was emotional abuse." My grandma's eyes fill with tears when she looks at me. "Can you ever forgive us? We should have tried harder. It hadn't even occurred to me that they would send you to Leticia's family. She's estranged from them, and Jocelyn had long ago been shunned by her family."

"It was smart of them. None of us considered looking overseas, especially when my PI did a search and there was no record of your passport having been used. What I want to know is how they managed that? We knew the photos of you and the MC gang were false. My PI figured that out after questioning the gang, and they claimed they had never heard of you. I confronted Eric and Leticia, but they were adamant. You had become addicted, and they kicked you out, so you ran away with them. Their story never changed. It was like they believed it." Grandpa bangs his fist against his knee. "To be honest, I thought that maybe you were dead. I never said anything to Vi because I still wanted her to have hope. I asked a friend from the FBI to look into it, but without a body or proof of any crime, there wasn't much he could do. I've also had him keeping an eye on Eric since, and now that I know you're safe, we can use everything he's discovered against them. They are going to pay. Up until now, I've turned a blind eye to their activities. I figured he was our son, and you took the good with the bad, but no more. He won't know what's hit him. If both of them don't end up in jail, I'll be surprised."

"Why didn't you contact any of us?" Mary finally speaks up, and I tense again.

"Well, my parents are excellent liars. I demanded that they give me my phone back, but they refused. When I arrived in London, I used Jocelyn's laptop to google Kash and Kira's information, but their Facebook pages came up first, and what I saw made me sick. Both of their pages had words of hate against me and showed photos of both of them declaring they didn't need me and they had other friends. At first, I thought that somehow my parents had doctored something up and were interfering with me finding their real pages. I was full of conspiracy theories back then, but Darcy and

Seamus did a search from a local internet cafe, one my parents couldn't have messed with, and found the same thing."

Mary winces and nods sadly. "Yeah, they both kind of lashed out when you disappeared and your parents told them those lies. Kira didn't last long and came to her senses after a week or two and removed those nasty comments. Kash lasted a little longer."

"I know, I saw it all—all the parties and different women—and then I just stopped looking. I was so sick and in and out of the hospital, and my family banned me from looking because it made my blood pressure high, so I decided I had to let it go for the sake of me and my girl," I tell her, and she grimaces and shakes her head.

"He's never going to forgive himself."

I shrug. "I've forgiven him. We all had the information we were working with. If I had been in the same situation, I might have done the same thing."

"Why didn't you return home sooner?" Louella asks, leaning forward in her chair. She's been quiet throughout my story. "Once Jorja was born, why didn't you return?"

"Because Mom and Dad said they would take her from me and I would never see her again. I was terrified," I admit, and the room explodes. "Jocelyn left me a letter in her will telling me that it was time to reclaim my life, that both Jorja and my grandparents and especially Kash were missing out on too much, and I would regret it if I didn't at least try. It's why she left me the house and a sum of cash, so I could at least support myself."

"Well, you don't have to worry about anything anymore. I will make sure of that." Grandpa stands up and pulls his phone out of his pocket. "I'm going to call my lawyer and my FBI friend and see if we can get the ball rolling on Eric and Leticia. They are going down." He leans in and gives me a kiss on the cheek and then my grandma. "I want to meet my great-granddaughter. Can you bring her up here?" he asks, but before I can pull my phone out, Noah already has his, and he calls Bentley.

Mary chuckles and shakes her head. "You know, I was kind of shocked when you said you were in a relationship with both Noah and Bentley, but it's perfect. You do know you're going to have to make room for Kash as well, right? There is no way he's not going to want to be in your and Jorja's lives."

Before I can respond, shocked that she's not screaming obscenities at me, Noah hangs up and grins at her. "We already factored him in, but that's it. We're not sharing our girls with anyone else."

Peaches giggles, but Mary stands up, goes over

to the open bar, and pours a big slug of whiskey into a glass before tossing it back.

"Buckle up," Noah announces. "We're about to be joined by the rest of the gang. Bentley's parents, Ginny, Kira, and Simon are coming with the girls and my parents. Dylan and Ethan are heading to the locker room to distract Liam and Kash if they get out early. Hopefully the press will keep them occupied for a while," Noah cautions, and I feel sick. I am not ready to face Kash tonight. I've already gone through an emotional roller coaster.

I groan. "I'm going to have to tell my story all over again, aren't I?" Mary comes over and drags me out of my chair and hugs me hard.

"Oh, my sweet girl, between us all, we can fill them in. Why don't you have a drink? You deserve it."

Peaches jumps out of her chair and goes behind the bar. "Come on, I'll shake you up a cocktail that's going to leave you feeling no pain."

I take a seat as everyone else talks quietly, discussing how they will share my story with the others. "You can do that? Aren't you a little young?"

She snorts. "My gran owns a bar, of course I know how to. I'll have you know that I'm an excellent cocktail maker."

I watch with nervous awe as she flips bottles

and shakes things and eventually produces a fruity cocktail in a flourish.

"Drink up, because here they are," she says, nodding toward the elevator.

The room gets noisy as the rest of the group piles in. I quickly pull Mary to the side for a moment. "I'm not going to tell Jorja that you are her grandparents tonight, mostly because all she will do is fixate until I cave and introduce her to Kash, and I need to get through her youth tryouts tomorrow before I fall apart." Mary's eyes cloud with sadness. "You know how you're going to dinner at Kira's on Monday? Well, we are too, it's so we could reconnect."

The sadness fades from Mary's eyes, and she rolls her eyes as her daughter approaches. "I thought Kira was going to tell us she was pregnant again. I have a bet going with Simon. I guess I lost this one."

"You should know better than to bet with Dad, Mom. Are we good here?" Kira looks between us, and Mary wraps an arm around both of our waists and pulls us in for a hug. "We are good, but don't think I'm not going to love on that gorgeous child like a grandma."

Simon catches sight of me. I expected the same kind of reaction as Mary, but he just pushes everyone out of the way, knocking Bentley into a chair in his rush to get to me.

"Mimi!" He gathers me in a hug and presses a kiss to my head. "God, girl, you are a sight for sore eyes. Where the fuck have you been?" He pulls back just as Jorja squeezes between us.

"Hey, Mama, we won! And my favorite player scored two goals, and Lola's daddy got two goals. It was amazing," she gushes, talking a million miles an hour. "I'm even wearing the same number as him!"

"Mama?" Simon frowns and looks between us. He puts two and two together and comes up with four. "I'm going to go out on a limb and guess you have a story for us?" he says, dropping his arms.

"Yes, she does, but she already told it once, so this time she's going to sit at the bar with Lola and Jorja, and Peaches is going to make them cocktails while I tell those who missed it exactly what transpired and what's going to happen." My grandpa returns, slapping Simon on the back and shaking his hand. "Your boys certainly dominated on the ice tonight."

"Calvin, good to see you, and yes, they did. Liam and Kash are going to be hard to beat if they keep going like that." Simon puffs up with pride.

"Come on, let me tell you a heartbreaking story

so my girl doesn't have to relive it, then we'll come up with a plan to protect everyone."

Bentley gets up from the chair he fell into and comes over and wraps his arms around me as my grandpa drags Simon away.

"Are you okay?" he asks. "When Kira told me you ran into your grandma and Mary, I wanted to come, but Noah sent me a text saying to wait," he says, looking guilty, but I just press a kiss to his lips.

"I'm fine. A huge weight has been lifted off my shoulders, and I learned a thing or two about my parents that backs up my thoughts that they were not fit to be parents. No one is to blame but them."

Noah steps up behind me and rests his chin on my shoulder, giving me his silent support. I can feel the weight of everyone's stares, and when I open my eyes, I catch sight of Bentley's Mom and groan.

"Fuck, how did I forget your mom would be here? How embarrassing! My college lecturer is going to know all the family dirt. I'm never going to be able to look her in the eye again, and she knows about our three-way."

Bentley pulls back and looks down at me with a cheeky grin. "Trust me, my mom won't be hearing anything about our three-way." He winks, and Noah chuckles behind me as I squirm between them. Now is not the time to be thinking about a three-way with these two delicious men, but my brain can see nothing but.

"Hey, Noah, did you kiss my mom and squeeze her bottom like Bentley did?" Jorja shouts across the corporate box, and I want to melt into the floor. I groan as the rest of the people in the room laugh.

"Not yet, but the night isn't finished yet," he calls back, and she gives him a thumbs-up before swinging around on the chair she's sitting on at the bar.

"I definitely need that cocktail now. Hopefully Peaches isn't light-handed with the alcohol," I tell my guys, pushing out of their embrace and joining the two girls at the bar, distracting them while the others talk about me.

CHAPTER 24

Bentley

This evening is filled with so many emotions—anger, hurt, sadness, and eventually, forgiveness and love. Calvin Kennedy fills in those who missed out on Mimi's story, giving them a condensed version with promises from myself, Noah, and Mary to give the others a full account when we get a moment.

Jorja is completely distracted by the mocktails that Peaches makes her and Lola, so she has no clue about the conversation going on behind her. Miriam, of course, does, and we can tell by her tense shoulders that she's listening while keeping the two little girls distracted, but finally, everyone in the room is up to speed. Our families are like one big entity, and if something happens to one, then the rest want to stick their noses into it. That's why I was so surprised to hear about Peaches' problems. Lou did a good job of keeping that from everyone, because if she mentioned it to anyone else, we'd all know about it.

Everyone wants to help bring Eric and Leticia to justice, but Calvin asks everybody to leave it with him for now. He doesn't want the two of them being tipped off to anything.

Dylan and Ethan were keeping the guys distracted, but Ethan sends Noah a text, telling him the press conference is about to end. None of us want Kash to find out like this, so we all go our separate ways. Everyone takes their leave, hurrying down to greet the winning players, while Noah and Miriam sneak out. Mary promises to keep Kash distracted. Tonight wasn't easy for her, and we want to be there for her.

Jorja goes with the others, excited to meet her new idol, still oblivious to who he is to her for the moment. I could see Mary and Simon were dying to smother her with love, but they restrained themselves for Miriam's sake. After Monday, though, the gloves are coming off. She's going to become one well-loved little girl.

Jorja is such a delight, and she spent the game sitting between Ginny and me, cheering her heart out for Kash. She has no idea he's her dad, but he sure is her favorite player. She was so excited to meet my sister, and I watched my ballbuster sister fall instantly in love with the little girl. She asked Ginny if she was a witch like the movie, to which Ginny winked and told her she couldn't let a muggle in on the secret.

Jorja squealed with excitement and asked her if she had a wand and an owl, and Ginny told her she would show her when she came to visit. I guarantee my sister will find the nearest Harry Potter store tomorrow so she can make it real.

I overhear Kash ask his mom what happened to her during the game, but Simon is able to head him off without needing to lie to him. They are all having dinner at Kira's place on Monday so they can tell him. Kira asked both Noah and me to come as well for support for Mimi. She's certain Kash is going to be mad and will probably shout a little bit but will calm down quickly. I know Miriam feels sick about it, but she's adamant that Jorja needs him in her life.

"Hey, buddy, you look like you have a lot on your mind." Kash comes over, and I give him a huge hug, patting him on the back. Fans surround us, offering their well wishes, but I know from the look on his face that he's ready for some quiet.

"Drinks at Lou's Place," I shout out to the crowd, and they cheer and start to disperse, knowing that they can get a chance to chat with their idols at the sports bar. The Titans always have the VIP section reserved on game nights.

"Ah, no, sorry, just not really in the mood to party tonight I guess," I tell him, and he frowns.

"You don't want to party? Why don't you invite your project partner? I'm sure that will put a smile on your face."

I grimace before I can stop myself, and he raises an eyebrow.

"That didn't go well?" he asks quietly, and I sigh.

"No, it did, but she has other plans tonight. Come on, I'll have at least one beer with you. You and Liam were on fire." I congratulate him as our families say their goodbyes and separate.

"Hey, I'm just going to walk the girls to the car, and then I'll get a lift with you to the bar if you don't mind," Liam says as he, Kira, and the two little girls approach.

"Yeah, no probs. Hey, Jorja, you want to meet Kash? He's the player who wears number fourteen," I tell her. She's holding Lola's hand and standing back a bit, but the moment I tell her that, she leaps forward.

"You were awesome!" she squeals and holds her hand up for a real high-five. I snort in amusement as Kash startles in surprise at the miniature hurricane's enthusiasm, but he recovers quickly and kneels down so he's closer to her.

"Oh hey, you're Lola's friend." He high fives her as Lola pushes forward next to Jorja.

"Hi, Uncle Kash." She throws her arms around him and gives him a huge hug, and Jorja's eyes widen.

"He's your uncle?" she asks, almost sounding envious.

"Uh-huh." Lola nods as Kash gives her a kiss on the cheek.

"You're so lucky." Jorja sighs, and I can see that Kash is amused by the little girls' interaction.

"Okay, shall we get going? It's way past both of your bedtimes." Kira steps in and pulls Kash back to his feet, giving him a kiss on the cheek. "Great game tonight. Don't forget dinner at our house on Monday."

They take their leave, but not before Jorja gives me a quick hug. "What was that?" Kash asks quizzically as the four of them walk away, leaving us in a now empty corridor.

"What?" I ask as I start walking, hoping that he'll be distracted.

"You and Lola's friend. I saw her with you and Ginny during the game."

I can't help but smile. Ginny was so good with her, which I wasn't expecting. Do I admit that she's the daughter of my project partner and omit who that project partner actually is?

While I'm deciding, we exit the arena and find Ethan and Dylan leaning against my car, saving me from having to answer Kash's question.

"Hey, are you guys heading to Lou's Place? Noah's already gone, so we can't get a ride with him," Dylan grumbles. "He's not even going. He needs to take his date home."

My eyes widen in panic, but Ethan subtly nods to me. Noah must have told them to keep a lid on the identity of his date. Liam joins us, and I'm thankful I went with the four-door Aston Martin, though it's still going to be a squeeze with five grown men in it.

"Yeah, no problem. Jump in," I tell them before Kash can ask questions.

Liam still has no clue either, but Kira says there is no way he could have kept it a secret from Kash. I feel guilty as fuck that we know and haven't told him, but hopefully he'll understand we were only protecting Miriam and Jorja.

During the drive, Ethan and I keep the discussion on the game, which completely distracts both Dylan and Kash. Dylan plays hockey himself and is hoping to get a scholarship to play for Storm View U, much like Kash and Liam did. He peppers them with questions about his diet and workout routine. They start gossiping about other teams, and so the conversation never swings back around to personal stuff. I wonder if that's why Ethan had Dylan tag along in the first place.

It's not long before I'm pulling into a parking space close to Lou's Place. The bar is packed, and it takes us a little while to make our way from the front to the VIP section. As we try to push our way through the crowd of well-wishers, I feel my phone vibrate in my pocket. It's a message from Noah inviting me back to Miriam's. He's worried about her and says she's been quiet since they left, and he wants me to come over and help cheer her up.

I can't leave immediately or Kash will be suspicious. It's already a break in tradition for Noah not to be here, but I'll have one beer and head over. I text him back, letting him know, and he sends me a thumbs-up emoji.

I tuck my phone back into my pocket as we make it to the VIP section. The bouncer lifts the rope, shaking hands with both Liam and Kash and congratulating them on a great game. There's a number of large booths in this area, and all of them are occupied by most of the Titans as well as a few of the coaching staff. The rest of the people in here are fans, and most of them are girls. I don't know how they can do this every season. It must get exhausting having puck bunnies throwing themselves at you.

One of the booths is half empty though, and there are no puck bunnies although they are hovering close by in case one of the players changes their minds. In it sits the rest of the first line. Captain Joe is married, but his wife is home with their baby girl. Vlad and Theo, the defense, chat animatedly with Zeke, the witch doctor, who is the Titans' goalie. He's also fucking hilarious.

"Bentley, my man." Zeke stands up when he sees me and gives me a hug. "Finally, someone who will drink with me. The rest of these guys are being lame." Everyone else exchanges greetings, and we pile into the booth, taking up the rest of the space. Dylan is in heaven, chatting with his idols, but Ethan is paying more attention to his phone than anything else.

"Hey, no work tonight," Kash teases him, and I

watch in surprise as he flushes slightly and puts it away.

Huh? Maybe our workaholic friend wasn't working, and maybe that was personal. Kash waves down a waitress who flutters her eyelashes, but no one pays her any particular attention. They are not supposed to bother the players. Lou will fire them on the spot for that shit, so it's not all that aggressive. We place our order, and everyone dissects the game while I listen on. I'm not all that interested, to be honest. I love watching it ,and Kash and Liam are my boys and I support them, but I don't need to do a play-by-play breakdown afterward.

"Noah told me what happened. Is Miriam okay?" Ethan whispers in my ear, and I shrug.

"I'm not sure. I'm going to check on her once I'm done here. Can you cover for me? Kash is still in the dark."

Ethan frowns. "Is that fair to him?"

"No, of course not, but no one wanted to fuck with his game. We never considered running into anyone Miriam might know and it all falling apart. She's telling him on Monday."

"Good. Don't leave it any longer so that he finds out from someone else. The circle that knows is getting wider."

"What about Dylan? Does he know to keep his

mouth shut?" I watch as the younger man talks to the hockey players.

"Yes, he doesn't know the whole story, and neither do I, but I agreed to stay silent because I like Miriam and don't want to see her hurt. Both of us plan on grilling Mom and Dad tomorrow. They know it all now."

"Yeah, and you're right. Kash usually keeps a low profile the day after a game, so hopefully we'll be in the clear."

The waitress returns with our drinks. One of the puck bunnies gets bold and tries to join our group, but Joe, who takes his role of captain very seriously, chases her off. He wants his boys focused on winning this year, not on chasing tail. If it were up to him, he'd have them all married off and producing children like he is. He thinks a player in a stable and committed relationship plays better than a single one who looks for nothing but the next fuck. I wonder what he will say about our relationship if Kash decides he wants to be involved.

I spend the next hour nursing my drink, wanting to be somewhere else, but I love my friend too much, and if I left too soon, he'd be suspicious, but after another text from Noah saying that he'd taken Miriam for ice cream and coffee, and they were now heading back to her place, I stand up.

"Where are you going?" Kash asks, and I shrug, trying to think of an excuse.

"Sorry, man. My project partner just messaged, and she's done with her thing." I wink, knowing he's going to assume I'm leaving for a booty call.

He chuckles and nods. "Alright, I'll see you sometime tomorrow."

"Are you okay to uber home?" I ask him, and Joe waves me off.

"I'll get him home. I'm only having two," he promises. "We have a niece's birthday party in the morning."

"Thanks, man." I wave my goodbyes. Zeke complains that I'm leaving before we've had a chance to chat, but Ethan distracts him.

"Hey, can I get a ride?" Liam stands up and stretches. "I'm done too."

"Yeah, no problem." Their place is only about ten minutes from Miriam's, so it's not like it's out of my way.

We wave goodbye and head out into the humid air. It's not that late yet, and there are still plenty of people milling around, but I finally feel my muscles loosen. I've been wound so tightly since we left the arena, my worry for Miriam making it impossible for me to relax, but now I can go and look after my girl. I might stop and grab some ingredients for mac and cheese. That's my go-to comfort meal when I'm feeling crappy or sad. It works for the guys too, so hopefully it will work for her. There is a late-night supermarket close by, and if a pint of ice cream with gummies falls into my basket, well, we can't let it go to waste, and I'll have to give it to Jorja.

CHAPTER 25

Miriam

Noah suggests coffee and ice cream after the game, and I don't have anywhere I need to be or a child who needs to be tucked in, so I happily agree. We go to a cute little place that serves adult coffee and ice cream in that they add alcohol to their concoctions. Noah tries to make conversation while I eat my Baileys covered sundae, but I know I'm being bad company.

"God, I'm so sorry. I'm being such a drag, but tonight just keeps playing over and over inside my head. All that new information about my parents... I'm seriously questioning every decision I made over the last six years, and it makes me sick. Everyone has missed out on so much because I was a coward," I blurt to Noah.

He's been so kind and patient with me. Shit, we missed two thirds of the game because he was helping me with my family drama. We haven't known each other that long, and that's the kind of thing you do with a long-term girlfriend, not someone you've only been on one date with. I wouldn't be surprised if he dropped me home and I never heard from him again. I'll be sad when I still run into him if Jorja is in Kash's life, but I won't be mad.

"Oh, Mimi, no, babe. Don't think like that. The past is the past, and you were operating with what you thought you knew. Regrets are futile in that kind of situation. You just have to look forward to the future."

"You aren't annoyed at how this all went?" I ask, wanting to know where we stand. "You're not ready to drop me at home and put me in your rearview mirror? Because I wouldn't blame you if you were."

He chuckles and shakes his head, picking up my hand and placing a kiss on it. "I think you are one seriously brave, badass woman, and nothing that has happened has even come close to scaring me off."

My soul swoons, and I swear there are hearts in

my eyes when I gaze at him. I'm already halfway in love with this man. Both he and Bentley have been amazing, and I'm not sure I deserve either of them.

What I discovered about my parents was shocking. I had no idea that my father wasn't my grandparents' biological child. I was devastated to learn that I have no blood relationship to either of them, though they assured me it never mattered to them, but I wasn't at all shocked to hear he was a sociopath. Not once did he ever stop my mother from belittling me, nor did he show that he cared about me in any way. We were strangers living in the same house. It's why I tried to be at my grandparents' place as much as possible. They were warm and caring, whereas we were practically strangers in my house. As long as I kept up appearances when they had parties, they left me alone most of the time.

"And I know B feels the same way. I sent him a message. He's going to meet us at your place after he has a beer with Kash. He's worried about you. I'm sure he's probably plotting what he's going to feed you, because according to B, the way to make someone feel better is to feed them."

This makes me laugh. "Well, he totally seduced Jorja to his way of thinking with his soup. Apparently, that's why I need to lock you both down according to her. You to help me fix everything around our house, and him because he cooks so much better than I do." I was messing around, but his smile turns decidedly predatorial, and his eyes narrow.

"Hmm, and what do you think about that? Because I can't say I'm opposed to her suggestion at all, although my superior handyman skills aren't the only thing I bring to the table."

The conversation takes a turn, and I grab hold of the distraction with two hands. "Well, I don't know, Mr. Wilson, I may need a demonstration of these other skills you claim to possess."

"Check." He holds out his hand to catch the attention of our server, and I dissolve into giggles, but before I know it, we're back in his truck and heading in the direction of my house.

"I'm going to show you so many skills, you're never going to let me go," he declares, his eyes on the road, and he may be driving slightly over the speed limit. All thoughts of what happened tonight slip away as my body starts to throb with delicious anticipation. It's been so long since I've had sex, but I remember really enjoying it. I only hope that I haven't forgotten what to do.

The rest of the drive to my place is quiet as my brain frets about what's going to happen. Thank goodness I shaved my legs and armpits before I got dressed, or that could have been a disaster. Aunt Jocelyn gave me a voucher to have a laser Brazilian for Christmas one year. I wasn't exactly sure why, because no one else was seeing it but me, but she claimed it was far easier than shaving every time we went to the beach. Now, though, I'm eternally grateful for the crazy old woman. It's like she knew I might actually want to use my vagina again one day.

What if I forget how this is done? Apart from the couple of kisses both the guys gave me, I have basically been a nun for six years. The most action my vagina has seen recently was when I pushed Jorja out of it. Hopefully everything went back into place. I shove my hands under my thighs and cross my fingers.

Noah pulls into my driveway, and I notice the lights are out at Fred and Mae's. Are they home and in bed, or did they head to my grandparents' place for late-night plotting? I wouldn't put it past them. I hadn't shared my whole story with them before tonight either, and they were just as horrified as everyone else. Fred suggested that there was probably a concrete slab somewhere that Wilson Construction needed to pour that we could shove their bodies into. Neither of them blinked at the poly relationship, and apart from a few raised eyebrows, no one had anything to say. There were no accusations of me being a slut or a gold-digging whore or anything like that. Everyone was super supportive and thought it was exactly the kind of relationship the three boys needed. We'll see if they are still singing the same tune once the media gets hold of the story and runs with it if Kash decides he does want to be involved.

My mind has been latching onto everything but the fact that we have now stopped and Noah is opening my door. This is it. Either I'm going to rock his world, or I'm never going to be able to look him in the eye again, and this relationship will be over before it's even started.

He peers in at me, one eyebrow arched in question when I don't move. "Hey, babe, it's okay. You seem to be overthinking all this, and it's no big deal. If you're not ready, then we can just go inside and have a drink and watch a movie together on the couch. There is totally no pressure. We go at your pace."

I jump down out of the truck and grab his hand. "No, I want this, I really do, but what if I forgot how to do it? It's been so long and you're so..." I trail off and wave a hand up and down his smoking hot body. "You, and I'm sure you've had lots of experience, and I have exactly six weeks. It's intimidating when you think too hard about it."

He just shakes his head and rolls his eyes at me. I want to be outraged that he thinks I'm being ridiculous, but before I can have a go at him, he throws me over his shoulder and walks toward my house, giving me a sharp slap on the butt.

"Right, you are so overthinking this. We just need to get you out of your head. Leave it to me." He holds out his hand for my keys, and I drop them into his palm. I hear him open the door, and as we step inside, he throws the keys in the bowl before letting me down. Before I can complain, he pushes me against the wall, surrounding me with his body and all his delicious weight, and kisses me.

I melt into him, his tongue tangling with mine as his hands drift to my hair. He uses my ponytail to angle my head, and I moan from the feeling of that tight pressure—I do like to be manhandled. His other hand drifts to my jeans and unbuttons them, pushing them over my hips and down my legs. I can't believe he can manage that with one hand, but I toe off my sneakers and step out of them. His hand leaves my hair, his mouth still attached to mine, nipping and sucking and completely making all thoughts leave my mind except for the feeling and taste of him. He tastes sweet, like whiskey and ice cream, and he smells intoxicating, all woodsy and manly. He surrounds me, sending every one of my senses spiraling out of control.

He steps back suddenly and lifts my sweater and shirt up over my head, tossing them to the side. I reach out, wanting the same thing, and he removes his one-handed, reaching over his shoulder in a move that's fucking click bait to women. His Titans jersey joins my stuff on the floor, and we both take a moment to drink each other in. Noah is cut. I think his muscles have muscles, but it's not that refined, I've been working out in the gym kind of sleekness. He's rugged, and I can tell it's from working hard. His skin is also this delicious golden color, his brown nipples are peaked, and surprisingly, one of them has a ring in it. I itch to put my mouth on it and give it a tug, so I do. I lick it before wrapping my mouth around the hard bud and using my teeth to tug it. He growls and crowds me again, pushing me back so I'm flat against the wall with my hands trapped in his. He takes my mouth once more in a scorching kiss, and my core throbs as I try to rub against his body.

He pulls away. Both of us are breathing hard, and there is a dark desire in his eyes. "Leave them there," he commands, releasing my hands and turning his attention to my breasts. He pulls down both cups of my bra, exposing my peaked nipples to his gaze.

I watch as he licks his lips before reaching up and pinching them. I groan, and my head drops back against the wall as I close my eyes against the exquisite sensation as he takes one in his mouth. Wet warmth engulfs my nipple as he rolls his tongue around it before sliding his teeth across it. I desperately want to run my hands through his hair, but I'm pretty sure he meant business when he told me to leave them in place. Something flashes behind my eyelids, and my eyes spring open. Through the open doorway, I see the headlights of a car shining through. I start to move, but he places one hand between my breasts and holds me in place.

"I didn't tell you to move. It's just B. Now stay still." He leaves his hand there but slides his body down mine until he's crouching at my feet.

I look at him with wide eyes, glancing between him and the open door. His hand follows the path of his body. There, he hooks two fingers in either side of my panties and slides them down my legs until I'm wearing nothing but my bra with my breasts hanging out of the cups.

I fight the urge to cover myself and squirm, but he shoves my panties into his pocket and pushes my legs apart. Just as I hear footsteps up the front porch, he leans forward and swipes his tongue through my folds before sucking my clit hard.

I couldn't stop the moan from leaving my mouth if I tried, my eyes meeting Bentley's green gaze as he steps through the front door. His eyes widen as he takes in everything, and then they narrow and he drops the bags he's carrying in each hand.

"Well, this looks like fun," he comments as Noah pushes away from my dripping core.

"Miriam is still thinking too much, B. Care to give me a hand in distracting her from her worries?"

"Abso-fucking-lutely," Bentley replies, closing and locking the front door behind him. "Just give me a moment to put these in the fridge. He picks up his bags and hurries away. I watch him retreat, but Noah's mouth is back on my pussy, and I can't keep my eyes open. My head thrashes back and forth at the intense sensation he's wringing from my body as he licks, sucks, nips, and probes. I'm so lost that I don't even notice Bentley return.

Suddenly, his mouth is on mine, kissing me hard as Noah slides one finger into my wet heat. My eyes roll back at the slight pinch that quickly turns to pleasure as he slides a second one in next to it.

"So tight. Going to have to stretch you a little," he mutters as Bentley nips my lip and pinches my nipple.

I gasp and groan, fucking myself on Noah's fingers as they quickly build me into what's going to be a mind-blowing orgasm. They play my body like it's an instrument, and they are virtuosos. The room spins as my orgasm builds, fierce and sizzling, fraying my self-control. My voice turns harsh as I beg for more as the two men overwhelm me with dual sensations. Pleasure trickles over every nerve ending, and my body detonates into a thousand splinters as they push me over the edge. I scream, and Bentley puts his hand over my mouth, lapping gently at my nipples as I ride out the astonishing orgasm.

"We don't want Mae and Fred to run over, thinking you're in trouble." Bentley chuckles as I come down from the stratosphere.

Noah slides his fingers out of my pulsing pussy, and I watch with awe as he reaches up and offers them to Bentley. "Taste her. You've never had anything so sweet," he says, and I swear I have a mini orgasm as Bentley leans in as instructed.

He doesn't look away from me as he does it, but I swear his eyes roll back in his head as my flavor crosses his taste buds, and he groans. "Fucking hell. I never want to eat anything else now."

I stare at him, my mouth open in shock, as Noah stands up. I blush as they stare at me and begin to grow self-conscious. I'm mostly naked, and they are still mostly dressed. Before I can say anything, though, Bentley scoops me up bridal style and heads in the direction of the stairs.

"Come on, we're not done yet. She's starting to think again. We have our work cut out for us tonight. I hope you don't need any sleep for tomorrow," he tells me, and as I look over my shoulder, I watch Noah prowl close behind us, his hand adjusting his very obvious erection behind his zipper.

"Sleep is for the weak," he growls, and my body flushes with pleasure. I only hope I can be as good to them as they have been to me.

CHAPTER 26

Miriam

The trip to my bedroom seems to take forever, but at the same time, not long enough. Bentley is right, I've started to overthink things again, but as we step into my bedroom, neither of them will let me get lost in my own mind. Bentley places me down on the bed and reaches around my back to release my bra before flinging it to the side. Noah takes a seat on the small chair I have, but not before he removes his jeans. Bentley and I watch as he leans back on the chair and shoves his hand into his boxers, stroking his hard length.

"Hmm, what do you think, Mimi? Noah took such good care of you. Don't you think it's time you took care of him?" Bentley stands behind me as he whispers in my ear, his fingers lazily plucking my nipples and sending tiny electric shocks through my system.

I rub my thighs together, wet from my last orgasm, trying to find some friction as my core throbs. I nod enthusiastically as Bentley's hands run over my body. He has calluses that create a scratching sensation that's a direct contrast to the way the rest of my body feels.

"Such a good girl," he whispers, and I groan. Do I have a praise kink to go along with enjoying being manhandled? "How about you get on your knees and suck his cock like the good girl you are?" He leads me over to Noah. The carpet has been ripped out by the contractors, exposing the wooden floor, so Bentley grabs a pillow off my bed and throws it down. Noah parts his legs, and I shuffle between them, my hands on his powerful thighs, his leg hairs tickling me where they touch my body. Bentley threads his hand through my hair so he can control me, and my eyes just about roll back in my head. Oh yeah, I definitely have a submissive kink, and these guys are playing directly to my needs.

"Such a pretty girl on her knees for you, isn't she, Noah?" Bentley croons as Noah stares down at me, still stroking his cock under his boxers. His eyes sear into my soul with dark heat. "She's going to look so pretty with your cock in her mouth."

Wow, Bentley has a dirty mouth on him. I probably would have guessed that if I thought about it hard enough.

He kneels behind me and turns my head up to kiss him while caressing my breasts. "And these tits would look so good with your cock sliding between them, painted with your cum."

I whimper as he turns my head back to face Noah and find he pulled his cock out for me to see. It's long and thick and glistens with precum, and my mouth waters. I can't wait to wrap my lips around it, but Bentley is controlling all of this, and I can't move because he has me trapped.

"Tongue out," he demands, and I instantly do what he says as he leans me forward and allows me to run my tongue along the length of Noah's cock.

Noah groans, and his head falls back.

Bentley pulls me away before I can lick the bead of precum. "Such a good girl," he coos. "You can use your hand. Wrap it around the base and make him feel good."

I don't hesitate, wrapping one hand around his cock while the other plays with his balls.

Bentley chuckles. "Looks like our brother taught her well. She remembers to look after the balls. Look how small her hand is wrapped around your cock." Bentley's words tease both me and Noah, and Noah grunts and opens his eyes. I can see the strain in his gaze, and I feel a wash of pride and pleasure from knowing I'm making him feel good.

"Spit on it," Bentley orders, and I lean forward and dribble a line down his length before using my hand to spread it about.

"You are going to be rewarded for your obedience," he coos as he strokes my head and his other hand slides down to circle my clit. "Now lean forward and take him into your mouth. Don't stop until your nose is against his pelvis," Bentley commands, and I mentally cross my fingers, hoping I can do this.

Noah's long and thick, but so was Kash, and I became pretty good at sucking dick. Unlike a lot of people, I enjoy it. I enjoy the rush of power I feel when I make a man feel good. Breathing through my nose, I wrap my lips around his cock, being careful with my teeth, and use my tongue to caress his length as I slide down. I gag slightly, and my eyes water, but I push past my limit until the tip of his cock sits in my throat.

"Fuck!" he shouts as he grabs my head and holds me there for a moment. Tears run down my face, but I swallow, and he jerks slightly, pushing himself deeper before releasing me and allowing me to pull back and breathe.

"Such a good girl, taking him so deep." Bentley strokes my back, whispering words of praise. "You looked so pretty with his cock in your throat. I can't wait to see you with mine in your throat. I think you deserve a reward for obeying so well. What do you think, Noah?"

"Yes, give her a reward," he mutters quietly, his eyes not leaving mine as he brushes the tears from my face. "I like seeing tears in your eyes from my cock," he says, and I shiver from the darkness in his words.

I have a feeling Noah likes to play hard, and I am so fucking here for it. They work together too well not to have done it before.

Bentley helps me to my feet, turning me to face him and kissing me, not at all worried that I just had his friend's cock in my mouth. Behind me, I hear Noah remove his boxers. Bentley gently strokes his hands all over my body, but he nips my lip, creating a direct contrast to his touch. It's like he's deliberately keeping me off balance, and my body doesn't know if it's coming or going. One of his hands drifts lower, and I feel a finger probing at my entrance before he slides two in, and I moan.

"Oh man, she's dripping wet. Such a good little

slut, ready to take my friend's cock in her tight little cunt. It's going to feel so good, like a fist wrapped around your dick," he tells Noah as he plunges in and out a couple of times, his other hand still holding my hair tight. "Condom?" he asks, and my heart sinks.

Fuck, I don't have any. I'm on birth control, but only to regulate my periods since I certainly wasn't planning on having sex anytime soon. "No, do you have any?" I ask him, and he grimaces and looks at the door.

"In my wallet downstairs. Noah?" I ask, and he groans, his chin falling onto his chest.

"I left mine in the truck." The three of us are quiet for a moment.

I really don't want either of them to leave to get them and break the moment. "I'm clean. There hasn't been anyone since I had Jorja, and I'm on the pill," I tell them quietly, hoping they don't think I'm trying to be sneaky or anything. My daughter is proof that I'm fertile.

"Thank fuck." Bentley rests his forehead against mine and looks me in the eye. "I'm clean, I've never had sex without one."

"Me neither," Noah chimes in.

"Good enough for me," I reply, hoping like hell that none of us will regret this.

"Well, how about you step back and spread your legs? I'm going to lower you down over Noah's cock, and you're going to ride him. Good girls get orgasms, and you've been such a good girl."

We're instantly back in the moment, and goosebumps erupt on my skin as he guides me into position. Noah has his legs together, and mine are on either side as he holds his cock in place so I can slide down on it. He slips it back and forth through my wet folds, coating it in my desire, before putting his other hand on my hip and helping me slide down.

"Oh!" My mouth rounds as he stretches me to my limit, but little by little, they work me up and down. Bentley's dirty words of praise and Noah's secure hands give me confidence, and soon, I find myself completely impaled on his cock. My inner core throbs, and the two of us moan.

"How does she feel?" Bentley asks, looking at where we're joined as he strokes his hand over my face and pushes my hair back. "She looks so good sitting on your cock."

Noah groans and gives a little thrust. "She's fucking tight and hot, and if I'm not careful, I'm going to blow my load before anyone else has fun," he warns, and I can't help the grin that creeps across my face as his hands drift up to cup my breasts.

"Oh yeah, she likes that, likes having power over

you," Bentley mutters as he removes his shirt, and my eyes widen in surprise when I see a big tattoo across his chest—there was no sign of any of them on his arms or legs, so I hadn't expected it—and glistening in both nipples are little bars.

He sees me watching him, and his own grin creeps across his lips as he runs a hand over his body before popping the button on his jeans and pushing them down. His thighs also have tattoos on them, but what draws my attention is that he's commando, and he has three piercings on the underside of his cock. My eyes widen with interest, and he reaches down and strokes the length of it, brushing his thumb against each of the bars.

"I think she likes your piercings. She just gushed on my cock," Noah murmurs, tweaking my tits with his rough hands and slowly circling his hips. "How about you lean forward a little, gorgeous, and show Bentley how good your cock sucking skills are?" He pushes gently on my back to angle me down as Bentley takes a step forward. I use my hands to balance myself on Bentley's thighs as Noah's hands go to my hips, and he starts to lift me up and down on his cock.

Sticking my tongue out, I swipe the bead of precum from the tip of his cock, the salty flavor making me groan as he slides his cock into my mouth.

Between the two of them, they work my body into another frenzy, using it to take their own pleasure. Dirty words of praise from both of them reach my ears and drive my lust higher. At this angle, I can't quite swallow Bentley all the way down, but I make up for that by using my tongue and decent suction, being very careful not to click my teeth against the bars. Getting a chipped tooth while sucking a dick would not be fun.

Bentley's hands caress my back and run through my hair, sliding down to caress my breasts, while Noah releases one of my hips to slide his fingers between us to play with my clit. My body is wound as tight as a clock, and the two of them pant like they ran a marathon.

"Are you there, man?" Noah asks as my pussy starts to ripple with my impending implosion.

"Yes, Mimi is going to swallow all my cum like a good girl, but I want to see her tits painted with both our cum later tonight."

Those dirty words and the thought of that is enough to tip me over the edge. I moan around his cock as my orgasm rolls through my body like a freight train. I clamp down hard on Noah, which has him shouting and planting his feet to thrust through my orgasm before filling me with his cum.

"Swallow now," Bentley demands as I feel his cock swell within my mouth before the salty seed splashes across my tongue. I swallow as fast as I can, trying not to spill any as I ride out my own pleasure. Their groans are like an instant trigger, and I explode again, shivering hard.

"Such a good girl, swallowing my cum and taking Noah's deep inside you. Such a good cum slut for us."

I shiver again as they caress me all over.

"She's going to be so much fun," Bentley mutters to Noah, who hums his agreement as I feel his cum leak out from between us as I lick Bentley's cock with my tongue.

He pushes me back, and I lean against Noah, my eyes drifting closed as they continue to stroke and praise me.

"Come on, let's get our pretty girl cleaned up, and then I'll make us something to eat." Bentley's arms go under me, and he lifts me off Noah. I feel a gush as his cum slides out of me, and they both groan again. "God, I had no idea I would be so fucking turned on by seeing that," Bentley says, and Noah mutters his agreement.

"All I want to do is push it back into her."

Bentley chuckles. "Noah is discovering a new kink—breeding Mimi. I like the sound of that. Why don't you do what you want?"

He carries me closer, and I crack my eyes open. We both watch as Noah gathers up everything that slid out of me and uses two fingers to push it back in. All three of us moan, and Bentley chuckles again.

"Oh yes, so much fun.

As promised, they cleaned me up in the shower, and Bentley made us the most amazing mac and cheese before the two of them used my mouth and tits to get off again, painting my body with their cum. Noah proceeded to mix it together and then used his cum slicked fingers to finger fuck me to orgasm, while Bentley whispered dirty words and played with my tits. Once more, they cleaned and dressed me before tucking me into bed and snuggling in next to me. I was out before they finished kissing me goodnight.

"No way! You had a sleepover without me?" My

daughter's words have the three of us sitting bolt upright in bed.

Thank fuck the guys thought to dress me before we fell asleep. My hair is over my face, and I push it back in panic as Jorja jumps up onto the bed and bounces around.

"Well, to be fair, you were having your own sleepover," Noah says as he reaches out and tickles her, and she giggles.

"Oh my god!" Another voice draws our attention to the doorway, where Kira stands wide-eyed and open-mouthed. "Shit, when I saw that their cars were here, I thought they'd come over early to bring you to tryouts."

"Damn, what's the time?" I ask, reaching for my phone and not finding it. Shit, it was in my pants, which are on the floor of the entryway.

"Yeah, I quickly realized that was not the case, but I was too slow to stop her. Sorry." Kira smirks as she leans against the doorframe. "Hey, Jorja, go grab your bag and give these guys a chance to wake up."

"Okey dokey, but next time I want to sleep over too," she calls as she rolls away and hurries out of the room.

Bentley groans and flops back on the bed, pulling the pillow over his head. "Jesus Christ." His voice is muffled, and Kira giggles.

"That is the best deterrent to your sex life ever. Kids are the biggest cockblocks, so have fun with that. I'll let you get dressed, but I can guarantee if you don't get ready quickly, both of them will be harassing you. They've been up since six. Liam groaned and rolled over and went back to sleep, so the three of you are lucky he didn't tag along."

"Shit, I hadn't even considered that," I mutter as I climb over Noah and search for something to wear.

"Twenty-four hours, and everyone who needs to know will know. My husband will need his ruffled feathers soothed, so the three of you owe me big time."

Noah runs a hand through his hair and grimaces. "The man has no chill. You know he wouldn't have kept it to himself."

She points a finger at him. "I know, and that's the only reason I agreed not to tell him, but don't ever ask me to keep another secret from my husband." With that threat, she leaves to wrangle both girls, and the three of us get dressed.

Most of the guys' clothes are here except for Noah's shirt. Both of them decide to run home to change, promising to see me at the ice rink later after heated kisses that can't go anywhere, leaving me hot and horny and having to play mom. Thank God we're going to the ice so I can cool down.

They wish the girls luck and depart, and I feel the weight of Kira's stare. I know she's dying to pepper me with questions, and all I can do is praise God that my daughter and hers are in the way. Cockblocks indeed.

CHAPTER 27

Miriam

The drive to the arena for tryouts is filled with loaded silence despite the girls talking the whole way. I feel Kira's gaze on my face every time she glances over, but I refuse to look at her. When we arrive, she's distracted by the flurry of activity it takes to get the girls into pads and gear. Lola and Jorja are trying out for the under seven age group, but it means Lola will probably be one of the youngest. When she and Jorja hit the ice, though, I see that it really isn't going to matter. Both of them easily skate rings around the rest of the kids.

I can finally take a breath when I sit down to watch the girls. I know it will only be a matter of seconds before Kira starts to grill me.

"Do you want coffee?" she asks, standing in front of me. I look up, and she grins. "I think this is going to be a two shot with caramel kind of conversation."

I groan but nod, and she heads off to the concession stand as the coaches try to wrangle the kids into some semblance of order, but it's like herding cats. As soon as they have them in a line, one falls over or their skates shoot out from under them. The coaches are spending more time putting kids back on their feet than anything else. When they are finally in a line, they practice their puck skills. They have to hit it back and forth between a partner—not too hard, just hard enough that the partner can stop it and return the puck. I snort in amusement, not envying the coaching staff at all. It was hard enough teaching one stubborn little girl, let alone twenty of them.

Kira sits down next to me and hands me a steaming cup of coffee that smells like delicious caramelly sweetness. Before she can ask me a question, I start to chuckle. Next to Lola and Jorja are another couple of skaters—their sex unknown under all that padding—but one of them had their skates slide out from under them and is lying on the ground. I can hear sobbing sounds, and I look around, but nobody is watching. Before I can get up, though, my daughter puts her stick on the ground and skates over, hauling the slightly bigger child to their feet and brushing them down. I hear her little pep talk, and it's one I've given her a few times.

"Come on, it'll get easier. You just have to keep practicing. If you give up now, you're only going to disappoint yourself." She smacks them on the helmet and then the ass and pushes them back to their spot.

"Holy shit, she really is a mini you. I remember you saying something like that to me when we first started, and I was horrible."

"In our defense, we were a little older and had developed a finely tuned sense of mortality. Jorja still believes she's invincible, so she just gets up and keeps going. She's also lower to the ground, and I swear it doesn't hurt her when she falls as much as it hurt us."

"Now, my sister from another mister, I kind of want all the tea, but I don't need details. Those men are like brothers to me, and that's just gross. What happened after you left the stadium?"

I give her the rundown but skip all the juicy details, and by the end, she's shaking her head.

"Don't get me wrong, I love my husband more than life itself, but you are living the dream. Then again, only time will tell if that dream turns out to be a nightmare. Imagine living with three men who don't put the toilet seat down or all fart while you're watching a movie. Not to mention you're going to need a bigger bed."

My eyes widen, and I hold up my hands. "Hang on, who said anything about living together?" I ask her, and she giggles, ignoring my moment of panic.

"Yeah, I guess my brother probably wouldn't want to spoon B or Noah. You're going to need a bed hopping roster."

"Look, I think you're jumping the gun here. Yes, I enjoyed Noah and Bentley last night, and I really like both of them, but who knows what will happen tomorrow night. Kash may never forgive any of us. He's their best friend and has known them for years. They may choose him over me, and rightly so if he decides he wants nothing to do with any of this."

"Pfft, you've known him just as long. Don't be so silly."

I shrug. "Look, I'm just not getting ahead of myself. We need to get through tomorrow night and see what comes from that, but at least I can say I've had an amazing threesome."

"An amazing threesome. Did you hear that, Noah?"

I jump as Bentley and Noah climb down a few steps to sit with us. Bentley holds his hand up for a high-five, and Noah indulges his ridiculousness while I blush bright red.

"Shit, I didn't know you were here," I hiss at him as they take a seat on the bench behind us.

"Obviously, but I like hearing you sing our praises. Don't get any ideas, Mrs. Worthington, you are a one-man girl. I can't see you convincing Liam to find a couple of buddies to play with."

She wrinkles her nose. "Considering two of his best buddies are like brothers to me, and one *is* my brother, I'm going to pass. If he asked Zeke to come play, though, I wouldn't be sad. That man is fine." She and I dissolve into giggles, even though I'm not actually sure what he looks like because I haven't seen the team without their gear on. I'm just going to take her word for it.

"Zeke is hilarious, man. I can actually see him keeping up with your crazy ass, but let's keep team harmony and not push our luck." Bentley pats Kira on the shoulder, and she flips him off, but Noah's eyes are glued to the ice as the coaches lay out a grid of cones for the kids to skate through.

They all line up to take their turns as Bentley asks, "Where are Jorja and Lola?"

I point out the two girls who are in the middle of the pack. Jorja is giving her new little friend another pep talk.

"You can do this, it's easy. You don't have to go fast. Go at the pace you are comfortable with. Speed comes after accuracy."

Again, another pep talk I've given her that she obviously memorized. How many times did I say it to the poor girl? Although Darcy and Seamus are the ones who got her up on skates, neither of them can skate worth a damn except to go around the pond, holding hands and looking lovingly into each other's eyes. It was up to me to teach my daughter how to do it, but I haven't been on arena ice since I left Storm View in the first place. It's always been uneven pond ice. I ache to find a pair of skates and glide around a perfectly flat surface, but I'll wait for another day. Maybe Jorja and I can find a rink to do a fun skate on.

"Holy shit, she skates like her daddy." Noah's mouth drops open in shock when it's Jorja's turn.

Most of the other kids slowly teetered their way through the course on unsteady skates. There are only a few who really know what they are doing, and you can tell they've been skating as much as they have been walking, Lola being one of them, but none of them take the course as fast or as precisely as Jorja.

I hadn't wanted her to learn to skate. The first time she went out to the pond with the guys, she caught a terrible cold and ended up with a chest infection. This happened a couple more times, so I put a stop to it. Both she and the guys were devastated, but her health came first. The doctors diagnosed it as asthma, a result of her premature lungs, but when she kept catching the same things, even if I kept her inside, I finally relented. She was going to be sick either way, and skating certainly put a smile on her face. I would cover her with so many layers that even if she did fall, she was perfectly protected from all the padding. Today I tried to put thermals on her before her pads, but Kira just snorted and shook her head and pointed out a shirt and some leggings.

"Trust me, she isn't going to be cold."

I feel an immense amount of pride when my daughter doesn't hit a single cone and uses some fancy footwork to make the fastest time through the course. The coaches are kind of speechless for a moment as they stare at the little terror in awe.

"Holy shit, where did she learn to skate like that?" Bentley is breathless with surprise as Kira puts an arm around me.

"That would be Mimi. She was a demon on the ice. I'm pretty sure that's what caught my brother's eye in the first place. She gave him a good run for his money when we would play scrimmages. Liam and I would spend more time trying to grope one another, but Mimi and Kash played for keeps."

We're quiet for a little while as we watch the kids. Although some of them aren't great skaters, all the teams in their league will be made up of similarly skilled players, so all the kids make the team.

A woman makes her way around to the parents sitting in the stands, handing out permission and insurance forms. "If you could all fill these out and bring them back before the next session, that would be great. practice will be on Mondays and Thursdays, and game days are on Sunday mornings. We are lucky enough to be granted permission to use this arena on Saturday and Sunday mornings, so our youth league is spread out over those days, but please pay attention to the roster, because sometimes we can't use it, and then our games are held over at Storm View U in their arena."

I take the forms she hands me, but she's not looking at Kira or me, instead batting her eyelashes at Bentley and Noah.

"Hi there, do you guys have kids down there? My son is playing this year. He's one of the best, so I'm pretty sure they will make him team captain. My ex-husband is going to be so happy."

Kira snorts next to me, and I smile to myself.

That wasn't very subtle, but you have to work with what you have when you're a single mom.

"Uh, we're here to support our girls," Noah says ambiguously. He could be referring to Kira and me or children down on the ice.

"Well, that's just great. Maybe we can sit together at the games. There's a roster of names going around for all the parents to fill out in case anyone needs a ride. My name is at the top. I'm Tegan."

Before either of them can answer, someone calls to Tegan from higher up in the stands. A flash of annoyance appears in her eyes before she waves goodbye and goes to help another parent.

I look around for something to lean on to fill out the considerable amount of paperwork, but I end up crouching on the ground and leaning on my seat.

"Would you look at this? There's a snack roster for after the game, and a drink roster too." Kira sounds bemused as she looks through the paperwork.

"Drink roster?" Bentley leans in, trying to have a look. "What's that? And what kind of snacks? I'm sure I can whip up something healthy and tasty for the girls when it's their turn."

Kira drops her papers and gives him a big kiss on the cheek. "You are the freaking best."

"It's where you provide the Gatorade for the big tub the kids fill their bottles up from, I think." I look over the paperwork, trying to make heads or tails of it.

"Hey, kids, that was amazing! We hope to see you all at practice this Thursday, but as a special surprise, some of the Titans have popped in to say hello to you."

The kids cheer, and my heart starts to race as I look up at my best friend.

"Please tell me that it's just Liam." I wondered why he wasn't here to cheer Lola on.

Kira's eyes are wide with panic, and she glances from me to the ice. "Fuck. I thought it was just going to be Liam and Zeke, but Theo, Vlad, and Kash are all here too. Fuck, it's too late for you to hide. He's already skating over here. Fuck, fuck, fuck."

"Hey, sis. Lola looked good on the ice, Liam is stoked." I get goosebumps at the sound of his familiar voice on the other side of the boards. "Listen, can you introduce me to her little friend's mom? I just want to tell her I think she has a future champion on her hands."

I shake my head, but Kira can't help her automatic reaction and looks down. I hear the door nearby open, letting Kash out from the ice. My body grows stiff as I hear him walk toward me.

370

"Hey, I'm Kashton Young. I just wanted to say your daughter has amazing footwork. Where did she learn that?"

I can't ignore him, so I sigh and stand up before lifting my head to look into the same Caribbean blue eyes that I see on my daughter every day.

Kash blinks, his eyes widen, and then his mouth drops open. "Mim?" he asks like he can't quite believe his eyes.

CHAPTER 28

Miriam

"Hey, Kash." I wave awkwardly.

"Holy fuck." That's Bentley behind us, but neither of us can look away from one another, both locked in an intense stare down.

"But... What? Where?" Kash stammers and shakes his head again like he can't believe what he's seeing. He tears his gaze away from me, his eyes narrowing as he glares at his sister. "What the fuck?"

"Hey, babe, did you see Lola? She was outstanding!" Liam skates up to the edge of the arena, oblivious to what's going on. "Hey, Mimi." He nods before doing a double take. "Holy fuck! Mimi?" He then narrows his eyes and glares at his wife. "I knew you were hiding something. You've been cagey all week."

Kash turns his attention back to me, and I can practically see steam coming out of his ears. "Where were you? Why did you leave? I thought you loved me." The question tears out of his mouth as he reaches out and grabs my arms, shaking me hard. I can't stop the tears from welling in my eyes when I hear the anguish in his voice.

"Hey, you big meanie head, stop shaking my mama!" Jorja appears out of nowhere and smacks Kash on the ass with her stick, pushing her helmet off her head so she can glare at him unimpeded.

He stops and turns slowly to look down at his mini me. I hear sharp inhales around me as those in the know wait for the fallout.

"Holy fuck," Liam mutters and looks from Jorja to Kash and then to me, connecting the very obvious dots.

Kash sinks to his knees with tears streaming down his face as he looks at his daughter for the first time.

Jorja's bottom lip sticks out in a pout, and she crosses her arms. "I'm sorry if I hurt you, but you can't touch my mama like that," she tells him, and he just stares at her in awe, making her shuffle a little on the spot, looking to me for reassurance.

"Oh, honey, it's okay. Thank you for defending me, but he was just a little overwhelmed to see me."

"You know him?" she asks, biting her lip and looking between us.

I sigh and get down on my knees. Kash is still frozen in shock, and I'm not sure which way his reaction is going to go. I reach over and pull my daughter toward me.

"Remember when you asked about your daddy, and I told you that there were reasons we couldn't be with him, but he loved you despite us not being together?"

She nods her head. "You said it was to keep him and us safe."

"That's right," I praise her, pleased she remembered. "Well, I have made some new friends recently."

"Bentley and Noah," she interjects, looking up at the two guys who are standing behind us, giving us space but still close enough if I need them. She waves, and Bentley winks and Noah waves back, and she giggles.

"Well, yes, but not just them. I've reconnected with some family members who are going to help make sure that we are all safe, so it means you can now meet your daddy."

Her face lights up, and she bounces on the spot.

"When, Mama, when? I want him to see how good I am on skates!"

"Well, that's the thing. He's already seen how good you are on skates." I nod to the man who's hanging on to every word like it's a lifeline.

Jorja looks confused for a moment, so I help her out. "Kash is your daddy," I tell her gently. We wait while she rolls everything around in her mind, and a grin suddenly stretches across her face.

"My daddy is awesome!" she yells and throws herself at him. "Lola, my daddy is just like your daddy!" Jorja shouts over Kash's shoulder as she hangs off his neck like a monkey.

Liam has picked Lola up, and they both watch us from the ice. Lola cheers, but everyone else remains silent as we wait to see how Kash is going to react.

I bite my lip, ready to rip into him if he denies his child, but he just sobs and wraps his arms around her and hugs her tight.

"She's beautiful and so smart and clever," he says to me over her shoulder as he holds her close.

"Yes, I am," she agrees, and everyone laughs, and it breaks the tension slightly.

"We have a lot to talk about, and I know you must be angry and confused, but you need to let me explain. If you still hate me after everything I tell you, I'll understand, but I won't stop you from seeing Jorja. We're back to stay now, and it's only fair you have a relationship with her. I just ask that you don't take her from me."

His eyes widen in shock, and he shakes his head. "No matter how mad I am at you, Mimi, I would never do something like that."

"Hey, we're needed on the ice. Can we table this for a moment?" Liam suggests, looking back at all the little kids who are waiting to speak to their idols.

"Yes, look, I promised the girls they could swim after tryouts since our pool is finally ready. Why don't you come over, and we can have that talk while they are swimming?"

"I'll pick up some steaks, and we can grill and make some salads for lunch," Bentley suggests.

"I don't have a grill," I tell him, and he shrugs.

"I'm sure Mae and Fred do. Noah and I can grab it from their place."

"And we can watch Jorja while you talk with Kash," Noah reassures me, and I see Kash narrow his eyes out of the corner of mine.

"Where do you all fit into this?" he growls, and Jorja pulls back and pats his cheeks.

"It's okay, Daddy. They are Mama's boyfriends, but you can be her boyfriend too. She might need a bigger bed, though, because I don't think you will fit in it with the three of them."

"Fuck my life," Bentley mutters, and Noah grumbles about chatty little six-year-olds.

I'm just frozen, but Kira quickly comes to our rescue. "Hey, how about we come too? Then Liam and I can watch the kids while the four of you hash this out."

I'm still frozen on my knees, unable to look at anyone. I can't believe she just said that. Talk about airing out all the dirty laundry in one go.

Kash stands up, still holding onto Jorja. "Fine, but I want to hear it all. Nothing gets left out." He looks pointedly between me, Noah, and Bentley. "But first I'm going to go skate with my daughter." I can see his chest puff up with pride as he looks down at our girl in his arms. She looks so tiny compared to him, even though she's wearing all those pads.

"Don't forget her helmet," I call, picking it up from where she threw it and passing it to him.

She grabs it out of my hands and shoves it on her head before wriggling in his arms. "Put me down, Daddy, and I'll race you," she tells him, and within minutes, hurricane Jorja is back on the ice with Lola, and the two of them are being chased by their daddies, giggling wildly. It soon turns into a free-for-all as all the kids decide to join in and chase the Titans players. There are smiles and laughter and shouts of joy, but all I feel is frozen inside.

"Hey, at least it's all out in the open now." Kira gives me a hug, squeezing me tightly. "It will be fine. Everything will work out, I can feel it in my gut," she whispers in my ear before pulling away.

We watch as Jorja stops and helps her new friend back to their feet again. I still can't see if it's a boy or a girl, but I'm proud of my daughter's kindness anyway. Kash slides to a stop, spraying them both with ice, and the kids giggle. I watch as he takes one hand, and Jorja takes the other, and they help the kid move around the ice.

"Excuse me." A quiet voice drags my attention away from the ice. Standing off to the side is a pretty woman. She looks younger than me and Kira, maybe nineteen, and she has long, thick brown hair that's parted into two braids. She's wearing skinny jeans and a big, bulky jacket that hides her figure, and she's pale with dark circles under her kind eyes, but she's smiling. "Is that your daughter?" she asks, pointing at Jorja.

"Yes, she is," I reply, smiling encouragingly.

"I'm Shaley, and that's my son she's helping. I just wanted to say that you should be proud of how kind and compassionate she is. Wesley has always wanted to learn to skate, but I haven't been able to afford it. The only reason he's here is because the league offers gear for kids who don't have any." My eyes drift back to the kid between my daughter and Kash. Now that I look closely, I can see that his gear is too big for him, but he's grinning from ear to ear with joy as they move around the ice.

"He's doing well if this is his first time. I'm Mimi, and this is Kira, Bentley, and Noah. Would you like to join us?" I offer politely, but she shakes her head.

"No, but thank you. I have to leave for work soon, but I didn't want to drag him away when he was having so much fun. He doesn't get a lot of joy in his life at the moment, but I try."

I hear the sadness and tension in her voice and realize she has her own problems.

"Well, if you ever need any help getting him to and from practice or the games, let me know. My number will be on one of the many lists," I joke, gesturing to the pamphlets, and her face falls.

"Thanks, but it's a bit more expensive than I can afford. I don't think he'll be joining the team.

"Oh, but there are scholarships you can apply for," Kira says, leaping forward as Shaley starts to walk away. "If you come on Thursday, we can organize the paperwork for you to fill out. It doesn't hurt to try."

"And if you come a little earlier, Jorja and I can

give him a lesson on the ice to help him get his footing," I offer, and tears well in the girl's eyes.

"Really?" She looks between the two of us. "Yeah, okay, that would be amazing. Thank you."

"No problem. We'll see you then," I tell her, and she moves away and waves her hand to get her son's attention. We watch as he thanks Jorja and Kash and skates over to his mom. He pulls his helmet off, and he is the cutest little blond with ringlet curls.

"Mom, did you see me? I was going fast!" His grin stretches from ear to ear, and his mom fusses over him as they remove his borrowed gear. He looks a little thin too, and I wonder if maybe Shaley is struggling to keep food on the table. If I hadn't had Jocelyn, I would have been in the same position, and she obviously had him when she was even younger than I was.

They leave without a backward glance, and Noah steps up and puts his hand on my shoulder.

"Are you okay?"

I nod. "Yeah, I forget not everyone is lucky enough to have an Aunt Jocelyn. That could quite easily have been me."

"Since when does the youth league offer scholarships?" Bentley asks Kira, scratching his head.

Kira shrugs. "Since today. Liam makes enough money, so why shouldn't we help out those who are less fortunate? Even if the leagues aren't interested in starting one, I will pay for his gear and fees for the year."

"And I will give him skating lessons so he'll be able to keep up with the girls."

"You two are too kind." Bentley chuckles, and I shake my head.

"No, we were lucky to have families who love us —or most of them anyway. I just want others to know the same kind of love."

"You can't save everyone, Mimi, and some people don't want to be saved. She might not want to take handouts," Noah cautions, and Kira snorts.

"What, do you think I'm stupid? That's why we'll donate gear for all the kids who can't afford it. That way she won't feel like she's being singled out. Liam will love it. He loves youth hockey and remembers how much he loved it when he played it. The coaching team is happy to have him around now, but they are going to be kicking their own asses when we get further into the season and he's trying to do their job for them."

I feel my body tighten with tension again as the coaches announce that the session is over and the two men and two girls skate back over to us. Kash hasn't let go of Jorja's hand since the little boy left, and Jorja is in daddy heaven.

"Is Daddy coming home to our place for a swim? Daddy should just move in now so he can read me a story and tuck me in every night." My daughter has such high hopes, and I hate the thought of disappointing her.

Before I can answer, Kash does. "Your mom and I have some things to talk about, but after that, we'll swim, and I'd love to tuck you in and read you a story before bed."

I'm glad he didn't make her any promises he wasn't willing to keep, because that is all doable.

"Okay, Daddy," she agrees and starts to struggle out of her gear.

I watch on with tears in my eyes as he automatically helps his daughter like he's been doing it for years. I point out the gear bag when he asks and watch as he packs it as he listens to her tell him all about our house, which we got from Aunt Jocelyn. His eyebrows jump up and down with surprise through the whole story, and I would laugh if the situation wasn't so serious.

"Alright, so we'll meet you all at Mimi's place. You guys are in charge of the food." Kira points to Noah and Bentley. "And you two are in charge of the inflatables." Kira points to Kash and Liam.

"Huh?" Liam scratches his head.

"The kids don't have any pool toys at my place

yet," I explain. "Ethan's pool guy only gave me the go ahead to use the pool yesterday."

"Ethan?" Kash's brow wrinkles in confusion. "How exactly do you know everyone?" he demands, but Kira pushes him out of the way and grabs Jorja's bag out of his hands. Jorja is still wearing her skates and is struggling to get them off, so I start to bend down to help her, but he beats me to it.

"Never mind that. It will all be explained shortly without little flapping ears." Kira looks pointedly at the girls sitting side by side, and they giggle.

"Our ears don't flap, Mommy," Lola tells her as Liam pretends to flap her ears.

"Oh, yes they do." The girls giggle some more, but their fathers carefully extract them from their skates. Jorja slides on her *Paw Patrol* Crocs and leaps to her feet.

"To the Batmobile," she shouts, her little British accent strong, and everyone stares at my child with surprise as I shake my head at the weirdo.

"Sorry, that's most definitely Darcy's influence. He said it every time we went somewhere. Seamus drove a black BMW."

"Seamus? Darcy?" Kash asks, and Jorja jumps up and down, grabbing his hands.

"Yes, they are the best uncles in the world," she tells him, and Liam scoffs with outrage.

"I will have you know that I will be your most favorite uncle in the world."

Jorja stops bouncing and stares at him, trying to figure everything out.

"Kira is Daddy's sister, which makes Liam and Kira your uncle and aunt," I explain, but before I can finish my sentence, she puts it all together.

"And Lola is my cousin. I didn't even need you to marry Noah to be cousins with Lola!" she shouts, and the two girls hug and bounce up and down.

"Nice to feel wanted," Noah mutters good-naturedly.

"Alright, let's get this show on the road." I take Jorja's bag from Kira, and the two of us make our way out of the arena, followed by everyone else. Parents try to stop the two Titans players to talk, but while they are polite, they don't engage.

"I have it on good authority that Jorja would like the biggest unicorn floatie you can find her," I hear Noah mutter to Kash. I smile but don't look back.

I knew there was a reason I trusted my heart and chose to be with these guys. He could have kept that information to himself, but he was happy to help his friend. I only hope they are still friends after we've all had our talk.

CHAPTER 29

Noah

The tension is high as we follow Miriam and Kira out to the car and get the girls and all the gear loaded into the back of Kira's SUV. I can see Kash side-eyeing us as Jorja and Lola, oblivious to everything going on around them, chatter happily. Jorja is absolutely over the moon to know that she and Lola are cousins in real life, and she can't stop referring to Kash as "my daddy," which practically makes him melt at the knees. He leans in to say goodbye to her once she's all strapped into her seat, and she grabs him by the cheeks and presses a sloppy kiss to his mouth.

"Bye, Daddy. See you soon," she calls as he shuts

the door, and she waves to the rest of us as Kira pulls her car out of the parking lot.

Miriam is tense the whole time, and she hops into the passenger seat once everything is loaded without a backward glance for me or Bentley. I can see the hurt in B's eyes as they drive away, but now is not the time to reassure him.

"Would someone like to explain to me what the fuck is going on?" Kash demands, his skates hanging around his shoulders and his feet slipped into his own pair of Crocs. Jorja declared that he needed some Croc gems to go on them, and I can't wait to help her find him something funny.

"I'd like to know the same thing." Liam crosses his arms, and the two of them stare us down.

Bentley leans back against my truck and shoves his hands into his pockets, glaring stubbornly at them.

"Last I heard, you were dating project girl, and you were going on a date with the girl whose house you were fixing up, Mae and Fred's neighbor..." He trails off and looks in the direction the truck went. "You said you'd borrow Mae and Fred's grill?" He points at me. "Does Mimi live next door to them?"

I nod and run a hand through my hair. "Look, I know how this must seem, but trust me when I tell you we had no idea who she was. Remember when Gramps called and told me a branch had gone through his neighbor's roof? Ethan and I went to help, and Dylan tagged along too. We still didn't know who she was, but Gramps and Grammy liked her, and we offered to help her with her renovations. Actually, Gramps volunteered our services, and you know we do anything he asks," I explain as Liam drops the tailgate on my truck and leaps up to get comfortable, but Kash can't sit still. He paces back and forth as he listens to everything I say.

"And I met her in class. We actually got off on the wrong foot, and I felt bad. I liked her long before I knew who she was to you." Bentley sounds defensive, which is probably not the right attitude to take while Kash is feeling so off balance, but here we are.

"Same. It wasn't until I saw Kira, Mimi, Jorja, and Lola next to each other that I put two and two together and worked out that she was your summer mystery girl who broke your heart. By then, it was already too late, and I was falling for her."

"Yeah, and I felt the same when Jorja was sick," B adds.

Kash stops pacing. "Jorja was sick?" he asks, going up to B and shaking him much like he did Mimi, but Bentley pushes him away.

"Yeah, man, stomach flu. She puked all over Mimi in the supermarket. That was Wednesday night. I helped them get cleaned up and took them both home. I made Jorja some chicken noodle soup for when her stomach felt better," Bentley tells Kash, and Kash stares at him wide-eyed for a moment. I'm not sure if he wants to hit or hug him. Hugging wins out.

"Thank you, man, for being there for my girl." Huh, that's interesting. Kash is calling her his girl. Maybe this isn't going to be as bad as I thought it would be.

"Your girl?" Liam sounds surprised. "I'm pretty sure you fucked your way through half the Storm View U campus when your girl disappeared." The fucker sounds like he's playing devil's advocate, and Kash blushes bright red. "I think you need to get a ticket and get in line, because these guys seem to be riding that merry-go-round."

I turn around and stomp toward the flippant asshole. "Don't you dare talk about Miriam that way. You have no idea what she's been through or what our relationship is."

He holds his hands up. "Whoa. Settle down." He looks unsure now, and B stabs a finger in his direction.

"Don't make me fuck up your pretty face. Your

wife may not love you anymore." The threat isn't handed out lightly.

Kash starts to pace back and forth again. "So let me get this straight. You two are both in a relationship with my ex-girlfriend, the mother of my child?"

"Yes," I reply, and Liam whistles behind me.

"Oh, hey, Kira was saying something about this the other day. There was an article in one of my hockey magazines that she was reading. Why she was reading it, I have no idea. She never reads them, but she said that two of the players from Ann Arbor are in a multi-person relationship. What do they call it?" He closes his eyes while he thinks. "Polyamorous? Yes, that's it." He opens his eyes and nods.

Kira has obviously been doing a little ground work for us.

Kash nods slowly. "Yeah, you were talking about that at dinner the other night." He points his finger at me accusingly.

"Yes." I don't deny it. "I'd just worked out who Miriam was, but B didn't know during that conversation. I was already half in love with her, and knowing that both of you felt the same way, I had to come up with something, or two of us were going to get very hurt."

Kash scoffs. "I used to be in love with her."

B just snorts as Liam shakes his head and says, "Yeah, man, keep telling yourself what you need to hear."

"Look, I don't know what's going to happen, but first you need to hear her out. Unless you are working with all the facts, you can't make an informed decision, and if Bentley and I can agree to share her, then I don't see why we can't make room for you too if that's what you want." I'm trying to be calm and rational, but Kash is making it hard.

"And she's happy being passed around like an easy hole?" Before I can stop him, B punches Kash on the jaw. Liam jumps down and holds Kash back as I grab hold of a fuming Bentley.

"Don't you dare fucking speak about her like that. It's not anything like that."

"Hey, man, calm down," Liam tells Kash as he rubs his jaw. I lift up B's hand to make sure he hasn't broken anything, but it looks okay, just a bit red.

"Come on, let's go get some groceries, and you can feed the girls. That will calm you down," I suggest, and B sneers at Kash before turning and climbing into the passenger seat of my truck.

I lift up the tailgate and slam it shut before shaking my head at my best friend. "Don't be a dick, Kash. I know you're shocked, but you're not this guy. Don't bring evil Kash back out to play. Remember how guilty you felt when you realized you'd been lied to? Well, think about what kind of lies Mimi must have been told, not to mention she saw your Facebook feed during those weeks of evil Kash. You don't have any stones to throw in this glass house."

He stops fighting Liam and sags in his hold, and for the second time today, tears stream down his face. "None of it matters if I've lost her to you two."

I step up as Liam releases him and grab his arms, giving him a little shake. "Don't look at it that way. Think about it. You're away almost eight months of the year playing hockey. Wouldn't it be a relief to know that B and I are here looking after them for you?"

Liam nods slowly. "I always worry so much about Kira and Lola that they end up going to Mom and Dad's while I'm away so I can concentrate on my game. I've been thinking about getting them a guard dog and installing a security system to make it less upsetting."

"Ah, man, I'm sorry. I hadn't thought about it that way." Kash slaps Liam on the back in support.

"And with B wanting to open his new restaurant, he's going to have some long hours as well, and you and I will be around when he can't be. And let's face it, it's not like we haven't shared girls in the past."

I drop that last suggestive comment, and he

glares at me again. Fuck, he's going to be a stubborn ass about this.

"Whatever, man. You do you, but B and I aren't giving up, so move and make room for us, because we are going to be in Miriam and Jorja's life whether you want us to be or not. Look, come or don't come for lunch, but if you don't, how do you think your daughter is going to feel? Decide now how you want to go on, Kash, and make the right choice."

With that bit of advice, I climb into the driver's seat and put the keys in the ignition. The truck roars to life, and I shove it into gear, peeling out of the parking lot, annoyed to hell. I watch them in the rearview mirror as I drive away.

"He's going to fuck this up," Bentley mutters, and I can't help but think that he's right.

We arrive at Mimi's place about an hour later. Bentley took ages deciding what to have for lunch and choosing all the groceries. After, I stopped by the liquor store and picked up some beer and coolers for the girls. I figured alcohol would help ease the tension some-what, so to say I'm disappointed when I pull into Miriam's driveway and only find Kira's SUV parked next to the house would be an understatement.

"He's not coming," B mutters, shaking his head. "What a fucking idiot." He climbs out and starts hauling the grocery bags inside. The door is unlocked, and he just walks through. I follow him with two more bags, hearing laughter coming from the backyard.

When we go out back, Kira and Mimi are sitting cross-legged on a blanket on the grass by the pool. She waves, and we head back there.

"I thought you guys might have gotten lost," she teases, but her eyes cloud when she realizes no one is behind us. She recovers quickly and smiles brightly. "Sorry it's not much of a party. I don't even have any patio furniture."

Kira scowls at the fact that there are two men missing, but she keeps quiet.

I crouch down and cup Mimi's face in my hands. "Are you okay?" I ask her, wanting to know how she's feeling after our run-in with Kash. "I'm so sorry. I had no clue he was going to be there, or I would have warned you."

She waves me off. "Don't stress. Kira said the

same thing. At least it's all out in the open now, and did you see how happy Jorja was? Whatever happens, that will always mean the world to me."

I give her a quick kiss on the forehead. "Well, if you need to talk, we're here," I tell her before straightening up. "Come on, B, let's check the shed for chairs before going over to steal Mae and Fred's grill. I'm pretty sure it has wheels."

Bentley bends down and cups her face the same way I did, but instead of kissing her on the forehead, he plants one on her lips. "I see you," he tells her, and she smiles at him, her eyes watering slightly.

"And I see you too, babe." She kisses him again, and he stands up.

I can see he's feeling reassured about where we stand. I think he was worried she was withdrawing when she didn't say goodbye, but I told him it was probably just too much for her and not to overthink it.

"Are you going to cook me some meat?" she asks teasingly, and he cups his junk and thrusts his hips forward.

"I've got your meat right here for you."

"Eww, gross, get away." Kira pushes his legs as Miriam giggles, which is music to my ears. We're going to be okay.

Bentley and I search the shed and find some

Adirondack chairs folded up and covered with canvas. We take two, carrying them back to the grass.

"There isn't a table, but there are enough chairs for all of us," I tell the girls as we place them around their blankets and towels.

"Hi, Noah. Hi, Bentley. Did you bring your swimmers?" Jorja waves from the pool edge. She looks around and frowns, and my stomach sinks. "Where's Daddy? Didn't he come too?" Her voice is so small, we can barely hear her.

Before I can come up with an excuse, however, the back door opens, and Liam and Kash step out carrying the biggest pool toys I've ever seen. The two of them do a couple of trips, and by the time they return, both girls are jumping around like crazy.

"Sorry we're late. It took a while to have them all inflated," Liam apologizes, going over to Kira and giving her a kiss on the cheek.

"Is this for me, Daddy?" Jorja asks as Kash hands her the biggest unicorn inflatable you can probably get while still fitting in a pool.

"Yes, baby. A special person told me you were hoping to have one," Kash tells her while looking at me. I can see the apology in his eyes, and I allow myself to feel a small amount of hope. "Here, shit head, this is for you." He hands Bentley a large poop emoji inflatable, and the two girls giggle.

"That's poop!" Jorja laughs and points to it. "You called Bentley a shit head. Hahaha."

Kash grimaces as Miriam joins us in scowling at him. "I think we're going to need to start a swear jar. Jorja, what have I said about that language?"

"That it's for adults only. Daddy, you owe the swear jar a dollar." Jorja doesn't look repentant at all, and Mimi looks skyward.

"Lord help me."

"Come on, Daddy, let's go for a swim." Jorja tugs on his hand, but he stops her.

"I'll be there in a bit. Uncle Liam and I are just going to help B and Noah get the grill from Fred and Mae's."

"Are you going to use the maze?" she asks and points toward the gate in their fence behind the pool.

"Ah, maybe not this time. We'll do it the easy way, because we'll be carrying the grill," I tell her, and she smiles.

"Okay, but grab your swimmers from Mae's place. She told me you and Ethan were always leaving your clothes lying around."

She and Lola struggle with their inflatables.

Lola's is a beautiful peacock, and both girls are gushing with compliments for each other's ride.

Kira and Miriam go to help them, and I lead the guys back through the house and over to my grandparents' place, pleased with the olive branch and effort Kash is making. Maybe there's still some hope after all.

CHAPTER 30

Kashton

My mind is buzzing with what-ifs and how comes and what the fucks, but I push them all to the side for the moment so I can spend the afternoon grilling with my best friends, my sister, the former love of my life, and our daughter. Holy fuck, our daughter! You could have knocked me over with a feather when Miriam told me that. I mean, how could I have missed it? It was like looking at a mini me, but I wasn't operating with all the facts, like Noah said. I feel like I was smashed into the boards by the defense and my head and heart are still reeling.

My emotions are all over the place, and at any moment, I'm sure I'm going to boil over, but I'm trying my hardest for the sake of my friendship with my boys and for my little girl. She's oblivious to the tension and such a fucking delight.

The four of us are quiet as we wheel the portable grill back from Mae and Fred's. To say they were surprised to see me and Liam is an understatement, and I think they probably know what's going on. How many people around us know? If I think too hard about that, my mind starts creating scenarios again.

Everyone was slow to appear to see us after the game last night. Does this have anything to do with it? Do my parents know and decide it was a good idea to keep me in the dark? I'm not sure if that's something I can forgive them for if that's the case. I'm already mad at my sister—so is Liam, to be honest, but he loves her and will hear her out.

When we return, Bentley begins making us some salads to go with the meat he's preparing, and Jorja and Lola drag Liam and I into the pool with them. She tries to convince Noah to join us too, but he makes the excuse that he's going to find us some more chairs and help Bentley. I think he's just trying to do his best to give us space and time. I can see that both of them have established a rapport with my daughter, and I can't deny that it's not a kick in the gut.

We have a blast throwing the girls around and giving them rides on their floaties, not that there is much room in the pool once both of the darn things are in there. The smell of cooking meat drifts over the pool, making Jorja sit up from where she was reclined on her unicorn like a queen.

"Is Bentley cooking?" she asks, looking around, and she sees him at the grill. She cheers and throws herself off the floaty, narrowly missing the side. She swims to the edge and hauls herself out. "Mama, Bentley is cooking for us!" she shouts and hurries over, and I watch as Miriam pulls a hooded unicorn towel over her head.

"Yes, but please go help your father get the floaty out of the pool."

Jorja pouts but happily skips back to help me. She pulls, and I push, and it soon sits on the side of the pool.

Miriam frowns and looks at the garden shed. "We'll have to store them in there so they don't blow away. I hope they fit."

"Silly Mama, we can just let the air out if they don't," Jorja says, and Miriam grimaces.

"Do you plan to blow them back up? Because I'm pretty sure your daddy had a machine do it."

Jorja isn't listening, though, and she runs back to the pool to help Lola pull her peacock out before turning cartwheels over the grass, while Lola gets her own hooded towel.

"Wow, it's exhausting just watching them." Noah approaches the pool with some beers in his hand. I pull myself out as Liam does the same thing, and we both take one.

"Lola will definitely crash tonight. Hopefully she'll stay awake long enough so when she does fall asleep, she'll be out for the night," Liam says, taking a long drink of his beer.

The silence is slightly awkward as we stand there, watching the girls dance around the grill and talk to B. He just smiles and patiently answers every one of their questions. I never realized how good he was with kids before. Jorja hugs him around his legs, and I feel a pang of jealousy. My daughter is so affectionate. Miriam really has done a good job of raising her.

In the car on the way over, I contemplated suing her for custody. Even though I said I would never do something like that, I was fucking mad, and I have the means to do it, but Liam just looked at me and shook his head.

"Who are you, man?" was all he said, and I put a stop to those thoughts. He's right, that's not me, and my mom would have smacked me around the ears if she heard me saying something like that.

"Here." My sister approaches and throws a towel at us. "Dry off. Bentley is just finishing the meat, and the salads and bread are done. The picnic blanket is our table." She points at where they were sitting. They've straightened out the blanket, and Miriam is setting down plates of salad and rolls. The girls run over, and I watch as they follow her back inside before very carefully returning with some paper plates and plastic cups. Miriam follows them, carrying a jug of some kind of juice and the cutlery. I take the moment to really look her over.

The awkward yet gorgeous teenager I knew and loved is gone, and in her place is a confident, beautiful woman. She changed out of the clothes she wore at the arena, and now she's wearing a strappy little romper that doesn't hide anything. Her breasts look bigger than I remember, and so do her hips. It must have been from her pregnancy. I quickly lower the towel over my crotch as I think about how she must have looked, rounded with my baby. I'm fucked if that's not one of the sexiest thoughts I've ever had.

I feel guilty because I wasn't there to support her through it, as well as cheated that she didn't allow me the opportunity. I'm sick of making up scenarios in my head, and it's time I learned the truth, but I can hold back for a little longer so I can enjoy my first meal with my little girl.

"Daddy, come on. Bentley's meat is ready," Jorja calls, and I can't help but snort. My sister rolls her eyes and walks away as Noah and Liam snicker like teenagers with me.

"Well, we better not keep Bentley's meat waiting," I call back, and she runs ahead to sit at the picnic blanket.

Bentley comes over carrying a tray of grilled sausages and steaks and some fancy-looking kabob things, and he mutters so the girls don't hear. "That's what your mother said last night."

Miriam, who had been taking a drink of her juice, spits it out all over the place, thankfully turning her head in time so she didn't hit the food. She blushes bright red and uses a napkin to wipe her arm.

"Oh my god, I'm so sorry," she apologizes quietly, and Kira giggles.

"No harm," B tells her, cheerfully placing the platter down with the rest of the food and giving her a kiss on the cheek before smirking at me. "Now eat up, everyone. Let's not let my meat get cold."

"Oh, for fuck's sake," Noah mutters and helps himself before sitting on one of the wooden chairs circling the blanket, putting his food on his lap. "I'm sick of hearing about B's meat."

Everyone else helps themself to food, but Jorja cocks her head to the side and looks at Noah with sad eyes. "Do you not like Bentley's meat? I love it, and even my mama says Bentley's meat is so good."

Kira gasps, stands up, and walks away. "Babe?" Liam calls, and she just waves her hands, still walking away as her body shakes with mirth.

"I'm good, give me a moment."

"Okay, how about we stop talking about Bentley's meat and just start eating it?" Mimi suggests to Jorja while the rest of the adults at the blanket burst into laughter. Her head drops. "You are all fucking children," I hear her mutter, and Jorja gasps.

"You said the F word."

"Yes, I did, now eat up, and I'll owe the jar a dollar when we get one."

The rest of us settle down, and the conversation turns light as it's dominated by the children. Jorja regales us with tales of picking fruit in the orchard with Mae, and now Lola wants to go with them next time.

Next, she tells me about going to the flower markets with Uncle Seamus, Darcy, and Aunt Jocelyn. I'm not sure who these people are, but I can tell that they have been a loving family to Miriam and

Jorja when I wasn't able to, and I will forever be grateful.

"Mama's going to take me along to the flower markets when she has her shop here," she tells Lola. "You can come too."

"I'm sure that's just what Mimi needs when she's trying to work," Kira says dryly before raising an eyebrow. "You're opening a shop."

Mimi blushes a pretty pink. "Yeah, Seamus and Darcy are backing me. It's why I'm taking business classes at college, but to be honest, apart from my marketing class, which I love, the rest are boring and not anything I don't already know from working with them in the UK. The only thing that differs slightly are the taxes."

"Did Dad call you?" Noah asks, leaning forward.

"Yeah. He and I are going to look at some places this week. I just hope they are in my budget. And Mae has helped me make a few contacts with some of the flower wholesalers. She's part of a flower arranging club once a month."

Noah chuckles. "Did she wrangle you to come and teach some classes?"

Miriam grins and nods. "Yes. I showed her some photos of some of the special occasion arrangements we did, and she wants me to teach them."

"Not sure why. All those damn women are rich

enough to just pay someone to do it. It's unlikely any of them will ever do it themselves," Kira remarks, leaning back and patting her stomach. "That's a good little food baby," she mutters before groaning. "Why oh why did Bentley's meat have to be so good?" We snicker like teenagers again.

Miriam shakes her head and stands up. "Right, how about we clean up some of this mess?" Jorja and Lola carry their plates back into the house as the rest of us gather everything else. When we get into the kitchen, Jorja pulls out a step, but Miriam shakes her head.

"It's okay, baby. We'll use the dishwasher today. Most of the stuff can go in the bin anyway."

"What was she doing?" I ask Mimi while Jorja happily pushes it away and opens up a rather old-looking dishwasher.

"Oh, because it's just the two of us, we usually just hand wash them. To be honest, I'm not even sure this one will work, but we can give it a go."

"How about Liam and I take the girls to get some ice cream for dessert?" my sister suggests, and Miriam looks at her and mouths, "Thank you."

They take their leave, and the four of us awkwardly clean up before Miriam sighs and throws her towel on the bench. "Come on, let's get this over with. I can't stand the tension any longer."

Miriam leads the way through the house. It's a little dark and cluttered, but I can see how nice it will be after it's had some work done to it. She leads us into what must be considered a living room, but the sofas are outdated and slightly threadbare. "Sorry, but I don't have a lot of options at the moment. It's still a work in progress," she tells us as we look around.

We take a seat, and she takes a deep breath.

"All I ask is that you hold your questions until the end, and I will answer them all. I've told this story too many damn times, and I am glad this will be the last time."

I nod, and she starts speaking. The longer she goes, the higher my temper rises until I'm just about ready to explode. There's a gut-wrenching ache when she tells me how she found out she was pregnant and that the maid told her parents before she could decide what to do. Then she tells me about how difficult her pregnancy was and how rough Jorja's health has been due to her being born early. By the time she's finished, all I want to do is grab a gun and annihilate her parents.

When I ask why she didn't reach out, she explains about seeing what Kira and I said on our Facebook pages. The rush of guilt is immense, and I feel tears well in my eyes once more. We both regretted those posts and later removed them, but I guess the damage was already done.

"I didn't say anything last night, but I'm fairly certain my parents paid someone to keep an eye on me in the UK. Every six months, I'd get a letter in the mail containing a photo of me and Jorja from somewhere we had recently been, with the words, 'We are always watching.' We took it to the police, but they could never trace it."

"Fuck, Mimi, do you think they know you returned?" Noah gets up and starts pacing around the room. I can see how much my friend already cares for my former love.

She shrugs. "The latest one arrived just before I left the UK, so they probably won't notice for another six months."

"And what about this?" I ask, gesturing to the three of them. "Is it something you're just messing around with, or are you serious?"

"We're serious." Bentley reaches out and grabs Miriam's hand.

"What are you going to tell your families?" I ask, shaking my head in disbelief. "They will never accept it."

"Actually, they all know, so do your parents," Noah replies, and I sit upright in my chair, my back straight. Before I can shout at them, Miriam reaches out with her other hand and grabs mine where it's curled in a fist.

"We weren't going behind your back, but there was a series of unfortunate events last night, and I couldn't avoid it any longer. We were all supposed to be at Kira's for dinner tomorrow to tell you, I promise."

I wrinkle my nose. "I thought they were going to tell us they were pregnant," I mutter, still not understanding how they are so calm about all this. "What was their reaction?" I ask, leaning back again, and Miriam smiles.

"Actually, they were all really good. They said it was the perfect relationship for them to be in because it meant they never had to put their friendship before a partner or vice versa."

"Your mom thinks that it's a smart idea." Bentley is still glaring at me like I killed his cat. I must admit, I like how protective he is of Mimi, but he really doesn't need to protect her from me. She's been hurt so badly, and he never has to worry about me hurting the mother of my child.

I mull the idea over in my head. "And say I decide to give this a try... How will it work?"

CHAPTER 31

Miriam

My heart is in my throat, and my stomach rolls with all the intense emotions and bone-aching tension filling the room, but finally, we get to the question I'd been anticipating. Apart from outrage, anger, and guilt, he took our story well... or as well as could be expected, considering his daughter's first six years were ripped away from him, but the relationship aspect is something that's hard to wrap your head around, looking from the outside in, despite it being very easy for the three of us.

I shrug in answer to his question. "There are no rules."

"Except honesty and transparency," Bentley adds, still glaring at his friend. I'm not sure what happened between them once we left the arena, but the tension between them has been very obvious, and I feel sick that I'm the cause of it.

"So far it's been easy, to be honest." Noah is relaxing on the threadbare sofa, his arm draped across the back of it. "We just take it as it comes."

"So does Mimi date you individually or together?" Kash asks, but what he's really asking is if I fuck them together or individually.

"Look, man, it's not like the plot of some seedy-ass porno. We're trying to feel this out as we go. Who knows if it will work?" Noah shakes his head at Kash, his disappointment obvious. "So far, we've both been on separate dates with her, but like today, we've all spent time together, and there will be times when we include Jorja in whatever we are doing too. You just have to make your decision. Are you willing to stop being a stubborn ass and give it a try, however it works, or are you going to deny something that could be amazing because it doesn't fit societal norms?"

God, I could just kiss him right now, and if it wouldn't set Kash off, I would. Noah's keeping this conversation on track and not letting anyone derail it.

"But one thing I won't do if you want to be involved is hide my affection for the others around you. If I want to kiss either of them while you're around, I will, so if that's not something you're down with, that's fine. I wouldn't force you to be in a relationship you feel uncomfortable in, but they deserve my full commitment." I'm firm on this, and I can tell by the tightening of his jaw that he doesn't like it, but he nods his assent.

He sighs and runs a hand through his hair, shrugging. "I don't know if it's something I'm interested in," he says, and my heart sinks. I still love him and hoped he might take a risk, but I understand. "I have the Titans to think about too. The media response could be crushing. They may not approve of it."

"Don't be a fucking pussy, man," Bentley sneers, but I shake my head at him.

"No, he's right. He does have his career to think about. The rest of us are lucky in that it shouldn't affect any of us, but they will rake him across the coals."

"Louella approved it," Noah says quietly, and Kash's head whips around, his eyes narrowed.

"How does she know?" he demands, and I sigh.

"She was there last night. My grandparents were sitting in her box."

"She pulled me aside as we were all leaving and asked me to tell you that if you decide you want to try this unconventional relationship, she will back you, but she would like to have a conversation with you and the coaching team first on how you are going to manage the media before we start making it obvious that your baby mama is dating three men. Also, she said not to leave it too long because these things have a funny way of getting out."

"The whole world knowing will add a layer of protection to Miriam and Jorja from Eric and Leticia too," Bentley tells Kash, still sneering at him.

"Why can't we just have them arrested and be done with it? Or pay someone to get rid of them?" Kash's hands are clenched into fists, and I can see how angry he is.

"We're working toward that. My grandfather's FBI man is getting all his ducks in a row, but it might take some time."

"Look, take a week to think about it. Spend some time reconnecting with your girls, and that may help you decide if you're in or out, but if you say you're out and break Mimi's heart, don't expect us to choose. We love you, man, but if you love us, you wouldn't make us. You would find some way to coexist." Noah says this calmly, but I hear the steel in his words. I used to think instalove was so cliché in my romance books, but this shit does actually happen. I'm not sure what I'd do without either of them anymore. We've become quite the unit in such a short period of time.

"Yeah, okay, sure," Kash agrees, but he doesn't really sound that optimistic. Before anyone can say anything, though, I hear Kira shout through the house. The others have returned.

The girls have another swim, and all the adults join in this time, meaning that the large pool toys had to stay out, but Kash and Liam picked up some other fun things that had the girls playing happily until we were all wrinkled prunes when we got out.

We ordered some pizza for dinner, but both girls' eyes were drooping, so the others took their leave around six. Kash was the only one who stayed. Jorja could barely keep her eyes open as her daddy read her a story and tucked her into bed, and she was out like a light with a smile on her face before he even finished the first couple of pages.

I turned out the light and pulled the door closed, leaving it open a crack. "You want coffee?" I ask Kash as we head downstairs, unable to stand the awkward silence any longer.

"Nah, but I could use another beer," he tells me, and I decide that maybe he's on the right track.

I grab him one and choose a fruity cooler that Noah had bought, and then we head outside to sit on the wooden chairs and watch the sun go down.

We're quiet, but I have nothing else to say to him. I've apologized, but we were manipulated by a pair of pros.

"I'm sorry about all the girls and the horrible things I said when you first left," he says suddenly.

I shrug my shoulders. "Don't worry about it. I probably would have done the same thing if it had been in reverse, and to be honest, it wasn't anything I hadn't expected once you got to college. I was just an immature senior cramping your style." I think back to all my worries when we had been hot and heavy.

He turns in his chair and grabs my hand. "No, Mim, we were end goals. You were it for me. I'd already planned that once I made pro, I was going to ask you to marry me."

I roll my eyes. "I guess that quickly flew out the door."

He drops my hand and hangs his head. "Yeah, I was angry and hurt. I was so in love with you, and you were gone, and I lashed out. I'm not sure I'll ever forgive myself."

"Kash, there's nothing to forgive. We were played. I stopped hating you as soon as our daughter was born. How could I hate someone who played a part in creating such a miracle? I didn't have the mental capacity to hate you with everything else I was worrying about, so I let it go."

He shudders with emotions. "I wish I'd been there for you both."

"Me too, but it's in the past. We just have to make the most of the future. Look, whatever you decide to do, we'll be okay. If you don't want to be involved in whatever I'm building with Noah and Bentley, that's fine, we'll still be the best co-parents a girl can have." I reach out and grab his hand, giving it a squeeze, and we sit in companionable silence as the skyline darkens and the insect symphony becomes loud. I don't want him to feel pressured, but I missed him, and feeling his hand in mine brings me happy memories of our summer together, even if it's only for tonight.

L ife goes on. Jorja and I continue going to school, and Kash is in and out of the house all week. Any time he's not at practice, he's at our house, spending time with his daughter. We still have dinner at Kira's on Monday night so Jorja can officially meet Mary and Simon in grandparent capacity. There are many tears and laughter, but things between Kash and me are still strained. I hate not knowing where we stand, but I need to give him the time to process it.

Bentley and Noah are attentive. They take me out while Kash connects with Jorja. We've been bowling and to a movie, but my favorite was just walking through Mae's orchard and making out like teenagers under the fruit trees. When we returned to the house, Kash could tell what we'd been doing by the state of our hair and clothes, but instead of being aggressive, he kind of seemed sad.

Finally, Thursday comes around, which is Jorja's first hockey practice day, but first I have an appointment with Noah's dad, Mason, to tour a few potential shop fronts. I drop Jorja off at school and drive to the first address. When I get out of my car, I'm surprised to find not only Mason, but Noah, Bentley, and Kash as well. I'd met Mason briefly at the hockey game, but now that I have more time, I notice that his sons really are carbon copies of him. He's rugged and built, like his sons, but now that Ethan has taken over the physical construction side of Wilson Construction, Mason is expanding into real estate. He doesn't want to do physical labor anymore and wants to spend more time with his wife, but at the same time, he doesn't want to get bored. It seemed like a logical transition.

"What is this?" I ask, gesturing at the three guys, and Mason rolls his eyes, chuckling.

"I asked Noah to come along for a reason, but apparently these bozos think you need their 'expert' opinion too. I tried to say no, but they just followed me here."

Next to Mason's truck is Bentley's Aston Martin. Well, I guess they are all getting on well enough to travel together, so that has to mean something, doesn't it?

"I'm here because I was hoping maybe there might be something suitable for me too," Bentley argues, and Noah scoffs.

"Yes, because Dad will be showing Mimi restaurant buildings." Noah does his own eye rolling and looks like his father's twin.

"I wasn't letting them come on their own." Kash shrugs, scuffing the toe of his sneaker on the ground.

"Aren't you supposed to be at practice?" I ask him, and he shakes his head.

"No, we had early morning conditioning, so I'm done for the day."

"Okay, shall we get started then?" Mason asks, pulling out a set of keys, obviously done with the three guys. "I think you're going to love this one. The location is amazing. If you look around, there is a mix of high-end boutiques and mom-and-pop stores, so it means you will get a larger range of clientele. It was previously a florist, so it already has a cool room, but there is also a very large storage area out back that I'm pretty sure we could section off and turn one of the sections into a hothouse for you."

"What happened to the previous tenants?" I ask him as he leads the way, the three guys follow along quietly behind us.

He frowns and looks at a stack of papers in one of his hands. "It says they retired and couldn't sell the shop despite it making excellent money. When I read that, I made a call and spoke to the owner. She and her husband wanted to retire to Florida and weren't prepared to wait the time it would take to sell the shop. Their daughter lives there and had a child or something. Anyway, she was happy to hand over the financials of the previous business because they really want to sell the shop."

"Oh, it's for sale, not rent?" I ask him, and he nods.

"Yes, it's slightly out of your budget, but I think with the foot traffic you're going to get, it will make all the difference. Have a look before you decide, and I can always refer you to our financial advisor."

I worry my lip with my teeth as Mason puts the key in and turns the lock before flicking on some switches and stepping back for me to walk in.

I gasp as I take in the room. The owners must have just shut the doors one night and walked away. The business is fairly intact with everything I need except for plants. There are display shelves and a large table for putting together arrangements. There are also boxes and ribbons and even a balloon and party supplies counter. The shop is way bigger than I had expected. "Wow, this is amazing."

"The price of the shop includes everything you can see," Mason explains, allowing me time to look without any pressure. I make my way around the building, touching and examining everything as I go. It's a little dusty, but nothing a good clean won't fix.

Bentley, Kash, and Noah do the same thing, poking and prodding bits of floral foam and messing around with the stuffed toys.

"What's this?" Bentley asks, pointing at a machine next to the balloon table that looks like an old-fashioned diver's helmet.

"Oh cool. I always wanted one of these, but Seamus said it was gimmicky. It's a balloon stuffer.

It opens the neck of the balloon wide enough so you can fit all sorts of things in there—teddys, baby clothes, flowers, more balloons. It's just a cooler way of wrapping gifts. I think it's fun."

"Why don't I show you the cool room and the storage area? I asked Noah to come along so he can make suggestions about the hothouse for you. I didn't want you to think I was unduly influencing you either way." Mason looks sheepish, and I giggle and give him a side hug.

"That thought never would have crossed my mind."

He leads the way out the back with Noah and I following him. Bentley and Kash stay out front, and I cross my fingers that there's no bloodshed. Bentley has been holding a mean grudge about something. I just hope they work their shit out soon.

The cool room is freaking perfect, and I just want to cry when Noah tells me exactly how we can divide the space so there's still plenty of storage and I can have a nice little hothouse for tropical flowers. I want to ask how much, but I'm scared it's going to be way over my budget. I'm sure Seamus and Darcy would help me if I asked them, but I want to prove that I can stand on my own two feet and support my daughter.

We make our way back out front. Noah is scribbling some numbers on a piece of paper he grabbed from somewhere. "Look, I can't be a hundred percent on figures, since Ethan is the brain behind all that, but I'm happy to build what you need, no charge for labor if I can fit it in around whatever jobs Ethan assigns me and my classes. This is a rough estimate on how much it will cost you. We'll need to wire the new room so we can regulate the humidity and maybe add a mister. I've never done one before, so I'll need to do some research and ask around to see if anyone else on the staff has experience." He hands me a piece of paper, and my eyes jump at the relatively low cost.

"Are you sure?" I ask him, and he grins and gives me a kiss.

"Of course I am. Isn't that what Jorja says I'm for?"

Mason chuckles. "Dad might have some ideas too, and if you get him involved, it will keep him out of Mom's hair."

"That's a good idea. He drove Ethan nuts supervising last week at Miriam's place. Ethan will owe me one. In fact, he may even throw in the cost of the materials to get Gramps off his back."

"Wow, I can't thank you both enough." I take a deep breath and brace myself. "Okay, so what do they want for this place?"

Mason mentions a figure, and I feel a little light-headed. "But I'm certain I can get it down to..." He mentions another figure that's a little more reasonable but still out of my budget.

I feel my heart sink, but I plaster on a smile. "Okay, how about you show me the other ones as well while I think about it?"

"What's there to think about?" Kash demands gruffly.

"You obviously love it, so why don't you get it?" Bentley chimes in, sounding like he can't understand what the holdup is.

I grit my teeth, annoyed at the rich boy's tone deafness. "Because I'm not sure I can afford it," I tell them, and Kash just shrugs his shoulders.

"I'll buy it for you." The room is silent for a moment as I stare at him in shock.

"Ah, I need to make a phone call. How about I give you all a moment?" Mason hurries out. That man is not stupid.

"What?" I stutter, not sure if I heard him right.

"I said I'd buy it for you. See it as an investment into my daughter. If her mother is happy, she will be happy. I haven't been able to help for the first six years, so it's the least I can do now."

"Kash, that's so kind of you, but I can't accept it."

"Why not?" Bentley demands, and my eyes swing to him and then Noah who shrugs. "He has the money, so let him."

"Look, if you are uncomfortable with me doing this, then we can work out a repayment system, but I won't charge you interest and you can do it at your own pace. Everyone is happy," Kash says lightly like it's no big deal, but I see him brace for rejection.

I can't help myself, and I wrap my arms around him and hug him hard. "Thank you," I whisper as his arms come up, and we embrace for the first time since all those years ago. He's wider and harder than back then, but he still smells the same, and I melt into him.

"You're welcome," he says, pressing a kiss to my hair, sounding pleased.

"Well, I say this is a cause for celebration. Let's go get lunch at Lou's before picking Jorja up for hockey." Bentley sounds pretty pleased with himself, and when I glance at him, he winks at me.

Why do I get the feeling he may have had something to do with Kash's offer? I won't worry about that now, I'm just happy they seem to be getting along better.

CHAPTER 32

Miriam

The paperwork for the shop takes a couple of hours, so it's almost one in the afternoon when we arrive at Lou's for lunch. It will take a few weeks for the transaction to settle, so I have some time to make plans, but I'm already writing lists in my head. I can't wait to call Seamus and Darcy and tell them all about everything that's happened. It won't surprise me if they get on the next flight over from the UK. Everything is just too exciting for them to be left out.

"Hey, look at this! You're out with all your beaus!" Peaches smirks as she comes to take our order.

"Shouldn't you be at school?" Kash growls

before I can dispute her claim. Now that he mentions it, she wasn't there last Friday either.

She shrugs. "I have free periods Thursday and Friday afternoons, so I might as well be making money, but slow your roll. Normally I'm out on the ranch helping with the horses, but one of Grams' server's kid is sick, so I've been helping out."

"Louella owns one of the preeminent cattle ranches in the state and breeds stunning quarter horses. Peaches wins plenty of rodeo competitions showing them." Bentley sounds proud and reaches over and ruffles the girl's hair.

She slaps his hands but grins. "You should all come out for a ride one day," she suggests, and Bentley turns white.

"Ah, no, I will stick to having all my horses under the hood of my car, thank you, and my balls thank me."

Peaches chuckles evilly, but before she can tell me the story, someone waves for her attention, so she tells us she'll be back in a moment.

"Not a fan of horses?" I ask him, and he grimaces.

"I am, but my balls aren't. We are all happier when I just abstain."

"How did we end up talking about Bentley's meat again?" Noah says dryly, leaning back in the booth and putting his arm around my shoulder. I see Kash eye it closely before turning his attention back to the menu in front of him.

I giggle, and Kash snorts, but Bentley just grins. "Because my meat is spectacular. Isn't it, Mimi?"

There's a moment of silence as we all wait for Kash to lose his shit at Bentley's insinuation, but all he says is, "Well, it certainly looks like a shish kebab. Maybe that's why Mimi likes it. I saw her enjoying those on Sunday."

Holy fuck, and now I'm dead. I thought for sure he wasn't interested, but he seems to be coming around slowly. Noah and Bentley burst into laughter as I feel myself blush hot with embarrassment.

"I seem to remember you quite enjoyed my meat-eating skills," I hiss at him, and a slow grin spreads across his lips.

"Yes, that's right. They have me to thank for your talents at eating meat, don't they?"

I squirm in my seat as I think about learning to suck cock in the back seat of Kash's Jeep, parked in a truck stop out of the way.

The sexual tension in the booth is off the fucking charts when Peaches returns. She's busy scribbling on her notepad, so she doesn't notice. "Alright, what will it be?"

Kash, Noah, and I all order the brisket and slaw,

and Bentley orders pork ribs and potato salad. The guys ask for a beer, and I look longingly at the margarita menu but opt for apple juice instead because I'm driving.

"If you want a margarita, have one. I'll drive your car and pick Jorja up from school," Noah suggests.

"Aww, Jesus, he's sweet. Why can't I find a guy who's sweet and can keep his dick in his pants?" Peaches mutters, and the boys all come to attention.

"Someone cheated on you?" Bentley growls.

"Who is it? We'll pay him a visit," Kash threatens.

Peaches smiles, but her eyes are sad. "It's fine. It was a while ago, and it's been taken care of. I'll get these, and you are having a margarita," she tells me before hurrying away so they can't ask her any more questions.

"How old is she?" I ask, and Noah's forehead wrinkles.

"Same age as Dylan, I think, so she just started her senior year. She just turned seventeen, if I remember correctly."

"Yeah, I was talking to her at the hockey game while I was trying to keep the girls occupied, and she told me she doesn't want to go to college. She wants to work on Grams' ranch and take over those operations."

"Yeah, Louella's late husband was a genius at investment and business, and Louella learned everything along with him. He passed before Peaches was born."

"Where are Peaches' parents?" I ask, and the three of them develop expressions like thunderclouds.

"That woman is a waste of space," Kash growls, and Bentley grunts his agreement.

"Nobody knows who her father is. Her mother wouldn't say."

"She basically handed her over to Louella when she was born and disappeared. Louella and her husband believed in working for what you have, much like your grandpa," Noah tells me. "She wasn't happy with that. She didn't want to work, she wanted to be taken care of and have money to spend. She's been looking for a sugar daddy ever since. I think she's scored more than a few, but they never last. She reappears for a moment, wreaks havoc in both their lives, then disappears when she finds someone else to con."

"Poor Peaches." I sigh as I watch the girl talk to the man behind the bar who's putting our drinks together. "I know how she feels."

"Yeah, I don't doubt you two could compare stories," Kash growls, and his teeth gnash together like they do every time my parents get mentioned.

The conversation turns to lighter topics, and the food and drinks are brought out. Before I know it, it's time to pick up Jorja. It was comfortable, and there was no tension except for an occasional rise in sexual tension. I start to feel hope for what may be, but Kash still hasn't committed either way, and I'm dying to know what his decision is.

"That was delicious. I'm stuffed. I hope Jorja doesn't want to eat dinner tonight, because I'm not sure I can fit anything else," I say as I throw my napkin on the table.

"How can you do that to the poor darling? She'll be starving after ice hockey," Bentley scolds me, and I shrug.

"I'll get her a happy meal on the way home."

He gasps like I suggested starving her. "You won't feed her crap. I'll get some groceries on the way home and make her some home-made chicken fingers and potato salad. This one was good, but mine is better." He waves at his empty plate imperiously.

Kash and Noah chuckle. "You've done it now," Noah grumbles, and Kash grins.

"Thankfully Mimi and I have to go pick up Jorja."

He slides out of the booth and offers me his hand. "Have fun," he tells Noah.

"Hey, I said I would drive Mimi," Noah calls as Kash hurries us out of the sports bar, paying the tab on the way out.

"What the hell was that?" I ask him as he guides me to my car with a cheeky grin on his face.

"Bentley acts like fast food has been put on Earth to spite him, and Noah will probably hear him grumble about how it's cheaper and a lot healthier for people to cook, blah blah blah, all the way to the arena."

I look back at the direction of the sports bar. "That was mean," I tell him, and he shrugs unapologetically.

"I may be coming around to the idea of sharing you, but it's still every man for themselves when it comes to Bentley and his fast-food hatred."

A thrill of excitement washes over me at hearing Kash admit that, and I happily hand over the keys when he holds his hand out. He unlocks the car and holds the door open for me, ever the gentleman I remember. These boys' mamas taught them right.

We drive to Jorja's school together and find Kira waiting under the same tree that I'd been under that first day. "Well, I can't say I'm not happy to see you two together." She raises an eyebrow at me in question, and I shrug. I still don't know either way. "How did the viewings go?" she asks me, and I can't help but bounce up and down with excitement much like my daughter does.

"Oh my god, we found a place, and we signed a contract. I can't wait. I'm not sure how I'm going to manage it on my own, but I'll work something out."

"We?" she asks, looking between us, and Kash shrugs like it's not a big deal.

"I'm helping her out a little bit."

"A little bit? He bought me the whole place. I'm going to pay him back of course, but he made it possible for me to have my dream. I don't know what I'd do without him." I throw my arms around him, hugging him hard again, hoping he realizes how much this means to me.

"Aww, you're such a big softy," Kira teases her brother, and I feel him flip her off as his arms come up and he hugs me back.

She giggles. "Look, I know this might be a bit pushy, but I've been looking for something to do now that Lola's at school. There are only so many lunches I can attend with vapid Felicia clones. None of the hockey guys are married except Joe, and while I love his wife and we're good friends, she has a newborn at home and no time to hang out, which means I'm stuck with the mothers here, and ugh, they are hard to take in little doses."

"Hey, Kira would be perfect for running the balloon section of your shop since she's full of hot air," Kash teases as he drops one of his arms so I can turn to look at her, but he leaves one wrapped around my waist, his thumb caressing my skin where my shirt has risen up.

Thank fuck I'm wearing a bra today and my nipples are hidden, because they would practically be poking Kira's eyes out with how hard they are just from his touch. I shiver, and he looks down at me and winks.

"Asshole. Also, can we keep the eye fucking to a minimum please? There are children around," Kira scolds playfully.

I blush and step away slightly, and I see disappointment in his eyes before he quickly hides it. There are a lot of people around, and I'm still not sure if he's all in, so we need to be more careful.

"I love the idea of the two of us working together, and if you don't like it, it's not a big deal. Although the sale won't be final for a few weeks, Mason says the owners are happy for me to have the keys on Monday. Why don't we get together after school drop-off and talk about it, and you can see the shop?"

It's Kira's turn to jump up and down. "That would be awesome, thank you!"

"Also, I'd love to hear if you have any ideas on local artisan suppliers for soaps and candles and shit."

She tips her head like she's thinking. "I don't think I know anyone personally, but I can ask around."

"Didn't you do a soap making workshop or something?" Kash hip bumps his sister. "I remember Liam smelled all flowery for a few weeks, and the guys gave him shit, but he happily bragged that you made it and he wanted to make you happy."

Kira groans. "Yeah, I did a workshop, and they only had a couple of choices as far as fragrances went, but I had a blast."

"Instead of sourcing it, why don't you make your own products? Then you will be keeping all your business in-house," he suggests, and I blink stupidly for a moment.

"What an awesome idea. The only reason I was going to source them was because I won't have time to make the product if I'm doing the floral arrangements, but Kira could."

Kira looks slightly stunned, but before she can argue, the bell rings. I'm not really paying attention because I'm plotting world domination in my head.

"Hi, Daddy, hi. Are we going to hockey now?" Jorja bounces up and down in front of us all of a sudden, and he picks her up, throwing her into the air before giving her a kiss.

"We sure are," he tells her, and she cheers as Lola hugs her mom and then wraps her arms around Kash's leg.

"Me too, Uncle Kash."

Kash puts Jorja down, who laughs with delight as he lifts his niece and throws her in the air too.

"Ms. Kennedy?" I turn around to find Mrs. Brady waving at me from the doorway to the school.

"I'll see you at the car," I say, and Kash frowns, but someone needs to watch Jorja while I speak to her teacher.

I make my way over, and she smiles hesitantly and asks me to join her in her classroom. I take a seat at her desk in one of the student chairs, feeling decidedly uncomfortable, and I don't know why.

"I just wanted to ask you a few questions. Jorja has been telling the class that she has three daddies now," Mrs. Brady says, and I'm not sure if she's asking a question or not, and I feel slightly defensive.

"And?" I ask, unsure what the problem is.

"She's also telling everyone that she and Lola are cousins. Now, I don't like to encourage lying in my class, and I was wondering if you could speak to her."

I feel a moment of panic. So far, we have managed to keep our story between the relevant families, but I hadn't even thought to ask Jorja to censor her words.

"Well, Jorja isn't really lying, so I won't be doing that," I tell her, my hackles rising at her insinuation.

"How are Jorja and Lola related?" she inquires, and I can tell she's being nosy.

"I don't see how that's any of your business now."

She frowns, and the woman goes down in my esteem. "Well, we need all that information for our school records," she argues, and I shake my head.

"I filled out my details and an emergency contact." I put down Mae Wilson. I will have to update them, but I'll wait to see what Kash decides either way. "That was all that was required. I'm not sure why anything else is relevant."

She sighs like I'm being difficult. "Look, it's part of the school policy that our families must not bring our organization into ill repute. If you are dating more than one man, then it may be a problem."

Oh, fuck no. "Excuse me, but my private life should have no bearing on Jorja's education."

"The school committee may see it another way."

She's trying to seem sympathetic, but I know she's annoyed that I haven't fed her need for gossip.

I grin. "Mae Wilson is on the school committee, isn't she?"

Mrs. Brady nods. "Yes, she is. Fine old family, the Wilsons."

"Oh, and Violet and Calvin Kennedy?"

She nods quickly, but it slows as she puts two and two together.

"Yes, the same Kennedy as my surname, my grandparents, and Mae is my neighbor, so I believe your threats may be a little empty, but feel free to take it to them if you feel you must." I stand up and make my way out of the classroom, anger warring with worry. Kash better make his decision quickly, or our daughter is going to out us before we're ready.

CHAPTER 33

Bentley

When Kash and Miriam arrive at the arena with Jorja, there's tension between them, and I swear I want to punch my best friend again. He's going to fuck all of this up, but I watch with surprise as they both help Jorja get ready. They work like a well-oiled machine, and before we know it, Jorja is on the ice. Kash disappears somewhere, and Mimi joins me and Noah in the first row.

"Is everything okay? You seem a little tense?" Noah asks carefully, and Mimi sighs and rests her head on my shoulder.

"What did he do? Do I need to pummel him again."

She raises her head and looks at me with surprise. "You hit him?"

"Yes, and I'll do it again if he deserves it," I growl, starting to stand up, but she puts her hand on my thigh, stopping me. My cock twitches in my jeans. We agreed not to flaunt sex in Kash's face this week, and he's always been around, so apart from making out in the orchard and at the movies, intimacy has been lacking.

"No, Kash hasn't done anything, I swear. He's been wonderful. I just wish I knew one way or the other. It was Jorja's teacher. She was being nosy and made some insinuations that slutty moms weren't welcome at the school."

"She did not!" Kira gasps as she approaches. Lola took a little longer to get ready because Liam isn't here. He had a meeting with his lawyer. His parents are making waves again, but he'll be here soon.

"Yeah, she did. I basically told her to fuck off in a polite way by reminding her that both my grandparents and my neighbor are on the school board, although I can't deny being in limbo is hard. I don't know where I stand with him. He hasn't even tried to kiss me. I think he's just not attracted to me anymore."

I clench my fists and have to hold myself back

from finding my friend and shaking some sense into him.

"Give him time. He's trying," Noah tells her, and she looks out over the ice, watching Jorja and Lola skate and hit a puck back and forth between them. We came early because Miriam offered to give the little boy Jorja befriended lessons before practice, but he and his mother don't seem to be here.

"Here." Kash appears out of nowhere, and he's holding a pair of skates for Miriam. They are not hockey skates, but actual figure skates.

Her eyes widen, and she looks up at him with surprise as she reaches out to grab them. In his other hand, he has his own pair of figure skates.

"I thought you might want to blow off some steam."

Her smile is blinding, and she quickly toes off her sneakers and pulls on the skates. Kash does the same before standing up and holding out his hand. He escorts her to the ice, and they step onto it and glide around together.

"What the hell?" I mutter as Kira squeezes between me and Noah and takes Mimi's vacated seat.

"Did you know that when Liam and Kash were about sixteen, their hockey coach at the time told them that if they were serious about going pro, they should consider taking some pairs figure skating lessons? He said it would help them with their foot-work. They scoffed but trusted their coach, so they signed up and dragged me and Miriam along. There was no way that Kash was going to do ice dancing with me, so he skated with her, and Liam and I were a pair. We were terrible, and both of us hated it, so we didn't last long, but Kash and Miriam were magic on ice. It was like they just clicked, to the extent that their figure skating coach wanted them to compete. They wouldn't because their love of hockey overruled everything else, but I'm almost certain that's when they fell in love, though they fought it for a little while."

We've been watching while the two of them skate around in circles, talking quietly. Miriam keeps shaking her head, and he keeps nodding, but Kash suddenly reaches for Miriam's hand as music comes on over the speaker system, and I watch in awe as they perform an elaborate routine. Jorja and Lola stop what they are doing and skate over to the side to watch with us.

Jorja sighs. "My mama and daddy look beautiful."

They really do. They move like one organism. My heart leaps into my throat as Kash bends and lifts Miriam over his head, her body upside down and her legs spread wide, the grin on her face is magical. He lowers her to the ice, and they come to a stop. She laughs, breathing heavily and holding her side.

"Holy crap, I can't believe you can still lift me! I've put on so much weight, and I think I pulled a muscle in my side," she tells him breathlessly, and he smiles and twirls her around before they skate back toward us. I know something happened while they were skating, or maybe it was before that, but I can see it in my best friend's eyes that he's all in.

"He isn't sure how to approach the physical side of the relationship with her," Kira says quietly out of the side of her mouth, making both Noah and I gape at her in surprise. "If you say I said something, I'll deny it, but I thought maybe you two could help." She stands up as the arena starts to fill with other kids and parents.

Miriam and Kash skate over to us, both of them grinning with joy, and I feel a rush of happiness. This is going to happen, we just have to help Kash get out of his head, and I have the perfect idea.

"You two looked amazing," Noah says as they step off the ice as children start to trickle out in hockey gear.

"Yes, you did. I didn't know you could girlie skate," I tease Kash, who looks around before flipping me off.

"Oh, that was so much fun, but gosh, I'm unfit." Miriam sits back in her spot now that Kira moved. "I need to do that more often." She unlaces her skates and pulls them off before pulling her shoes back on. She picks them up to hand them to Kash, and he shrugs.

"They are yours."

"Mine?" she asks, blinking with surprise.

"Yeah, I got them from the pro shop in the lobby. Maybe we can skate together more often. I've missed it." He sounds unsure, and I want to crow that my big, badass pro hockey player friend is struggling with a girl. I guess when they actually mean something, you don't want to fuck it up, but from the smile on Mimi's face, I'd say he's doing alright.

"I'd like that," she tells him, "as long as I get to go one-on-one with you too." We all know she's talking hockey, but we're males, and our brains go elsewhere, so when his eyes narrow and become heated, I shift on my seat to make room in my pants for my rapidly hardening cock.

"I'm sure I can figure something out," he promises her.

Noah is watching them with his scheming face on, and I know he's thinking about what Kira said.

It's Kash's turn to get out of his head, and I have the perfect plan.

I stand up and give Noah a nudge, and thankfully he must be on the same wavelength. "Who wants coffee? We'll get them while you watch the kiddies," I suggest, and they all put in their orders.

"Oh, there's Shaley and Wesley. I'm going to go speak to them. Liam and I made an anonymous donation early in the week specifying that he had to be one of the recipients. I have some fake forms to fill out, but Louella is going to ensure he gets what he needs. She's arranged for the pro shop here to help them after today's practice." Kira hurries away, and Miriam looks at the two of them thoughtfully.

"What are you thinking?" I ask.

"I was just wondering if we are going to need another person in the shop to help out."

"That's sweet of you. I'm sure both of you could benefit from having an assistant. All three of you have children, so there are going to be times when someone is sick or has needs," Kash says.

We leave the two of them and make our way to the concession stand, our heads together as we plot. Miriam's submissive side is going to play perfectly into my plans to get my friend well and truly committed to this relationship. I make a phone call to

Peaches, knowing she has access to the arena, begging her for help. She agrees but makes me promise never to speak to her again about our sex life.

By the time we return, we have hashed everything out. We arrange for Jorja to go home with Kira for dinner and promise her that by the time we're done, Mimi and Kash will be back on track.

"Don't fuck this up," is her only warning.

Practice wraps up, and Miriam is surprised when Kira tells her she's going to take Jorja and Lola out for a happy meal and then home. It's the only part of the plan that I'm not happy with, but I can't very well leave to make them real chicken nuggets and still be involved with the plan. We watch and bide our time, keeping the two of them occupied with conversation so neither of them realizes everyone has left except us. Peaches gave us the security code and assured us that the cameras will be switched off for a few hours. No one is in the arena but us.

Noah and I separate the two of them. Noah asks Miriam to follow him to the pro shop so she can point out something he can buy Jorja as a gift, and I offer to give Kash a hand with the equipment. They both look at us strangely because yeah, the ideas suck, but it was the best we could come up with on short notice.

Kash and I chat happily, the animosity gone between us now that I know he's all in even though he hasn't said anything. Finally, he becomes aware that Noah and Mimi have been gone for a long time.

"Where are they?" He looks at the watch on his wrist, but I ignore him.

"So have you decided?" I ask him firmly, and he sighs and looks me straight in the eye.

"I still love her, man, and if that means I have to love her along with you two assholes, then that's okay with me. Over the week, I've seen that both of you are all in. I was worried it was just a bit of fun for you, a novelty," he says, and I go to argue, but he holds up his hand. "But I can tell you're committed to making her happy, and that's what matters to me, so don't fuck this up," he growls, and I arch an eyebrow.

"What, like you have been?" I retort, and he groans.

"I'm trying, man. It was so easy before, we just sort of fell together, but I don't know how to leap over everything that's between us now."

"Dude, you are so fucking overthinking this. Just grab her and kiss her."

"Easy for you to say since you're not carrying around a whole heap of baggage."

I shake my head and lean back in my seat. "Did you know that Mimi's quite the little submissive?" I say conversationally.

He grunts like he doesn't want to talk about it, but he leans toward me, and I know I've got him.

"She likes to be told what to do, loves it when you praise her, and fucking gushes when you take her choices from her."

He clenches his fists and glares at me. "She doesn't consent?"

"Whoa, no, hang on, it's not like that, I promise. It's not rape or even no consent. It's just a part of her likes to have all the decisions taken out of her hands. She likes to feel caged and wanted and needed."

My phone lights up, and it's a message from Noah telling me they are ready. I stand up and tap him on the shoulder. "Come on, I'll explain it." I walk along the stands in the direction of the Titans' locker room. Kash looks down at the gear at his feet. "Leave it. We'll come back for it."

Curiosity must weigh out over concern, because I hear him behind me, and I smile. Got him.

I bring him into the corridor that leads to their

locker room, and Noah meets us just outside the door. I can see through the frosted windows that the lights are out.

"Where's Mim?" Kash asks, sounding confused.

"She's in there." Noah nods to the darkened room. "Somewhere." The Titans' locker rooms are a huge labyrinth of lockers and hockey and workout equipment, not to mention the physical therapy tubs, saunas, and steam room.

"What do you mean somewhere?"

I grin and start to strip off my clothes, and Noah does the same.

"We're playing an adult version of hide-and-seek. The first to find her gets to fuck her, and she's handcuffed. She's going to look so pretty on her knees with my cock in her mouth," I taunt him when he seems frozen on the spot.

"She agreed to this?" he asks Noah, whose hand is on the buckle of his pants.

"Not only did she agree to it, she was dripping down her thighs when I stripped her naked and let her go."

"She's naked? What about cameras?" Kash looks around, and I shake my head.

"Turned off. Come on, man, are you going to play or not?" I know I got him when he starts to remove his clothes. "When I get to her, I'm going to bend her over and fuck her doggy style. She's going to love the feeling of my piercings in her pussy."

He starts to strip faster, not even realizing that Noah and I haven't gone any further than our jeans.

"I can't wait to paint her tits with my cum," Noah says, and when he adjusts himself, I know how he feels. Kash is going to owe us.

"Her safe word is pineapple. Anything goes unless she says that," I tell Kash, who nods his assent. He nudges off his shoes and socks and pulls his jeans down just as Noah shouts, "Go!"

Kash tears through the doors like a bat out of hell, and the two of us grin wickedly at each other.

"You're both very welcome," I say quietly as Noah and I redress. Noah lays Mimi's clothes with Kash's on the floor. He adds a note, telling them that we'll see them at home and we'll pick up Jorja. I'm whistling as we gather all the gear on the way out to the car. As we leave the arena, Noah puts his arm around me.

"We did good, but he fucking owes us. I'm as hard as a rock. Miriam is so responsive. I want to play this game in my grandparents' orchard one night."

"I'll be down for that," I agree, hoping none of this backfires.

CHAPTER 34

Miriam

I'm so confused when Noah drags me toward the pro shop. "Isn't it closed?" I ask him, and he chuckles and nods.

"Yup, it is, but I had to get you away from Kash for a moment," he says as he guides me to the left. We wind our way around the arena until we get to the players' corridor. We turn down it and head in the direction of the Titans' locker room.

"Why? What are we doing?" I ask him as we stop in front of it. There is no one around, and I know that everyone is leaving the arena as we dawdle here.

He pushes me back against the wall next to the door, and I shiver with desire. I love it when these men surround me, but we haven't had any opportunity to be together since the first night except for a bit of fooling around in the orchard.

He smirks before leaning down and whispering, "A little bird may have whispered in my and Bentley's ear and told us that Kash is nervous about rekindling a physical relationship with you."

"He is?" I ask, unable to hide the surprise in my voice. "He still wants me?"

Noah chuckles darkly, and my nipples pebble at the sound. I love it when his dominant side comes out to play. Both he and Bentley excel at hitting kinks I didn't even know I had.

"Oh, baby, how could you think he doesn't? We see him watching you constantly, but both of you have so many issues the two of you have to get over."

"But how?" I ask him, and he pushes his body against mine, and I melt into him.

"Because you're going to be a good little girl and play a game with him for us, aren't you?"

"A game?" I ask breathlessly, completely turned on. "Here?" I look up at the camera I can see out of the corner of my eye and feel my panties grow damp. Shit, another kink, but maybe not for anyone's viewing pleasure but my guys.

"Yes, here. No one is around. It's just going to be

us and you. We're the predators, and you're the prey." He pulls back and grins wickedly at me. "And you're going to run from us. Whoever catches you first gets to fuck you until you come. Then they'll let you go, and the game continues."

Holy fuck. My eyes roll back in my head, and my core throbs with need.

"And if I get away?" I ask, and he just grins wider.

"You won't because our girl likes to please her men. You will pretend to struggle, but secretly, you'll love it because you're a good girl."

Ugh, just fuck me now, I'm yours, my body begs as I rub against him.

"I need to hear your words, Miriam." His tone is firm as he wraps his hand around my ponytail and angles my head so I'm looking at him.

"Okay." I'm breathless and needy, and his eyes brighten with excitement.

"Good girl. You're going to do everything I tell you, aren't you?" he says, and I quickly agree. I would agree to anything right now.

He releases my hair and steps back, grabbing my hand and leading me into the locker room. "I'm going to let you have a look around so that when the lights are out, you don't hurt yourself."

"It's going to be dark?" I ask as he lets me get the

lay of the land. The locker room is huge, and I quickly take note of a number of hiding spots.

"Yes, it wouldn't be fun if we could find you right away." We return to the front door, and Noah steps back. "Strip," he commands, and I peel off my clothes so all I'm in are a bra and panties.

"Uh-uh, those too."

I shiver from excitement as I reach around and unclasp my bra, letting it fall down my arms to join my other clothes. I shimmy out of my panties, and they also join the pile. Noah stalks toward me and leans in, running his nose up the column of my neck.

"Look at those pretty nipples just begging for me to bite them, but I better not get a head start, that's not fair to the others."

He squats and picks up the clothes at my feet, but not before he leans in and takes a swipe of my clit with his tongue. My knees buckle, and he catches me before I can fall to the ground. "Delicious. I have your scent now. Turn around," he commands, and I do. He draws my arms back and uses my panties to tie my wrists together. "Now run." He slaps my ass, and I squeal and take off like a lion is after me. Well, maybe not a lion, but the big bad wolf, and he wants to eat me.

I don't get very far before the lights turn out. Noah does his best to scare me by making loud noises and banging his fist against the locker. I have to move slower now, but my adrenaline is racing, and I can't stop myself from panting. Without the use of my hands, my progress is practically at a snail's pace, and I'm kind of lost.

The noises die away, and my heart skips a beat. Have they started hunting for me? I was going to hide in the empty ice tub, hopeful they wouldn't think to look there. A small glow in the dark sign tells me I've made it to the physiotherapy room. Through this door are the ice tubs, hot tubs, and the steam and sauna rooms as well as a few of the massage tables for rub downs after a hard game or workout.

I hear the front door slam open, and I can't help the gasp that escapes my mouth. My whole body is trembling with the rush of pheromones, and I feel myself leak down my legs. I'm so desperate to be caught and fucked, but I want to make them work for it.

"Come out, come out, wherever you are." The voice echoes through the rooms and has an eerie quality to it. I can't even recognize whose voice it is, which makes the anticipation even higher.

I push through the door and try to let it close slowly behind me, but it's difficult with my hands tied behind my back, and it slips from my fingers.

"Gotcha. I'm coming to get you," the voice calls. It sounds closer but no less clearer.

I wonder who it is. As much as I would like it to be any of them, I'm secretly hoping it's Kash. I think this was a way to get us both out of our heads, but I hope my submission isn't going to turn him off. We didn't play any of these kinds of games when we were together previously, so this is new for him.

There's a little bit of light in this room, since the hot tubs have internal lights that didn't go out when the rest did. Shit, that's going to make it easier to find me. My eyes slide to the sauna. It's turned off, and I think I can make it in there before he comes through the door. Hopefully he won't think to look in there in his rush to find me, whoever it is.

I move as fast as I can given the circumstances, but my heart sinks when I get to the door. I need to push down on a handle to open it. Fuck, with my hands tied behind my back, I don't think I'm going to be able to manage it.

The door to the physio room suddenly slams open. I'm out of time. I squint as I try to make out who caught me, but the low lighting makes it hard. I turn and try to hurry in the direction of the workout area, but I'm not quick enough, and my body gets gently pushed up against the wall so I'm surrounded by the large body that has caught up with me. I bite my lip to hold in my moan, not wanting to give away how turned on I am. I struggle, but let's face it, it's halfhearted. Heavy breathing sounds in my ear, and calloused hands slide across my stomach, one going up to cup a breast, and the other gliding down to slide a finger through my wet folds. It has to be Noah or Kash then, because Bentley's hands are softer from all the washing he does as a chef.

"You know, when Bentley told me you were a submissive, I almost scoffed. I remember how you used to ride me on the back seat of my Jeep with wild abandon, so I thought there was no way my pretty girl was a submissive, but then I remembered how you used to gush all over my cock every time I said you were a good girl, and it all started to make sense." Kash's breathing is ragged, and his skin is scorching hot as he presses me harder into the wall, his thick cock rubbing against my naked ass through his boxers.

"Do you like to be told what to do, Mim? Do you like having all the decisions taken out of your hands? Does my pretty little girl like to please her masters?"

I shiver, and a whimper escapes. Kash is pushing every one of my buttons at the same time as he circles my clit with a finger dipped in my juices.

He slides it through my folds again. "You're dripping wet and just dying for my cock, aren't you?"

I still don't say a word, and he tugs on my hair, making me turn my head so I can see him slightly. In this light, he looks devilish, and it sends my heart racing faster.

"Answer me," he demands.

"Yes I want your cock," I pant out as he brings his finger up and sticks it in my mouth. "Suck it. Taste how needy you are for me."

Oh my god, this is a new dynamic for us, but fuck, I am here for it. Opening my mouth, I latch onto his finger, sucking it like I would suck his cock.

"Bentley was right, you're going to look so good on your knees with my cock in your throat. Has he seen you with a cock in your throat before?" he asks, and I whimper and nod my head, and he smiles wickedly.

"My girl is cock hungry. Well, I should give her what she needs. Those other bastards will be here any minute, and I want you all to myself for the first time. Do you remember what it was like, Mimi? How good we were?"

My eyes close as I picture what it used to be like, but obviously, he wants a verbal answer, because he tugs my hair again.

"Answer me."

"Yes, I remember." I'm just about sobbing with need. My pussy pulses, and I feel tears stream down my face.

"Well, that was nothing, pretty girl. I am going to wreck you, and you are going to beg for more." Kash drags me over to the hot tub by my hair. He whirls me around to face him, and I can finally see him properly for the first time.

His eyes rake over my body, and I can practically feel his gaze scorch my skin. He leans forward and sucks on one of my nipples, using his hand to tweak the other one. My arms are still behind my back, and I'm trapped, unable to move.

"I like seeing tears stream down your face in need. Such a needy girl. Do you ache? Would you like me to fix the ache?" His words caress my soul as his hands roam over my needy body before they leave it, pushing down his boxers. "Words, Miriam. I need to hear the words."

"Please, Kash, fuck me hard," I beg him, and he spins me around and bends me over the hot tub, running one of his hands over my ass before he pulls back and slaps it. I cry out, but it's followed quickly by a moan as he caresses the sting away.

"I love hearing you beg for it. Say it again."

He nudges my feet apart and bends me over more so that my whole upper body is lying over the hot tub, my face hovering just above the water. The hair on his legs tickles my skin as I feel him line himself up with my opening.

"Tell me how much you want me, that you've missed me, and that no one fucks you better than me," he commands, and I hear a touch of desperation in his voice.

"Please, baby, I need you. I've missed you so much." Before I've even finished, he slams himself home, and I scream, my voice echoing through the concrete room.

"Oh fuck, you're tight," he mutters. "I wasn't expecting that, sorry," he says as he reaches around and plays with my clit as my body adjusts to his intrusion. He mutters words of praise, and I relax as he strokes my hair and back and every inch of skin he can touch.

"Such a good girl, taking my cock like that. Your pretty pussy squeezes me so tightly, like a fist wrapped around it. So fucking good."

The pain flows away as his words of praise tick every kinky box in my arsenal.

"Oh yeah, you like that. I can feel your cunt flutter and get hotter and wetter. That's a good girl, taking every inch like my cock was made from a mold of your cunt." He starts to slide in and out, slowly teasing me and playing my body like a fiddle.

One hand plucks my nipple, and the other circles my clit as his powerful thighs drive his thick length in and out of me, my body trapped between him and the hot tub, using it for leverage. I can't drop my head because I may end up drowning, so my muscles strain to hold it up.

My eyes roll back as my entire body starts to pulse like little electric shocks are running up and down my limbs. He pounds into me much like he plays hockey, relentlessly and unforgiving, and the whole time, he mutters dirty words of praise, promising me that he and his brothers are going to have so much fun using my body for their own enjoyment. His hand moves away from my clit before I feel him push against my asshole.

"Oh, you like that. I can feel your pussy tighten. You're so close, I can tell. Would you like it if Noah, B, and I used all of your holes at the same time like the perfect little cum slut you are?" He chuckles darkly as that thought throws me over the edge and into one of the biggest orgasms I've ever had. Again, my scream echoes off the concrete walls.

"That's it, oh yeah, your pussy feels so good. I'm going to fill you with my cum so it drips down your thighs." I can't do anything but moan as Kashton does just that. I don't even care that we haven't discussed going bare, I love the feel of his cum filling my pussy, and it sends me into another orgasm.

"Such a good girl, milking my cock for all its cum. I can't wait to stuff it back into you." Kash groans as he leans against my back, his cock still pulsing deep inside me. He places tiny kisses up and down my spine and circles his arms around me, holding me close like I'm precious to him.

"I missed you so much. I'm so happy you're back," he mutters quietly before pulling out, and my heart soars. He releases my arms and massages them before turning me around and lifting me up onto the side of the hot tub. He gets eye level with my cunt and watches as his cum drips out, smiling darkly as he pushes it back in. "I want them to feel that I was in you first," he tells me, his competitive side appearing.

I giggle quietly, and he looks up at me. "I think we might have been set up," I tell him when he raises a questioning eyebrow.

"Huh?" He closes my legs so nothing can drip out again before pushing them to the side so he can get close to me.

"We were very loud. If they were going to find us, they would have already."

Understanding shines in his eyes, and he grimaces before shrugging. "I'll have to thank the assholes for setting up the best night of my life." He leans in and kisses me, and it's like I've come home. Everything about him is familiar and comforting, and I wrap my arms around his neck so he can't get away. I'm not sure how long we kiss, but when I shiver from getting cold, he picks me up and lowers me into the hot tub. "We may as well make use of it while we're here."

The next time we make love, it's face-to-face and reminiscent of our previous love making but with a twist of dirty words, a combination of new and old making it freaking amazing.

CHAPTER 35

Miriam

We found our clothes. Thankfully, Noah left them where it was easy to find them. After we redressed, we left the arena hand in hand, the doors locking behind us. We drove back to our place to find a very smug Bentley and Noah. I must give them credit, because their plan worked, but we made them sweat for a little while.

The following day, Kash has an appointment to speak to Louella Eastern and team management about our situation to concoct a plan to deal with the media. I have my early morning accounting class, and then we're all meeting at Lou's Place to grab lunch. Bentley is spending the morning with

Mason, looking at suitable properties for his business venture, and Noah is working with Ethan on one of their jobs.

My class finishes a little early, and I head over to lunch, thinking if Peaches is there, I can chat with her for a little while, but my phone rings just as I pull into a parking lot a little bit down from the sports bar. It seems to be busy today. I frown as I go to grab my phone, but then I smile when I see it's Seamus calling.

"Hello, I was just thinking about giving you a call," I answer, and I hear a dramatic, put out sigh.

"Are you sure you weren't just too busy with your new life over there in the colonies?" I can hear him pouting through the phone, and I roll my eyes.

"I would have thought you'd be happy that I was making friends."

"You've made friends?" I must be on speaker phone, because that's Darcy. "Male friends?"

I giggle. "Yes I've made some male friends."

"Some?" I can hear the glee in their voices, so I put them out of their misery and tell them everything that's happened since I last spoke to them. They gasp and hiss in anger and pepper me with questions through the whole thing, but finally, I get to the part where I tell them I'm trying a polyamorous relationship with three men.

"Ow wee, girlie, you get yourself some!" Darcy praises.

"Mother would be so proud of you," Seamus says, and there's a moment of silence as we think about our beloved Jocelyn.

"Well, as soon as we get off, we'll make inquiries for flights. You are going to need our help in setting up that shop."

I shake my head, starting to argue, but I stop myself. Why not? We've missed them, and it would be nice to have them here, even for a little while. If they don't do it in person, then they will just nag me by phone. "Can't wait to see you," I tell them as my phone tells me I have another call.

"I have another call. Text me your flight details, and I'll pick you up. I'll clear out one of the spare bedrooms for you."

"You're not living with your beaus?" Darcy asks, and I grimace.

"Yeah, not yet. It's a little too soon, don't you think?"

"Miriam, honey, when you know it's right, you know. Why waste time? Life is too short to worry about what society thinks. Look at what happened to Mum. She was taken from us without warning."

I assure them I'll think about it and answer the other call.

"Mimi, it's Grandpa. We got the ball rolling on that investigation into your parents. We think we'll have some solid evidence to put them away for a long time by the end of the week."

"Hey, Grandpa, that's actually a relief to hear. I've been worrying about them in the back of my mind. I don't care so much about me, but their threats about Jorja worry me. I'm not so sure how secure her school is, and I don't want them to be able to get access to her there."

"Well, aren't you lucky you know someone on the board? I'll hire a security guard for a week or two. No one is getting to her who hasn't been approved."

"While I have you on the phone, I want to talk to you about something." I tell him about Jorja's teacher. He's suitably outraged and says he will keep an ear out for complaints. "If the principal is stupid enough to bring her complaint to the board, we'll spank both of them."

We hang up, and I head into the sports bar. I must have been on the phone a long time, because I find all three of my guys already waiting in a booth.

"There you are. We saw that you were on the phone and didn't want to disturb you, so we grabbed a booth." Bentley shuffles over so I can sit next to him this time. All three of them have glasses of beer in front of them, and they are half empty. I groan.

"I'm sorry. It was Darcy and Seamus, and those two can talk. I was filling them in on everything that happened—they will be here next week—and then it was Grandpa updating me on my parents' case."

I want to kiss them all, but I am very aware we are in public, and I don't want to out us before Kash is ready, but I slide my hand under the table and take a hold of Bentley's. I can at least give one of my guys affection. He grins at me and squeezes my hand.

"How did it go?" I ask Kash.

"Coach was fine with it. He said as long as it wasn't affecting my game, he couldn't care less. Upper management grumbled, saying it could paint a bad light on the Titans." I feel my heart sink as he says this. "But Louella told them to keep their bigoted opinions to themselves. As long as a player isn't doing something that brings the team into ill repute, she doesn't care what they do in their private life. Her words, and I quote. 'They are not having orgies in public or filming that shit, so leave them the hell alone.'"

"So, no sex tapes?" Bentley jokes, and I giggle but blush, thinking about my response the other night.

"They aren't holding a press conference. They think if we make a big deal that the media will think we have something to hide and dig deeper. They are issuing a watered-down statement about supporting players in whatever lifestyle choices they make as long as it's not harmful to the player and the game."

"At least one team is. The NHL is notoriously close-minded compared to other pro sports leagues." Noah grabs a peanut out of the bowl in the middle of the table.

"It will blow up for a little while, but hopefully, it will blow over quickly. Just be prepared for some media scrutiny," Kash tells us.

I'm glad Grandpa is going to get a security guard for Jorja now.

"Don't worry. We've got this, man." Bentley holds his free hand out for a fist bump.

Kash rolls his eyes but complies, then a waitress who is not Peaches approaches our table, and we place our order.

The news broke over the weekend after the Titans won their game. Kash was hounded during the after-game press conference, but he stuck to game information only. Because they didn't get any sound bites, though, they came after me hard. Fucking hell, the press is brutal. I know I was warned, but I found myself surrounded as they flung questions at me from all directions—gross ones insinuating disgusting things—but I just gritted my teeth and didn't engage. I figured if I'm boring, then they'll lose interest, but our faces are splashed all over trashy tabloids across the nation. If my parents hadn't known I returned, they sure do now, unless they are oblivious, and I very much doubt that.

Thankfully, after a week of being badgered, the press lost interest. There was a scandal out in LA surrounding another hockey team, the Neighpalm Shockwave. Two of the players' wives were photographed snorting coke off each other's boobs and being involved in a bukkake party with some visiting Japanese businessmen, so the heat disappeared—mostly.

"You're such a slut. One day, Bentley is going to come to his senses and realize he needs a woman who makes him her priority."

Bentley and I have been sitting quietly, working

on our project in the back of the lecture room. Sure, we can feel the occasional stare, but people mostly leave us alone. I think it's because Sarah is in the classroom, and I will take that as a win, thank you, but Rebecca is pushing her damn luck. She and her partner moved closer, and she has been whispering insult after insult the entire class. Bentley tried to clap back, but I stopped him. If you give them attention, they thrive, but if you ignore them, hopefully they will shrivel up and die. That's what happens with plants anyway.

"I assure you, Bentley is very much my priority. Do you feel neglected, babe?" I turn my head to look at him.

His eyes sparkle with amusement. Yes, I know what I said. Do as I say, not as I do.

"Not in the least." He leans in and kisses me deeply. I get a thrill that I can be affectionate toward my men now.

"Excuse me, but do you think we can keep all PDA for after class?" Sarah calls out, but she sounds amused more than annoyed.

Bentley salutes her. "Sorry, Mom, just reassuring Rebecca that I don't feel the least bit neglected."

Sarah rolls her eyes. "Maybe Rebecca should worry about her project." The whole class hears the threat, but Rebecca is an idiot.

"But don't you think he would be better off with someone who is not such a slut?" she asks loudly, hoping that Sarah is on her side, but she's barking up the wrong tree.

Sarah crosses her arms and stares at the girl. "Why is Miriam a slut? Because she happens to enjoy the attention, love, and affection of three men? Because they are establishing an open and honest relationship where all of their needs and wants are seen to? Damn, I wish I was as lucky as her."

Other girls in the classroom cheer and shout their agreement, and I smirk at Rebecca as the subject turns back to our projects.

She huffs and stops staring at us. Miriam, 1. Rebecca, 0.

"Oh, did I tell you that Grandpa called last night? Mrs. Brady and the principal did approach the board, saying she was concerned about our relationship and Jorja's well-being."

"Oh?" Bentley looks worried. I love how invested he is in both of us.

"The board issued a statement they prepared earlier, knowing it could be coming. It is not up to the staff or parents to judge how someone chooses to live their life as long as the child in the care of that family is well loved, cared for, and provided with the necessities of life, and shows no sign of mental or physical abuse. If a staff member shows prejudices or judgment toward a child because of their own ideals, then that staff member can choose to find employment elsewhere."

"Whoa, go Grandpa." Bentley sounds impressed.

"Yeah, the principal quickly backed down, but Mrs. Brady is now seeking employment elsewhere without a reference from the school. You know, it's sad. She was so kind to Jorja and Lola on their first day. I had such high hopes."

He leans in and presses a kiss to my forehead. "Everything will work out for the best. Have you heard anything from your parents?"

The guys have been bombarding me with this question every day since we went public, but it has been radio silence. I, for one, am okay with that. Jorja still has a security guard on her, and I am not very often alone in public. If the guys aren't at school with me, then Ginny is my constant shadow.

"No, still nothing. I'm not sure whether to be relieved or not."

"I guess only time will tell," he says, turning his attention back to our project. We're working on things for my flower shop today since I actually have a premises and he doesn't yet.

Kira and Shaley are both going to come work for me. Shaley had been working at a service station and was barely getting enough hours to keep food on their table. She burst into tears when I offered her the job and promised that she'd work hard and I wouldn't regret it. I have plans to put her through the same kind of design course I did. Both Kira and I will probably want to have more kids one day, and having her fully trained will only benefit my business. I can't wait for Seamus and Darcy to arrive. They are going to take one look at the wounded little bird and smother her with love much like they did me when I arrived in England.

The bell rings, and we go our separate ways. Bentley has another appointment with Mason, since they still haven't found him a place he's happy with yet, and Ginny will meet me out front and walk me to my car.

I've been waiting fifteen minutes, though, and Ginny still hasn't arrived. I promised Noah I'd meet him at the new shop front so he can do some measuring. Giving up, I walk over to my car. The campus has students everywhere, so nothing bad is going to happen. I pull out my phone and dial Noah to let him know I'm running late. I arrive at my car while it's ringing and find that my car is blocked in by a dark sedan. I walk over and knock on the tinted window, hoping someone is in there, and the back one lowers. My stomach rolls as I see the gun pointing at me, and behind it is my father's icy glare.

I hear Noah answer, but I'm frozen.

"Hang up the phone and get in the fucking car, Miriam, or the men I have tailing your pro hockey player will ensure he never plays again."

CHAPTER 36

Miriam

I quickly do as he says, shoving my phone into my pocket, deliberately forgetting to discon-nect, and open the door. My father shuffles over, his gun still pointed at me, and I climb in, pulling the door closed behind me. The car quickly glides away.

"Well, I must say I never thought you would have the capacity to surprise me. You were such a boring child, but you turned into an interesting adult," my father comments like he didn't have to point a gun at me to get me to cooperate.

"And a bit of a conniving slut too. Imagine my and your mother's surprise when we saw the news, and there was a huge kerfuffle about a pro hockey player and his newfound baby mama and child, and it was you." He glares at me. "You never said Kashton Young was the father of that whelp." He points his gun at my stomach like I'm still pregnant.

"Why would I?" I say calmly. "You just would have used it against him.

"And now you've secured yourself a place in two of the other wealthiest families in Storm View. It's a pity Louella Eastern doesn't have a child your age, or you could have made it a quintet."

"What do you want?" I ask, bored and terrified by his ramblings, but he isn't listening.

"You know I'm pretty sure Jameson Greyson does. He's new to town, a hotels and resorts mogul. I heard rumors of him and Louella Eastern joining forces. How about you spread your legs for him too? Then you'll have a clean sweep of the town's richest families."

Oh my god, my father is trying to pimp me out, and he sounds serious. I grit my teeth and repeat my question. "What do you want, Eric?"

He shakes himself out of his daze and smirks. "Can't I just catch up with my poor, estranged, drug-addled daughter?" He chuckles at the story he spread around the town. That information was dragged back up during the media frenzy, but it was quickly denied with a statement from my grand-parents.

"You made us look like fools," he hisses, his true self finally appearing. "The church asked us to leave, and I've had investors jumping ship in droves, wanting to take their money with them, questioning why it's taking me so long to cough it up. I'm fucked."

"What did you think was going to happen? That I would never return to my life? That once I was gone, I didn't exist anymore?" I ask him, unable to control the anger in my tone. He hauls back and pistol-whips me. Pain explodes across my cheekbone as I slide back on the seat, blood welling in my mouth from where he cut my lip.

"You mind your fucking mouth, missy. I can easily put a bullet in that little bitch head of yours or sell you off to the Russian mafia. They like whores who are happy to take it in every hole. You may actually make me some money."

"Grandpa won't let you," I argue, not to mention neither will any of my boyfriends, but I don't think he needs me to add to his annoyance at the moment.

Eric chuckles. "The old man has become a nuisance. Now that you're back in the picture, he'll probably change his will, so he's going to have a nasty car accident tomorrow."

My stomach rolls, and my heart races. Why is he telling me all this?

"Unless you do something for me." He smiles greasily, knowing I won't have any choice but to do whatever he wants.

"What do you want?" I ask him yet again.

"There is a high society party being held at the Eastern estate on Sunday. It's a celebration for the opening of the hockey season and an auction to raise money for the youth league."

I nod. I know about it. Louella put it together when she realized that others than just Shaley struggled to find money for their kids to play sports. The guys and I received an invitation. I dab at the cut on my lip with my shirt, my face throbbing in pain.

"I want an invitation, and you are going to convince your boyfriend's families to invest their money with me. If they don't, bad things will happen to all of them. I know people who can make it happen."

I grit my teeth in anger but agree. I need him to let me leave so I can tell people about his plan.

"I have someone following everyone. One wrong move, and I will make sure people will die."

"No one is going to believe me," I argue, and he chuckles as the car pulls into the driveway of my grandparents' estate, but instead of going right and heading to their house, it goes left toward my old childhood home.

"That's why you're here. You are going to tell everyone we had a meal and reconciled, and that we were so very grateful you were okay and were falsely led to believe what we told everyone."

The car glides to a halt, and Eric gestures for me to get out. I consider making a run for it, but the gun convinces me not to, so I follow his instructions. We enter the house, and he tucks his gun away. My mouth drops open as I stare at the debauchery that's taking place. It looks like I've fallen into a cheesy, seventies porno. There are naked bodies writhing everywhere, and drug paraphernalia and alcohol on many surfaces. My stomach rolls from nausea this time. My parents have lost their damn minds. It smells of sex and sweat.

I watch in horror as my father approaches a group where a man rails into a woman from behind. Her face is planted in the pussy of another woman in front of her. He pulls a little bag of white powder out of his pocket and assembles a line on the woman's bouncing ass. The man fucking her pauses as my father leans in and snorts the line of coke before licking the remaining residue.

He slaps her ass and says, "Look, our prodigal daughter has returned, Leticia."

My horror increases as the woman raises her head and blinks at me.

"Oh, you found the bitch, did you?" The woman who she had been eating out also sits up, and to my disgust, I find it's the maid, Macy. Well, I guess that explains a lot.

I take a moment to really look at them, and I'm happy to find the years have not been kind. My mother's body is ravaged by drugs. She's thin and emaciated, and she obviously had breast implants, because they are the only part of her that seems to have survived. My father has a pot belly and a receding hairline. I feel immense satisfaction in seeing this.

"I thought we were having dinner," I grit out through clenched teeth.

Eric chuckles, leans in, and sucks on Macy's obviously enhanced tits. "I am." She moans like a porn star and drops back as my father pushes my mother out of the way and starts to go to town on the maid. The whole time, my mother has been railed by the man behind her. She seems bored but makes all the right sounds.

"What am I supposed to do?" I ask, crossing my arms, and she shrugs.

"From what we hear, you have three boyfriends,

so you must like to fuck. I'm sure someone here will be happy to indulge you."

The man railing into my mom leers at me. "I will," he says in some thick, Eastern European accent. "She's beautiful." I shiver at his unwelcome stare and start to leave. I'm not staying.

"Fuck off, Miriam." My mother glares at me, obviously jealous of the attention the man is paying to me. Seriously, though, she can keep it. "You aren't wanted here, you never were."

She thinks she's hurting me, but she's not telling me anything I didn't already know. It was her go-to insult. It hurt the first few times, but now it's nothing, like words on the breeze.

"If you don't pretend to have dinner with us, I'll give the go ahead to break your hockey pro's knees. I can't imagine he will ever play hockey again." My father's face is glistening as he looks up from Macy. I want to gag at the sight, but I'm not sure what kind of reaction that would get.

"Fine. Is my bedroom still where it was?" I ask, hoping I can escape up there and maybe they haven't discarded all of my stuff.

"Just the way you left it." He grins before returning to his task, and I turn on my heel to leave.

"Remember our deal, Miriam. You get me those

accounts, or I will make sure everyone you love pays."

Unlikely, asshole. If anyone is going to pay, it's you, I think but keep it to myself. I flip him off, and he laughs like it's the funniest thing he's seen. I head up to my bedroom, not willing to risk that he might be telling the truth for today, but when I leave, I plan on going straight to Grandpa. We have to finish this soon.

As I make my way upstairs, I take my phone out. Noah is still listening on the end of the line. I assure him that I'm okay and explain that I'll play along for now and fill them all in when I get home.

"Are you in any danger?" he asks, and I laugh a little hysterically.

"Define danger. I think they are all distracted and will be for hours unless the drugs run out and wear off."

I pause at the door to my bedroom. "Can you please come and get me in two hours? That's as long as I'm willing to stay. Bring the truck. I'm taking any of my things that remain from when I lived here before."

"I'll be there," he promises, and we disconnect.

I open the door to my room and a wave of nostalgia washes over me. It's like they closed the door and never set foot back in here. There is six years' worth of dust covering everything, but I spend the next hour gathering everything I want to keep. I'm not sure I fit into the clothes anymore, but I know they will fit Shaley, and she probably needs them more than I do, so I pull everything out of drawers and closets, leaving only the underwear behind. I find a couple of suitcases in a hall closet and stuff everything in them before running them down to the door.

Nobody even notices me except for the man who had been railing Leticia earlier. Leticia, Macy, and Eric are passed out in a pile on the same couch they were using while people still fuck all around them.

The other man has now moved on and is standing in the middle of the room, and at his feet is a masked, bound man sucking on his cock. The sub is struggling as the other one holds his head so he can't get away. Tears and snot dribble down his face, but the man who stares at me holds on. I think he's going to choke the guy, but the sub suddenly arches his back and orgasms, painting the floor in front of him with his cum. The other man releases his head and winks at me, waggling his tongue suggestively, which makes me feel ill. I shiver with disgust and run back the way I came. I won't wait the two hours. Fuck this. My blood relatives won't even notice I've left.

I grab the last suitcase and walk out the door without looking back. I walk over to my grandparents' place, struggling with all three cases. Halfway there, I decide to leave them and get them on the way out. I run the rest of the way to my grandparents, worried that my parents will chase me down and force me to return. I burst through the front door, the familiar smell bringing me comfort.

"Mimi?" My grandfather appears from his office, wringing his hands. "Noah called and told me what happened. Are you okay?" he asks, sweeping his thumb over the developing bruise on my face.

I shake my head, bursting into tears. "No, not even remotely," I tell him, and he wraps me in his arms, giving me a tight hug before leading me to his office. There are two men I don't know. I would say they are probably slightly older than Eric but not as old as my grandpa.

"These are the FBI agents I told you about," he introduces us, and they question me about everything my father said. We go over the interaction for so long, Noah is waiting for me in the parlor with my grandmother when we finish. When he sees my face, he tries to leave, threatening Eric, but the FBI men convince him to stand down.

We tell them goodbye, and we take our leave. "I need a shower and some bleach for my eyes," I tell him as he drives down the driveway, stopping to pick up the forgotten suitcases.

I tell him exactly what happened.

"What did the FBI say?" he asks. "Are they going to arrest him?"

I groan and slump in my seat. "No, they said it's my word against theirs. They can't act yet. They are putting together their final bits of evidence, though they assured me they have men trailing Dad's men."

"Fuck!" Noah shouts and slams his fist against the steering wheel. "That's bullshit."

"Yeah, so for now, I have to play along. We spoke to Louella, clueing her in, and she said she would send them an invite to the gala, but I've decided to send Jorja, and Lola—if Kira and Liam are okay with that—back to the UK with Seamus and Darcy. They land tomorrow, and we're just going to turn them right around. The girls will be safe over there, and the boys will dote on them. I'll call them when we get home."

The rest of the trip is filled with tense silence. I

know Noah is not angry at me, but feeling helpless at the situation.

"What happened to Ginny?" I ask, and he growls.

"It looks like your father paid someone to waylay her. She's okay, just annoyed," he assures me.

When we get back to the house, Bentley and Kash are both there, as are Kira, Liam, Jorja, and Kash's parents, Mary and Simon. Kira and Liam readily agree to send Lola away with Jorja, but Mary says she'll go with them so Lola feels more comfortable. She's never been to England, and all three of them are excited. Kash gives me his black credit card and tells me to book all five of them business class flights.

"Darling, we don't fly any other way," Jorja tells him with her nose in the air, mimicking Seamus.

I roll my eyes, and the two little girls giggle.

"I was looking forward to meeting them. Hopefully once this is all over, they will return," Bentley says, and I scoff.

"Wild horses couldn't keep them away, and I am very much worried at the kind of trouble the three of you could get up to," I tell him, and he grins.

We make the arrangements, and Kash and I pack

a bag for Jorja, while Kira and Liam return to their house to do Lola's.

"I hate that I just found her, and we have to send her away," he says, sitting on Jorja's bed with her Paddington Bear in his lap, looking forlorn.

"I know, I hate it too, but hopefully it won't be for long, and she will be safer over there."

"I know. Listen, the guys and I were discussing it, and you should move in with us while all of this is happening." I think he expects me to argue, but Aunt Jocelyn didn't raise an idiot.

"I was thinking maybe you guys could move in here. There is more than enough room, and I don't want to give up my house. I'm comfortable here, and that's what I need for now."

"Sure, no problem. My house was just convenient. I have no attachment to it, and neither do the guys."

"Why do I get the feeling that this sounds a little more permanent than just for now?" I stop what I'm doing and stare at him, and he blushes. It's what I've always loved about him—the big, badass hockey player blushes like a virgin bride. He blames his mom.

"Well, what I mean is that we're in this, so we might as well go all in. I don't want to miss another minute of Jorja's life, and us moving in together just makes sense. I'm starting away games soon, and Bentley's business will be up and running before we know it."

I cave and let him off the hook. Dropping the shirt I'm holding, I approach him and climb into his lap, planting a kiss on his lips. "You don't need to give me excuses. I would love to live in sin with the three of you."

He starts to stammer, and I put a finger over his mouth.

"I'm teasing. That will happen in its own time." We take another couple of minutes to make out, but when he pushes me back, I remind him that we're on our daughter's bed, and he jumps up. I laugh, and we finish our packing before heading down-stairs to have a final meal with our daughter for the near future.

CHAPTER 37

Miriam

Many hugs and tears accompanied our goodbyes to the girls and Mary. Darcy and Seamus promised to look after them all like they were their own, and they were already making plans for all the wonderful sightseeing they were going to do. Although I'm going to miss my daughter like crazy, and it's the first time we've been apart for any length of time, I know we made the right decision. I can breathe a little bit easier when I get a notification that they are safely in the air.

Kira and I spend the next day shopping for fancy dresses. Everyone is invited to the gala, and they are aware of the roles they need to play. Leticia and Eric are going to be welcomed into the fold like long-lost loved ones and lulled into a false sense of security until the FBI can finalize the case against them.

I feel ill that I'm asking Noah's and Bentley's families to participate in the charade. Simon, Liam, and Kira have already assured me that they will do whatever they can to make it so Mary and Lola can return quickly.

Kash organizes a limo for the four of us to take to the gala. It's a tense, quiet ride, but we all indulge in a couple of drinks.

"If I have to pretend to accept your parents, I'm going to need a few of these," Bentley growls before tossing his shot back.

When we arrive at Louella's vast cattle ranch, her gorgeous house is lit up with party lights. It's overflowing with people taking advantage of the perfect night and gathering in the beautiful gardens. Servers in black and white mingle, offering canapés and a variety of beverages. The items on auction are displayed in the ballroom at the back of the home. Music plays, and the occasional tinkle of laughter can be heard. Most people are enjoying themselves, but as I look around and catch sight of our families, I can't miss the tension in their eyes despite their smiles.

"Welcome," Louella greets us as the line makes it to her and Peaches, who are welcoming their guests. She gives us all warm kisses on the cheek, her floral perfume tickling my nose. Peaches looks gorgeous in her peach-colored satin gown, but she seems uncomfortable. I'm almost certain she's going to bolt the minute she's allowed to.

"Do you need a lifeline?" I whisper as I give her a hug. Her hands tighten painfully on my arms.

"I will give you my first born," she responds as I pull away, giggling.

"I'm not sure we need to be so dramatic." I turn to her host. "Would you mind if I borrowed Peaches? I need to use the bathroom."

"Of course not, but rest assured we all know our roles today," Lou tells me. "I think you are the last to arrive." She looks over our shoulders, and sure enough, there is no one behind us.

"My parents are already here?" I ask, and she frowns.

"No, but if they are going to be late, then they don't deserve to be welcomed." She turns to Kash. "I have someone I want to introduce you to. Jameson just moved to town a few months ago. He keeps a horse here, but his younger son is crazy about a certain hockey player and would love to meet you.

His older son is around your age and could probably use a friend or two who aren't after him for who he is and how much he's worth."

My boys smile, and Kash holds out his arm for Louella. "Lead the way."

Noah waits and looks at me. "I do need to pee. I'll catch up with you," I assure him. I can see him war with himself, but eventually, Peaches just shoos him away.

She shows me to the bathroom, and then the two of us are joined by Ginny and Kira. Together, we find a spot off to the side, and the three girls fill me in on all the gossip from Storm View high society.

"That's the mayor. Rumor has it he's gay, and his wife is his beard and enjoys affairs with her son's friends on the side. He plans on running for governor, but all the dirty laundry in his closet is going to be his undoing," Peaches shares, and we look at her with surprise.

She shrugs. "Grandma believes that knowing everyone's secrets is good business practice. You never know when you might need to use them."

I'm getting a whole different view of Louella Eastern. It's no wonder she is one of the richest women in the state. She's smart and ruthless.

"Well, she'd have a field day with what I saw at my parents' house the other day." I point a finger.

"See that couple there?" The girls look at where I'm pointing.

"That's my father's boss from the hospital," Kira says. "Simon is a highly respected knee surgeon."

"They were at my parents' orgy yesterday." I wrinkle my nose as I have a flashback, and the girls gag and groan and make appropriate noises of disgust.

"Those are two words I never want to hear to describe my parents." Ginny shudders, and we giggle.

A sudden commotion catches our attention. We wander out onto the patio and discover flashing lights speeding down the driveway to the house. Peaches wrings her hands as Louella greets the officers who get out of the police car. Driving up behind it is another vehicle, and my grandpa's FBI friends get out of it. I see him join Louella and watch as an intense conversation takes place. I put my arm around Peaches, hoping that whatever happened doesn't involve her or her grandma, but as one, they all turn and look at us.

"Shit," Peaches says as the FBI, Louella, and Grandpa wave us over. We exchange a glance, and the two of us hurry over to find out what they want. It turns out it's not Peaches they want at all—it's me.

"I'm sorry, Miriam, but your parents have been in an accident," Grandpa says, and I blink in shock. That wasn't what I was expecting him to say.

"Huh?" I'm confused, and Peaches slips away, returning only moments later with my guys. Noah slides an arm around my shoulders as the main FBI man takes over.

"I had men trailing them in the car on the way to the party. They reported that the car was swerving all over the road like the driver was intoxicated."

I scoff. "They probably were."

The man nods. "Yes, but unfortunately they hit a slick patch on the road, and one of Louella's cows happened to escape and run in front of their car, and they swerved and went off into the ditch."

A strange sensation rushes over my body. It's not concern, but hope.

"Are they okay?" I ask, secretly crossing my toes that they aren't.

"I'm sorry to report that the car went up in flames. By the time the men tailing them arrived, it was too late to save them. The firefighters can't get close either, because it's an EV, and the lithium battery has caught fire."

I frown at him in confusion.

"They can't be put out by regular means," he explains.

"So they are dead?" Bentley asks, voicing the question that's been blaring in my brain.

"Yes. I'm afraid there will be no survivors. We'll have to wait for an autopsy to identify them, but we think it was your mother, father, and the house maid, Macy, in the car. Our men reported three people."

I sag against Noah, and Kash leaps to help hold me up, but I quickly recover and look at my grandpa who's watching me carefully. I guess he's waiting to see if I break down.

"I want to see it," I tell him, and he doesn't look shocked or judge me. He just nods his head and hurries off to have a car brought around. The guys declare that they are coming with me, and as we walk away, I see Peaches talking to her grandmother out of the corner of my eye. She looks irate, but Louella just smirks, gives her a hug, and wanders off to continue entertaining her guests.

I don't have time to think about that because the guys quickly hustle me into the limo Grandpa poached, and the four of us and Grandpa ride silently until we get to the accident site. It's far enough away so we couldn't see the flames from the homestead, but you can't miss them as you get closer. There are flashing lights from paramedics, firefighters, and police, but they are all standing around, watching the fire burn. The firefighters water the paddocks on either side so it can't spread in the hopes that it will just burn out naturally without causing any more damage.

I climb out of the limo and wrinkle my nose at the smell, but I carefully make my way over to join the line of people watching. The car is a mangled mess and engulfed in flames. There is no sign of any of the doors being open, but I scan the remaining area just to make sure. When I don't find any bodies, I heave a sigh of relief and lean back into my guys who are gathered around me.

"It's finally over." I sigh, and the immense relief that washes over me makes me lightheaded.

"They aren't going to be able to cause any more trouble ever," my grandpa promises me. There are tears in his eyes, but I think they are from what could have been, not because he's sad Eric and Letitia are in flames.

I refuse to leave before the fire dies down, and I know for sure all three of them were in there. They were the cause of all my troubles, and I want confirmation that they are gone. The sun is rising, and guests from the party have all driven past on their way home, but I still stay and watch. Louella and Peaches joined us at one stage, bringing food and jackets, but I didn't need one, because the fire kept me warm. It's only as the sun creeps across the horizon, lighting up the sky with its brilliance, that the firefighters can finally extinguish the fire. I haven't moved from my spot, although I did get rid of my heels—my feet were killing me. As they cool the metal with their hoses, one of them is able to peer in the window. I watch, my eyes locked on him as his eyebrows jump and he grimaces before backing away. He talks quietly to the police chief before he turns and approaches us.

"Was it my parents?" I ask, and the police chief sighs. They are burnt beyond recognition, so it's impossible to get a formal ID. The coroner will need to use dental records, but there are three people in the car."

"What was he surprised about?" I ask, pointing at the firefighter who peered in.

The police chief sighs. "It appears that the passenger may have been giving oral sex to the driver, which may have contributed to why they were slow to react."

Fuck my life.

"Right, okay. Please let me know when you get a formal ID," my grandfather says as I stare at the car in shock. Of course that's how they came to an end.

I turn and don't look back, disgusted that I could have come from either of those deviants and thankful that neither of them can threaten me or mine again. I'm also thrilled that I can call Seamus and tell him to bring my girls home.

"Let's go home," I tell my guys, who have been with me the whole time. "I need to wash the stench out of my hair."

EPILOGUE

Miriam

Because the FBI was involved, we got the results very quickly. They confirmed it was Eric, Leticia, and Macy. I didn't ask where each body was, because that was information I didn't need to know. I already have a horrible reminder of my parents floating around in my brain, and I'm going to need therapy, so I didn't want to add to it.

The case the FBI was building fell apart. Without my parents, they had no proof of who they were involved with. The money my father embezzled from their church remains lost, but they were able to recover some for his other investors. I'm not sure why, but they named me their heir in the will, and I had been given bank account details from the

Cayman Islands. I wanted nothing to do with anything from them and handed it all over to the FBI. For now, their house will sit empty until my grandparents and I decide what to do with it. I would like to turn it into a home for teen mothers who have nowhere else to go, but that's a plan for the future.

We also spoke to the girls and Mary, who are going to stay in London for another week so they can see everything Seamus and Darcy planned before all five descend on us.

Exactly a week after the fire, Kash had an away game on Saturday, but he's due home on Sunday. The guys have lived with me all week. I didn't see the point of them returning home despite our troubles resolving themselves. We are enjoying establishing our relationship without the pitter-patter of little feet. We lived, laughed, and loved—boy, did we love. We haven't had a foursome yet, though, which I'm feeling a little sad about.

I wake up Sunday morning feeling a little like my vagina is broken after last night with Noah and Bentley. They like to dominate me, and I love to be dominated. It makes me feel sexy and wanted and needed, but I think I'm going to need a break today.

I crack my eyes open, becoming aware that it's quiet in my bedroom, and I can't feel any bodies on either side of me. Yawning, I sit up and yelp when I find Noah sitting in the seat in the corner of the room. Just like that first night, he's naked except for a pair of boxers, but he has something in both hands, and I can't make out what.

"Hi." I smile at him, but he has his dom face on. "Babe, normally I would be up for an early morning romp, but I think you guys broke me last night," I tell him, wincing as I gingerly move my legs, my pussy crying out in alarm.

He smirks his dark smirk, and my pussy's cry of alarm turns into a small whimper.

"I mean, I guess I could take one for the team," I say, and he chuckles darkly. My nipples peak, and I squirm with anticipation. He stands up and prowls over to the bed, and I wiggle with excitement. He pulls back the sheet I had over me, exposing my naked body to his heated gaze.

"Are you going to be a good girl for your boyfriends?" he asks, his voice sending chills down my spine. Although I'm mostly submissive, I occasionally like being a brat. It makes them all growly and stern.

"What's in it for me?" I sass, and his eyes dilate as he crawls up the bed.

"What about another game of adult hide-and-seek?" he suggests, pushing my legs apart and settling between them.

My pussy convulses at the thought of my game with Kash. "Who's playing?" I ask, and he grins wickedly.

"All of us. And the same rules stand. He who catches you gets to fuck you however they want." He swipes a tongue through my folds, and I sag back on the mattress, my clit pulsing with the attention he's giving it.

"Where are we going to play?" I ask, worried about the safety of doing something like that in my house.

"We're going to wait until the sun goes down, and then we are going to take advantage of the fact that Fred and Mae are out of town for two days. The maze and the orchard are the playing grounds," he tells me while lapping at my pussy.

I just about come on the spot when he tells me this. "I am so in," I tell him, and he chuckles against my pussy, then I hear the pop of a lube bottle.

"Such a good little girl. Our little cock slut wants to be chased and pounded by her men, don't you?" I'm panting now, but I stop suddenly in surprise when I feel him push something against my asshole.

"What are you doing?" I ask him, completely turned on.

"It's time our little cum slut let us use all her holes. Your daddies are going to fill you with their cum until you're dripping with it."

Oh my god. Did he just call him and the other two my daddies? Am I into this? The gush from my cunt tells me I am.

"Holy fuck, you like that?" Noah sounds surprised, so I guess he'd been testing it out. "Oh yeah, you really like that. Breathe out for me," he commands as his tongue goes to town, cleaning up my pussy. He slowly pushes the lubed butt plug into my ass. He hasn't even gotten it halfway in, and I detonate, my orgasm screaming through my body. He shoves the plug the rest of the way in, and there's a slight pinch of pain as it pushes past the ring of muscle, but it just adds to the exquisite pleasure already racking my body.

"Such a good girl," he praises as I come down from my high. He licks and sucks, praising me constantly. When I look down at him, he's staring at me with lust-glazed eyes.

"You will wear that all day. You can't remove it until one of your daddies tells you to," he orders, and I quickly agree, my pussy throbbing at his words.

"Good, now get up and spend the day relaxing.

Nap, eat, and bathe, but that plug stays in. Meet us at your gate to the maze at dusk." He stands up and walks back to the chair. "Wear nothing but this." He hands me a little red cape, and without another word, he leaves.

I drop my head back and close my eyes. Fucking hell, that was intense, but I can't help feeling excited for what's to come—me, hopefully.

The guys are gone all day, but I do what he told me to. There is a large breakfast waiting for me when I go downstairs. I feel a little awkward walking with the plug inside me, but I soon get used to it. I eat and then take a long, relaxing bath before watching a movie and having a nap.

I take another bath and shave myself from head to toe before applying moisturizer all over my body. It's this iridescent shimmery kind that makes me look all ethereal. When I'm done, the sun is starting to set, so I put on the cape and make my way into my backyard then down the path to the gate to the maze. My footsteps stutter as I get there and find all three of them wearing the exact same outfit, and each of them have a wolf mask on their heads. They must be wearing padding to disguise their bodies, because I can't actually tell who is who with all of them being the same height.

"Good girl," one of them praises, their voice

distorted by the mask. "You know the rules. If we catch you, we get to fuck you until we come. Then, we'll release you and try to catch you again."

I shudder on the spot, the long grass tickling my naked legs.

One of the others takes over. "We'll fuck you however and wherever we please. Feel free to fight us, because we love it when you struggle."

"We'll only stop if you use your safe word," the final one says. "Tell us your safe word."

"Pineapple," I reply, looking down at my feet like a good submissive.

"Are you ready? Once we start, there is no stopping until we say so."

I nod and look up at them, my heart pounding and my core throbbing from the anticipation of them catching me and doing whatever they wish. I'm not sure I'm going to get very far.

"Good, you get a ten-minute head start. Run fast, little girl, because the big bad wolves want to eat you. Go!"

AFTERWORD

Thank you all for reading Ice Me Out. This idea was rolling around in my head for a while but I ignored it while I worked on other things but then I won an image from the wonderful Wander and I saw this and it fit my idea of Kashton perfectly, so I rolled with it.

I hope you enjoyed the book. It's the first standalone I've written and it was a bit of a learning curve trying to balance story and steam and make it plausible in 100K words.

It would be super awesome if you could leave a review wherever you bought it, because I love to hear what you thought of the story.

I have plans for the Storm View world so make sure you keep an eye on my Facebook group for all things Lexie.

In the mean time why don't you check out one of my other series. You can find everything on my website at

www.lexiewinston.com

Acknowledgments

Firstly I need to thank Bobby Kim and Wander Aguiar. I won a competition run by Bobby and the prize was a Wander image. Blaze on the front cover is that image. I couldn't be happier with how my cover turned out so thanks to both of you.

To my cover designer Natasha of Dazed Designs. She took that amazing photo and made it just what I wanted. Love your face.

Thank you to Jess at Elemental Editing for being the flexible, wonderful person that you are. You regularly talk me down off my ledge and boost my self esteem. I couldn't do this with out you.

Thank you to Tara Von Doodlebug, Sandra Stocker, Chloe Bianca Vines for your name suggestions so many months ago when my brain was not working. A shout out to Elizabeth Hutchin-son. Although I didn't use your suggestion it made me laugh out loud.

Kerry Keller. You are the bestest alpha a girl could want.

And lastly to you guys the readers. I love what I

do, and probably would do it regardless if anyone read them or not, but you guys make it that much sweeter so thank you.

Until next time, happy reading!

Lexie

www.ingramcontent.com/pod-product-compliance
Lightning Source LLC
Chambersburg PA
CBHW020239120726
47904CB00001B/28